LAST BORN

DAUGHTER

Also by Kastie Pavlik

<u>Children of the Morning Star Series</u>

The Arrival Reawakened (1)

Confessions of the Second Born (2)

Last Born Daughter (3)

Eternal Light Descendant (Final)

Additionally

How to Make Lemonade

Praise for *The Arrival*

...providing a degree of psychological and philosophical dimension...there is still some fresh blood to be drawn...

~The BookLife Prize

...an author with a genuine flair for originality and character driven narrative storytelling. A deftly crafted and unfailingly compelling read from beginning to end...

~Midwest Book Review

...gorgeously written, with a great page-turning plot and complex characters...

~Serene Conneeley, Into the Mists & Into the Storm Trilogies

...the premise is clear, and so well thought, not good nor bad, vampires [s]imply are...a great start to a new series...

~Ruth Miranda, The Blood Trilogy

Pavlik's descriptions are scrumptious, a delight to the senses...a new world of vampire mythology where love and faith in the Almighty are pivotal pieces of this delightful page turning puzzle.

~M.K. Deppner, Photographs of October

Praise for *Confessions Of The Second Born*

...the world Kastie Pavlik creates is nothing short of fascinating...it left me craving more...

~Ruth Miranda, Heir of Avalon Trilogy

...infused with powerful darkness, aching light, and scenes which threaten to rip the reader's heart out...[y]ou'll want more when you finish...

~M.K. Deppner, Photographs of October

...kick-ass new characters, lots of action, a little romance, a plot twist or two, and lots of magic and intrigue...a new spin on vampires and their history, lore and world...Jonathan's...back story is fascinating...

~Serene Conneeley, Into the Mists & Into the Storm Trilogies

Praise for *Last Born Daughter*

Prepare to have your heart ripped, because that's how Ms Pavlik rolls and I love her books for that.

~Ruth Miranda, Heir of Avalon & The Blood Trilogies

...a compelling world that will draw you in and make you cheer for your favourite characters — then break your heart when you realise not all will survive. It's a masterfully crafted tale of love, loss and sacrifice, perfect for fans of vampires, myth, legend, and paranormal romance and suspense.

~Serene Conneeley, Into the Mists & Into the Storm Trilogies

Thrilling...devastating, but satisfying. A riveting read you'll have trouble putting down.

~M.K. Deppner, Photographs of October

...I dread and thrill in equal measure for where Pavlik will take us. So much hangs in the balance, and with an ending to Last Born Daughter that left me in stunned silence, this series still has so much more to come.

~Julie Embleton, Turning Moon series & Voyager Chronicles

Praise for *How To Make Lemonade*

Beautiful prose and an unexpected story...Ms. Pavlik delivers unique twists and leads the reader through the darkness toward the light...or does she?

~M.K. Deppner, Photographs of October

I simply could not put it down...I was left replenished, satisfied, my thirst slackened by this fresh glass of lemonade!

~Ruth Miranda, The Preternaturals Series

LAST BORN DAUGHTER

CHILDREN OF THE MORNING STAR BOOK 3

KASTIE PAVLIK

DEDICATED TO MY MOTHER & FATHER

FOR RAISING A WEIRD NERD WITH A
PENCHANT FOR VAMPIRES, WRITING, AND
ALL THINGS CREEPY CRAWLY.

...THEY WERE GROTESQUE...
THERE WAS MUCH OF THE BEAUTIFUL,
MUCH OF THE WANTON,
MUCH OF THE BIZARRE,
SOMETHING OF THE TERRIBLE,
AND NOT A LITTLE OF THAT
WHICH MIGHT HAVE EXCITED DISGUST.

~EDGAR ALLAN POE, *THE MASK OF THE RED DEATH*

TABLE OF CONTENTS

Reference Map.. ..
Chapter One: The Eyes of a Fallen Angel............................1
Chapter Two: Lionhearted.......................... 20
Chapter Three: Rainne Blood Pathos.................... 30
Chapter Four: Pillars and Stars 41
Chapter Five: Sacrificial Blood 64
Chapter Six: Black Shuck Rises.................... 90
Chapter Seven: Caged Birds 99
Chapter Eight: Heartstrings........................116
Chapter Nine: War Hound 135
Chapter Ten: Falconry........................... 151
Chapter Eleven: The Unfortunates 165
Chapter Twelve: Killing Them Softly 180
Chapter Thirteen: Blood Loss 203
Chapter Fourteen: Frightened Among Us 213
Chapter Fifteen: Thy Grief, Thy Joy, Thy Hate, Thy Love 230
Chapter Sixteen: Sire thy Rage 242
Bonus Chapter: The Promise 259
The story concludes 270

NOTATIONS..271
Author Note (Updated) 272
Historical Notes & Character References...................273
Timeline 275
Author Sketches 276
About the Author...............................279

Reference Map

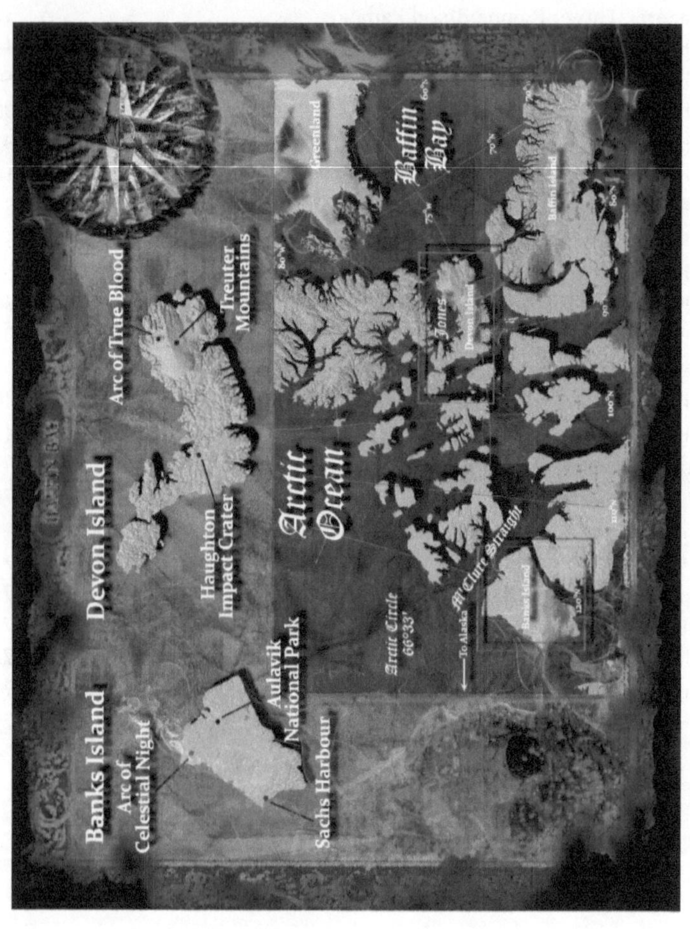

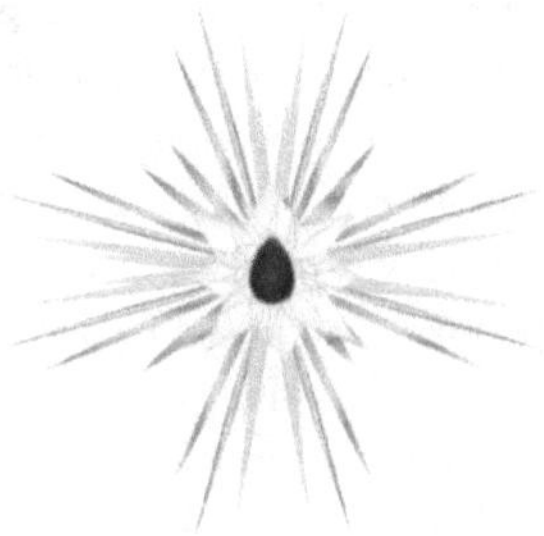

Chapter One: The Eyes of a Fallen Angel

I

South of the Tropic of Cancer, Africa, 5th Century A.D.

The black veil split in twain and spit her into a world rent asunder. Fearsome war cries shredded the heavens and earth alike, and the bloody spray of battle formed a sticky mist that fell upon mounds of bodies, mutilated and lifeless, gnashing and thrashing—dead or alive, all danced to Death's violent chorus.

Naked and shivering on unsteady legs, she collapsed into warm, blood-soaked mud. She curled into an upright ball, slicking herself with putrid slime, gaze swinging wildly, claws carving chunks of flesh from her body. Folding small enough might return her to the Nothing of Before.

Gore and grime were thick upon beautiful beings whose skin shone brighter than the setting sun. Feathered wings, once a pristine white and now stained vermilion, towered from their backs, and their stately robes rippled as they swung flashing silver blades and angled shields that mirrored their gilded radiance into blinding, blistering rays.

A searing beam gleamed, and she yelped, jabbing her fists into the sockets, disbelieving that such magnificent warriors wielded their beautiful light as a weapon. She peered through teary slits at their opponents: demonic creatures with blood-splattered paraffin skin, bottomless black pupils, and veiny, engorged eyes.

Long claws and sharp fangs formed crude, biological armaments, and tattered scraps of cloth and torn red cloaks revealed harsh ridges in the muscles clinging to their bony frames. Shadowy auras spewed forth a fortifying, murderous miasma that draped half the battlefield in darkness.

Instinct demanded she join the slaughter. She covered her ears against its thundering, internal voice and cringed at the urges carved into her brain before her consciousness had become aware of itself.

A streak of silver clipped her world to the tip of the sword flying at her heart. She shrank inwardly, squeezing her eyes shut. Instinct's voice quieted and the cacophony of light and dark faded. Sticky warmth splashed her head, trailed by the scent of ambrosia. Pangs of immeasurable thirst knotted her stomach.

Blood streamed from her attacker's body overhead, his limp wings sheltering her from madness until he and his sword thudded into the mud. A masked woman in a red cloak flicked the gore of his death from her weaponized arm, oblivious to the sword swinging at her back.

Instinct sprang her up to defend her masked savior. The blade landed square in her gut. The world tilted askance as she met the winged warrior's eyes with tears streaming from hers.

Studying her with curious sorrow, he tugged his sword free. She clutched her belly and collapsed, her hip and shoulder sinking into the mire. Brilliant blue fire flickered in his eyes as he planted his shield upright and dropped to his knees.

He offered his hand but her feeble reach failed. The masked woman twisted at the waist and struck with cold precision, and was already thrusting at another foe before his body—or head—hit the ground.

Her lips trembled in horror. Half a second longer. An inch farther. Scenarios alighted in her mind of ways he might have survived. An offer of aid to his enemy had cost his head and hunched his body against a useless shield, his hand forever outstretched without regret.

Nagging urges and persistent hunger paraded purpose as an illusion of memory—imposters incapable of explaining her existence or why this warrior's death carved a black chasm into her heart. Blood and mud swirled into the tears dripping off her jaw as she drew herself up and grabbed the warrior's sword. The blade sliced her fingers. Crimson beads raced down its gleaming length leaving no trace behind.

She longed to disappear so cleanly.

Walking her fingers to the hilt, the tip inched closer and bit into the skin at her breast. She cast a mournful glance upon the headless warrior and glimpsed a blond man in the distance, his clothes frayed and worn, barefooted legs coated with the muck of battle. His penetrating gaze trapped her in snuffed orbs that had once burned. Movement shimmered at his back: ruffled, dirt-covered feathers weighted by thick chains crisscrossing his torso. Unarmed, he approached seemingly unnoticed by either side.

Wet drops splashed her face. She wiped her cheeks. Blood slicked her fingers. The masked woman gurgled overhead.

A blade pierced the masked woman's chest, but silver-tipped claws had deflected a fatal blow to the heart. The chained man suddenly swooped down and plucked her up from the sucking mud.

"She did not save you, child," the man said, cradling her against cold metal chains as he raced away. "Anyone in her path is doomed to die."

The woman removed her white mask. Starkly pale lips moved as she lifted onto her toes, fingers splayed and tipped with double-edged blades the length of short swords. She swung her arms out wide and pulled into a tight spin trailed by severed heads and throats spraying crimson—fanged or winged, it mattered not. A river of blood flowed in her wake.

"That creature is death incarnate." The chained man's voice rang with a prowess imbalanced with the natural world. "The most lethal weapon created and the Morning Star's failsafe to end this war."

The ground was a lush green where he took her. White clouds dotted the deepening blue of the horizon, and youthful laughter and birdsong filtered over the distance. There was no violence, no blood, no screaming.

"I like this place," she tried to whisper. Thirst held her voice hostage.

The chained man knelt on damp grass and propped her against his chest. "You are but an infant who has lost too much blood to survive this wound."

He nudged her mouth to his throat. "Follow your instincts and you shall live on to make a difference in this world. Drink from me. Take my blood."

Instinct honed her to his swishing veins, his pulse on her lips, the sweet aroma released with each beat. She bit into his jugular, famished and eager, and dug her claws into his back, latching him tight. He gasped and palmed her head. A satisfied growl rumbled in her throat.

Each swallow restored strength and erased the insanity of battle. The chained man's blood was sorrow in liquid form that bonded with primitive urges and planted a seed deep within her psyche to seek a life beyond wanton brutality.

It was a balm on the dark hole in her heart.

"I am called Hawkiel." He emphasized a long "i" in his name as his hand stayed her head. "Finish when you are ready, child; you can't take too much. I shall walk the plains and shores of this Earth for as long as it exists. Death has turned its back to me. Unlike you, I am cursed with true immortality."

Comfortable in his arms, she relaxed, unaware of ceasing or falling asleep. Dazzling pinpoints of light dappled the sky of night when she awoke.

"Good evening, Little One," he whispered, searching the heavens. "Have you recovered?"

"Aye," she said, staring in awe. Under the moon's soft light, his skin glimmered like a polished blade beneath a thin coat of dirt. "Who are you?"

"I am Hawkiel. I once watched over this realm as part of that constellation there." He pointed at the stars directly overhead. "Humans call it 'Orion, the Hunter of Night.' Somewhere above us, perhaps even there, my brother watches now, but he is blind to me and I to him."

Filth and blood caked his hair and skin, yet he bore a distinguished visage of perfect symmetry with prominent cheekbones and a defined jawline. She thought his cheeks might dimple if he smiled.

"What is your name, child?" His gaze drifted down from Orion. Though muted and dull, she knew it had once outshined the stars.

"How do I know?"

"What do you imagine others calling you?"

A large black bird materialized in her mind's eye. "Raven?" she asked uncertainly.

"Lucifer has moved onto the emerging Norse beliefs, then. Ravens are Odin's trusted companions, flying about the world to tell him of what they see and hear." Muted eyes reflected the stars. "It's a beautiful name. Ravens are majestic birds. Highly adaptable and intelligent. They're associated with death, but are splendid when one pauses to admire them."

"Raven." She repeated her name a few times and studied the golden-brown locks she twisted in pale, slender fingers. She turned her hands and feet out and looked over her arms and legs. Hawkiel had dressed her in his outer gown. "I don't feel majestic or beautiful. I feel like a monster."

"You are no monster, child. You are an anomaly who can bring peace to your kind. You know true justice in your heart." He paused. "There are two others, but neither embraced their gifts as swiftly as you. Like me, you do not wish to fight."

"I don't want to go back there," she whispered, shrinking behind her knees.

"You are my hope." He stroked her hair. "When this conflict arose within the Celestial Curtain, my twin brother, Darkesiel, and I didn't share the Morning Star's ideals, but we didn't desire to strike him either."

He sighed. "In a war with only two sides, we chose to remain neutral. As punishment, we were sentenced to an existence of walking until we find something worthy of a fight. Our wings were bound and our lights extinguished. We were cast out from the Celestial Curtain—my brother to the heavens and me to Earth, struck blind and mute to each other so that we may neither see nor hear the other."

"But you look for him anyway?"

"Every night. I search in vain. I can't see my brother, and yet I search."

"I am sorry for you, Hawkiel."

"Do not mourn for me, child. This conflict began with the Morning Star—Lucifer. Because of him, I have watched my brothers kill each other for more than four hundred years. I am a fallen angel, but not one of the Fallen Host, and, as my hope, you are a gateway to ending this torment for us all."

A flash of blinding blue cracked the sky open and struck the earth. A plume of dust rose before them as thunder grumbled throughout the heavens. Raven cowered within Hawkiel's embrace.

"Brother Gabriel?" A note of surprise tuned Hawkiel's voice.

The earth-shaking being looked much like the winged warriors, yet bore no stain—mud or blood or otherwise—and was unsullied and perfect, weaponless, and haloed in pale blue.

"Do not looketh upon me thou fallen star," he said in a melodious voice not meant for the natural world to behold. "I desire to witness what hath made thou shine. We saw warmth spark within thy heart, and it began twisting the fibers of light and dark as far as our vision can see. That spark momentarily renewed our hope that thou shalt rejoin us, but alas, my view has shown that it shalt touch humanity with greater effect."

"I cannot raise a sword against my brothers," Hawkiel replied. "Spark or not. The Hand of Divinity should intervene and end this war. His children do not deserve this any more than the Heavenly Host."

"Speaketh not of those thou chose not to protect," the being, Gabriel, spat. "The Hand of Divinity hast chosen to intervene—based on the spark in thy heart—thou *fallen* star."

"He will end the war?"

"Nay. He hast stripped the Morning Star of his power of creation."

Hawkiel's breath caught in his throat. "Stripped? Why only that when He can end this? Why intervene at all? They are both too stub—"

"Do not question His ways!" Gabriel snapped. "That frightened beast cuddled to thy breast shalt be the last of her kind to curse this earth."

"She is not like the others, Brother Gabriel. Have hope for them and hope for an end to our differences."

"Thou speaketh of hope, yet refuseth to fight for it? Thou believeth in love, yet do nothing when others vie to wipe it from this world?"

"I will not raise a sword in a battle of misled innocents."

"And yet they chose to follow and thou chose not to choose." Gabriel paused for a moment. "Alas, henceforth thou shalt be known as the herald who shalt usher this world into darkness at the End of Days. Thou shalt cometh on the heels of a horseman and reduce this world to ash with the light of thine own ray when thou hast finally chosen to fight. And this creature shalt be the harbinger of thy coming. Give her thy mark, thou fallen star. And a name. She can surely end this war and succeed where thou refuseth to try and fail."

"No."

"Then I shalt erase her from existence now, alongside your hope."

Silence hung off his final word. The muscles under Raven's fingers tensed as Hawkiel drew in a tight breath.

"I name her Hawkings," he said at last. In that instant, the fire of a sun blistered Raven's newborn skin. Screeching in agony and reeking of charred flesh, she futilely fought to escape Hawkiel's steely embrace.

He pulled the gown off her shoulder. "There, Brother Gabriel. My mark. This girl shall be known henceforth as Raven Hawkings, harbinger of the End of Days, and the only one of her kind with true justice in her heart. She will be immune from intervention by both the Heavenly Host and our fallen brethren."

"Fair thee well, thou *fallen* star," Gabriel said, his voice fading alongside his materialized form. "Watch this one lest she fail Destiny and doom every soul on this planet."

II

Orison Crossing, Summer 2006

"Ground Control to Commander Raven." A rough finger jabbed her bicep. "Is your circuit on? Ground Control t—"

"I heard you the first time, you daft idiot," Raven snapped, slapping Alex's outstretched hand into his cheek. "This is hardly the time."

"Hey! I'll stop slapping myself if you stop spacing out." Shifting from foot to foot, Alex poked her again. "Our world's going to Hell and you're in La-La Land with the Gingerbread Man. Did you catch him?"

She wrestled his nose between her thumb and forefinger, and yanked him within inches of her face. "I caught you, so what do you think?"

Beyond Alex's whimpers, she eyed their shell-shocked lords. Master Jonathan stood beside Eric sitting in his desk chair, their absent gazes betraying an inability to comprehend Lord Lucien's evacuation order.

"I need them clearheaded," she said lowly to Alex before shoving past him. "Master Jonathan?"

He wasn't entirely present, but he looked up, at least. "Another attack may be imminent and *he* will come if we don't contain this."

"Lucien is aware." Master Jonathan's voice was distant, but his black and gold irises finally focused on her—*hard*. "He lifted Endymion to the third seat days ago. We'll discuss it later."

To himself, he muttered, "Lucifer will probably move again soon, too."

Eric's face rose sharply. "What was that?"

"You're alive. His return is inevitable." Slicking his fingers over his brow, Master Jonathan scoffed and straightened his spine. "We need to secure both entry points from Animus Hollow to ensure the High Council's safe arrival. Raven, take point with Rainne and Lucien. Alex, you and the pack attend the Elders."

"I cannot leave you three alone," Alex replied. "I'll assign Heron and Cyprian, sir."

"Acceptable." To Raven, Master Jonathan said, "Rainne is presently in sleep mode under the care of six hunters. When she awakens, initiate the Hawkings Protocol and input command 'beta echo zero.' Ensure there are no lingering effects from her activation."

Raven flinched. "Lady Rainne was activated? When? By whom?"

"Corben sent her after the Sacred Vessel. Endymion put her to sleep. I cannot chance that she will reactivate when she sees Paresh—"

"*That woman is not coming here!*" Eric stabbed the desk with his index finger. Hostility flared from his aura. "I put Molly in the ground *today*— and now this? What the hell am I supposed to do about the High Council's arrival with 'full escort?' What does that even mean? Why are they coming here? How many are coming? Where does Lucien expect me to put them?"

"Many are coming," echoed the Chief of the Orison Crossing Police Department. All color had drained from Walter's face. The sagging bag of soup he'd brought for Paresh slid through his fingers. "What..."

Raven caught the bag before it spilled on the crimson and cream rug covering the hardwood floor of Eric's office and escorted the ghostly lawman to a recliner. "Here, put your head down. Now, breathe."

Gathering her black peasant skirt, Paresh swiveled on the corner of the desk to face Eric. "You said Dad left the mansion to a skeleton crew. Is it habitable?"

All eyes—except Walter's—landed on the young woman. Their surprised vampiric auras prickled the books lining the built-ins, but her...this girl—their Sacred Vessel—undulated serenity and embraced their fear.

Picking at her nails, she glanced around uncertain about the sudden scrutiny. "Is that a bad idea?"

"No, it's a great idea," Eric said, slightly dumbstruck. He grabbed the handset of his desk phone. "I'll pull the crew—no humans on site."

Master Jonathan's head bobbed in agreement. He reached for Paresh's hand and visibly relaxed upon making contact, inhaling deeply and smiling halfheartedly. "It's perfect, Pare."

As Eric arranged the caretakers' offsite housing, Raven tied the soup bag upright on the coffee table and sat on the recliner arm to catch Walter if he passed out. Eric hung up and patted Paresh on the thigh. Cords of tension in his neck unwound as he settled into his chair, his hand lingering on her knee.

"The Arc of Celestial Night—" Master Jonathan scowled, disgusted. "They want to distract us. Donovan said victory comes amid chaos. There will be more."

"Aye," Raven said, "but their success depends on our failures."

"Well, we're starting where we can. The mansion won't be up to the Elders' standards, I'm sure," Eric said, "but it's there and ready. How many are coming?"

Raven tucked a strand of neon pink hair behind her ear. "The Chthonic Knights and Crimson Guard are on security detail en masse and will arrive alongside the Elders and arc heralds. That's twelve, eh, no—*eleven*—Elders, plus Lord Lucien, four heralds, and, what? Seventy-five hunters?" She visually queried Alex.

"At least fifty-three of mine—the rest are already here. I don't know how many Nallura's got up there," Alex replied. "No need to worry about lodging the hunters, though; we're nomads. Goody, we should go."

Take-charge Alex is back, Raven thought, momentarily sidetracked by the freshly tailored seams and sharp creases in the black suit he'd worn to Molly's funeral. Squared shoulders sloped over a tapered body that was all muscle. Limber and graceful as a high diver, he was always fierce and alert on duty. Despite his aloof affect, he only *played* the fool.

Catching her staring, Alex made an impatient "let's go" gesture and then addressed his hunters. The first and second officers of Master Jonathan's pack, Heron and Cyprian, had charged in upon learning of the blast on Banks Island. Their subordinates were likely awaiting orders in the lobby.

"Mind Master Jonathan's wound. If you have the choice of fight or flight, take flight and request backup."

Heron and Cyprian balled their fists to their chests and said in unison, "Yes, Commander."

The hunters resembled humans of Middle-Eastern descent, nearly twins with cropped black hair and dark tiger-stone eyes despite Heron's pale complexion and Cyprian's olive-toned skin. They shared the true blood's regal features and lengthened canines, and wore the Crimson Guard's standard uniform of black cargo pants and form-fitted black and red sleeveless shirts.

"The pack's with me. Call them in." Alex produced his Vampiric Star and tapped the silver prong for Animus Hollow. Master Jonathan's pack filed into the office and the endlessly rolling white haze of the dimensional divide between Heaven, Earth, and Hades split open.

"Goody?" Alex pointed at her and tossed his thumb at the portal. "The Elders will be here any minute and that Gingerbread Man ain't gonna catch himself."

That didn't last long, Raven thought dryly, rolling her eyes. She patted Walter's shoulder and stepped from the lawman's line of sight. She mouthed to Eric, "Take care of him."

She swatted Alex into the portal. His hunters followed, but Raven hesitated to watch Paresh sit beside Walter. She hoped the girl's presence soothed humans the same way it did vampires.

With a final nod to her lords, she stepped into the Hollow's mouth, and the crumbling reality she'd unknowingly been holding together cracked and shattered. The peace she'd fought to bring to her nation was gone.

Her First Officer had turned rogue, the traitorous Elder had activated Rainne Blood Pathos for the first time in centuries, and Lord Lucien had elevated Lord Endymion to his rightful seat—anticipating Hawkiel's arrival. And now, he was evacuating the Arc of True Blood while the Arc of Celestial Night burned to ash.

The sensation of a hand slipped into hers and pulled her into a body-heated cloud of masculine pheromones and notes of the sun, organic green, and seaside. "Alex…"

The Hollow's mist secreted her whisper from his ears. Beneath her fingers, the black silk of his shirt and the muscular ridges of his chest were a sensation of memory, but his racing heart was real—electrical energy remained a tangible part of the Hollow's molecular conversion.

For a split second, she enjoyed him as her version of Heaven. He was a contradiction in their world that belonged in nature amongst glittering sand, salty spray, and sparkling blue waters. He was the smiling warmth of daylight and the sweetness of dew-kissed leaves.

"You aren't alone." The Hollow threw his voice far away, but his breath caressed her ear.

In a time when friends hadn't existed, before love and souls, the Hand of Divinity had engrained the instinct to protect in Alex. She'd always had him—one of few who knew the truth of her existence—which made her a dangerous distraction.

She broke free and yelled, "They're exiting at the fixed point in the forest. Redirect them to the variable point at the Hawthorne Mansion. I'll set up a security net."

"As you wish, High Commander." The conspicuous absence of his vocal squeak flared resentment and guilt in Raven's gut. No matter his effort, Alex couldn't stop the inevitable. Only the Hand of Divinity held that power—the same Hand that refused to end a war raging under a modern veil of free will.

Eric and her eternal lords possessed the power of fallen angels, but she had the blood of one in her veins and viewed the world through his eyes. The Vampiric Nation's turmoil threatened to eviscerate the delicate balance between the stars and the Lamb, to unleash the power of letters and scrolls, to pull the lynchpin between life and death.

It didn't matter if Lucifer moved again. The Morning Star commanded great power and a preordained role in Final Judgment, but he wasn't holding the trigger to a premature Apocalypse.

Hawkiel was the catalyst and he was coming.

III

The tide of Paresh's calm ebbed and left nothing to douse anger's rising flames. Eric had gotten his three days and buried Molly, but it'd been asking too damn much to finish the evening free of the Vampiric

Nation's theatrics.

"Lucien made it clear that I'm ignorant by choice," he said too lowly for Walter—and Paresh, he hoped—to hear. Through a thick fringe of lashes, he spied their new security detail before flicking an irritated gaze at Jonathan. He jabbed his splintered desk. "But you tell me what I need to know, *now*. If anything happens in my town due to this evacuation, your nation isn't going to like its newest Arch Elder."

"No worries there. They've never liked you, Brother." Jonathan nudged his chin at Heron and Cyprian, their interest piqued under thinly veiled confusion.

"Master Jonathan?"

Of course, it was Heron. He seemingly spoke for both of them. Jonathan's lips parted as Eric was about to respond.

"Don't you dare speak for me," Eric growled, halting Jonathan with an impatient hand. To the hunters, he snapped, "I don't have time for archaic traditions. Jonathan and I are equal to Lucien. Mind your post and don't interrupt."

Upon facing Jonathan, the ferocity in Eric's gut roiled. His brother was nodding, meaning the two hunters had sought visual confirmation behind his back.

Deliberately splaying his fingertips in line with the desk's wood grain, Jonathan looked askance and spoke in a faint, controlled voice. "Those 'archaic traditions' protect the flow of sensitive information— particularly items known only to Lucien and me. As a former soldier, you should understand that. We will talk when we have adequate privacy."

A raised finger silenced Eric's protest. Jonathan returned it to the desk. "Let's begin with Rainne."

Motioning for Jonathan to sit opposite him, Eric eased back into his chair. Nauseating arrogance rolled off his brother as he studied the smaller leather chairs. Newfound brotherhood be damned—his fingertips whitened as he pressed off the desk.

"Rainne was the twelfth true blood created," Jonathan began, shoving an unstable paper stack aside and leaning against the edge. "We didn't know it at first, but Lucifer needed a way to exterminate us after we eradicated mankind—"

"Starvation would have worked, I'd think," Eric muttered, straightening the leaning tower.

"Perhaps, if humans were our only nutritional source." Jonathan cocked a smug brow.

Sucking down a restrained breath, Eric closed his eyes and stole a quiet moment in darkness. Beaming a tight smile at his brother, he let the air trickle between his lips. "Did you tell me any full truths? Ever?"

"It's doubtful." Jonathan shrugged. "Shall I go on?"

"By all means, *your highness*, please, do continue."

Eric got a look of warning, but merely crossed his arms and glared back. Jonathan, wearing the haughty air of a man in control, settled comfortably and folded one arm under the other with supernatural ease. "I'm not the one evacuating the arc."

"Are you seriously telling me to redirect my anger?" The chair squeaked as Eric leaned forward. "Because if you think I'm not angry as hell at you, you're dead wrong."

"Okay—" Jonathan tossed his hand out. "Then, do you want to fight or talk? I'm an easy target so take your shot." He tossed his other hand aside and stood.

Eric stewed in silence. Jonathan tried to hide it, but he favored his left side anytime he moved. The scarred tissue from the wound Donovan had reopened remained a critical risk for hemorrhage.

"You should be resting," Eric grunted with a huff.

"Nice of you to care." Jonathan failed to pass a grimace off as a smirk.

"For once, I won't fight you on that," Eric replied. "And you're right. You're not the source of my frustration, but you need to take better care of yourself. Here—you. Sit."

They swapped places, Jonathan unable to hide his discomfort and Eric's worry creasing his forehead. Jonathan grinned and whispered behind the back of his hand. "Look at us, acting like civilized siblings."

He winked and sank into the chair's cushioning leather. "All I meant was—the true bloods were created to fight in the Great Holy War against the Host, which—much like humans—*He* made in His image, at least in their earthly forms, so their blood—"

Clearing his throat, Eric ran his hand through his hair. "Yeah, yeah…roaring war machine, glory days, etcetera—got it. No starving. Avoid saying something you don't want *overheard*."

Jonathan's gaze drifted over Eric's shoulder. "She knows I fought in the war, but not what that truly means."

"It's for the best." Eric sighed. "I promised her I wouldn't ruin how she sees you, but I can only do that if you help."

Jonathan nodded. "Suffice to say that the true blood protein can't infect angels and we would have turned on the Fallen Host as an eternal supply."

"Enter Rainne?"

Jonathan nodded again. "Lucifer usually shoved new true bloods into battle uncaring if they lived or died—"

"Might've been your first indication of things to come," Eric muttered, getting another visual warning.

"But," Jonathan said tightly, "he presented Rainne personally—"

"What does he look like?" Eric interrupted again, gripping the desk and slightly straightening under the power of human curiosity.

"I…" Lowering his gaze, Jonathan distractedly traced the splintered crater atop the desk as though truly seeing it for the first time. Hooded eyes posed a silent question—he hadn't angered Eric enough to warrant such violence, so who, then?

Feeling his ribs shrink around his lungs, Eric drew in a shallow breath. He tipped his head to Walter. Jonathan's gaze followed and returned to the damage.

Lifting an interested brow, Jonathan pursed his lips and drifted into thought, pressing raised splinters flat. "When?"

Huffing with exasperation, Eric said, "Before you got here. It doesn't matter; answer me."

Jonathan continued his repair and whispered, "Lucien might know. I've only seen him through possessions, like with Nicole."

"But you're his favorite—"

"Ha," Jonathan chuckled lightly, "of the creations he hates more than humans. Why else present Rainne, speaking the truth of her abilities, but lying about his motive for creating her? The first time we activated her, she shredded everyone to ribbons. It didn't matter which side they were on."

Emotion seeped from Jonathan's aura, carefully and deliberately directed to reach him and him alone. Eric recognized the pain of betrayal and briefly thought back to his father's desperation for that last drop of whiskey to numb his grief. He understood that kind of abandonment too well. He wiped his face to clear the memory.

"You keep saying 'activated' like she's a machine. What is she?"

"Lucifer's failsafe. If *he* ever activates her—" Jonathan's darkening gold eyes lifted. He held up four fingers. "Mere words. That's all it takes. Four words from Lucifer's mouth and Rainne takes all our heads. In his hands, she'd kill everyone on Earth."

"And he…he was *here*," Eric whispered, falling into a different memory, one of blood and death better suited to a nightmare.

"I'd think Rainne would be his primary target. Not you. Not her."

Jonathan nodded at Paresh. "And certainly not an arc of ancient vampires sleeping their lives away. But Corben had the chance to take her and didn't. None of this makes sense."

"How did he——" Rolling his hand through the air, Eric searched for the right words. "——make such a *thing*?"

Jonathan shook his head again. "She's a true blood, but she's also the most efficient killing device on the planet. We can program her with codes and enforce access restrictions, but no one supersedes Lucifer's authority. Lucien issued a standing kill order if Lucifer is ever remotely close to being within her hearing range."

The heat of anger expanded in Eric's tightening chest. "And yet he let her walk up to Paresh like that? How close was she——*really*——Jonathan?"

Jonathan stared at the fractured wood, fingers frozen, lips silent. Finally, without looking up, he clenched his jaw. "Too close. I don't know why he hesitated."

"He wanted to see if she'd affect me." The barely audible response came from Paresh. Perched beside Walter, she lifted a gaze filled with melancholy and disappointment. "One of these days, you'll realize that you can't keep hiding things from me, no matter how quietly you whisper. Lucien knew he could stop her despite the bravado."

"Don't take her lightly, Pare," Jonathan warned. "She's too unpredictable to take that gamble."

"Why didn't *you* stop her?" Eric asked.

After another moment of jaw-grinding thought, Jonathan tossed his chin at Heron and Cyprian. "Wait in the lobby."

The hunters bowed their heads and stepped out, the room flashing blue twice behind them to confirm the button blocking noise both ways. Jonathan eyed Walter, hunched on his elbows under Paresh's soothing hand crisscrossing his back. A flash of steel gray from beneath her blond mane made her focus clear——no more hiding; she was part of their conversation.

Eric acknowledged her with a subtle nod and addressed Jonathan's surveillance of the lawman. "I guarantee he's thinking about how to keep his officers from noticing increased activity at the mansion—— especially given the news release about David's involvement. He's not paying attention to us."

"Very well." Tugging at his black cuffs, Jonathan hesitantly revealed, "Lucien and I are immune to Rainne so we can command her, but——"

He threw out an agitated hand. "You saw her. Once she's activated, she's difficult to control, and…sometimes my commands don't stick."

Jonathan shrugged somewhat helplessly at Paresh. "My only thought was putting myself between her and you."

Facing the ceiling, Jonathan ran his tongue along his upper teeth. "He shouldn't have waited. Lucien's authority is law, even to her."

Copper strands escaped the crimson ribbon at his nape as he shook his head in frustration. "But if Lucifer's got command, our immunity doesn't matter. We'll succumb to exhaustion from fending her off and then she'll take our heads. I assume it's the same for you." Jonathan pointed at Eric. "But Pare? I'm certain Lucien was curious less about immunity and more about her effect. I wasn't there when Rainne received Paresh's blood."

"Why do you keep her alive at all?" Eric demanded at the same time that an appalled Paresh asked, "Why risk losing that control?"

Paresh added, "Isn't she a threat to the Vampiric Nation? I thought threats were dealt with swiftly."

Jonathan quieted, stewing as he fidgeted with his jacket. His jaw bulged when he smoothed down the left side. "We withdrew from the war as a nation of bloodthirsty creatures suddenly forced into peace. Lucien needed leverage."

"Always the Iron Fist." The words tasted so bitter, Eric nearly spat them out.

"It's cruel," Paresh agreed. She grabbed two water bottles from the refrigerated sideboard along the interior wall and coaxed one into Walter's hand.

"That is why I don't want you exposed to my world, Pare," Jonathan said. "It's not about keeping secrets. You see the world as beautiful, but I live in a place where fear and hope are weapons used to rule a nation."

"Your world is my world, Master Jon." She sipped her water.

"Just Jonathan, Pare." He swept his fingers over closed eyes. "Raven is our safety net for Rainne. It's why Lucien made her the VaSH High Commander against so many objections. The particulars are restricted to a confidential few."

The worry that suddenly crinkled Jonathan's brow roused Eric's unease. "You know something?"

"No, but *Donovan* knew things about Raven that we didn't think even Lucifer knew. He must be involved if they're calling themselves the Children of the Morning Star—"

"The COMS—" Paresh interrupted as Walter said, "I'm sorry about the folks you lost in that explosion."

The lawman patted Paresh's leg and stood. "If this place needs to be your haven, then it will be. If you have wounded, bring them here. Juliet at the blood bank can make arrangements. I'll do whatever I can."

Walter looked utterly defeated. Shrugging limp shoulders, he said, "Just…tell me what I can do. There has to be something. We've lost people. You've lost people. We're in this together."

Paresh threaded their fingers and nodded at Jonathan and Eric. "It's hard for them, too, Walter." She squeezed his hand. "They don't know what to do, either."

"We'll minimize our presence at the Hawthorne Mansion to avoid causing you trouble," Jonathan said.

Shaking his head, Walter said, "Don't worry about anything like that. This town should be there for Eric like he's been there for it all these years, and that extends to you."

"Thank you, Walter, really." Eric gave him a half-smile of understanding. "It's been a rough couple of weeks."

"That's an understate—whoa!"

Walter lurched sideways as Paresh's legs crumbled. Landing on her knees, she gripped her throat and groaned. Eric sprang over his desk and Jonathan left the chair spinning in his sprint to stop Walter from crashing down on top of her.

"Pare, you need to drink or you will never heal properly!" With a confused Walter half-dangling over his arm, Jonathan swore through clenched teeth and scowled at Eric.

"Ohh," Paresh moaned. "I need…soup."

"You don't need soup!" Jonathan barely contained his disgust. "You shouldn't even be able to eat human food!"

Her hands dropped to her sides as she slumped against Eric. "But it's what I want. It's all I can think about."

Eric cupped her face, studying her carefully. "You aren't hiding anything from us, are you?"

"Ironic." She smiled weakly. "When the pain comes, it's like fire. No hiding that."

Eric pressed his forehead against hers, stroking her nape. "One day soon, I promise, this will end."

"Why not go to The Greenery?" Walter suggested, awkwardly righting himself as Jonathan bumped him off and yanked his sleeve straight. "If we're only going to hurry up and wait, does it matter where we are?"

"If the 'COMS,' as Paresh calls them," Jonathan replied, "or Lucifer, attack, we're vulnerable regardless."

"Well then, let's get this young lady some of that soup she's craving," Walter said.

Eric rocked back on his heels. "Jonathan, have your hunters cloak themselves. You've sparked enough curiosity in town; I don't need more after that scene at the church." He rose, pulling Paresh up with him. "We'll go the analog route and leave a note."

Jonathan tipped Paresh's chin down and doled a kiss onto her crown. "You shouldn't be eating soup, but if you want soup, then so be it."

"Thanks, Master Jon."

"Just Jonathan. You are far too important to call anyone 'Master,' especially me."

Their weakly constituted plan restored a blush of color to Walter's face. Eric motioned for the lawman to lead the way out and muttered to Jonathan, "I echo Walter's offer of safe haven, but I don't want that weapon here."

Jonathan slipped an arm around Paresh's shoulder. "Rainne Blood Pathos shall not step foot in Sunset Grove. I vow it with my life, Brother."

IV

South of the Tropic of Cancer, Africa, 5th Century A.D.

Only when Gabriel's light vanished did Raven dare open her eyes. Black ash flaked off as she gingerly inspected her charred flesh. Whimpering and revolted, she smeared sooty fingers on grass slicked with dew.

"The pain won't last long, Little One." Hawkiel gently took her hand and cleaned her fingers with his raiment. "I required the heat of a star to boil your blood and burn your skin; stain and needles do not suffice on creatures with restorative powers, I'm afraid."

"But why?" She craned her neck in vain to see what he had done to her.

"I cannot say. I know not of Brother Gabriel's, or the Almighty's, plans. My mark gives them access to you, but how they choose to use you remains to be seen."

As the pain faded, she brushed off clumps of dead and burnt flesh. Blackened flecks drifted on the breeze. A raised welt met her fingers. Unable to form a mental image by tracing it, she pulled the cloth over and protectively hugged her arm.

Lifting his sleeve, Hawkiel revealed a tattoo on his left bicep of two upright and intertwined crescent moons, the same pale blue of his eyes, which intersected at two points over the center of a blood red, twelve-pointed star. "A reminder of my former glory. Red and blue—the colors of the blood that binds us. This is my mark—the mark you shall bear henceforth."

A lump gathered in her throat. "I don't understand," she croaked.

"Ah, child," Hawkiel said, embracing her. "Lucifer's methods are cold. Jealousy has blinded him to love's warmth, and bestowed upon him the cruel hand that shaped your form and threw you into battle before you had even once opened your eyes. Whether you follow instinct into the slaughter or perish, he cares not. One must wonder if he cares about the Fallen Host or his other brothers anymore. Perhaps hatred has thoroughly consumed him.

"The Morning Star cannot see that good exists within the Realm of Man. You need only watch humans unaffected by the war. Its reach is mighty, but not all encompassing."

He pointed at flickering lights along the northern horizon. "That is a small village where humans live in simple structures and subsist on little more than grain and fish. Everyone has a purpose there—the men work hard, and the women cook and rear their children. Families revel in their love for each other and the love of God. They are not without strife or suffering, but are inherently at peace and pray for the blessings of God to befall them. They have shown me kindness and offered shelter in harsh weather even though I am a stranger."

"They would not be so kind to me," Raven thought aloud, tucking her knees to her chest. If the Earth was large, perhaps she could fold small enough to disappear into one of its crevices.

"Why do you believe such a thing?"

Raven hugged her knees closer. "I feel it, deep inside."

"Look into your heart. You will feel differently soon enough. Come and see." He stood and offered his hand.

She was wobbly upon rising and thankful for Hawkiel's steadying arm.

"Can you walk?"

"Aye," she said, but the world was spinning beneath her feet despite nothing in her visual field moving. She desperately clung to Hawkiel. "It wants to cast me off!"

"Your race is so sensitive." There was a note of awe to his voice. "Lucifer doesn't appreciate the miracle of your existence or his craftsmanship. No other angel has such ability."

Holding one index finger straight up, Hawkiel pointed his other index finger down and circled the first finger. "This is the planetary design for many of the celestial bodies within the cosmos. The Earth spins in place on an axis as it orbits its star through space, like this. Much time has passed since I last noticed it, and humans aren't aware of it—human astronomers believe this world is the center of the Universe."

"The Earth is spinning? Now?" Raven incredulously looked down and wiggled her toes. "Why am I not cast off?"

"You ask a great many questions, Little One. I shall answer them all; we have time. For now, come see humans through the eyes of an angel and be enlightened."

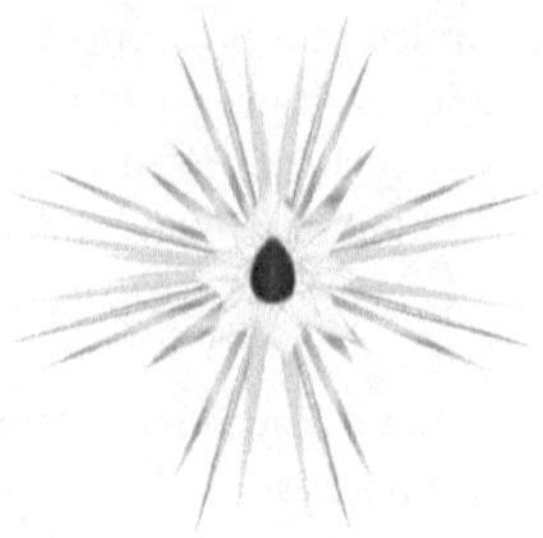

Chapter Two: Lionhearted

I

Orison Crossing, Summer 2006

Animus Hollow's endless white haze split into an oval of fragrant green between rows of squat and twisty apple trees. The fruit's budding perfume lingered atop notes of bark and humid undergrowth, and the buzz of working insects brought the grove to life, the antithesis of a day engulfed in death.

Raven had opted to match Alex and worn trousers instead of a skirt to Molly's funeral, but she wasn't equipped to handle an evacuation of this magnitude. She'd only come prepared to set up a security grid at Eric's house.

They say to be thankful for small miracles, right? she thought, the points of silver-tipped darts pricking her fingers as she dug a cluster from her pocket.

She threw the darts in a wide arc. Slicing through branches and foliage, each one burst open at its zenith and spat gravity-defying blue sparks that crackled and connected along tiny, electrified pathways. Raven collected the emptied shells, tucked them into her pocket, and grabbed a new handful.

Those silver barbs scattered horizontally, leaving a wake of blue sparks mere inches above the ground. Zigzagging like alternating current, they connected and leapt hungrily at the overhead arc to form a net.

Additional darts carved a path out of the orchard, through a derelict garden with broken statues and an empty scalloped fountain, to embed into the mansion's rear wall. The sparks there linked together and jogged back to their source, creating a protective tunnel to keep the

Elders unseen and unheard.

She shoved a final grounding dart into the grass with her heel. A central beam shot down from the peak and fused with the exposed metal dot, forming a thin coating of silicone that contained coding and security data pertinent to the grid. Raven peeled the chip off and the net flickered into transparency. She stuck the tiny circle beneath her left breast, close to her heart—the safest place on her body to keep it.

Barely a minute passed before a ripple through the silicone chip indicated an interruption of circuitry. The auras of her unseen visitors announced the arrival of her remaining squad. "The Crimson Commander is directing the Council here. The proximity net is in place. Secure the house."

"Yes, ma'am."

"Do not alert your presences to any humans," Raven ordered. "One caretaker resides onsite—Lord Eric has arranged for offsite rooming. The rest live elsewhere and are off today for the funeral."

"Understood," Jocathian replied, cloaked a few rows ahead. "By all appearances, the structures are presently empty."

"The communicators are compromised. After the Elders arrive, give verbal status reports to the Crimson Commander."

"Yes, ma'am," her hunters replied in unison. Another ripple announced their departure.

Where are you, Alex? Impatiently tapping a prong on her Vampiric Star, she opened a portal across from the variable point and straddled the two realms.

Hawkiel told her many secrets about Animus Hollow that no one else knew—First and Second Born aside. The Hollow's fold transformed all entrants into concentrated energy, which, for vampires—whether true blood or altered—meant temporarily fusing their bodies and symbiotic auras.

Hawkiel had taught her how to block that fusion.

She released her aura to scout the endless haze and found the Elders at the exit. The exasperation within Alex's energy signature indicated it hadn't been a peaceful trip. She pulled her aura back and closed the Hollow.

An instant later, the variable point opened and Alex appeared apart from the fog. He popped his mouth wide, rolled his eyes up at the early evening sky, and mouthed an exaggerated, "Wow!"

Lady Ambrosia shoved her way out pursued by Plathius and Danaë, her security detail. Garbed in the Crimson Guard's black and red uniform, Danaë snatched Lady Ambrosia's wrist. Her partner struggled while the High Elder waved the other wildly, yelling, "Do not touch me! Unjustly sequestered to quarters and then ordered to leave—I will not be treated as a criminal!"

"Lady Ambrosia." Alex gave a reverent nod. "Lord Lucien ordered you and Lady Lucasta into custody. My hunters cannot permit you to wander free—"

A loud slap resounded off Alex's face and down the row of trees. Glowering and poised to strike again, she spat, "Tilting your chin? You *kneel* before me! I am a High Elder of this Council!"

As Alex briefly touched his inflamed cheek and nudged his sunglasses straight, an apathetic voice drifted through the portal. "I shall relieve you of that burden, Ambrosia."

The High Elder paled as her gaze shot into Animus Hollow. "How did you…?" She glanced uncertainly at Alex. "But he hasn't left the arc."

Lord Lucien's disembodied voice again floated through the rolling mist, "Commander Alexander, place Ambrosia into secure custody."

"As you command, my lord," Alex replied with a lopsided grin.

He nodded for his hunters to hold Ambrosia's arms, but she was too shocked to resist. Alex cuffed her wrists with a hinged, silver ring and stated, "Ambrosia, former Higher Elder of the Fifth Seat, I hereby place you into secure custody as ordered by Arch Elder Lord Lucien the Eternal."

A fleeting shadow in Ambrosia's expression rang Raven's internal warning bell. "Alex," she said, "hang back with the others in the Hollow until she's secured. Danaë and Plathius, take Ambrosia into the house, now—Chavnia and Jocathian are securing the interior. They will assist. Seal her in a room with a barrier set to block all noise and a minimum of two hunters with eyes at all times."

Alex's crinkled brow questioned Raven as his hunters marched Ambrosia toward the house. Ignoring him, she asked, "Is Lord Lucien truly at the arc?"

"Yes," came an emotionless voice.

"Is Lady Rainne with you, sire?"

"She is."

"I request permission to detail your departure personally."

"Allowed."

She re-activated her exit portal and faced Alex, who was standing half in and half out of the variable point. "Once Ambrosia is properly secured, escort the Council inside with apologies for the delay from the

High Commander. The proximity net is centered here—"

She indicated the metal head in the grass. "—and extends to the rear of the house. Chavnia or Jocathian will present verbal status reports. Secure and anchor the entirety of the grounds and remain here until I summon you to assist with escorting Lord Lucien and Lady Rainne."

"As you command, ma'am," Alex replied, balling his fist over his heart, but not tucking his chin. As Raven stepped backward into her portal, his fern green eyes locked onto hers through his garnet lenses, seeking answers to questions he didn't need to ask.

☽ ❊ ☾

Security protocols at the Arc of True Blood restricted Animus Hollow's access to Snowblood Square, the center of the arc, and the Elders' meeting hall. Set to match Sunset Grove, the atmospheric half-light of evening broke through a patchy sky. Streams gurgled, frogs whirred, and bamboo fountains clanked hollowly. With the privacy grid down, the arc seemed empty and largely devoid of life. Abandoned.

"Commander."

"Oh!" Startled, she whirled in place and dropped into required reverence. "My lord! Apologies for not greeting you in proper form."

"Rise. Matters are far too pressing for formalities."

"Aye." Raven stood. "May I speak freely?"

Upon receiving a subtle nod, she asked, "How certain are you that this arc is vulnerable?"

"Our defenses are impenetrable."

"Then why evacuate?"

"To deny the traitorous Elder access to our security panels and equipment. Surely, you don't question the Arc of Celestial Night was destroyed from the inside out by the COMS?"

"I don't," Raven replied. "The…COMS?"

"Children of the Morning Star."

"Oh, of course," she said. "If I may, I have reservations about taking Lady Rainne from here."

"As do I. Endymion will guard her. The others shall believe I sealed Rainne into an iron casket—Endymion will prepare it for transport upon your departure. Bare your shoulder."

The black sleeveless blouse under her jacket gave him a clear view of what he wanted to see. Her breath caught when his icy fingers stroked Hawkiel's mark.

"The communicators aren't compromised, but I've switched the security frequency as a precaution. Use Alpha One." He traced the pale blue crescent moons on her skin. "The enemy acted faster and more erratically than I expected. I will make short appearances at the mansion."

"Understood. Lady Rainne and Lord Endymion will stay here with you?"

"Correct," Lord Lucien said. "Should the need arise, you shall return immediately to execute Rainne."

"Aye, sir," Raven said quietly.

"It's becoming visible. Keep it covered." His hand fell to his side.

"Aye, sir."

"Why did you wish to see me?"

Slipping into her jacket, she said, "I felt a negative jolt during Ambrosia's outburst—all that noise was a show to announce her location. She didn't know I'd cast the proximity net and hoped to catch us unprepared since Alex and I attended the human's funeral out of uniform."

Slipping his hands into the sleeves of his black kimono, his countenance and affect were as cold and flat as an arctic desert plain. "Connall, Corben, Ambrosia."

"All High Elders. Same batch. Same dose of traitor."

"Perhaps," Lord Lucien said, nodding to himself. "Lucifer experimented with 'The Gilded Lady' to test metal density and defense. Lucasta was created separately, as was Endymion."

"How certain are you that it's Ambrosia?"

"Your negative jolt speaks for itself."

"No other suspicions?"

"By miniscule fractions not worth mentioning."

"Master Jonathan said Corben activated Lady Rainne—"

"Yes, yes," Lord Lucien interrupted, patting the air with uncharacteristic impatience. "Jonathan questioned Corben's reason for leaving Rainne behind. I suspect Ambrosia was to activate her to take out the High Council."

Another chill shuddered down Raven's spine. "My lord—"

"I am quite certain," he continued, "that she was instructed to do so after the Arc of Celestial Night was destroyed. Lucifer would never expect me to evacuate this arc. The puppets he controls are equally as ignorant."

"May I speak with Lady Rainne before I enact the Hawkings Protocol?" The catch in Raven's voice rippled through her eternal lord's aura as surprise and manifested as a single black streak in his left iris.

"The Sacred Vessel's blood has affected you?" He inched closer, studying her reaction.

"Not enough to interfere with my duty to you, I vow it." Under his intense scrutiny, she dared not move. "The gravitation is not as strong as with the others."

"I expected you to be immune. Tell me again what Hawkiel said to Gabriel."

"I'm immune to intervention by the Heavenly Host and the Fallen Host."

"Only to angelic interference, then." Pondering in silence, he glided past Raven toward his private quarters near the arc's outer rim. "You may visit with Rainne. Endymion, too, if you wish. Take the time you have."

A lump lodged in Raven's throat. As Lord Lucien moved out of her sight line, she blew out a slow breath. "My lord?"

Lord Lucien stopped without facing her.

"Why do I feel this way? This wasn't supposed to happen." Anxiety added a tremor to her voice.

"A seraph designed our vessel's existence, but the blood in her veins is from *Him* and her essence is a side effect. No one is immune to *Him*—no one at all." Standing still as stone, Lord Lucien's aura grew heavy with anticipation.

No one is immune. Every part of her begged for silence, but her lips were already moving. "Even you?"

Anticipation stiffened into an impenetrable barrier. Where she thrashed in the shallows, he was solidly rooted.

"Endymion will awaken Rainne for you, Commander. Jonathan gave you an order."

His retreating form grayed under the shadow of a simulated cloud, but his silver strands gleamed in the light. He truly was their nation's shining grace—their pillar of strength—standing strong atop quaking ground.

☽ ❋ ☾

Dozens of oak trees, as ancient and grand as the arc itself, shaded Lady Rainne's residence and speckled the evening sun as gilded champagne upon Lord Endymion's white silk robe. He greeted her at the courtyard gate with a kiss on each cheek.

"Ah, my dear! How are you this evening?"

Raven curtsied with a reverent nod. "My lord honors me with his welcome." Straightening, she beamed a spirited smile and winked. "As usual, Endymion."

A welcoming cloud of lavender took her in as they embraced. "How I'm doing is of no consequence," she said. "Master Jonathan told me of your restoration to the third seat."

Endymion cupped her cheeks. Perceptive chartreuse eyes paler than sea glass and a melancholy smile sobered his visage. "It worries your heart. You have no need to hide it. The hunters inside cannot hear us and we keep no secrets from Lord Lucien."

She leaned into his warmth. "Hawkiel's mark is showing."

Heat tingled where his thumb stroked her cheek and traced her lips. "The dark spot is moving, as well. 'Twould appear the brothers may reunite at long last."

"The Second New Age has only begun. It isn't supposed to be like this."

He contemplated her in silence, his gentle touch maddening. She yearned to pause the moment into forever—and he knew it, lingering, savoring it all the same. But, he also knew the weight of her obligation.

"Too many truths of this world are better left unknown, my dear," he said at last. "The balance is always in danger, and the violence on Banks Island may create havoc not seen in the Realm of Man since before the Treaty of the Lasting Peace. The human race must not learn of our existence again. The ensuing fear and panic would fuel Lucifer's army through the End of Days, premature or otherwise."

"Aye, agreed." Sighing behind closed eyelids, Raven felt soft lips, affectionate and tender, press against hers. His aura deliberately serene, he grasped her nape, pulling her closer. She melted into him.

Endymion was her escape—an ever-expanding, moon-kissed field of lavender and serenity that whisked away all uncertainties, doubts, and worries. His presence denied time and space—as though stopping the Earth's rotation—and affected ethereal vertigo.

He broke away, raking her lip with a sharp tooth. He whispered into her ear on a lonely breath she knew was a lie, "I don't get to see you enough, my dear. Perhaps you might call on me at my quarters when matters are not so pressing?"

"Of course, my lord," she whispered back, licking at the blood pooling on her delicate skin.

"Not as your lord. I shall never order you to come to me."

"And you'd never need to." Raven smoothed her palm down the silk covering his chest, craving to touch the pale skin beneath.

"I am sorry about the Arc of Celestial Night," he said. "Initial reports did not indicate survivors."

Raven tensed the side of her jaw he couldn't see. She'd deliberately avoided those reports. "Aye, the Silent Vespers are securing the site and expect me shortly. I must tend to Lady Rainne. Master Jonathan's orders."

"The Nation comes first." He kissed her gently. "I am sorry nonetheless. I shall awaken Rainne. Come."

II

Isle of Wight, England, 897 A.D.

"Aha!" Smiling over her shoulder, Raven held up the slippery bass wriggling in her grasp. "Dinner tonight, Salea! Your papa will be proud!"

The braids and wavy curls in her companion's dark hair bounced and red fruits jumped from the folds of her skirt as she turned in surprise. The fourteen-year-old had been gathering ripening raspberries along the River Medine.

"The trap worked?" Salea gaped in disbelief. "It worked!"

"Show your brothers this trick of yours and they won't tease you anymore."

"Won't you stay to eat with us?" Salea asked. "Papa would invite you." Innocent brown eyes pleaded with Raven to say "yes" for once.

Lightly fingering the girl's hair, Raven said, "Your family's done enough to clothe me for the last ten years. They don't need to feed me, too."

"Will you stay the night, then?" Salea pointed to the overcast sky. "The rain will come. And Mama tells us the best stories before we sleep."

"Do not worry about me," Raven said. "Has your mother finished weaving my second garment?"

Salea shook her head. "She was almost finished when I left this morning."

"Then tomorrow I shall bring your family a deer from the mainland that will feed you for a month."

A man with curly blond hair appeared in the distance along the riverbank. The robes gathered on his back gave the illusion of a hump despite his upright posture. Hawkiel only covered his wings when he'd be in human sight, a rare occurrence that had become more frequent after Raven befriended Salea.

A shimmer rippled over his form he as crossed into the visible spectrum of light. He waited until he was closer to ask, "How is Salea today?"

The girl beamed a proud smile and pointed at the bass in Raven's hand. "I caught a fish! Can you believe it?"

Salea's exuberance was infectious. Four hundred years ago, when Hawkiel first introduced Raven to humans, she never expected to grow fond of one. Salea made her smile—Raven hoped the girl would do the same for Hawkiel.

He impassively studied the gasping creature. "If you caught it, why is Raven holding it?"

Salea gave him a pointed look. "Raven grabbed 'im while I was plucking berries. *I* made a trap in a shallow pocket using sticks, and baited it with a dead frog."

"You've both been here all day?" The intensity in Hawkiel's stare prickled Raven's skin.

"You said we had time," she replied too low for Salea to hear. "That the battle hadn't yet crossed the English Channel."

He shook his head.

"The settlement?"

His muted eyes empty, Hawkiel pulled two crimson cloaks from beneath his robes. He tossed one to Raven.

"Ah! Mama finished her weaving!" Salea switched her hands around to hold her makeshift basket of berries steady while she stroked the cloak's fabric. "Mama said this was difficult to work with—she's never seen these fibers before."

"Your mother is the only weaver I've met that can repair these cloaks." Forcing a smile, Raven patted the girl's head.

Eager to examine the damaged fabric, Salea's mother had stopped them when they first came upon the homestead. The mysterious red wool, scavenged from the battlefields, protected them and their identities as they walked among Lucifer's ranks and was difficult to cut or mend. It had taken ten years using foraged cloaks and patchwork for Salea's mother to repair and successfully stitch new hems on both cloaks.

"The line is advancing." Hawkiel's words drew a sharp look from Salea.

"They are coming?"

Word had recently reached the island inhabitants that the Great Holy

War was advancing across the European shores. With little firsthand testimony, many were tempted to dismiss frightful rumors of winged creatures and ferocious beasts as lore, but the war itself—and its wake of destruction—sparked great fear as it shifted north.

"What of Salea?" Raven dropped the fish into the river and hurried into the cloak.

Hawkiel eyed the girl. "Send her home to join the ranks and fight on the front lines with the rest of her family and village. Send her north and hope she can outrun the battle. Make her yours and give her the power to defend herself. It is not for me to choose."

"Nothing is, is it?" Raven grunted, flipping her long brown hair from beneath her cloak to hang freely down her back.

"Raven?" A deep furrow etched Salea's brow. Her lips quivered.

"We only have two cloaks," Raven said to Hawkiel. "Will you watch over her while I retrieve another?"

"I will not fight. You know this."

"That's not what I asked!" Heat surged beneath her ribcage. "I may view this world through your eyes, but you and I do not share perspective! There is no justification in doing nothing for an innocent soul beyond the war's reach! *Sending her back is not an option.*"

Hawkiel blinked slowly with unnerving patience. "Choosing sides means choosing one brother over another. I cannot do that. You may do what you will."

"Then I am getting her a cloak." Her lips formed a grim line under the fire of her glare. She shrugged off her crimson wool and draped it over Salea's shoulders.

"Hold this tight and keep your head covered," Raven told the girl. "Run north. Hawkiel will stay with you, but if there's any danger, hide the best that you can. I will find you, I promise."

Raspberries spilled like blood at their feet. Salea grabbed Raven's arm. Her whole body was trembling. "Mama?"

Raven hugged the girl. "Run, Salea. Don't stop."

To Hawkiel, Raven said, "Sides be damned. You stay with her. If Death comes, she shouldn't be alone."

"I will do as you ask, but surely you know our travels will exhaust this girl."

"Only as long as she is human," Raven replied.

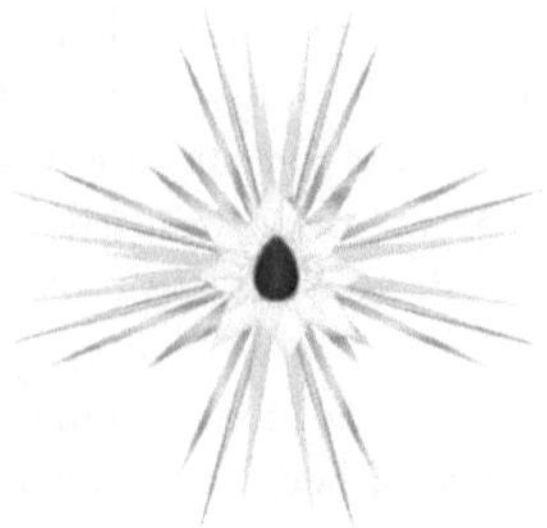

Chapter Three: Rainne Blood Pathos

Backtracking along the River Medine's bank, Raven gained speed and momentum until the water, trees, and sky streaked into colored layers, her heart thundering like the hooves of warhorses. Fishermen, goat herders, farmers, carpenters, bricklayers, blacksmiths, weavers, hunters—over the past four centuries, Hawkiel had introduced her to many peaceful, hardworking families. All had fallen prey to war's brutal march.

Not Salea. Not this time.

An obeisant stillness hung over the village's thatched roofs and wooden and stone structures. No unearthly growls, anguished screams, or rending of flesh from bone—it was quiet, eerily so, as though the people had vanished.

She ducked off the riverbank into a patch of tall, feathery grasses. A flash of metal zipped by her nose. With a flick of the wrist, she caught the projectile—a thick silver coin, Greek in origin. She recognized it instantly.

"Alexander?" she whispered.

"Turn back." His cryptic response came in a lower tone. "This isn't a battle where you can whisper about rebellion. You will die if you interfere."

Raven tossed the coin to a flattened patch where she thought Alexander was crouched. The coin disappeared when he caught it.

"You don't seek fledglings from this village?" she asked.

"My master cannot create fledglings; he is bored." A warm pocket developed beside her and an unseen hand twisted her face away from the village. "He wants blood. If you stay, you will perish. You cannot persuade him."

"I am not here for persuasion." Her chest swelled stubbornly. "And I don't care about your commander's desires."

"He's here with Rainne," Alexander replied quietly. "For the last thousand years, he has preyed upon the lands of Asia and brought death to the learning center of human civilization with the First Born at his side. Know what you're facing before you rush in and lose your head, and your progress. Many in the ranks are beginning to see the world through your eyes."

"I've planted a seed that will grow whether I am here or not. Doubters need only look at Rainne to see Lucifer's intent to destroy you all."

"Us all," Alexander reminded. "Aligning yourself with a fallen star doesn't save you from whatever fate shall befall us."

"So be it." She parted the grasses, but an insistent hand prevented her from crawling through.

"It's my *commander and Rainne*," Alexander insisted. "He is as strong as the Fallen Host. You've never faced anything like him before. Leave. Live on as the leading edge of our collective future and let this go."

"How can I do that? I am only recognized amongst the ranks with such great importance because I don't fear your commanders or that weapon they wield with a flick of their tongues!" She yanked free. "If the cause is truly as close to your heart as you would have me believe, then you can continue without me should I become a martyr."

"If you die today, all hope of withdrawing from this war will die with you."

"Then I won't die today." Raven flashed a smile and tapped Hawkiel's brand. "I bear the mark of success, after all."

"It's your hide. Don't be surprised when he flays it from your bones once he finds out who you are. He'll display that mark as a trophy."

Raven pursed her lips and fortified her aura to protect herself before slinking toward the village. She'd walked countless battles with Hawkiel, weaving between bloody claws and blades, whispering to pause and admire an untarnished world. Many of her brethren wanted more from life than brutality and killing—like Alexander. With his help and Hawkiel's shadowing, she'd avoided the ruthless commanders the others feared with reason. Usually, she was not so foolish to ignore the threat they posed.

So why now? Alexander can easily get Salea a cloak.

Maybe it was the quiet. The eerie vibe. The masked woman who had saved her life. Or perhaps the curiosity of seeing the beast she'd had the fortune of never meeting.

Timing her movements with the breeze, Raven inched through the grass. She knew what Rainne was. And that the creatures who commanded her were merciless killers in direct contact with Lucifer and the Fallen Host.

Everything she didn't know drove her forward.

Why did they willingly allow Rainne to kill her own? Were they truly ignorant of the purpose to her existence? How had Lucifer disillusioned them against whispers of hope?

Without the ear of one of those men, her rebellion was doomed. Fear was a powerful tool they brandished with efficient skill.

The buildings were close and she was about to lose her cover. There was no chaos, no war. She didn't understand what she was seeing: young and old, man and woman, the settlers crowded the village's center, quiet and unmoving, their backs to her. Raven maneuvered sideways to peer around them.

A woman stood there, her face tucked and the hood of her crimson cloak coiled about her shoulders. Her gorgon mane bounced and swayed of its own unearthly accord, possessing no color of its own and instead absorbing the surrounding light, reflecting gray clouds, earthy stone and thatch, and green and gold switch grass. A gust hooked beneath those strange locks and Raven gasped.

Rainne's mask was off.

The visible part of her countenance was stunningly beautiful with perfect symmetry and smooth skin paler than winter snow. Long, black lashes framed closed eyes that hid irises aglow with insatiable bloodlust. That stunning combination of vermillion on white trapped any who gazed upon her in helpless adoration—even as her claws lopped off their heads.

With few exceptions, only the angelic hosts were immune and humans were especially susceptible. In battle, vampires attacked villages for fledglings to use on the frontlines, but Rainne's solo presence confirmed Alexander's warning. The Grim Reaper already held dominion over their souls.

Apart from the crowd, a man in a mismatch of colorful, princely clothes leaned against a hut, his arms crossed and one leather-laced foot propped against the stone wall. His long silk tunic, embroidered with golden thread, was the iridescent blue of a peacock, and a gold fibula, encrusted with jewels and colored glass, fastened his crimson cloak— one of the cleanest and brightest she'd ever seen.

A flat affect of utter boredom dulled a visage more regal and chiseled than any statue she'd seen in Athens or Rome. The crimson ribbon at his nape secured his long auburn locks and fluttered with stray strands that flew on the breeze.

If not for a sharp pang in her heart, Raven might not have noticed his pupils focusing on her. His lips had paused mid-command, holding the final word hostage in the shadows of his mouth. A sneer carved demonic arches into his face as his gold-flecked eyes narrowed and his foot dropped off the wall.

"…rain." He started toward her as Rainne whipped into a fury. His aura shot ahead of him and stripped Raven's bare like it was nonexistent.

Defenseless and suddenly too aware of her vulnerability, she dashed for the closest hut. She eyed a fallen pitchfork and rolled to grab it before boosting herself into the air feet first.

She sailed over the corner of the thatched roof and landed on the other side, breaking the man's line of sight. Still, his eyes burned into her very essence. She had successfully claimed every drop of his attention and would never win in a fight against him—that certainty pained her to the bone.

She forced her breathing to slow and listened to Rainne's movements. Clutching the pitchfork, she squeezed between the huts.

A bloody mist rose as Rainne cut an effortless dance of death through bodies falling one after the other. Their heads, briefly held aloft by an upward slice, dropped a second later. The villagers had lost the mental capacity, and will, to flee, scream, or plead. Rainne was Death's silent, efficient ace.

Bolting from the narrow passage, Raven went airborne, twisting to land behind Rainne already ducking and weaving in synchronized movement to avoid her claws. Keenly aware of the auburn-haired commander's piercing attention, Raven stabbed the pitchfork into the foot of Lucifer's greatest weapon and quickly hooked her arm around Rainne's neck to undo the cloak's clasp. Rainne's bladed fingers swung with surprising reach and nicked Raven's cheek.

Her heart slammed in her chest as Raven dropped to the dirt. She bundled the crimson garment and rolled from Rainne's swooping claws. Raven back-flipped away from the scene, boosting off her palms for more height and a faster spin.

Possessing no will of her own to pursue, Rainne pulled the pitchfork from her foot and resumed her deadly dance. The auburn-haired man, Alexander's commander, seemed content to watch her escape through pointed slits. At the far side of the settlement, she pressed the cloak against her bloody cheek and darted perpendicular to the western flank seeking cover in the tall grasses.

She ran hard and fast, farther out of her way than she needed to go, before adjusting course for the Medine's banks. The river came into view and a silver coin whizzed past, clipping her ear and drawing blood with its worn, rounded edge.

Catching the coin by instinct, she cried, "What's this!" and smudged blood between her thumb and forefinger. Alexander appeared behind her, took his coin, and pressed into her as his hands landed on her hips.

Grazing her wounded ear first with his tongue and then with his lips, he whispered, "I didn't know you were immune to Rainne." He nibbled on her ear, drawing more blood. "Which means neither did he. He's ordered me to capture you."

"Better than flaying the skin from my bones."

"That may come later," Alexander mumbled down her neck. "I warned you against charging in and doing something stupid. If you needed another cloak that badly, I would have gotten you one."

"I need to go. Hawkiel's waiting on the northern shore."

"Watch your voice," Alexander warned. "It's not going to be like that. My commander has given me an order. I can't be certain that he can't hear us now as it is."

"No more niceties, then?" Raven dropped low, swept Alexander's legs, and shoved the heel of her palm into his sternum. Lashing claws left four bloody streaks down his cheek and a kick off his gut propelled her toward the riverbank.

Taking a shallow leap, she dove headfirst into the water, but Alexander caught her by the ankle. She crashed onto the rocky shore, winded and gasping for air that wouldn't come. He roughly flipped her onto her back and straddled her wearing a mischievous smile. "You're a nimble little nymph! Don't think you can escape. I warned you— you've never fought in real combat to know—"

Raven threw fistfuls of sand and rocks into Alexander's face. She bucked up and rammed her head into his abdomen, angling her palms into the ground to slide out from beneath him. She lifted her torso over her legs, tucked her feet, and sprang up and backward into the water.

She splashed into the Medine and sank into the currents dragging her safely from shore. When she surfaced, she waved to Alexander. "Converse less; fight more next time, yeah?"

A shadow clouded Alexander's features. His voice skimmed the water and hit deeper than the coldest chill. "You have no idea what you've done. He will never stop hunting you."

) ❋ (

A thorough search of the River Medine's northern hamlets led Raven past a small outcropping and into a wooded area where Salea, dwarfed in crimson wool, was wedged between the exposed roots of a giant oak tree. The girl, hugging her knees, rocked in place with a silent lullaby falling from her lips. Partially exposed to the visible spectrum, Hawkiel shimmered nearby, a silent watcher.

Hooking him on an insinuating glare, Raven turned and headed for the outcrop's boulders by the riverbank. He followed, briefly eyeing her cloak and wounded cheek and ear.

"Why didn't you tell me?" she demanded, shedding her drenched clothing.

"It wouldn't have made a difference."

"Perhaps not, but I thought I was going into battle and instead revealed myself to one of their commanders. Walking among them will be more difficult."

"By your choice."

She laid her wool tunic flat against the limestone. "For someone supposedly incapable of love, why do I seem to care what happens here more than you do?"

"It wouldn't have made a difference," he repeated.

She peeled off the cotton sheath clinging to her body and squeezed water from it in sections. "Aren't you supposed to love all things? Or did you fall out of love when you fell out of grace?"

"You made a choice. Direct your frustrations where they're due." He sat on the rocks and gazed skyward. "Night comes soon. What will you do with her?"

Frustration nipped her ribs. Raven gritted her teeth. "I'm going to catch her dinner. Did you tell her?"

Hawkiel nodded. "About her family. Not you."

"A girl her age has few options for a good life on her own." Raven shoved back at thoughts of Salea falling prey to human marauders and vampires alike. "She deserves a choice, but we need to keep moving."

Hawkiel stiffened. "You were pursued?"

"I've finally ruffled your feathers."

"Were you?" His muted blue eyes echoed the question. A tense ridge split his forehead and matched his grimly set lips.

"Aye, by Alexander, with warnings of others to come. He knows you're here and of my immunity to their weapon."

"This girl is not worth all that you have accomplished thus far! And yet you have risked it all."

"I enjoy her company," Raven retorted, lifting her chin. She laid her underdress on the rocks and pulled her long brown hair over her shoulder to wring it dry. "Too many innocents have died in the war, but at least they died for something. These deaths meant nothing. He was bored. He killed them for entertainment."

"The Second Born saw you?" What passed for alarm straightened Hawkiel's spine and rattled his chains. "He knows you're immune?"

"I'll have you flying at this rate, eh?" Raven said, shrugging. "He had long reddish-brown hair."

For the barest moment, she thought Hawkiel might faint. He shook his head as though all was lost. "That is their second born. The first one is too apathetic for such things."

"Alexander said his commander could not be persuaded."

"Not that one, no. But the First Born is logical and not controlled by bloodlust."

"If they capture me, will I be allowed to speak with him?"

"Unlikely. Their second born will kill you."

"Hmm…" Raven waded into the river. "I have his attention, so I must survive it."

Fish were a much easier catch than the deer Raven had hunted for Salea's family. Mammals fled before she could gauge their proximity, but fish weren't as sensitive. A few large bass swam by before Raven speared one perfect for a Salea-sized dinner.

"Please start a fire," she said with her back to Hawkiel, "and select a flat rock for this fish while I gut it."

"Do you intend to keep her with us, then?"

Coming ashore, Raven shot her winged companion an annoyed look, "Does it matter? She's my charge, not yours."

"Will you also take her into battle?"

Growing increasingly irritated, Raven knelt and cracked the fish's head against a rock. "Do you care about her well-being? Or that she'll hinder my ability to do what you need me to do?"

"Hawkiel?" Rubbing her eyes, Salea emerged from the trees beyond the outcropping. Upon glimpsing Raven below, she broke into a run. "Raven!"

Salea paused beside Hawkiel, her cheeks flaming at Raven's

unabashed nudity. She shrunk inwardly and fidgeted with the cloak's hem.

"I got you dinner, Salea." Raven sliced open the fish's belly and flicked its innards into the river.

"Is it true?" Salea asked in a small voice. "Did you see them? Are they dead?"

"There's no one left." Raven angled an eyebrow at Hawkiel. "Fire?"

Salea sank to her knees, tears welling, lips trembling. "Mama? Papa? My brothers?"

"I won't leave you behind, Salea. I'll protect you." Raven folded the girl's desperation and grief into her aura before they could consume the entirety of Salea's being. She rinsed the fish and her hands in the river.

"The war did not destroy your home or murder the people you love. One of the beasts acted alone." She took the girl's hands in hers. "The war's lines are blurring and slowing because many of the beasts don't want to fight anymore. But the war *is* coming and the beasts will arrive. He was simply the first of many. We can't stay here."

Tipping Salea's chin up, Raven captured her gaze. The girl's tears dried and her pupils dilated. Those dark, empty portals opened a path to her damaged soul and impressionable mind.

"Eat for strength and then sleep," Raven commanded. "Can you do that for me?"

"Yes," she replied in monotone.

"Good girl." Raven stroked her face, hoping for forgiveness.

Hawkiel returned with dry grass and branches. He arranged them on the bank and set a loose wad of grasses ablaze with heat generated from his palm. Once embers began to crack and pop, Raven filleted the bass and laid it on a flat stone at the center of the fire.

Hawkiel frowned at the girl's vacant stare. "You're not giving her a choice."

"If time allowed for explanations—" With lengthened nails, Raven speared the fillets and flipped them. She shook her head. "Alexander knows we're here, so we need to get off the river. Maybe backtrack to the European mainland, skirt the war's reach, and find someplace safe in the wake. None of that is hospitable for a human."

Satisfied that the fish was cooked, Raven plucked the stone from the fire. The scent of seared flesh blended with roasted fish and churned her stomach. She set the stone at Salea's side. "It's hot. Eat and rest."

Her motions perfunctory, the girl ate in silence until nothing but bone remained. Hawkiel sat with his back to Raven as Salea curled onto her side and fell into an entranced sleep.

Habitually scanning the overcast sky—searching in vain for his brother—Hawkiel said, "I suppose, then, you'll need me to feed her?"

Raven's response was quiet. "I was going to ask."

"After you altered her? It would be too late then. You're making a lot of choices tonight."

"You don't like this."

"I have chosen not to choose; what I like and don't like is of little consequence."

"Thank you, Hawkiel."

"I have plenty of blood to spare." It was a simple statement of fact. "She will be a liability until she awakens."

Raven brushed dark locks from Salea's throat. The pulsing jugular prickled her teeth and peppered anticipation along her tongue. She'd only ever fed on Hawkiel, but instinct responded on a molecular level that transcended thought.

"Don't linger or you'll kill her," Hawkiel warned.

Crimson draped her visual field as Raven hovered over Salea's throat. She savored the rhythmic pulse on her lips and the smooth, even bursts of breath caressing her cheek.

"Don't linger."

"I am not one of those beasts who lose control on the battlefield," Raven snapped in a raspy voice.

"Let the thirst build too much and you will be. You aren't different enough to ignore your similarities."

The thirst was gaining momentum. Saliva dripped from her fangs. The voice of instinct screamed for blood—craved every last drop. "I embrace my similarities to control them. My ability to do so makes me different."

Her blood-tinged gaze flicked over Hawkiel. Even with his back to her, his judgment and disapproval stung. He'd branded her centuries ago, but he didn't trust her, and that wariness had grown with each new ally she gained.

And now she was altering Salea without consent.

She punctured Salea's jugular. Barely a drop of blood landed on Raven's tongue before the infectious protein entered the girl's bloodstream. She withdrew and applied pressure to the wounds. The crimson view faded and her teeth receded.

"Hawkiel," she said, "my goal is to change the way they think, not become more like them."

He quietly contemplated the clouds.

"I didn't do this because I desire her blood. It's mercy."

The fire's crackle was the only accompaniment to the river's rumbling for a time. Raven cradled Salea's head in her lap and stroked her hair. A bead of sweat formed on the girl's forehead.

"Are you so very sure about that?" Hawkiel asked at last. "You are trying hard to persuade me of your noble intentions."

"I know true justice in my heart," Raven whispered. "How could I send her home to be slaughtered or off on her own to become somebody's slave?"

"You have forced her to become what killed her family."

"If she hates me for it, then so be it. I've given her an advantage to survive."

"And if she attacks an innocent when the bloodlust grows too strong to bear?"

"For someone who supposedly loves all things, you are a determined pessimist."

"I've walked the Earth twice as long as you've been alive. We do not share the same perception of the world—regardless of love." He pointed at the sky. "Do you think he searches for me as I search for him?"

"Aye. When the clouds clear later, I will find him for you."

Raven tucked the girl into the cloak, pulling the hems to cover her skin, and gestured at the old oak where Salea had soothed herself earlier. "I'll lay her down there. It's faint, but I sense someone coming."

"Don't assume it's Alexander."

Trotting to the tree line, Raven replied, "I don't, but hope it is because we can't outrun them. Our scent is too fresh and I can't take her into the river like this."

She tucked Salea between the tree's cradling roots. "Snuff the fire and stay here, out of sight. She should be protected enough to go unnoticed."

"The Second Born may have chosen to hunt you himself." Hawkiel approached with her garments and stolen cloak.

"Do you find joy in your negativity? Or does some small part of you actually worry about me?" Raven slid the cotton under garment over her head. She draped the woolen gown over a tree branch to drip dry and then swung the cloak over her shoulders. "Have faith in me. I'm not as careless or naïve as you think."

"Your thoughts are so transparent that I can see them, and that's what worries me." Hawkiel's golden curls bounced as he shook his head. "Do not get captured. Your only chance is with their first born, not the second. He will hunt you for sport."

"If I'm not back by morning light, take Salea across the river and head east. They won't take me easily. I will find you."

"You are making her my burden," Hawkiel said lightly.

"I am asking you to stay by her side. Whether or not you do so is your choice."

A faint glimmer flared in Hawkiel's eyes as Raven threw his words back at him. "Very well. East across the river, though I hope you return well before the morning star rises."

"Aye," she agreed. "May I use Animus Hollow?"

With a nod, Hawkiel uncovered his left bicep. Raven sliced into his tattoo with a lengthened nail. Blood streamed down her arm and pooled into fat drops at her elbow. A flick of her wrist cast his blood into the air where it spattered against an invisible barrier and formed the outline of a twelve-pointed star and two intertwined crescent moons. The cushion of energy that divided the Realm of Man from the spiritual dimensions appeared as a large white slit in the fabric of time.

"Open along the River Medine at the midpoint between our current position and Salea's village." Raven flicked additional blood into the Hollow and stepped inside. Gossamer fingers stroked her cheeks and blew whispers across her skin as she eased into its welcoming calm and prepared to face the monster waiting on the other side.

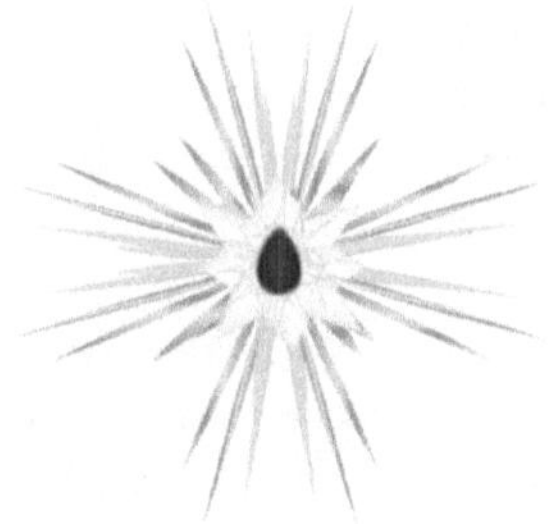

CHAPTER FOUR: PILLARS AND STARS

I

Orison Crossing, Summer 2006

The setting sun drenched the shaded glass panels of The Greenery's greenhouse with golden light. Perked by Paresh's essence, ferns uncurled and palms stretched tall. Japanese maples shook summer yawns from burgundy leaves and their chartreuse counterparts flaunted their lace-leafed glow. Even the pond rippled with glittering peaks and mysterious valleys as koi with long, flowing fins glided under the surface.

Eric had closed the restaurant and given the staff a paid day off in honor of Molly's funeral and reception. The volunteers who helped cater the Sunset Grove Parish had earned overtime for working there, but this building was otherwise empty.

Eric tried to excuse himself for kitchen duty, but Walter nudged him down the hall, dismissing his protests that he'd been human once and knew how to operate a microwave. "As the only human in a pack of vampires," Walter declared, "I will heat Paresh's soup in the appliance that you sure as hell didn't have in the 1860s, so go sit."

Smiling in spite of himself, Eric crossed through the heavy double doors held open by the newest members of their entourage, the largely silent Heron and Cyprian, to join Paresh at the pond's edge. She always greeted the fish first, hoping to catch Kabuki, the locally famous white koi, in the act of his theatrics. But, in the thirteen days since she'd arrived home, he hadn't jumped once. As with the creatures of the forest, the koi gravitated to her, gulping at the surface and swimming in close circles.

Eric pecked her cheek. "Your essence backfires here."

"What do you mean?" She squatted and stuck her finger in the water. She smiled when Kabuki nibbled on it.

"Every animal in town is under your spell." He gestured at the gathered koi. "They've never been this calm. Maybe stress was making Kabuki jump, after all."

"Hmm." She swirled her finger and the koi caught it again. "That's sad if it's true. But I guess that means he's better now."

"Are you conversing about a fish?" Seated behind them, Jonathan propped his feet atop the bistro table's mosaic tiles. He winked at Paresh and patted the chair beside him.

She touched her palm to Eric's chest for a heartbeat before clasping his hand and joining Jonathan. Given the security nightmare presented by a glass room, the hunters moved to the periphery and melded into the shadows.

"On my second night back, Eric told me about the white koi, there," Paresh said to Jonathan, pointing at Kabuki, "and how he jumps out of the water like a dolphin. I haven't gotten to see it yet."

Jonathan chuckled and eyed Eric. "Please tell me life here isn't really this boring."

Knocking Jonathan's feet off the table, Eric replied, "I'd welcome a return to boring, personally."

"That sounds very much like you, Brother," Jonathan muttered.

"Coming through!" The doors muffled Walter's yell an instant before he backed in hunched over an oven mitt-wrapped bowl. "Hon, this is hot, so be careful."

"Microwaves are tricky, huh?" Eric asked, pointedly staring at vigorous steam puffs. "How long did you set that? It only needed a minute."

Smirking at Eric, Walter presented the soup to Paresh and a produced a spoon from his rear pocket. "Let's call it cooked and leave it at that."

Eric split his fingers over his eyes and sighed. His chest rose and fell as though under a heavy weight.

"You okay, Counselor?" Chair legs scraped concrete as Walter sat beside him.

"Yeah." Eric waved a dismissive hand. "Everything was just nicely normal for a second."

Grunting agreement, Jonathan returned his shined Oxfords to the tabletop despite Eric's glare. Walter slumped with a sigh, hands clenched between his knees, and Eric rested his chin on his palm, watching Paresh hungrily stare down the green bean poking from the bowl's center. She drew infinity loops through the broth and scattered ghostly ribbons with her breath. She started with a tentative spoonful, barely grimacing when the boiling liquid burned her tongue.

Waving the scent off, Jonathan scoffed. "Pare, how can you eat that stuff?"

"Sarah hits a perfect balance of pepper and basil with the tomato—oh, it's so good!" Too famished for etiquette, she slurped the spoon dry and perched the bowl upon her lips.

The chief grinned. "Boy, Molly would've had something to say about this bean pole finally putting some meat on her bones."

With a sniffle, his smile faded. "Even though she's not that skinny…or a bean pole—"

"Say—" Eric slapped him on the back and threw his thumb at the doors. "Grab a drink with me. We'll bring something back for the others."

He exchanged what had become their "you've got Paresh" look with Jonathan and warily surveyed their security detail. Quiet and alert in the corners, they were antonymous to their seemingly loose, dimwitted Commander, but Eric knew Alex was sharper than he acted.

Surprisingly, he wished Alex were here instead. His goofy antics made Paresh giggle, and that alone would put them all at ease. Safe as they may be with Heron and Cyprian, their stoic guard evoked unintentional tension. Then again—maybe they needed that to stay grounded.

He led Walter through the dark interior to the mahogany bar. He switched on the recessed lights and excused himself to grab a few bottles of his "private reserve" from his office. When he returned, a soft beam spotlighted the lawman tossing back a shot of whiskey behind the counter.

"Hey," Walter mumbled, sloshing another round into the tiny glass. He capped the bottle and turned to shelve it.

"You should switch to a whiskey tumbler or a Glencairn glass, and keep the bottle," Eric suggested, padding across the maroon and black carpet. "Otherwise, you'll be back in here every other minute."

"God, you make me sound like an alcoholic." Sheepishly hugging the bottle, he slugged the shot and snagged a tumbler from the shelf, pausing to point at the Glencairn set. "And I'm not fancy enough to drink from a tulip."

"Well, at least drop that rotgut and grab the black or blue label—

whatever you want," Eric said, nodding at the scotch whiskey selection. He held up the bottles in his left hand. "You're not the only one drinking today, Old Friend. A small fusion of chilled cabernet won't kill us."

"It's not the cabernet in there that bothers me, you know."

As Walter's red-rimmed, glassy eyes drifted over the bottles, Eric wondered how many shots he'd downed. His blood didn't smell strongly of alcohol, yet, but it would catch up fast.

"Will Paresh...?" Walter asked, trailing into an expression of uncertain revulsion.

"Hmm, I doubt she will." Eric indicated the refrigerated chest under the wine rack. "She's partial to chardonnay. Grab it and I'll get stemware and a corkscrew."

Walter slapped the counter. "Wait! Can you get drunk? Sammy's off, so there's no designated driver."

"Okay, if we're pointing things out," Eric said, placing five wine glasses and his bottles onto a round serving tray, "technically you're drunk on duty and serving wine to an eighteen-year-old girl."

Walter's cheeks burned scarlet. Eric patted his friend's arm. "No—I can't get drunk. So, you take a sick day and enjoy the quiet while it lasts, okay?"

Walter exhaled a shaky breath. "What's going to happen here? They blew up one of their own arcs. What if they—"

"We'll deal with it, whatever *it* may be," Eric interrupted.

With a halfhearted nod, Walter added the chardonnay to the tray and sidled around the bar. He slipped onto a stool, tears welling in his eyes.

"I, uh—" Walter tried to clear the catch in his throat. He gave up with a helpless shrug and tapped his thumb along the tumbler's rim. "I don't know what to do. What to tell my officers. How to deal with this. Where do I fit in? And *Molly*...God, she's—"

He closed his eyes, unleashing a torrent down his aging cheeks, and bit his lip to stop it from trembling. "Molly's...*g-gone*."

He sobbed into his hand, shoulders heaving. Eric passed him a stack of cocktail napkins, his grief further ruptured by memories of Lucinda and Darien, of Andrew and Felicia, of young Paresh, so suddenly gone. He missed Molly and grieved for her, but she symbolized all the connections of his past and future, and that struck him the hardest.

Walter blew his nose and huffed at the ceiling. His hand shook as he guzzled his whiskey. Refilling, he blew out a heavy breath. "She was this town's anchor, you know—" A pained laugh fell softly into his glass.

"That unique piece that fit perfectly between you and everyone else. She——"

Sniffling, he scrubbed his cheeks with his shirt cuff. "Yeah, she made this town whole, you know? I'm already lost without her. I barely know that the sky is up and the ground is down." Nodding to himself, he pursed his lips and turned the tumbler in a tight circle.

Eric eyed the Art Deco-styled bottle boasting a large "XO" label tucked behind the register. The "XO" was accurate, but the bottle was a decoy. Molly had always called it her favorite brandy, but it was truly among the best cognacs in the world, and, given its value, no one but Eric knew what was really in it. It only mattered that it belonged to Molly.

He selected two snifters and streamed the bottle's liquid gold into both. He motioned for Walter to take the fuller of the two, and raised his glass. It'd make him sick, but she was worth it.

"I'm not feeling particularly *found* myself, either, these days, Old Friend," Eric said. "My guiding light has dimmed, but her memory shines bright through us—all of us—so we can't stay lost forever."

Fresh tears welled as Walter choked out, "To Molly," and sealed the toast.

Remembering how Molly habitually swirled and sniffed first, and then drank slowly, savoring the flavors and smiling—always contented and sometimes nostalgic—Eric rolled the glass with his wrist and released scents and flavors he couldn't enjoy. He quickly tossed the drop back and grimaced through the burn down his throat.

He wiped his mouth with the back of his hand, leaning over the sink and taking measured breaths, praying Walter wasn't aware of the angry dragon roaring to life in his belly. Thankfully, the lawman was distracted with composing himself, but grief was a stubborn, sticky thing.

Eric ran tap water into a clean glass and sipped, focusing on the variances of the grain in the bar's rich wood. It ran the full length from a single cut, protected by thick, glossy shellac that reflected the canned lights as prismatic stars.

Dragon fire quieted to hot steam and the nauseating burn subsided. Smoothing his hand over the ageless blue eyes mirrored in varnish, he whispered, "I always hoped she'd get over her feelings for me and see how perfect you were for her."

He quieted a moment. "But I'll never know if she saw it. She and I were family, but you were her best friend."

"Shit, Eric!" Shock bolted Walter's spine straight and struck him dumb. His lips moved, but nothing came out.

Nudging the tumbler into Walter's hands, Eric said, "Take a drink. I'm sorry, I shouldn't have—" He waved an agitated hand, trying to swat the words away.

Drinking as ordered, Walter came to and cried, "Damn it, you can't just drop something like that on a guy! B-but, yeah…she was my best friend. God knows…I loved her."

"Me, too."

Silence eased between them, punctuated by the solace of Raven's buttons. The restaurant itself seemed strangely alive, expressing its vibrancy in refrigeration compressors, cooling fans, and a dim electrical hum that lingered unbroken over creaking beams and settling walls.

"You know," Eric said, his voice loud by comparison, "depending on how the Earth is tilted and where you're standing, the sky might be down and the ground up, so you might not know as much as you think."

In slow motion, Walter slumped over the bar and his head lolled to the side. "What now?"

Eric grinned. "Think on that for a minute."

Sitting up with a groan, Walter muttered into his glass, "Smart ass. I'm not paid enough to think like an astrophysicist."

"You say I always have the answers, so I might as well try."

"Yeah, well, up, down, whatever—before long, vampires will outnumber humans in Sunset Grove."

That tied a knot in Eric's stomach. He wiped his face and sighed. "Before all this, I was thinking of taking Paresh to that bed and breakfast in Vermont that Felicia loved. I thought that maybe if I left, things would settle down; hell, maybe if I *had* left, Bill, Rebecca, and Molly wouldn't be dead—"

"Your weakness is the people you care about and the COMS know it. *That* is why Molly is dead; don't ever steal Donovan's blame," Jonathan interrupted, strolling in from the alcove. He leaned against the counter at the far end. "If you leave, they might follow, but they'll definitely keep killing humans here until you return—"

"You would know," Eric grumbled. The dragon belched under his ribs.

"—but going might be best for *her*," Jonathan continued, frowning his irritation. "With the High Council and the VaSH here, this is the safest place on the planet. Targeted? Yes. But also guarded."

Jonathan drummed his fingers on the bar in thought. "Yes—once the Elders are settled, you should take Raven and Alex, and go. Give Pare a break before that archangel gives her another damn vision. This isn't what I wanted for her when I sent her home."

Eric's expression hardened. The knot tightened and squeezed the dragon into releasing another burst of fire. He managed to mask his groan as frustration. "Regardless of what you want or wanted, it's too late. The vision of your encounter with Donovan wasn't the only one she saw."

Jonathan peered through narrowed slits. "What else did he show her?"

"Pillars of fire so hot it sears her eyes shut and smoke so thick it chokes her. She wakes to it every morning, describing a screaming man at the center who burns like a candle. He collapses in a moment of silence and then emerges with wings that touch the sky."

Jonathan's pallor grayed. "Wings of light?"

"*Of course* you know something about it." Eric needed a real drink to douse his tribute to Molly or it'd keep flaring. "Gabriel called it the 'wings of the light hawk' or something, and added that she wasn't supposed to see it—it's not her burden to bear. She didn't want to worry you."

Eric picked up the tray and headed for the alcove. "But she's determined to visit Grandfather Wisdom to get answers."

"Gabriel?" Walter swiveled too fast on the stool and caught the counter to steady himself and face Jonathan. "You said 'archangel.' Like, *the* Archangel? Gabriel?"

Jonathan rolled his eyes and joined Eric. "You can't be surprised. You know we're real, and that the Devil killed Pare and Eric. Of course angels and your god—"

"Knock it off." Eric jabbed two stern fingers into his brother's chest. "A penitent heart is a sympathetic heart."

To Walter, Eric said, "You're falling into our world too fast to take it all in. Remember that up is up and down is down."

"Except when up is down and down is up, or you don't know where the hell you are and you're lost," Walter retorted, staggering off his stool.

"If nothing else, take it as an affirmation of your faith. You're here to protect this town. Who better to have as backup? It's not too shabby with God on your side, right?"

All color drained from Walter's face. His knees buckled.

Jonathan tossed his thumb at him. "Sympathetic or not, he's human. I'm not catching him again and he's going down."

Eric shoved the tray at Jonathan. He took Walter's bottle and glass from his slackening fingers, and hooked an arm around the lawman's chest.

A disgusted noise came from Jonathan's throat. "Humans are such fragile things."

Plunking Walter's items onto the tray, Eric glared at his brother. "You're not helping, so don't bitch."

"I'm not the one who told him his god is on his side."

Leaning Walter against his shoulder, Eric marched through the bar's alcove. At the greenhouse doors, with Jonathan on his heels, Eric stopped abruptly. "Did you leave Paresh alone in there with hunters she doesn't know?"

"Check your perception, Brother." Jonathan shouldered past and pressed his back to the door. Light shot in through the crack. Jonathan tipped his chin and Heron widened the opening to take the tray from him.

Smoothing his hair with regal fingers, Jonathan propped his foot against the door. "You're too distracted. Pare's in the bathroom. That's why I came out. Go on in. I'll wait for her."

Eric crossed the greenhouse's threshold and deposited Walter into the closest chair. Spinning on his heel, he marched back out. "She's in there vomiting!" he growled through his teeth, his nose almost touching Jonathan's. The beast was stirring, which meant the dragon was the least of his worries, now. "Did the soup make her sick?"

Jonathan's eyes fleetingly flashed like they did in the old days and it roiled Eric's stomach. He was never drinking anything undiluted again. Nausea forced him back a step. Jonathan mistook it as a gesture of something else and tapped his index finger against Eric's sternum. "You and I need to spar, properly, to get our past out of our systems."

"I thought we were done with this—"

"Oh we are," Jonathan interrupted, "but I'll always enjoy a good fight and no one else can go head to head with me."

"That's hardly important now!" Eric tried to push past, but Jonathan threw up a blocking arm.

"You know it's part of the process. She shouldn't be eating human food at this point."

"You are unbelievable."

"She asked me to wait outside." Jonathan's voice was quiet. He didn't meet Eric's icy glare.

"Eric, I only need a minute. I'm okay." Paresh's voice traveled through the walls on a pained whisper.

Eric and Jonathan stared at each other as time slowed to a crawl, their auras charged with worry and the unspoken promise of blood, and their faces mirroring differing levels of agitation and the excited unease that came before a battle cry. Jonathan's lust may have subsided, but under that new, calm demeanor, the old Jonathan craved for them to tear into each other, unrestrained and unrestricted. It was a freedom he hadn't felt in a thousand years, and, despite everything that had happened between them, Eric certainly understood the suffocation of regulated freedom.

"You need to heal first if you want a fair fight, *Brother*," Eric said tightly under his breath. "Otherwise, I'll kill you whether I mean to or not."

Jonathan cracked a grin. He nodded in concession and the energy between them defused. "I accept that as a future promise, then, *Brother*."

The bathroom door swung open and Paresh stepped into the hall. "You are both unbelievable, okay? I can use the bathroom on my own, thank you."

She walked between them, touching both under the chin as she passed. "You worry too much and act like barbarians when I'm not around. Maybe I'll force Alex to tell me all those things you don't want me to know."

Her smile didn't quite reach her eyes. The fatigue she exuded made Eric reach for her. She slipped away, but paused to glance back. He closed the gap, turning her at the hip to search her face, seeking answers he already knew. He lightly stroked her jugular. Donovan's attack had damaged the progress she'd made healing from Lucien's bite.

"Tell me my worry's not warranted and I'll stop," Eric said. "Nothing else matters but you."

She winced and gnawed her lip. As she swung her gaze away, she saw Walter slumped in the chair. She gasped and ran over to him. "What happened?"

"He's overwhelmed," Eric said, "but otherwise fine."

"I can sympathize. We've been through a lot." She stroked his wrinkled brow and knelt, whispering his name.

The two Crimson Guard hunters gravitated to the concerned shift in Paresh's aura. Eric swallowed the urge to order them away. The need to be close to her was beyond their control.

Day in and day out, killers orbited her at every turn—including him. He hated restricting her life like David had. She'd never known true freedom and she might never get to.

Without a way to pinpoint traitorous rogues, he certainly couldn't ignore the skillsets of the hunters approaching her now. They had participated in the sparring maneuvers that scarred Jonathan with the injury Donovan had critically reopened. They complimented each other and formed a perfect whole in battle, hunting in tandem, competent enough to fight the bloodthirsty Second Born for days.

They'd been nothing but professional, but the memory of Jonathan nearly dying in a pool of his blood mixing with Molly's fueled distrust. Heron and Cyprian might lead separate units of Jonathan's pack, but they were a pair in everything they did. If Donovan had acted in a partnership like that—

"Any word from Alex?" Paresh interrupted Eric's grim musings with a knowing look as though she could read his mind, but the question was directed at Heron. She smiled softly as he edged nearer.

"No, milady." The hunter's dark eyes gleamed with curiosity as he studied her and the hand he had unwittingly extended. He clenched it into a fist and pulled it down to his side.

Her essence was a magnet, her touch a lure, her blood ambrosia—the food of the gods. She was their flame and they were her moths. In a single night, Paresh had become a potent drug and an irresistible temptation. She'd never be safe no matter what Eric did or where they went.

Cyprian was close enough to touch her, as well, yet he, too, refrained. In his eternally calm voice, he added, "That is a good omen, I am certain, milady."

Both Jonathan and Alex had faith in the hunters honor bound to protect the Second Born, but were the first and second officers of his pack more trustworthy than the rest? How could they be when Raven's First Officer had emerged as a predator among predators?

"And no word from Lucien?" Paresh asked Jonathan, again eyeing Eric with an intensity she knew only he'd feel. He wanted to grin away her concerns, but she'd read the lie in an instant.

"Nothing yet, Pare." Jonathan elbowed Eric in the ribs. "Look who's taking charge. Maybe we do worry too much. She's a natural."

Eric couldn't take any more. He swatted off the hunters and shook Walter awake. The chief groaned to life and wiped his face. Paresh knelt at his knee like a little girl, but she wasn't a little girl. She was a woman with her own power—possibly stronger than Lucien—but Eric couldn't help worrying. Like grief, it was a tricky thing with a tendency to stick.

"Everything okay, Walter?" she asked with an innocent tilt of the head.

The chief snorted. "Yea—wegotch gahd onrside."

Squinting at a sun that had yet to set, he rubbed his eyes and slumped deeper into the chair. "God, will this day ever end?"

"We'll be all right, Pare. Give it time." Jonathan sat at the table with Walter. He visually directed Eric to the dry, empty bowl a few tables over. Eric frowned. If Paresh vomited after finishing her soup, Jonathan was right: she shouldn't be eating human food.

He swept his fingers along Paresh's shoulders as he crossed behind her to sit beside Jonathan. Her essence pulled on him even stronger than it had at their first dinner together. Wanting nothing more than to take her home and never leave his bedroom, he forced his focus on filling the stemware with the fusion of chilled blood and cabernet. He almost poured a fifth, but chose not to put Paresh on the spot. He offered the chardonnay to her, a freshly refilled tumbler of whiskey to Walter, and invited the hunters to join them.

"How was your soup, hon?" Walter asked.

"Good. Thank you for heating it up for me," Paresh replied, taking the seat next to him.

"It's honestly the easiest thing I've done since you got home. Molly would've—" His voice caught and eyes watered. He lifted his glass.

Eric took his lead and raised his glass. "To Molly."

The others followed in kind. "To Molly."

Casting a dark look at Jonathan over the rim of his glass, Eric spoke in a low voice Walter couldn't hear. "Regardless of your feelings on the matter, humans take priority for protection here. Lucien singlehandedly made this town a bigger target than it already was. If the COMS attack, the Elders are to evacuate to the Arc of True Blood and the hunters focus on preserving human life. Am I clear?"

Jonathan took his time finishing his drink. He set the glass on the table, turning the stem to center it perfectly in front of him. A thin slit twisted his lips into a sinuous shape. Eyes darker than black coffee fell softly upon Paresh and hardened as they shifted to his brother.

"Firstly," he began in the same, low voice, "*Paresh* takes priority. Secondly, if you have orders for the hunters, give them to Raven or Alex. I've already told you I'll support any decision you make here. It's your town."

Licking his lips, Jonathan's grin widened. His eyes glinted

mischievously. "Brother, you've declared your eldership. Stop acting through me and wield your power. The COMS will never defeat us when we stand together. I dare Lucifer to return himself and try again."

II

Isle of Wight, England, 897 A.D.

Animus Hollow opened along the River Medine midway to the remnants of Salea's village. As Raven stepped onto cool pebbles and a damp shore, a gust of wind, scented of soil, river water, and a foreign flower, snaked around her with strangely viscous intimacy, and stole and held her breath captive.

Every inch of her skin prickled; the tall grasses on the rocky terrace ahead were stock-still. The gust shot skyward, lifting her long, wet locks and vanishing. She sucked air into desperate lungs as her hair slapped her shoulders.

A presence lurked near the rocky terrace, but it wasn't Alexander or the Second Born. Someone else had joined the hunt and she'd surrendered any advantage she'd hoped to gain.

The presence evoked fear and a warning that this odd, one-sided stalemate would end the instant she moved. She studied the rocks where she thought the vampire was perched, but otherwise stood inert. Her predator seemed content to observe in kind.

Thick clouds and shifts in the sun's muted light marked time's passage. Only after hidden stars governed an overcast sky did a shadow shimmer on the rocks. Slender and effeminate, yet definitively male, he materialized with fair hair and skin kissed silver by night's monotone. Crimson wool draped his shoulders—the ultimate protection for Lucifer's battle-hardened creations.

As the shadows cracked off his face, an involuntary gasp parted her lips. In Athens and Rome, she'd been awed by beautifully carved, flawless marble gods and goddesses. She'd thought of them when she saw the Second Born, but this man, this creature, was beyond them. Transcendent. Ethereal.

His unnaturally pale eyes, the color of a peridot stone, gleamed with amusement. Somehow, he knew her deepest and most secretive thoughts, but there was no malice in his aura. He was neutral in body, mind, and spirit, almost like—

He vanished from the outcropping and suddenly stood before her. He was nearly a head taller, which forced her to look up. He grasped her jaw, his touch gentle, fingertips soft, and spoke in a voice more soothing than she'd expected.

"So you are the troublesome one."

She tried to step back. "You have me at a disadvantage."

"Yes, I do." He cupped her face with both hands—insistent, not forceful—and captured her gaze.

The first twinge of panic surfaced in Raven's mind. This man commanded alarming power within his gentle gestures. She wholly doubted her ability to handle this situation.

"So young," he cooed, tracing her lips with his thumb, "and only a drop of human blood in your veins…"

He leaned closer. The heat of his breath made her belly quiver. His thumb smoothed an arc over her cheek. "Ooh, barely even that."

He inhaled deeply. "Ahh! You don't feed on humans." His eyes dusted her lips with an insinuated kiss as his hands slid down her throat. "No— you travel like *them* and have *their* blood. Which Host? The Fallen or our foes?"

Shuddering as his fingers splayed across her collarbone, she heard herself reply in a breathless voice, "Neither. He is a neutral star punished for not choosing sides."

"The phantom that walks the battlefields by your side." His pale orbs dove into hers. "He's the silence that shields your whispers from the First and Second Born."

"Aye. A fallen star expelled from the Celestial Curtain." Her brain screamed to shut up, but her mouth and body weren't listening. Her gaze dropped to his mouth, velvety as a rose petal, and her lips parted.

Satisfaction flickered throughout his aura and tickled her stomach. A slow tingle travelled down her legs as his perfect lips formed a devious grin. "Do you fear me, young one?"

"Should I?"

He lashed her wounded ear with his tongue, drawing blood. "'Tis a shame Alexander's silver coin bit you first, although smart to prove the effort of his failure. The Second Born kills for much less and rarely only punishes."

She swallowed hard and watched him with large eyes. He pulled back and grinned. It was unsettling. And exquisite.

"Hmm, you think he prefers surviving to dying? Ask Alexander in five hundred years. Punishment is *endless*." Licking his lips, he blinked slowly, his long lashes curling against the high slope of his cheekbones. His hands tightened around her throat. "'Twould appear you are but clay in my hands. Twisting your pretty neck would put a swift end to your meddling. You may be immune to Rainne, but, with me, you are pliable and *easily* bent."

Those peridot depths tugged harder. She was drowning under his spell.

"Shall I prove it?" Accepting her silence as consent, he parted her lips with his tongue.

A fire roared in Raven's belly. He tasted like the sweetest nectar and smelled of the continental lavender fields long since scorched by the war.

She whimpered when he pulled away. He hooked her bottom lip with his teeth and lapped at her blood with his tongue. He grinned, his concentration intense and palpable. "So pliable—of your own will, no less. Alexander must enjoy the pleasures of your flesh. Given his willful participation in your rebellion, one might wonder about the swiftness with which he saved his hide by revealing your rendezvous point with Hawkiel on the northern shore."

Panic chomped her ribs with unforgiving ferocity. Was someone else tracking Hawkiel and Salea? Her mind screamed to run. Her feet refused. Her mind screamed to escape. Her body yearned to surrender. She licked her healed lip, exhaled, and closed her eyes. Dying by his hands would be a delightful torture, a pleasure to the end of consciousness and life itself.

The grip on her throat loosened. His fingertips were lighter than feathers as they spread out to her shoulders. "I am the Third Born," he revealed. "Lucifer's first vampire, ally to Alexander, and your highest ranking conquest."

The questions stacking in Raven's mind tumbled with her eyes to his lips, to the crimson stain of her blood there—the start of ritualistic pairing. She hesitantly touched it, imprinting with her finger to claim him as hers.

After Hawkiel's branding, she thought she'd never claim anyone—ever. Hawkiel's contract had stolen her free will and chained her to him—and to Gabriel, whom she hadn't seen again. But, claims between vampires were symbolic of bonds that respected free will and marks on humans were territorial.

Bewildered, she met his eyes, asking silent questions, but his mysterious, chartreuse orbs yielded no answers. Bonding was rare and usually completed by the dominant vampire. Why had he voluntarily reversed their roles when she was clearly the submissive? Logic tried to shoulder its way between them, but her body knew what it wanted from him, and it didn't care about words, intentions, or symbols.

"My name is Endymion. Do not fear me."

"Endymion," she repeated, finally realizing that, as Lucifer's first vampire and first infectious protein carrier, he was the oldest of her kind—a commander of all and a leader with his own army.

"My, how nicely it rolls off your tongue," he purred. "A scent of purity trails you and lingers on those with whom you share company. I have longed to taste you, Raven Hawkings."

Her hand fluttered to her throat. "An ally?"

"An ally." He brushed her fingers away. "I prefer to partake in an unorthodox manner of sorts. Arteries are far superior to veins."

His hand dropped to her waist and glided down her belly. "They call me a deviant. I do rather enjoy how the body's heat gathers in great concentrations here." His fingers pressed into the crease of her inner thigh.

The fire in her core flared. Adding pressure to his fingertips, he slid from the pulse of her femoral artery inward until she lifted onto her tiptoes with a gasp. She clawed into his shoulders.

"The Second Born would have me take your head now," he said with a heavy, deliberate breath against her ear. He gripped the nape of her neck and pulled at the hem of her meager cotton underdress.

"It doesn't appear that you want my head," she panted.

"I suppose not. My interest does lie elsewhere."

Her heart erupted at his touch, but he was calm and assured. Merely imagining his teeth sinking into her inner thigh drove her to the edge of delirium, and yet he was confident, every action calculated. He knew the tortures of his pleasure and delighted in her vulnerability.

She feared ever seeing him in battle. Ally or not, no part of her doubted he was a ruthless tyrant when pitted against the Heavenly Host. Under that peaceful façade loomed power and darkness.

His palm slid up her thigh beneath her dress. "Oh how your heart flutters when I touch you. Get your blood hot for me, my dear Raven."

Clinging to him, she whimpered and moaned, crushed by both pleasure and pain, and physically aching to tear into him like a wild creature. "Ahh," she panted, "yo…you're too cruel…"

"Quite so, my dear." He pried into her thighs with his knee and spread her legs. His hand continued its maddening upward trek along her thigh until he reached an intimate place only Alexander had touched before. She cried out and clawed deeper into his shoulders as his fingers slipped inside and he stroked her most sensitive area with his thumb.

The scent of blood struck her immediately.

It was his. Her fingers had carved into his flesh through his protective cloak. He merely grinned and stroked her with more pressure, forcing out another gasp and cries of pleasured anguish. She arched and pushed his fingers deeper inside her body. He tightened his grasp on her nape and held her as she writhed against him, both fighting and craving his touch.

At the edge of unearthly euphoria, her breath raggedly caught in her throat. All of time stopped. A moment of nothingness came before a pain too concentrated to hurt and a pleasure too pure to feel good. When she hit the zenith of the arc and time resumed, tremor after tremor rocked her body and her legs shook uncontrollably. She fell against his chest, reliant on him to stay upright. Still, he stroked her, mercilessly releasing body-shattering waves that crashed over her endlessly.

Gasping too hard to speak, she clawed his muscle down to bone. Her body shook so hard she couldn't think. Her eyes couldn't focus. He had dropped her into the epicenter of a hedonistic supernova.

"Ah, yes. There's the heat I want," he said with a distinct note of satisfaction. He lowered her to the ground. She squeezed her legs shut to contain the intense pulsations exploding from his thumb and tried to roll onto her side.

He held her flat on her back with an insistent hand and kissed her. His lips were dewy soft, but firm, and he bit her lip again as he pulled back and slid down her body. He caught her eyes, trapping her in his peridot arrogance. He flicked his tongue against the spot where his thumb had stroked her, and then his aura shifted hungrily and his fangs sank into the crease of her inner thigh.

A rough, hybrid moan and cry of rapture raced past her lips. She buried her bloody fingers in his hair, writhing again beneath him. He cupped her buttocks and shoved his teeth deeper. She moaned louder as unearthly ecstasy consumed her body totally and ruthlessly unlike anything she'd ever felt before. Nothing she'd shared with Alexander came close to what this man was doing to her, the power he commanded over her, or his ability to bend her to his desires. Endymion's touch was fire and she was melting snow.

Pinpoints of light flashed at the edges of her vision. Her muscles clamped tight and her veins burned. The entire Earth jolted beneath her and a crushing weight landed on her chest. She gasped and whimpered, surprised at how weak she sounded. The fingers curled in Endymion's hair loosened. Parched and burning from the inside out, she gulped and gasped. "En...dym..."

Each breath was a battle. Her hands fell limply to her belly. Her head rolled to the side, aiming her eyes across the river. This path to Death truly was the most blissful imaginable.

Darkness tunneled through flashing lights. Her heart pounded hard and slow as it struggled to pump a depleted reserve. Chills shook her body even as she went numb. Her eyes lost focus. Her breaths grew shallower and farther apart. Her heart shuddered. And then it stopped.

☽ ✳ ☾

Pitch.

Blood.

Warmth.

Threads as soft as spider silk swept her cheek. Pressure on the hinge of her jaw forced her mouth open. Drops of sticky, sweet blood splashed her lips.

She lapped at them with a dry, shriveled tongue. The thirst hit at once, a great pain that burned from her toes to the top of her head. Had her voice worked, she would have groaned and cried and screamed.

Blindly lifting her mouth, she hit something soft and smooth—something with a pulse that pumped wildly against her teeth. It smelled masculine and pure.

Hawkiel.

He pressed insistently at the back of her head. She weakly bit into his throat. With each swallow, anger nipped harder at her ribs. He had warned her, but she never listened and always rushed in.

You fool.

Disgust, humility, and anger took turns beating her ego. She'd been too self-confident to see her naivety, too quick to believe Endymion's alliance, too dismissive of the power wielded by the vampiric command—

"'Tis apparent you are more fragile than you seem, my dear."

Winter-cold shock froze her solid, horrifyingly trapped in *his* arrogant grasp. Determination drilled into her anger. She tightened the seal of her lips and sucked with vengeful greed.

And yet...emerging from Death's shadow with *him* snuffed her anger. She grasped at it, yearning to hold on, but it sifted through her fingers like fine sand. Painful thirst gave way to hunger. She savored all that she took from him and replenished her strength with every beat of his heart. He released her head and propped himself up as she latched onto his shoulders.

He was still on top of her, between her legs, clearly aching to finish what they'd started. She slowly tugged him down, craving the heat of skin on skin and bodies moving in unison. She whimpered and dug her fingers into his hair. A carnal moan came from low in his throat.

"Oh, not yet, young one," he said, his voice velvety and seductive as she curled her legs around his thighs. "'Tis easy to lose myself in you, my dear. I do not wish to pull away. Take your time and get stronger."

She relaxed in his embrace. They were fused, connected and bonded in a way she'd never known possible. She was always strong and always brave, never permitted to yield in the mission forced upon her. But here, for the first time in her wretched existence, she was alive and unburdened—free to make her own choices, regardless of consequence—free to enjoy her life.

Maybe trusting Endymion was foolish. But, maybe it was right. Panting as she withdrew from his throat, she whispered, "I am clay in your hands by my choice and I am strong."

With a hungry growl, he pressed her against the ground and took command of her mouth. He fidgeted with his cloak and garments, and she hiked the hem of her underdress up to her waist. When he entered her, she tightened her thighs around him and exhaled a ravished moan. He buried his face into the crook of her neck and panted heavily against her skin, thrusting deeply inside her and moaning painfully as though he couldn't go far enough.

He nipped at her throat and licked the pooling droplets. A rough growl reverberated in his throat. He grabbed her hips and thrust harder and faster. She dug her fingers into his back, clinging tightly, her heart racing and lungs burning under labored breaths. Every grunt and moan ignited her pulse, every thrust lit her nerves with fire, and every heartbeat made her blood burn hotter.

Raking her nails through his cloak and down the skin of his back, she bit into his trapezius muscle. He growled again, ever satisfied. Even by choice, she was little more than his plaything—his marionette. Was this what it meant to be at the bottom of their hierarchy? Was free will an illusion?

She issued a throaty growl in return and thrust her fangs in deeper. He ground her hips into the shore and grunted roughly, his body pulsing inside hers. Huffing heavily, he loosened his grip. She withdrew her fangs and he dropped against her chest, struggling to catch his breath. She threaded her fingers into his hair and held him there, her heart galloping in his ear. His body pulsed inside her and he moaned again.

From her vantage point, she saw little of his face, but there was no mistaking the gleam in his eye or the curve of his mouth. Her heart skipped a beat.

The curve sharpened as he glanced up. "Merely gazing upon me makes your heart flutter, my dear? Even now?" He grinned mischievously. "Does Alexander make your heart flicker so?"

Heat burned her cheeks.

"Ah, I thought not. You are too strong to become his clay. With him you are a rock."

He pulsed again inside her. Gentle fingers caressed her face, brushing stray hairs away. "Promise always to be clay for me, my dear Raven. Be hard as a diamond in battle, yet soft and pliable with me."

Staring across the river in silence, she wondered if he had charmed her with some hidden power or possessed her like a demon. Her body and thoughts seemed like foreign things.

"My request surprises you, my dear?" His voice was smugly satisfied. "No one can possess you—not even me."

Her heart skipped another beat.

His voice grew more insistent, almost begging. Perhaps her choices truly were her own.

"Promise," he said. "Give me a vow, my dear Raven."

"I promise," she whispered.

His smile was pleased, his eyes intense. She had played into his hands, again. He was a demon, after all. He commanded Lucifer's army, adept at manipulation and killing. He reveled in torturing his victims with pleasure or death, or both.

"Your smile never changes," she said. "Not in moments like this or moments in battle, does it? It's a cruel thing."

"One must enjoy what one does, my dear." His lips twisted with dark satisfaction. "I choose to enjoy the path I walk, regardless of where I go."

"And you're always in control. Your prey can never escape."

"Ah! I could devour you again—although, I doubt you'd survive." He sliced her throat with a lengthened nail and collected the blood that appeared. Licking his finger, he said, "No one escapes unless I let them go."

He cupped her cheek and caught her gaze. "We are allies, now," he said, his words paced and deliberate. "I can gain you an audience with the First Born. His growing concern is for the greater good of our species. He will listen to your logic. However, I shall require time."

"How much?" Hope sparked in her belly.

"Whilst the majority of our force wishes to withdraw, fear holds them to battle. Those who disobey do so at great peril." Darkness lit his eyes. "Alexander is fortunate to have the Second Born's favor, but he will know that favor intimately well for the rest of his life because of you. Most are not so *privileged* after failing so fantastically at such a simple task."

The panic center in Raven's mind sounded an internal alarm. "What is your intent, Endymion? What if you fail?"

"I never fail." He flattened his palm and shoved her face sideways against the mud and rocks. "I was ordered to kill you."

Her heart stopped an instant before panic gave it a jump-start. "Wh-what?" She wanted him off. *Now.* "You intend to kill me?"

He licked her throat and moaned, "I do have a tendency to follow my orders, my dear, and your life means less than my own. I am cruel, remember?"

She ground her teeth and glared from her peripheral. His eyes glinted black as he flashed a bloody grin. "The advantage was mine from the beginning. You made it quite easy. *No one escapes unless I let them.*"

Shoving against his chest did nothing. He was immovable. There was another pulse inside her. Acidic blood rushed up her throat. She gagged. "So me not dying was a fluke, then? Or did you resurrect me to finish having your fun first?"

Shoving harder was futile. She squeezed her eyes shut and screamed, *"What is your intent?"*

"You made a vow." His voice was lofty, commanding, and authoritative. "I *never* fail, Raven Hawkings. I am quite skilled at killing my prey, and I've developed abilities that allow me to return life so I that may take it again and again—even to the soulless. Do you require more proof? I can kill you again."

His blood burned her throat as it regurgitated into her mouth. She spit it out and shuddered beneath him. "You're a monster."

"Hmm. Your vows must mean as little as your trust in me." He licked her throat again and lifted his palm. "Your heart stopped. You stopped breathing. Your consciousness no longer registered on this physical plane. I will truthfully report to the Second Born that I killed you, because I did."

She slapped at him, kicked her legs out, and screamed for him to get off. He pinned her hands above her head. She spit his blood into his face.

"You promised to be clay, but you are turning into a rock." He kissed her forehead. "I never fail. I take what I want. I am a monster. I am cruel. I am much like the Second Born in many ways."

He kissed her again. "Alas, I was an ally when I arrived here. I was an ally when I stopped your heart. I was an ally when I started your heart. I am your ally now. And because of our shared pleasure, when I report to the Second Born, I will bear undeniable proof: your angelic blood has flooded my veins, and my cloak, hair, and flesh bear the scars and blood of a passionate battle. I am far more competent in not failing my duties than Alexander. No one else shall come after you, my dear. You are free."

A knot formed in Raven's throat. Tears stung her eyes. She hadn't cried since she met Hawkiel—the day of her birth more than four hundred years ago. "You came here to kill me."

"And to revive you."

Raven clenched her jaw and balled her fists. He released her arms. "I am here because you foolishly displayed your abilities to the Second Born. I am the Third Born—only two others rank higher. Fortunately for you, my dear, I also share the Second Born's favor, and his ear, as an advisor."

"He was going to come himself?"

Endymion nodded. "He and the First Born can cloak themselves beyond detection. He would have killed you the instant you appeared and returned brandishing your head to quell the rebellion."

Raven shuddered beneath him. As his lips curved at the corners, a spark lit in her mind. "If you're Alexander's ally, does that mean you're the other anomaly in the ranks?"

"I am far from normal—"

"No, I felt something. Something similar to Alexander."

The curve widened. "Alexander and I do have more in common now."

Heat rose to her face. Fangs poked through Endymion's grin and his eyes shone with anticipation. A retort lingered on her tongue, but she no longer wanted to play the puppet, so she cut her strings and glared at him in silence.

He cried out with delight. "Ah! There's the dominance he likes in you!" He withdrew from her and lay on his side, stroking her face. "Keep your promise to me, my dear Raven. Be his rock, but be my clay—only for me."

Rolling onto her side to face him, she caught his hand and nuzzled his palm with her cheek. "It cannot be a coincidence that you and Alexander are both close to the Second Born."

"I have the First Born's favor, as well," Endymion replied. "He is cold and keenly aware of the happenings under his command. 'Twill not surprise me if he sees through my deception immediately."

A nervous breath caught in Raven's throat.

"Favor comes in many forms. The Second Born craves desire and blood. The First Born seeks truth and trust." Soft fingertips traced an arc from her eye to her lips. "A heavy burden rests upon you, my dear. No matter your will or strength—when the weight grows too much, it will crush you. Worry not about me."

"Of all Lucifer's vampires," she whispered, "only I have never killed a Heavenly Host or human in cold blood. I am proof we can live in peace."

"What of the human blood presently in your veins?"

"I enjoy the company of a young girl whose family lived in the village your commander decimated. She was with me when..." Raven's voice trailed. If an angel couldn't understand her intentions, she certainly couldn't expect it from a vampire. "Casting Salea into the world alone seemed barbaric."

"You took pity on her?"

Raven's eyes widened. He understood. Hawkiel had been disappointed. "At morning light, Hawkiel will take Salea due east. We're skirting the battle and going south behind the warpath. That will give us the best—"

"No," Endymion interrupted, "the Fallen have scavengers and soul collectors lingering along destruction's trail. Direct your traveling companions north. The war's progression is slowing as reluctance grows, but we continue to push the Heavenly Host's line back. Let Alexander and me unify our brethren. I shall approach the First Born at an opportune moment with a logical suggestion that he shall heed."

"But the ranks? They'll believe me dead. Alexander doesn't believe they possess the will to continue—"

Endymion silenced Raven with a finger to her lips. He dipped the tip inside and pricked it on a sharp tooth. She suckled the wound as he said, "We need to push the ranks to think for themselves. Your rebellion has gained a commander—the commander who supposedly killed you. The humans say to have faith? Worry not. I never fail."

He grabbed her by the nape and pulled her to him. He kissed her deeply. "'Tis imperative you stay off the battlefield—stay dead. I shall contact you via couriers that can leave unnoticed. Many years may pass before I can gain you an audience with the First Born and trust that he will not kill you on sight."

"I can travel like the Host," she replied, "and meet you or Alexander anywhere at any time. Hawkiel will insist I return. He won't like me entrusting my mission to a vampire, let alone the vampiric command."

"No risks. Focus on your Salea. If she remains pure hearted like you, she will boost your cause—additional proof that we monsters can coexist with the natural world."

"Aye," Raven admitted. "She possesses great potential."

He kissed her again, his teeth scraping her bottom lip. "My scouts are loyal. They follow orders and will shake off your scent before returning to me—which is unfortunate."

He groaned. "I cannot taste you again soon enough! Time is a thin barrier between us, but it will be daily torture. Be assured that we shall see each other again before the humans mark the end of this millennium."

"That's nearly a hundred years away!"

"What's another century between us?" he asked in a playful, seductive voice. "Imagine how satisfying it will be to come together after so long, my dear. My clay doll—I shall mold you again and again, and ensure that you enjoy every second of every moment twice as much as I—I am yours, after all."

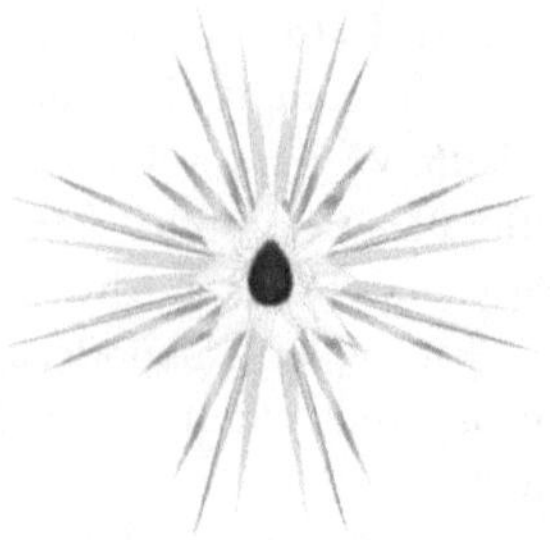

CHAPTER FIVE: SACRIFICIAL BLOOD

I

Orison Crossing, Summer 2006

Shades of rich apricot and deep persimmon blanketed the sinking sun beneath vivid swathes of pomegranate and the indigo beginnings of night. Strands of clear mini lights and solar lamps sprang to life and transformed the greenhouse into an intimate, magical place. Dots of light reflected off the pond as sparkling stars and cast mysterious shadows beneath the leaves.

The group had fallen into silent musing after an hour of sharing memories, laughing, and crying. They'd received word that the Elders were settling in and that Raven's duties as VaSH High Commander would keep her away until morning. Alex was stuck at the mansion, charged with overseeing the High Council's security detail, so Heron and Cyprian were theirs for the night. The evening had otherwise passed in relative peace.

Now that the conversation had stalled, Paresh realized she'd never sit in this place with Molly again, and, for that, she was sad. The older woman had been kind and reminded her of her mother in many ways.

But then there was Master Jon—Jonathan—who had survived despite what Gabriel had shown her. The room tilted sideways as she melted into her palms. The chardonnay buzzing through her veins made her feel light enough to float.

Her auburn-haired guardian had remained mostly quiet, sipping his cabernet fusion, contented to listen to Eric and Walter reminisce. He'd known little about Molly and seemed genuinely interested in learning about the woman he'd risked his life to protect. The fact that he had chosen to live made Paresh immensely happy—despite the cost.

He caught her staring and shook his head at Eric. "This is the worst possible time for Paresh to get drunk."

"She's okay."

"Hmm," she murmured. "She's right here, too."

"And not going anywhere." Eric's gaze was like a warm shroud as he reached across the table. Her fingers tingled when they made contact. "We should call it a night and rest up for tomorrow."

She nodded with a sigh, not wanting to admit that she'd been fighting off droopy eyes for the past ten minutes. "Your house?"

Eric deflated subtly, but smiled and dipped his chin in agreement. "Walter? You going home or do you want a nightcap?"

The lawman stretched his arms high overhead and yawned. "I'm good if you drop me off at my house. I'm in no shape to drive." He pointed from Eric to Jonathan and back. "Now that your people are taken care of, one of you had better make sure that tiny thing—" He nodded at Paresh. "—sleeps tonight and takes better care of herself."

Jonathan straightened, ruffled at being chastised. *By a human, no less*, Paresh thought, hearing his voice in her head. A small giggle escaped her mouth. The sound drew their attention and that made her laugh harder. The room was swimming now. Or she was swimming in the room. The last time she had laughed in here had been with Molly and Don—

She slapped her palms on the table. The world jerked to a stop.

"What the hell?" Walter cried, his chair skittering into another table as he jumped up and Heron and Cyprian launched from their dark corners to land at her side.

"Sorry, Walter—guys. It's n-nothing," she said sheepishly, rubbing her arm under the flame of humiliation. Butterflies flopped in her belly. They weren't the good, fun kind that Eric gave her, but rather a type that shouldn't exist. They were vicious, stinging and gnashing monsters that made her sick.

She leapt up. Her bare feet slapped the greenhouse's shellacked concrete as she ran for the heavy double doors yelling, "I'm fine, don't worry!"

She grabbed her belly and stumbled into the ladies' room. Unable to make it to the sink, she blindly scrabbled for the garbage canister she knew was by the door and held on tightly as her whole body heaved until she ran dry.

Wiping her mouth, she slumped against the wall and slid into a heap on the floor. Blackness spun around her. She squeezed her eyes shut to hide behind her own darkness.

But demons lived there, too.

Donovan's bloody smile cracked open over her mind. The butterflies kicked and slapped at her stomach. She groaned and fell onto her side.

The tiles of the floor were cold against her cheek. Her fingers scratched at the grout lines in front of her face, grounding her to a reality where she knew she was safe—even if she didn't feel like it.

The door creaked open behind her, throwing a dim puddle of light upon her. It swung shut and a warm body sat beside her, smoothing a familiar hand over her back while repeatedly assuring, "It's okay, it's okay."

"I'm sorry for scaring you," she said. "All you do is worry about me."

"What—" Eric's voice cracked. "What can I do, Paresh?"

Tears stung her eyes. Her lips trembled. She sniffled as quietly as she could.

Eric curled on the floor behind her and wrapped her in his arms. He buried his face in her hair at the crook of her neck. "You have nothing to apologize for. Ever," he whispered.

Silence lapsed. His scent—raw masculinity and pheromones under neroli blossom, bergamot, and musk—was lulling and comforting as it cushioned her from the dark emotions that lingered within the protective shield of his aura.

"I know it's not about me," he whispered. "I should have been there. I should have seen it. I never should have let him—"

A heavy breath brushed her neck. "I'm sorry. I'm here. I've got you." He combed his fingers through her hair. "Anything you need. I'll do anything I can."

Within the safety of his cocoon, the world stilled. The blackness calmed. She heaved a breath in, fearing the stomach cramps would flare up, and exhaled slowly when they didn't.

"Will you sleep tonight?" he asked. "We'll sleep in my bed and have breakfast together, just the two of us?"

Her mouth started watering. A metallic sensation burned into her teeth. She gurgled and pulled herself up to the waste can, vomiting into it. Eric rose with her, gathering her hair and whispering something she couldn't decipher.

Her stomach heaved again and her hold slipped. She lurched forward, slamming her ribs on the hard plastic edge before Eric caught her.

"This…can't…" she panted, bracing herself, "be normal."

"It's not," he said, the depth and pain of his concern making her wince. "I…I don't know."

She closed her eyes and hung her head over the edge until her new nose told her things about that garbage can she'd rather not know. She straightened, thankful for Eric's steadying hands.

"I feel weak…" Shadows swirled and crossed her eyes under heavy lids.

The evil butterflies seared a line across her belly. She slumped into Eric's arms. He was whispering again, from far away. She couldn't hear him. A fiery, sable cloud emerged from the blackness and pillars of fire roared through the cityscape forming in her mind. The growls of a monstrous behemoth shook the earth and the cries of the tormented flowed with thick black smoke down her airway.

Unable to gag or choke, but desperate for air, she silently stared at the chained man at the center of the blaze. Slender and tall, he burned like a candlewick, and his screams…his screams were too horrendous to bear——like a bell tolling for Death's inevitable arrival.

II

Arc of True Blood, Summer 2006

The Elders' private residences resembled traditional Japanese wooden post and beam structures with removable shoji panel walls and fenced courtyards. The interiors were largely the same: a sprawling room with tatami mats and rice paper or canvas screens splashed with watercolor nature scenes, low tables dotted with crimson cushions, and down-filled futons and pillows for sleeping and lounging. Lady Rainne's home, however, was merely a façade of uniformity.

A wall of empty gold frames and a narrow hall greeted Raven and Lord Endymion upon entry. The right path led to Lady Rainne's sitting room that overlooked the private garden where she meditated each morning. The left path led to the same space, but also hid the entrance to the central room where Lady Rainne rested.

Securing her had been the highest priority after Lord Lucien signed the Treaty. Her "prison" was built long before the Arc of True Blood's completion. It started as a box with three-foot-thick walls made from a mesh of concrete, iron, and steel. The exterior was coated in layers of gold, silver, and copper, and the interior was lined with diamond and tungsten panels. As her residence came together, the box was encased in camouflaging materials and the doors were hidden with the same technology used at Snowblood Square.

On approach, there were no visible seams in the wall. The entrance only appeared on the northern face for authorized true bloods. Unlike the gaping black hole at the meeting center, Lady Rainne's chambers opened through a medieval gate with studded wooden doors with iron bolts and huge locks. The formidable appearance concealed the redundant gridded electronic circuits used for surveillance, defense, and offense, and the sound barriers that worked in conjunction with the arc's privacy grid to block all noise. When locked down, nothing got in or out.

The first gate lifted and three Crimson Guard hunters met them on bended knee. They rose in silence and lowered the gate when Lord Endymion activated the mechanism to open the next gate. Iron spikes grated against concrete and stone, and the floor shuddered as the gate slammed shut. The hunters secured the doors as the Elder unlatched the second set. The vestibule interlock was one of the simpler, but effective, countermeasures.

Another trio of hunters met them in the second vestibule with the same reverence and interlock sequence. The hunters and Lord Endymion simultaneously released and locked the latches, and the final door swung open into a dim room aglow with candlelight.

Hundreds of paraffin stubs flickered in candelabras, sconces, pedestals, and ancient chandeliers, dripping to form waxy stalagmites and stalactites. The scent of sulfur mixed with cinnamon and clove oils to mask the strong, metallic odor of Lady Rainne's blood. It was nauseatingly concentrated, repugnant and odiferous, and only a potent combination of fire, oil-infused wax, incense, and ventilation made it tolerable. Her essence was vile and repulsive.

The space itself, resplendent with cast-iron metalwork, evoked the gothic aesthetic of a queen's medieval bedchamber. Satiny damask wallpaper in tone-on-tone deep crimson hid the stark metal walls behind ornate curves and sharp tips. Gilded and black lacquer frames of every size and shape hung empty on the walls. Black and blood red velvet textiles, and braided, golden cords and tassels complimented the beautifully carved and lacquered Baroque furniture—chaises, high back chairs, and the hulking centerpiece of her bed.

There, surrounded by carved rosewood gargoyles and silk pillows in crimson and gold, lay Lady Rainne. Covered in champagne-colored lace, only her snow-white hands and feet were exposed. Lace draped her hair, its scalloped hem softening the edges of the white mask that hid her face. Laid out like a corpse with her hands folded over her chest, her appearance inferred a delicate fragility that her aura shattered. Despite her dormancy, she emanated more power than any beast imaginable.

Lord Endymion secured the door and joined Raven at the bedside. "Ready, my dear?"

Focused on the sleeping Elder, Raven nodded.

"Resurrectio, Rainne Blood Pathos."

Lady Rainne stirred to life, her initial motions mechanical and reminiscent of early robotics before transitioning into natural movement. Each precise, positional shift transitioned smoothly with a dancer's grace. Sitting up and sweeping her feet over the edge of her mattress, she extended an impeccably sculpted hand, her fingers tipped with pure silver claws sharper than any blade in the VaSH's arsenal.

Lucifer had not designed his weapon to think like a humanoid. She processed logic like a machine. Every move was calculated, every word articulated and never arbitrary. Much as with Lord Lucien, when Lady Rainne spoke, others listened. No one else shared her view of the world. No one wanted to.

She was near flawless with a single vulnerability. Raven's sworn oath to protect her—or to destroy her—had allowed an unlikely kinship to bloom. Lady Rainne responded to Raven with a fond affect not allotted to the others.

Kneeling in reverence, Raven kissed the back of Lady Rainne's hand and bowed her head. "Milady. I am glad to see you are well."

"And I, you, Little One." Her voice was rich and sensually husky, ringing of prowess and darkness, and hinted at a smile behind her mask.

Cold slate tiles met Lady Rainne's silver-tipped toes. The delicately woven gown hugged her lithe form and the fabric loosened at her wrists and ankles to drape scalloped hems over her feet and hands. Her gentle touch burned like ice as she palmed Raven's cheek. "I shall not resist my punishment, Vampire Hunter Raven."

Folding the Elder's hands into her own, Raven replied, "Milady, I'm not here to punish."

"I am a threat to the Servator, am I not?"

"Aye, milady."

"Then why am I awake?"

"Threat assessment and enhanced restriction."

As Raven stood, she lowered Lady Rainne's arms to her sides.

Steeling her grip, she held the Elder's palms flat against her thighs. "It is better than the alternative."

"For you." The words fell softly on a note of sadness.

Raven's mind flashed to the battlefield and the Great Holy War's bloody blooms, tattered feathers, and torn flesh. On that day, her first day, she had witnessed firsthand the carnage her mistress reaped when activated.

"Elder Rainne Blood Pathos," Raven said, affirming her resolve. "Acknowledge High Commander Hawkings."

Lady Rainne stiffened. She'd never willingly accept a protocol born from an angel other than Lucifer, but the appearance of Hawkiel's mark had elevated Raven above Lord Lucien in her control hierarchy. With permanent remnants of Hawkiel's blood in her veins and body, Raven was the only one who could render Lady Rainne useless to their enemies and the High Council alike—including Lord Lucien.

But not to Lucifer, Raven thought bitterly. That sole vulnerability dictated death.

The nails on Lady Rainne's toes and fingers doubled in length, lethally sharp. Her spine snapped in line with her center and her shoulders squared to form an unnaturally stark right angle between her jaw and throat. When she spoke, she no longer sounded like a living creature. Her consciousness barely existed within the shell of her body. Once activated, all control ceded to instinct and her master's desires.

"Current operational authority falls under Endythree, Vampire Shadow Hound High Commander."

Raven's knuckles cracked as her fingers tightened around the Elder's resistive wrists. "High Commander *Hawkings* supersedes Endythree. Acknowledge."

The white mask swiveled to Lord Endymion. His chartreuse gaze betrayed no emotion, nor did he move or make a sound.

"Ra...ven."

"No," Raven growled, "*Hawkings* has manifested. Acknowledge High Commander Hawkings as your master."

Minutes of silence passed.

Lady Rainne's arms trembled.

Her body shuddered.

The mask snapped to Raven.

Slipping free with ease, Lady Rainne threw her arms over her head and arched backward, planting her palms on the mattress and lifting into the air. She touched down on the other side of the bed and flipped back twice more. Her metallic toes clicked the slate as she landed. She stood defiant and tall with one hip thrust forward.

"High Commander Hawkings acknowledged. Input command."

Temporary relief trickled out on a slow breath. The Hawkings Protocol was an untested theoretical safety measure. The machinations within Lady Rainne's mind were intricate and infinite—no one truly knew how she worked.

"Deactivate all attack modes," Raven said.

"Attack modes deactivated. Input command."

"My lord," Raven said without looking away from the white mask, "might I suggest you wait outside?"

"Of course, my dear." In barefooted silence, he padded to the door and deactivated the chamber's sound barrier before securing the entrance. From the vestibule, he said, "Should it become necessary, the hunters and I will intervene with defensive and distraction maneuvers, High Commander."

"Aye." Raven studied Lady Rainne with a wariness that settled deep into her bones. She braced herself with a huff and then whispered, "Let the blood rain."

Time thinned and stretched like ice crystals forming atop a lake. Maybe it was seconds—or perhaps a bare fraction of a second. It seemed like forever. Time was the only barrier between them, dominating the uncomfortable stillness. If Lady Rainne removed her mask, a life that had spanned centuries would become a memory—but which one?

Lady Rainne straightened. Raven's fingers jerked.

"Invalid command. Rainne Blood Pathos is not engaged."

Raven blew out a heavy breath and sagged with relief as she took a small step back. "Input command beta echo zero. Excluding Zero Zero One, Zero Zero Two, Endythree, and High Commander Hawkings, erase all access codes. Under the authority of the Hawkings Protocol, you are hereby restricted from removing your mask until expressly ordered by High Commander Hawkings. Breaching this protocol results in immediate self-termination. Acknowledge."

"Command beta echo zero acknowledged. Erasing access codes." After a brief pause, Lady Rainne added, *"The Hawkings Protocol is active. Input command."*

"Peto somnus."

Bones cracked on slate as Lady Rainne collapsed into sleep. Raven turned to leave.

"My lord—" Raven reactivated the button and opened the door. "She's all yours."

Lord Endymion's fingers brushed her hand. "A word in private before you leave the arc, High Commander?"

Raven dipped her chin. "Aye, my lord."

"We shall prepare the casket for transport. Wait in my quarters."

III

Orison Crossing, Summer 2006

The door clicked open and Jonathan slipped inside. A faint glint of annoyance flashed through the darkness.

"I know you loved sneaking around my bedroom before, but can you not make it a habit now?" Eric asked dryly.

"Funny," Jonathan replied, closing the door. "How is she?"

"Vitals sound good, but she's still out. She didn't even wake up when I bathed her or changed her clothes."

A pang struck Jonathan's heart. "I've never seen anything like this."

"So taking her to one of your medical units is pointless, then?" Exhaustion weighted Eric's voice.

"They aren't getting anywhere near her. But Raven has medical training," Jonathan replied, leaning back with his arms crossed. He wondered when Eric last slept. It'd been nearly a month for him and he was feeling it. "I doubt she'll know anything we don't, though."

"I was lucky you put me into a coma for my alteration. Maybe I would've been like this. Who knows how certain interventions have complicated things." Eric sat up, careful not to jostle Paresh. "Gabriel might know, but he won't tell us."

A quiet sigh fell from Jonathan's lips. The pain of Pare's suffering nipped at him through her aura.

"Seriously, why are you in here?" Eric asked with a note of caution.

"Nothing happened, don't worry." Jonathan tossed his hand dismissively. "It's just...Lucien called me to the arc."

He reluctantly added, "I have to go."

"Now?" Eric asked in disbelief. "Doesn't he know—"

"Oh, he knows everything," Jonathan said, shaking his head and flipping his hand again. He'd argued every reason possible against leaving. "But, she's asleep, the town is protected, and you're under the guard of my pack. I can 'spare' the time."

"Of course you can. Because time stops for you." Coils of anger slithered through Eric's aura.

"Cut him a break," Jonathan said, thrusting his head against the door. "He cares for her the same as us, but he can't show it, and your power struggles are draining."

"All those years of calling me the Hawthorne's dog and you go running at Lucien's first call," Eric retorted. "This has been hell for her, and you have the gall to tout that Lucien 'knows all' when he can't even tell us what's happening to her? Or if she's still in danger of dying from his bite?"

Jonathan straightened.

"You hadn't thought about that?" Eric flung a disgusted arm at him. "Just go. I survived a hundred and forty years with you hunting me. I think I can handle a few hours without you."

"That's not…I didn't know you were worried that she might die because of Lucien," Jonathan replied. Eric's words bit harder than usual. "She'd be dead by now if that was the case. Donovan's attack might have aggravated the wound, but starvation and anemia are the real dangers. That's why I'm appalled at her human appetite."

"Well, she's not tolerating it despite her cravings." Eric's jaw bulged at the hinge as he gazed upon the sleeping girl. "At least those other things we can prevent."

"True." Jonathan surrendered to the pull of Paresh's weakened aura and crossed the room. "I don't care how much damn soup she wants, she needs to drink blood every day. As long as she does that, she'll heal and should get better."

"Should," Eric echoed, slumping against his padded headboard. "There're too many unknowns."

Paresh's subconscious essence concentrated on Jonathan. With a reluctant sigh, he squatted beside the bed and watched her sleep.

"It's like our old stargazing days, isn't it?" Eric asked.

Jonathan grunted. "Maybe for you. I was always a bit too distracted to enjoy the stars when I was with you."

"And now?"

Shaking his head, Jonathan replied, "I can't explain it. Like I said: it's gone." He smoothed his thumb across Pare's cheek. "It's like with her. No temptation, only familiarity."

Jonathan dotted Paresh's forehead with a kiss. "Sleep tight, Pare. I'll be back before you wake up."

"Make that a promise and get going," Eric said. He made a shooing motion with his hand.

"You need to sleep, too. We both do," Jonathan said, pressing a long prong on the Vampiric Star pinned to his lapel. A ghostly white mouth split the blackness behind him. He saw Eric nodding and shooing him, so he stepped in and let the endless haze enfold him.

The security protocols at the Arc of True Blood deposited him at Snowblood Square. The arc's atmospheric conditions were set to match Orison Crossing: dark and overcast. Eyeing the emptiness surrounding the marble dome of the High Council's headquarters, he muttered to himself, "Why isn't this under guard?"

"I'm monitoring all comings and goings." Lucien's voice sounded close. "Join me in my courtyard."

Jonathan surveyed the residences along the outer edge of the casements. Locked out of Animus Hollow's other access points, he was stuck with the minor inconvenience of walking or running the miles between them. He opted for the latter and arrived at Lucien's shoji screened entrance within minutes.

Kicking off his shoes, he slid the panel open and stepped inside, not surprised to find the eastern wall open to the night's air with Lucien meditating on his deck. The scent of cherry blossoms, summer algae, and vanilla incense wafted into the room, and the clanking of his bamboo fountain formed a rhythmic beat for the whirring frogs that lived in his pond.

"Paresh is not well," Jonathan said. "This is a bad time to call me away."

Lucien rose and met him at the tea table, absently smoothing the creases in his black kimono without looking up. "You are an Arch Elder of the Vampiric High Council. You have other duties. Let the girl sleep."

"This is why I never wanted to be on the Council in the first place. I don't want this added responsibility—or the restraint."

"The restraint?" Lucien echoed, his eyes swinging up slowly. "Did the Crimson Commander brief you?"

"Yes. The mansion is secured and the Elders are settling in. Alex mentioned that they're acting like entitled toddlers claiming rooms as territories." Jonathan shifted his weight to one foot. Maybe this wouldn't take as long as he thought. "But I haven't heard a peep from Raven."

"She activated the Hawkings Protocol successfully. Endymion prepared an empty casket for transport. At morning light, the three of you will escort it to the mansion and place it under heavy guard."

"Morning light?" Jonathan scoffed. "That's hours away. I can come back for that. Besides, Paresh will awaken long—"

"I need you here."

"Why?" Jonathan brushed past him and stepped onto the deck. The air wasn't humid like it was in Orison Crossing. A simulated summer night was nowhere close to the real thing. "No one other than Eric knows I'm here. If you wanted a show of force, I should have left with more witnesses."

When Lucien remained silent, Jonathan glanced back. His master's mouth was moving, but there was no sound. He rolled his eyes. "I know you can speak over your privacy grid, so do you care to repeat that?"

"Astute." Lucien's eyes narrowed. "But your tongue has grown quite sharp of late."

That caught Jonathan off guard. When had their interactions become this easy? "I…I'm sorry."

Lucien's brow lifted with indifference. "After the coffin is secured, High Commander Hawkings shall assess the damage on Banks Island and Endymion will return here to guard Rainne Blood Pathos. For the short duration that he is gone, I will oversee her confinement."

"Raven hasn't assessed the Arc of Celestial Night, yet? What has she been doing all this time?" Jonathan threw his hands out to the side and crossed the threshold.

"Endymion," Lucien replied simply. "And sleeping, as per my order through Endymion. I need my High Commander rested for the coming days—"

"*Our* High Commander," Jonathan said, strangely tempted to poke at Lucien in dominance as he would with Eric. "And you do realize that Endymion's version of 'sleep' won't include much rest?"

"Are you accepting your title, then?" Lucien asked. "*My* Arch Elders cannot be so fickle."

A deliberate, ebbing flow formed in Lucien's aura. "What are you hiding?" Jonathan asked suspiciously, stepping closer.

Lucien's eyes lost focus as he retreated inwardly even further and the sensation disappeared. "Once your assignment is complete, I want you three to separate yourselves from the High Council. Everyone in one place is too large of a target."

"I can't evict Eric from his hometown," Jonathan objected, irritated at how Lucien kept shifting his mood and their conversation. "He opened the mansion for us! Where else would you have sent the Elders?"

"I directed them to the mansion before I called. You told me it was empty during your confessions, so it was logical."

Jonathan threw his head back, running his hands over his hair. He paced in a small circle. "This is unbelievable." He shook his head and pointed a stern finger at Lucien. "You know, Eric tenses up every time you issue a new order. I told him to cut you a break, but——"

"You are barely accepting my orders yourself." Lucien's quiet voice rode a pained undercurrent.

"Yeah and I'm just as confused by that as you——" Jonathan stopped pacing. "Hold on——that actually bothers you?"

Lucien's expression flattened like stone. Jonathan was about to call him out when he remembered Eric talking with Walter about Vermont. He resumed pacing, directing his attention to the courtyard. "Eric mentioned leaving. I can get us away from Orison Crossing, at least for a little while, without him fighting me on it."

"Good," Lucien replied. "I expect our situation to escalate drastically. Hawkiel's mark is appearing on Raven's shoulder."

Jonathan froze. He tried to form a question but no longer had a voice.

"If other matters weren't more pressing, I would have told you sooner. That is why I ordered down time for her with Endymion." Lucien's aura shifted with unease. "I——"

"You lifted Endymion with instructions to watch the dark spot for movement, but that doesn't matter if that mark is visible!" Jonathan exploded with a spray of spittle. He threw an arm in the direction of Snowblood Square. "Your order to kill Paresh triggered the damn Apocalypse and you sent *Raven* to guard her! She never should have been sent anywhere near a divine nexus, let alone our Servator! I should have sent Alex!"

"You're right," Lucien admitted quietly. "But I disagree about Paresh. Lucifer killed her. He was the trigger."

Pacing faster with his hands on top of his head, Jonathan's voice rose with panic. "It's doesn't matter who triggered what!"

He kicked Lucien's table into his cupboard. The teacup collection within shattered and the table cracked down the center. Shaking his head, Jonathan whispered, "What is happening to us?"

Reality crashed down, callously dragging his shoulders and slackening his arms. His voice was empty as he gestured at the damage in apology. "What the hell…it's the end of the world."

Lucien's vanilla warmth drew physically closer and his aura's embrace radiated confusion, regret, and hesitation. This was not the same Lucien he'd long known——not that he hadn't changed, as well. A butterfly flickered to life in his belly as a frustrated sigh fled his lips.

"No one knows what that mark truly means." Lucien hesitantly gripped Jonathan's shoulder, sparking more butterflies. "Gabriel locked her into a contract sealed with the world's fate and that's all we know. I have faith in our Second New Age. This world will not end easily with her fighting for it."

Jonathan nodded absently. Even if he had a thought in his head, he couldn't respond. The heat of Lucien's palm set the butterflies ablaze, but everything was too much of a mess to give in to them.

"I do need you—" Lucien exhaled an unstable, melancholy breath. "I...I'm not myself. I need to hold onto the unshakeable façade that's expected of me, but my mind has splintered and I am failing."

He paused for a shallow breath and his hand tightened painfully. "I'm failing at every turn and I can't stop. These emotions are too strong. How can I affect apathy when I feel everything? I don't know what to do—I think about asking you, but I shouldn't need to ask, so I don't. But...I can't go on like this."

"What...does that mean?" Jonathan peered back. An undefinable edge had appeared in Lucien's aura. It was the dominant element and fluctuated rapidly with his internal battle.

"Either I regain control or I crumble and anarchy wins. I cannot help the way I feel. I cannot control it." Lucien's bony fingers curled in quiet agony. His hand dropped off Jonathan's shoulder, leaving a cold spot behind, and slowly formed into a fist that unfurled as equally slowly. "I feel them—fissures in my mind that crack open faster than I can seal them. Only—I don't want to simply close them—"

He swallowed hard and moved his lips, but there was no sound. His averted gaze drifted over the fibers of the tatami mats and his muscles tensed. "I...I want to fill them," he whispered at last. "With you. *You* are in there."

Sucking in a shaky breath, he tapped his head. "Consuming my thoughts. Always there, like you've always been there, since the moment I met you. You knew what to do, how to live. You were given purpose. You've never seen it, but you led. I followed. You showed me how to live. You've shown me—no—you *are*...my love. *You* are the warmth in my heart."

Lucien lifted his face and stared out over his courtyard, probing deep into the simulated night. He seemed...troubled, wistful, pensive—*so beautiful*—much as he had *that* night, and the same irresistible urge to touch him popped the butterflies like hot embers.

With all that had transpired, it felt like a sacred taboo, an intimate gesture too casual for the roles of their formal hierarchy—but their bond had evolved and they were no longer the men they once were.

What did Lucien want their relationship to be? Thinking back, Jonathan realized that he'd been hinting at this since that first night he'd confessed to feeling warmth in his heart. They'd shared their first truly passionate kiss and *made love* for the first time by Grandfather Wisdom. And then Lucien had stood in the rain and listened to his confessions. Fingers that had shredded thousands during the Great Holy War had stroked his face so tenderly—so uncharacteristically caring—and Lucien had barely managed to compose himself in front of Endymion, too.

Lucien had been hinting to him, showing him, trying to avoid saying it outright. It'd been crushing him, driving him insane—his biggest secret, his worst fear realized—something he could only share with Jonathan, his lifelong companion—*his love.*

Jonathan knew he should say something, but he was sick of talking. Lucien was so close, yet seemed so lost. His swathing body heat lit Jonathan's nerves ablaze and fueled the maddening urge to touch him.

His fingers twitched as he brushed the back of Lucien's hand. Jonathan licked his lips to quiet his quickening breath as his hand lingered in place a little too long before his index finger lightly raked Lucien's skin.

Fire ignited deep within his core, but he didn't dare move. A charge built within their auras. He couldn't tell if it was from his, Lucien's, or both.

They were both still. And silent.

Too still. And too silent.

Always restrained. Always detached.

Jonathan had never possessed Lucien's discipline or patience. His heart was galloping and every breath dusted a feverish caress upon his lips that aroused his awakening body. The lust of his yearning flooded into his aura and draped them both in thick, viscous layers. His eyes downcast, Lucien seemed unaffected—his mind apparently stuck on his revelation—but his pulse throbbed fast and hard, and his chest rose and fell rapidly.

Jonathan licked his lips again, nearing a breathless state that felt hollow and lopsided. Was this love? He didn't have a reference; he didn't know. But he physically ached from the *need* to touch him. The need to be touched. The need for the silence to end—

The charge buzzed Jonathan's temple, heady and dizzying, dropping him into delirium. He staggered off center and shuffled back a step, his hand falling away from Lucien's pulse and his warmth.

"Love will doom us all," Lucien said matter-of-factly—confirming and accepting both the statement and the consequences—before capturing Jonathan's hand.

The fire at his core exploded into a raging inferno. Jonathan's breath caught in the back of his throat. He glanced at their intertwined hands and threaded their fingers. Lucien firmed his grip, but wouldn't look at him.

Jonathan loosened his hold and tightened it again. A heated shudder rippled through Lucien's aura.

A fresh flame rushed over Jonathan's nerves and surged the burning butterflies upward into his ribs. Oh, how his body craved Lucien's touch! Time slowed as Lucien continued to battle within himself. He was so beautiful—and so...*his*.

Jonathan panted a sigh, eager for Lucien's walls to crumble and erase the restraint of their past. His pulse drummed too loudly and his heart was too alive, but so was his lust—cocooned in a simmering body that understood a visceral memory his possessive mind had never experienced.

He couldn't be more awake or more erect. The fabric of his trousers rubbed enticingly over his arousal with the subtlest of movements and everything around him lurched through space.

The inferno turned into a throbbing ache that quivered uncomfortably within his chest. Coming unhinged, Jonathan fantasized about grabbing fistfuls of Lucien's silvery silken strands and tearing into him after millennia of detached pleasure. Lucien wanted heat; he wanted to make Lucien burn.

"It doesn't have to," Jonathan whispered on a heavy breath, his ears ringing over his voice. "Doom us, I mean."

Lucien lifted his piercing gaze at last. His normally quartz crystal eyes were smoky and edged in a polished black that betrayed little emotion. Yet, within his quiet stillness, he infused energy into his aura until static crackled between them—two poles, one north and one south, drawn to each other by the magnetism of love, lust, and blood.

Jonathan's control spiraled as he matched pace with Lucien's transformation and his fangs descended. His breaths came faster and hotter as they locked eyes and he saw a flash of virginal nervousness in Lucien's gaze despite their lengthy sexual history. Jonathan barely repressed a hungry moan.

Panting and near breathless, he said, "What is Endymion always crooning to Raven? Something about being his clay doll instead of the rock everyone else sees?"

"How does that apply to me? I am the pillar that *cannot* rust." A blaze sparked in Lucien's darkening orbs, but that vulnerable uncertainty remained and Jonathan planned to devour it. "But I am rusting. Fast. I am rusting too fast."

"Then rust *only for me.*" Shoving his painfully throbbing fingers under Lucien's silver strands, Jonathan yanked him by the nape into a bruising kiss, his heart hammering, his injury protesting, his body screaming for release.

Damn their history, predetermined roles, and empty sex. Leaping blindly beyond his depths, Jonathan seized control to guide Lucien into a secret abyss where no pillar could possibly stand. The shining light of their nation was free to go dark, to fall and lose himself, to trust in Jonathan to find and return him to solid ground.

Lucien's tongue dove into Jonathan's mouth, feverish and unrestrained, and his hands were everywhere, popping buttons and ripping his delicate silk shirt, claws scrabbling his muscled chest and shoulders, drawing lines in blood. His rust splayed him open like a newborn blossom on an ancient root—he knew what to do, but it was like experiencing the first sunrise or first kiss of rain—that awkward newness of fumbling fingers, clumsy motions, and the primal hunger that came with self-deprivation.

Their Atlas had dropped the world.

For him.

A satisfied growl rumbled in Jonathan's throat. He scraped Lucien's slender neck with the tips of his thumbs to release his blood scent and tilted his head back, freeing his mouth to explore the lines of his beautiful blue throat. Gliding his tongue over muscles and tendons, he sampled the succulence that pumped beneath the surface. He growled again, thirsting and aching—his lust scorching him from the inside out.

Always quiet. Always controlled. Lucien had chosen apathy over emotion, always tamping down Jonathan's fiery bloodlust. Lucien was his only dominant partner, a reversal of his usual dynamic that reduced their sex to a methodic and scripted exchange of blood and body—the only variable formed within their auras by mutual pleasure.

But that emptiness was gone. Lucien's heart was finally smoldering.

Gasping and digging his claws into Jonathan's back, Lucien jerked their aroused bodies painfully closer. Jonathan grinded against Lucien's hardened response, moaning under a crashing wave of pleasure. He nipped at his throat with his cuspids, pinching but not breaking the skin. His breath came hotter and faster, and he grinned as Lucien's talons sank deeper with a desperate yearning to enter him. But, he didn't intend to let Lucien surface any time soon, and sucked that spot on his throat, teasing him with his teeth and tongue while he shrugged out of his jacket and tore off the tattered remnants of his shirt.

He unknotted the sash at Lucien's waist and let it fall freely, cringing internally when the most powerful Vampiric Star in their nation landed with a careless and heavy *thunk*. A chill from the days of old—the days of less than two weeks ago, anyway—briefly rushed over Jonathan.

Lucien didn't seem to care. His fingers danced over Jonathan's chest, traced the muscular ridges of his back, and slipped over the sloping muscles of his arms. But then he loosened the crimson ribbon at Jonathan's nape, symbolic in itself as the first gift Lucien had given him, and held it out to the side where he let it flutter down to drape over his star on the floor.

"Heh," Jonathan grunted, a fresh burst of flame chasing away the chill. "So that's how it is."

His grin widening devilishly, he rushed Lucien, wrapping an arm around his bared waist and knocking him off balance. Lucien's unsecured kimono flew open and they tumbled together amid streams of black silk and lengths of auburn and silver hair.

Jonathan landed on top of him, chest to chest, skin on skin, his coppery locks melting into frosted strands. Naked beneath him, Lucien's skin had taken on a lavender hue from the heat and pressure of his blood. His engorged, hematite eyes were open, watchful, and filled with want as the intensity in his aura intimately stroked every inch of Jonathan's body.

He pulled Jonathan down by the neck into a kiss that ignited under the fuel of their desire and embryonic love. As they moaned together, Jonathan parted Lucien's lips and their kiss flourished into something more powerful—the urgency, the need, the passion, the hunger— breaking this kiss meant death. Jonathan ached so badly to sink with him, into him, to relinquish control and flourish under Lucien's love as he discovered his own, but he needed a modicum of sanity to be Lucien's temporary pillar.

Black silk surrendered to Jonathan's fingertips as he traced the lines of Lucien's collarbone and shoulders. His skin was velvety smooth and softer than cashmere as Jonathan's hands roamed the muscles and bones that cut severe crests and valleys over his shoulders and back—harsh reminders of his beastly creation. Lucien wasn't merely a man hardened by life; he was a creature precision built for function: solid, lean, sharp, and lethal. He'd never been meant for love…or to be loved.

Gravity pulled Jonathan's lips down Lucien's chin, his jaw, his throat. He hovered excruciatingly long seconds over his throbbing jugular before trailing kisses down his collarbone and chest. Lying back and sprawling beneath him, Lucien closed his dark eyes and moaned—husky and guttural—spurring Jonathan lower, down the firm angles of his abdomen to reach his most sensitive spot. He kissed him there, taking him into his mouth, tantalizing and teasing again with his tongue and teeth, not permitting release even as Lucien arched beneath him, clawing at his hair and loosing a strangled cry.

He might have grinned had it not sounded so alien or ignited new embers within his own core that he didn't understand. He took his time, enticing and kissing, sucking and teasing—this new dynamic thrilling and scary, foreign and freeing. Jonathan wanted to soar on this high with him into eternity.

He crawled up Lucien's body, kissing and biting a return path to his rose petal lips. He met the wild yearning in Lucien's gaze with deliberate eyes, and his newly stoked fire crested. He growled, rough and low, and Lucien replied with a growl and a tug on his belt.

Hurriedly shedding his remaining clothing, Jonathan bent at an awkward angle to kick off a sock and Lucien jabbed the heel of his palm into the crook of his elbow. He rolled with him as Jonathan fell to the mat, catching him to cradle his tender injury, and smiled—an odd articulation of fangs that curved to the contours of his mouth. He lowered as if to kiss him, but instead spoke against his lips to order: "Command code zero, zero, one. Arc simulation adjust air effects ten knots, dimness adjust twenty-three hundred hours, waning crescent moon, twenty-degrees, east, weather adjust rain…steady."

Rhythmic pattering drummed overhead and in the courtyard, and Lucien smiled again. He embraced Jonathan in steely arms, interwove their legs, and threw his weight to one side to roll them closer to his deck where nightfall bloomed under a crescent moon and prismatic stars, and rain misted their entwined bodies.

Unable to hide his surprise, Jonathan met Lucien's smile with stunned eyes and a partial grin. "But you hate the rain."

Water beaded on Lucien's moonlit hair like glittering diamonds. He kissed a trail to Jonathan's ear, where he nibbled on his lobe and whispered, "I will rust for you—and only you—but I still get top bunk."

He laughed then, another foreign and light-hearted sound that brimmed with genuine amusement, and his cheeks flushed with embarrassment. Shadows shrouded his face as he ducked to peck at Jonathan's throat.

Lucien's breath was hot—and his lips soft and supple—on his skin. Thrusting his head back with a moan, Jonathan stared at the exposed ceiling beams, enjoying Lucien's heat and the rain's cool kiss as he mulled his admission. He grunted and pulled Lucien up to his mouth. "I'll grant your request, as long as you never hide your face from me—especially not after you call in the rain."

He didn't let him answer. If Lucien was going to rust for him on a caveat, then he was taking every remaining facet of control. He took command of his mouth, moaning and tugging Lucien down on top of him, and tightening his thighs around his waist.

"Make love to me," he ordered on a whisper.

"As you wish, my lord." Lucien gnawed on his earlobe, grabbed his hips, and entered him with a sultry, ravished moan.

A pleasured sigh raced off Jonathan's lips as he enfolded Lucien in his legs, prodding him to drive swifter and deeper. They joined as one, rocking and writhing to a new, impassioned rhythm fueled by throaty growls and gruff grunts, eager to explore each other with fresh curiosity, hands caressing and stroking, mouths ravenous, kissing, and biting. They formed an amalgam of pure ecstasy, slicked with rain, sweat, and blood, no longer knowing where one began and the other ended.

But oh how Lucien strummed his body and made it sing! He reached the pinnacle of something he had never felt before—a type of euphoria that soared beyond the highest of imaginable highs. He entered sensory overload, and bit at Lucien's throat and muscles, gasping as the world tilted sideways. Lightheaded and dizzy, he clung to Lucien, alternating between fisting his hands and digging his claws into his flesh, not wanting him to stop yet breathless and desperate for release.

They neared the excruciating edge of orgasm. Moaning and panting, Lucien began to slow his hungry thrusts. He tightened his strokes on Jonathan's arousal, and the building pressure of imminent release rolled

Jonathan's eyes back in his head. He gnashed wildly and hooked his fangs on Lucien's ear with an animalistic growl. Lucien issued a carnal response and thrust harder, striking Jonathan's pleasure center repeatedly and stroking firmer and faster.

Jonathan shuddered so hard and growled so deeply it physically shook them both. Lucien froze for a bare instant as their auras plunged them into a state of thrilling torture. The infused energy looped near endlessly, a brutal mix of lust and love that stroked the entirety of their beings, sinking farther than skin and bone, pricking them with blazing needles even as it cast them into a rolling sea of rose-colored love and lifted them higher than either had ever gone.

Then Lucien's fangs plunged into his throat, his hips drove hard, and he tightened his grip—deliberately stroking and flaring Jonathan's fire beyond control. The crescendo dropped over the edge and his throbbing body fell into churning waves of pure ecstasy. He howled as rapture shot him to the peak of that pulsating high and he came so violently that he ripped open his internal wound. He cried out as blindingly-hot pain tore across his abdomen, but he didn't care— *couldn't* care—not while drowning in his own enthralled high with Lucien grinding between his legs and pulsing inside him, his primal growl coursing down his fangs and vibrating deep into Jonathan's core.

Lucien stilled and Jonathan gasped for breath. In an injured body heated by friction and cooled by rain, he moaned, whimpered, and growled, his duty to guide Lucien back to solid ground long forgotten. His teeth prickled, anxious to penetrate Lucien's flesh. He tugged him down, wanting more, never to let go, to break Lucien again, and burn him even hotter. Kissing and pawing at him, Jonathan sank farther into their ravished abyss, so lost he didn't notice the black flies flickering at the edges of his vision until a railroad spike seemed to stab his head and the floor fell out from under him.

A telling, brittle ache stretched down his fangs. "Lucien…I need you."

A line of concern bridged Lucien's brow as he rose up on an elbow and realized that Jonathan was barely teetering on the right side of consciousness. "Your wound?"

"It tore—" Jonathan's eyes lost focus and the pain in his head mounted sharply.

Lucien tossed his hair over his shoulder and cradled Jonathan's head at his throat. Jonathan's fangs plunged into Lucien's jugular. He formed a tight seal with his tongue and pulled.

Lucien brushed damp strands from his face and stroked his hair. "My beautiful Jonathan…"

His voice trailed. To where, Jonathan didn't know, but the tenderness within peppered Lucien's life force with a newfound sweetness and draped him in calming warmth.

In that moment, he thought he finally understood love—and not the type he shared with Paresh. He supposed it wasn't meant to be so literal, but it was pain at the thought of living without someone, the will to die for someone, instinctive and implicit trust, a connection that defied description—a need to be together, to share a life, to become a singular whole. Maybe he was wrong and he'd never truly understand, but he knew enough: love was love, and he loved Lucien.

The internal bleeding gradually stopped as his injury re-seamed itself. With a sense of relief, he relaxed in Lucien's arms. Still somewhat settled between his legs, Lucien eased down on top of him, his eyes voicing his concern and love as he whispered, "I will rust for you. Only for you."

His voice was the calm after a storm Jonathan never wanted to forget. Through hooded eyes, he watched Lucien gaze wistfully at the moon, smiling into the misty breeze. The days of "less than two weeks ago" encompassed thousands of years, yet they were forever gone, sacrificed to restore the Vampiric Nation's pristine pillar and to form a bond that transcended all he'd ever known.

Jonathan committed Lucien's smile to memory. It belonged to him and to him alone. Then he pulled Lucien into a tender kiss and mumbled, "You are forever mine, and I'm not done with you yet."

IV

Arc of True Blood, Summer 2006

Unlike most true bloods, Endymion didn't surround himself in shades of blood. His haven celebrated nature's neutral tones, replicating the lightness of the pinewood posts and beams in bamboo furnishings like his folding tea table and the small altar that burned lavender oil. His watercolor dividing screens were splashed with green foliage, and the satin and silks of his bedding were a pale hue of jadeite that made the grin in his peridot eyes shine like polished sea glass.

"I am quite pleased you chose to come, my dear; waiting to taste you again was a pleasant torture."

"I shouldn't be here, though," Raven said, absently twisting a strand of Endymion's flaxen hair, wondering if the Elders had settled in or if

Paresh had slept. The sun of a new day would rise in Orison Crossing before she'd find out—and she had yet to assess the damage on Banks Island. "My duties are stacking against the clock."

He pursed his lips, studying her. "Leave those burdens from here. They're not what trouble you, young one. Tell me."

"I don't know that I can say. This is Lord Lucien's domain."

"'Tis alright," he whispered. He traced the outline of her ear and trailed his finger down her throat. "The Arc of True Blood may be Lord Lucien's domain, but this is my bed—"

His finger dipped low around her breast and spiraled in toward her nipple, teasing and rousing, but not soothing the ache at the peak. Her moan turned into a pained groan, which prompted another grin—ever satisfied.

"My clay doll may say and do anything she pleases within my walls. Lord Lucien permits me a privacy not afforded to the others." He kissed her and nibbled her bottom lip, drawing blood. "'Tis wonderful that a mere look makes your heart leap into such a tizzy, my dear."

His eyes poured into hers—bottomless, crystallized pools of concentrated delight that made her heart leap. "Does Alex make your heart skip so?"

She licked her lips. "It's complica—"

"Yes or no will suffice, child."

"No."

"Ah!" He rolled onto his back and stretched his arms out to the sides, sliding one beneath her neck. "That brings me joy."

Raven propped up on her elbow. "Do you want me to choose between you?"

The slight curvature of his lips was arrogant and knowing. "You may be anyone else's rock as long as you are my clay."

She started to smile, but then he added, "However, Alexander may wish for you to be his rock and nothing for anybody else."

"Alex—"

"My dear." Endymion rolled onto his side and pulled her closer by the hips. "I will never make you choose. However, I also will never allow someone else to make you choose."

He dipped his thumb into her mouth, nicked it on a sharp tip, and pressed it against her lips. His satisfied gaze watched her lick the blood off. "I am cruel, after all. Now, tell me what troubles you."

She mulled her thoughts a few seconds. "I should hate Donovan, but my heart is nagging me."

"You were once hunted as a threat to our existence. 'Twould not surprise me if you shared base sympathies." His expression hardened and his irises darkened to a dusky forest green. "'Tis a superficial comparison, however. You were branded to change the world. That rotten snake and his brethren seek to destroy all that you and my council mates have created."

"I don't question myself. The justice in my heart knows Donovan is a traitor who has earned his punishment."

"Then whom?"

Raven clenched her jaw. A hesitant edge cleft Endymion's aura. The cords in his nude form tensed slightly, the lines of his muscles forming shadowy ridges and his veins bulging blue at the surface.

"Whom?" he whispered, coaxing her to speak, his finger sinking lower and tracing circles onto her belly.

"Master Jonathan."

Endymion's statuesque expression didn't change, but his finger froze.

"Donovan went after what he wanted—same as Master Jonathan when he was bored and slaughtered Salea's village. And with Eric—he killed off the Hawthornes trying to win him as a prize—and he did win: Eric's at his side. My heart doesn't see a balance."

She brushed at something crawling down her cheek and pulled her fingers away in surprise. They were wet.

"I..." Humiliation burned her body hotter than Endymion's touch. "I wondered why Master Jonathan was alive after Molly died—why he'd been forgiven. He and Donovan are both masters of manipulation, entitled, take what they want—"

"Enough." His voice, quiet and firm, pulled her gaze up. The murky depths there simmered.

"I'm sorry, my lord. I shouldn't—"

"Don't." The hand that slipped under her jaw was gentle, but the roughness in his voice betrayed the effort required to control his tone. Raven hadn't noticed the transitional shift in his aura, but the veins in his eyes were thick and throbbing, his pupils were dilated, large black discs, his jaw had stretched at the hinge, and the sharp ivory fangs of a bloodthirsty predator poked over his lips.

"Lord Jonathan is nothing like that snake." Disgust clipped each word as Endymion's lips curled into a snarl. He took great care not to scratch her with his lengthened nails. "I will tear out his heart for making you cry."

A lump grew in her throat that formed a hurdle her voice couldn't jump.

Endymion's claws combed her pink locks. He kissed the wet stains from her cheeks. "Lord Jonathan was created with entitlement and brutality. He knew of no laws in the natural world. 'Twas not the world he was a part—until the Treaty."

"None of us were," Raven whispered.

"True, my dear, yet be my clay doll and listen awhile."

Another surge of cursed liquid scorched her eyes. "What the hell is wrong with me?"

"Anyone who does this to you must pay a price. Donovan shall give his life." Endymion folded her to his chest and tucked her head under his chin. For an instant—and an instant only—she gave in, closed her eyes, and allowed her vulnerability to bloom. She released her burdens and fears, lost in the ballooning of his lungs, the blood swishing through his veins, and the vocal chords rumbling against her ear.

"After the Treaty, Lord Jonathan fought daily to obey. None know him better than Lord Lucien and I, my child. Lord Jonathan hungers beyond comprehension, and yet, he tamed his beast. He found stimulation in sparring with his pack and training you, and wandered the Earth because standing still meant losing control. 'Twas not until he met Lord Eric that his control began to wane."

"He began to stand still," Raven said to herself.

"Lord Jonathan wandered less, his temper flared, his control spiraled, and he left a trail of destruction that birthed our salvation. The Heavenly Host share equal blame for the Hawthorne deaths. Their intervention drew Lord Jonathan to Orison Crossing; they wrought two bloodthirsty beasts upon that family. Lord Eric is too similar to Lord Jonathan to live amongst humans as he does."

"His morality gives him control."

Endymion pressed his fingers to Raven's lips. "Lord Eric's human heart tempers his rage and thirst, yes, but both rival what Lord Jonathan conquered in one day. Lord Jonathan is not so different from *you*, my dear. He may not have known what he was doing or why, but he selflessly disobeyed Lord Lucien to restore Paresh's life. He delivered our Sacred Vessel—the mother of our Second New Age—and her Anointed Strength, who once made Lord Jonathan's beast roar like none other."

He drew Raven's index finger into his mouth. Nipping at the tip and curling his tongue over it, he savored her blood with a moan. He pulled back and firmly pressed her crimson print onto his bottom lip.

"Getting what you want in life is wonderful, my dear. I wanted a diamond that melted like ice." The malachite sliver in his engorged eyes flashed mischievously. "I, too, bear a sense of entitlement and always get what I want. 'Twould be a shame if that is the marker by which the justice in your heart judges."

"Endymion—"

"Ah!" he cried. "How I adore the way my name rolls off your lips. Say it again."

"You're so cruel. *Endymion.*"

"And yet, snakes like Donovan are nothing like me, you, or Lord Jonathan."

Sneering, he said in a gruff, raspy voice, "That one knows right from wrong. That one was second in command of the highest ranked hunting squad. That one was next in line for eldership—nearly as old as I. *That one made my dear Raven cry.*"

"Endymion—"

"Lord Jonathan came from darkness, yet light got in and prevailed. He struggles with the same issue your heart feels. Donovan, however, is rotten to the core. He seeks not the thrill in the kill, but in evading capture within the squad designed to exterminate rogues like him—in reporting to you with the scent of his deed upon him."

An image of blood-tinged darkness flashed in her mind. It hit like a gut punch. *No, please—*

A low growl built in Endymion's throat. "He got what he wanted not from entitlement. There is no aristocracy in *that one.* No nobility. No respect. No justice. Only lust and greed for the sake of being lustful and greedy, by *choice.*"

"Aye," Raven agreed distantly. Her eyes roamed his pale green bedding, not seeing the fine threads or white silk embroidery. Instead, memory rushed in with darkness that promised to reveal a hidden truth. The past filtered in on a ghostly current of a village divided by screams of witchcraft and cries of innocence...

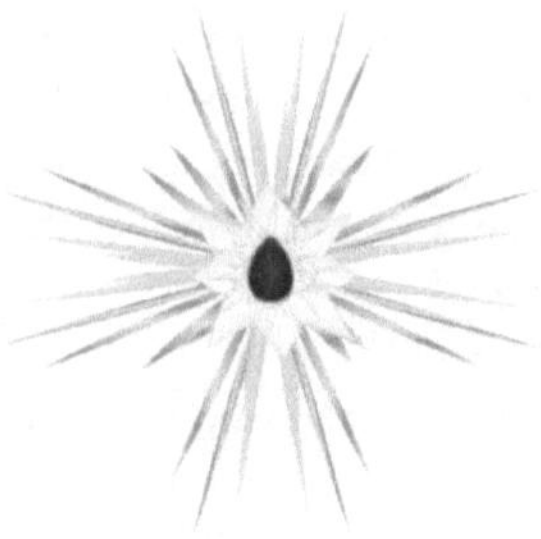

CHAPTER SIX: BLACK SHUCK RISES

I

Snowblood Square, Arc of True Blood, 1692

On bended knee, Raven and her First Officer waited in the pitch black chambers for the Vampiric High Council of Elders. Having discussed her written report prior to calling them in, their request for Donovan's presence meant she wasn't going to like their orders.

A herald draped in black emerged at last and announced the entry of the Eternal Blood High Elders and Arch Elder Lord Lucien the Eternal. Source-less beams illuminated the vampiric high command as usual, but Raven and Donovan remained shrouded in darkness and the herald didn't call the session to order.

Unease chewed on Raven's ribs as additional beams spotlighted the True Blood Elders one at a time until the entire High Council surrounded them. The herald disappeared and a sourceless glow rose about her and Donovan. Forgoing all session formalities, Lady Lucasta, the Fourth Seat High Elder, spoke first.

"High Commander Hawkings of the Vampire Shadow Hounds and commanding officer of the Wraith Reapers, do you swear by the accounts provided in your statement?"

"Aye, milady."

"Rise, Commander," Lord Corben, the Sixth Seat High Elder, instructed.

Raven stood with her arms rigid at her sides as she surreptitiously glanced at the other Elders. Lady Arria seemed apprehensive—disturbed even—but the remaining True Blood Elders veiled their faces within the shadows of their hoods—including Lord Endymion.

Unease chomped the bone.

"If the situation in Salem is this dire, then we find ourselves in a regrettable situation," Lady Lucasta said with a sharp tongue. "He is killing innocents. You are to terminate the rogue immediately, *no matter the cost.*"

"You are expected to follow this order tonight, regardless of the toll." Lord Corben was gruff and authoritative, as though scolding a child.

Raven sucked in her surprise and took an involuntary step forward to beseech Arch Elder Lord Lucien. "With respect to my Elders, I, especially, cannot kill a member of the Flock."

Lord Lucien's gaze lifted. Her entire body burned under his attention.

"Alas, sadly, 'tis regrettable, but the situation must be contained—even at great cost." Lord Endymion's reassuring voice came from her left. "Allowing this rogue to kill more innocents risks our entire nation."

Lady Arria bowed her head and clasped her hands at her bosom. "We have measured this decision against all possible outcomes. It is the only way."

Lady Rainne's quiet voice of reason rose from behind Raven's back. "He has entranced an entire village and enticed them to kill one another under the guise of doing so in His name, but they are only giving souls and strength to our creator. This rogue uses the Flock as a shield to elude our hunters; therefore, the shield must be eradicated."

Gritting her teeth, Raven met Lord Lucien's apathetic eyes, seeking a reason hidden within his silvery depths. Donovan and most of the Elders didn't know what he knew—her bond with Hawkiel restricted her from spilling innocent blood. "This order puts the Vampiric Nation at risk!"

"By any means, Commander," Lord Lucien replied in an empty voice.

A tap on her boot heel reminded her of her place. She stepped back in line with Donovan. "As you command, my lord. We'll leave straight away."

"We await word of your success." Lord Corben directed his disdain down his nose.

"Aye, milord," Raven replied. "You won't wait long." She crossed her heart with her fist and bowed, then opened Animus Hollow. Donovan rose and followed in silence.

☽ ✳ ☾

Waves beat a jagged, rocky shore, churning ocean spittle into a fine, salty mist that coated her lips and skin. Patchy fog slithered through the grass and caught the moon's faint radiance like wispy ghosts. Out of habit, she located the dark spot amongst the stars. It had stopped moving after the Treaty was signed and Hawkiel's mark had disappeared from her skin.

Her gut coiled in on itself. She had hated New England since long before the Vikings or English had sailed ashore. She'd never wanted to return, but it was inevitable. This was Hawkiel's Celestial Landing Point. Despite his brand fading, their contract remained intact—otherwise she wouldn't have discovered the treachery in Salem or returned to this dreaded island.

"That report of yours was rather detailed," Donovan said, exiting the Hollow behind her. "Do you think Arian's behavior proves that we can only fight the beast so long before it wins?"

"No." Raven palmed a communicator. "Lady Rainne is astute. Arian acted swiftly, using children to exploit the humans' paranoia of the supernatural. He went undetected here for almost a year and could have lasted longer had I not found him. Arian is fully aware of what he's doing."

"Leave it to you to find something this huge and trace it back to a true blood." Donovan huffed. "It can't ever be the humans or our creator. No—first Lord Connall, then the rogue Shadow Hound in Eastern Europe getting all werewoofy, and now this."

He shoved his hands into the pockets of his long coat and kicked a rounded stone. Hungry waves swallowed it with a roar. His eyes drifted over the harbor to lanterns flickering on the Marblehead Peninsula.

"We're far enough from Salem and the bay to stay undetected for now," Raven said, following his thoughts through his quiet stare. He must be nervous. Donovan rarely stopped talking.

"Why do they call their women 'Goody'?" he asked softly. "There's nothing 'good' about this."

"It's a term of address." Raven attached the communicator to her lower jaw. "Chavnia, Jocathian, appear forthwith at my location."

"Good day, Goody Woman!" Donovan said in a high-pitched, overtly English accent. "Are you well today?"

Switching to a demure tone, he shifted in place to reply, "I'm quite fine on this lovely day, thank you for asking."

"*Ah ha!* Thou art a witch!" he proclaimed in the first voice, jumping aside and pointing a stiff finger where he had been standing. He whirled around, covering his mouth, aghast at his accuser. "But, oh no! It is a lie!"

He turned again and gasped. "Oh my! Thou hast a devil's tongue!" Shaking his head and moving his hands in an ushering motion, he spoke in a deeper, masculine voice. "We cannot have this be. Off to the gallows! Right this way, if you please, Goody Woman. Goody—"

Raven's sapphire glare stopped him mid-act. He tossed his hands at the mainland. "They're doing it!"

"Innocents are dying because of a rogue true blood. They do not deserve such mockery."

Donovan rolled his eyes. "Are you going to do it?"

Ignoring him, Raven spoke into the communicator. "Alexander. Rendezvous at Marblehead Island, directly."

"Damn it." Donovan fed another rock to the sea. "We don't need the Crimson Guard tripping us up."

"Regardless of the High Council's orders—" Raven turned to face Chavnia and Jocathian as they appeared through a hazy portal. "We hunt Arian tonight without taking an innocent life."

"You can't disregard our orders," Donovan said.

"What does he mean?" Jocathian asked, sharing a quick glance with Chavnia. "Donovan met with the Elders?"

Before Raven could respond, Donovan answered, "The High Council ordered her to kill Arian by any means necessary, specifically stating that if he uses the Flock as a shield, we are to eradicate the shield."

"Truly?" Chavnia asked, golden curls bouncing off her cheeks as she swung her head toward the targeted village across from Marblehead. "Such a thing is too blasphemous to think, let alone speak aloud or order."

Raven's heel flew into Donovan's jaw. He reeled onto his backside and wedged between two wave-battered boulders. "Directives given at Snowblood Square are not yours to divulge," she snapped. "The Elders requested your presence as witness to controversy. Lord Lucien stated, 'by any means,' and I intend for the Crimson Guard to be those means."

"Bene, bravo!" an excited voice whispered in her ear. "Qualcuno è arrabbiato stasera?"

"No, I'm not angry." Raven faced Alex wearing an irritated façade. "Inglese, per favore. The English settled here."

"I prefer Greek myself, but Italiano is the language of lo—" An uppercut to his chin clamped his teeth onto his tongue and knocked his head back. Alex groaned and wiped a trickle of blood from his mouth. "Scusi! Nessuna necessità di violenza!"

"If you buffoons acted within your stations, I wouldn't need to get violent." Raven shot stern looks at Donovan slicking mud off his coat and Alex rubbing his jaw.

"Is your First Officer telling the truth?" Alex asked.

"Aye. While we go after Arian, you will protect the Flock. I'd rather kill the Guard than the guarded."

Sidling up to Raven, Alex whispered, "Is this you being 'Goody' and wholesome? Or looking to kill my hunters for the hell of it?"

Irritation cascaded a dark ribbon across Raven's visage. "Shall I make it an order, Commander?"

"Aw, *Goody* Raven's serious tonight. That's no fun." As Alex pouted, he met her gaze through hooded, deliberate eyes. "No need for orders. Master Jonathan's pack will suffice. They will report soon."

Alex leaned in and whispered in a seductive voice reserved for her, "That was quite a kick. I enjoyed watching that First Officer of yours fly, and was about to tell you how much I *adore* your aggression tonight, but then you went and drew blood on me. Now, I owe you the same, *Goody*."

Raven jabbed his chest. "The High Council is waiting. Get the pack here. And *never* call me that again."

☽ ✳ ☾

A hidden flame flickered at the top of stairs tunneled in crimson-hued darkness. Minute blood droplets, both human and vampire—albeit one more than the other—burst open on her tongue with each breath. A weighted pit formed in her gut. The stairs seemed to ascend infinitely, teasing entrance to the door cracked ajar.

The house was eerily silent except for the fire that crackled behind that door. A button was actively blocking all sound in and out, and not knowing why aggravated the ghosts of Raven's unease. Nothing about this mission felt right.

The final step creaked as she reached the landing. The metal doorknob was warm on her fingertips as she peered into the crack. A large wooden table had been tossed against the door, blood pooled on the floor planks, and arterial sprays patterned the walls and ceiling. Shattered glass glittered golden in a puddle of burning oil that masked the gore under scents of clove and sulfur.

Wood screeched against wood as Raven shoved the door open.

Arian's body lay twisted and crumpled in the facing corner, his silvery hair matted and bloodstained. One eye dangled from its socket and blood oozed down his cheeks. Gashes marred all visible skin, large chunks of flesh had been rended from bone, and one of his ears smoldered near the hearth's fire. A gaping hole exposed a chest without a heart.

The table, its benches and chairs, a small armoire, and a washbasin had been flung aside or destroyed, clearing a path for the bloody footprints that traced the battle's progression. Dying flames in the brick and stone fireplace baked blood onto ash-coated logs as they lapped hungrily at a waxy, white substance—one of Lady Rainne's special candles.

The footprints led to Donovan slumped in a pool of blood in the shadowy far corner. A young woman lay limp in his arms. Blood coated him head to boots and made determining his injuries difficult, but the girl was dead. Two crimson ribbons streamed from her throat and a golden hilt bearing the Wraith Reapers' crossed scythes betrayed the blade in her heart.

"I'm sorry," Donovan said, trembling lightly as he cradled the girl. "He had her in here. I couldn't help it—"

"Are you injured?"

"The bastard put up a good fight, but I'll heal."

"Then we accomplished our mission. Leave her. Wash up. You will accompany my final report to the High Council. Alex and the pack will take point on clean up, and Chavnia and Jocathian will erase the residual effects of Arian's mind control. We can't heal this village's scars, but without his influence, they will cease this nonsense."

Donovan began lowering the girl to the floor, her long dark hair folding into the blood pool, but he paused. "I should take her with me."

"This village is in a fragile state. If a local goes missing they'll start crying witch on their own."

"She wasn't from here. She spoke a foreign tongue commonly heard near the Arc of Ebony Stars."

"Siberia?"

Donovan nudged his chin at the boarded up window to indicate the townsfolk beyond. "Arian wasn't preying on the pieces in his twisted game. He fed closer to his original home; no one ever saw this young maiden." He glanced up at Raven for the first time. "She cried to go home, but she had no home because he killed her husband when he took her."

Raven's brow furrowed. "She was alive?"

Lifting the girl's corpse to his chest, Donovan stood and huffed in Arian's direction. "Why do you think he looks like that? He had her when I came into the room, so I lunged."

Raven conceded with a nod and turned her back to Donovan. She walked down the seemingly endless stairs and out of the dark-paneled house, and sucked in deep breaths of sea salt and organic, woodsy air, aching to rid her lungs of blood, cloves, and sulfur, and to escape the stench of innocent death that no longer lingered only at the gallows.

Her heart cried for the members of the Flock manipulated by Arian even as her predator eyes shaded everything the color of blood. A haunted chill prickled her skin and shook her to the bone. She bolted into a run, fumbling with her Vampiric Star to open the mouth of pristine white. She leapt into the Hollow's mist far preferring Lord Lucien's icy gaze to standing a moment longer on Salem's tainted soil.

II

Arc of True Blood, Summer 2006

Raven's heart hammered against her breastbone and sweat slicked her brow. She darted up and disappeared behind a folding screen brushed with watercolor weeping willows. Dropping to her hands and knees, she vomited blood into the porcelain floor basin that doubled as Endymion's sink and shower. Seeing the crimson spatter nearly made her vomit again. She rinsed it down the drain and splashed her face with cold water.

Her shoulder burned under the heat of a star. Prickly tendrils crept down both blades of her back. Clawing madly at the intense itch, she craned her neck and found Hawkiel's mark almost whole. Forcing herself still, she closed her eyes and took in breaths of the warm, lavender breeze blowing in over Endymion's gardens through his open courtyard wall.

The pale Elder's calming aura enveloped her like a blanket. He ran a white cloth under the tap and gently dabbed the gashes along her shoulder blades, dotting kisses along both lengths. He paused a moment before nudging her to stand and wiping blood from her chin. "All the burdens you bear."

Saying nothing further, he led her to his futon. He collected two silk robes and gave her one before slipping into his. Blood from her nose dripped onto the delicate fabric and bloomed into a crimson flower.

"Donovan told Paresh the prey of a Reaper doesn't live long enough to speak," she whispered. "That it's easy to shift the blame of a nibble."

She eased into the robe. It was cool on her skin and smelled like Endymion. She knotted the belt at her waist. "In Salem, Donovan never said Arian bit or killed the foreign girl. When he said he couldn't help it, I thought he meant—"

She shook her head. "But no, the look in his eyes and the clove and sulfur—that girl ran to him as a savior, crying about her husband's murder and being taken away, and he realized no one was looking for her."

Hawkiel's mark flared. She groaned and dug the heel of her palm into it. The ache crawled over her entire back. "She escaped one demon only to die in the arms of another."

"My dear, you had no reason to doubt your First Officer's account. 'Twas a difficult order to accept…" He gazed out over flowering purple mounds. "And to give."

"Hawkiel's brand draws my heart to imbalances—it led me to Arian's treachery, but not Donovan's." She eased onto her back and sighed at the ceiling beams. "But…Alex saw it."

"Perhaps your heart overlooks those closest to you," Endymion said softly. "Surely you didn't believe Alex was a rogue worthy of death or you would have killed him."

"Aye, but it's clear now. The differences between Donovan and Master Jonathan, I mean." Bile burned her esophagus. "Master Jonathan taught me so much after the Treaty was signed and I've not once thought about how it is for him now. Between his hatred and cruelty, it was impossible not to see him as the monster I found in Salea's village for so long. The empathy he feels for Eric must be killing him."

"'Tis true. He loves Lady Paresh like none other, and now knows—and understands—the fear of protecting someone under constant threat. It physically pains him."

"And everything he's done to Eric and the Hawthornes—" Raven bolted up right. "Bloody stars! He killed Paresh's parents."

"Lord Jonathan shall atone. 'Tis not our place to meddle."

The simulated sky suddenly changed to a clear night ruled by a crescent moon, the wind kicked up, and a steady rain pelted the courtyard. Endymion smiled and sat beside her. "Speak of the devil."

"Why would Master Jonathan leave Paresh at a time like this?" Raven peered out at the rain puddling on moss-grouted stepping-stones.

"Ah," Endymion said, "when Lord Lucien calls, one answers—even him. I am certain 'twas not an easy decision. He is not alone in learning about love or the yearning to protect these days. Love forms the basis of every emotion, after all——one cannot help but feel its touch."

The fire in her shoulder flared anew in her chest. "Love? You?"

"Mm," he cooed. "Add an 'I' and say that again, my dear."

He kissed the back of her hand. "Love has brought me unimaginable joy. But, that joy has blackened the darkness that comes when someone hurts the one I love."

He kissed the silk covering Hawkiel's mark. "Before the Second New Age, your heart skipped with a look."

Grasping her nape, he kissed her forehead. "Now it skips and leaps at memory."

He kissed her cheeks. "Love has strengthened us."

He kissed her lips lightly, gently, leaving a heated tingle without drawing blood. She met the satisfaction in his gaze with surprise.

His expression added a malicious twist to his smile. "I am protective of my clay doll. I am the cruelest true blood and I get what I want. With all that love has given me, imagine the fun I'll have when I next lay sights on my enemy."

His intensity made her lips curl up. Endymion's love granted her freedom from the burdens of her existence. He offered her a respite, brief as it was. He opened her unease, clarified it, and helped her relax in her own skin.

Only Hawkiel or Gabriel could douse her burning brand.

Endymion smoothed her hair and caressed her cheek. "Perhaps you should sleep, my dear. Become harder than a diamond for your pending duties."

She smiled and leaned onto her side, not surprised when he lowered on top of her and shifted her onto her back. "You said 'sleep,' my lord?"

Sharp fangs poked through his grin. "I said *you* should sleep, my dear."

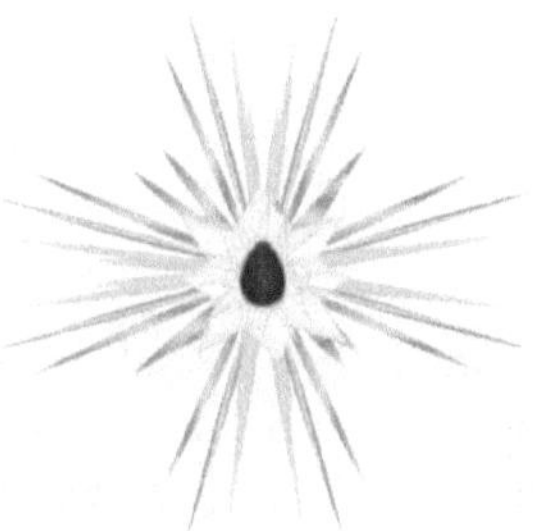

CHAPTER SEVEN: CAGED BIRDS

Orison Crossing, Summer 2006

Paresh awoke to the dark comfort of Eric's bedroom and his protective arm curled around her waist. His breathing was rhythmic, but she knew he was awake.

"Did you sleep at all?" she asked, groggily rubbing her eyes. A tired, nondescript noise sounded in his throat, which she took to mean 'no.'

Scents of soap and shampoo lingered on her skin and dampened hair, and she was wearing one of his white cotton t-shirts. "Thank you for cleaning me up last night," she whispered. "I don't remember much."

"How do you feel?" he asked, giving her a light, reassuring squeeze.

"I'm thirsty."

"There's a glass of water on the nightstand." He rose up on his elbow. "Do you need some light?"

"No." She rolled to face him and tugged him down. "I need you."

He palmed her cheek. "Anything I can do, I will do."

Blue light flooded her view and pressure mounted behind her canines. She inched closer, not yet familiar with her aura moving on its own.

Tilting his head back, he exposed his throat with an enticing growl. As she bit into his jugular, he moaned and embraced her as though afraid of letting go. She pulled his sweet nectar into her mouth, his pleasure vibrating against her teeth, his heartbeat pulsing against her lips, and his love streaming into her aura like warm honey. They were two hearts joined and loving as one.

She withdrew from his throat and kissed him deeply, longing to disappear in him. She stroked his hair, whispering, "Make love to me," and stole his murmur of agreement with a kiss. She then freefell into their mutual euphoria, tangled in Eric's sheets and in him, lost in the deepest, purest well of love, wishing never to surface again.

☽ ✳ ☾

The scorching ruler of day cut through a cloudless sky and kissed the forest canopy. Alex lifted his face, welcoming the heat on his skin despite the light searing his eyes behind his red lenses. Tears dripped freely off his cheeks as he leaned back onto asphalt shingles that burned his palms. Pain rarely fazed him; he'd adapted long ago to feel *life* instead. Despite the dangers of sun gazing, this was his contentment: a rooftop view of endless green and undulating leaves whispering in the breeze to a delicate chorus of distant birdsong.

He was elated that Jonathan had recalled him from the chaos at the mansion. Freed from the Arc of True Blood for the first time in a millennium, the Elders were like spoiled brats exploring and claiming new territories. At least Ambrosia's outbursts were manageable. Composure and adherence to social station and VaSH status added technical difficulties to overseeing security for the others.

Heron and Cyprian's appearance at the mansion had surprised him. Jonathan hadn't mentioned switching the guard when he and Lord Endymion arrived with Lady Rainne's sealed iron casket. After securing it in the Hawthorne basement vault, Lord Endymion had given instructions for its detail before secreting his return to the arc, and Jonathan had made a quiet exit while Alex placed his hunters.

Alex had scolded the pair for leaving their posts, but Jonathan and Eric had wanted a detail with a higher security clearance, and orders were orders. Besides, as two of the strongest creatures alive—even with the Sacred Vessel between them—their security was tricky. If they came under threat, most hunters would merely get in the way.

An engine roared up the forest lane and shut off at the carriage house. Alex stared down his nose at the break in the woods. His aura scouted the perimeter and he shifted the directionality of his hearing. He smiled at the increasing surge of animal pitter-patter.

His lords and lady emerged into the sunny clearing. Jonathan and Eric looked like real brothers, strolling leisurely with hands tucked into their pockets: Eric in his usual black and Jonathan in royal blue with matching fedora. Neither wore ties with their crisp white shirts, and both lagged behind Paresh, who bore a healthy flush on her smiling face.

Wearing a vintage blue sundress with a floral print waistband, she chased a butterfly partway up the flagstone before noticing him on the roof. She shielded her eyes with her hand and yelled, "Hi, Alex!"

Chuckling, he tapped his ear and softly said, "Yes, milady? I didn't quite hear you."

Cheeks burning pink, she gnawed her lower lip and mumbled, "Ah, sorry."

"You're too adorable for apologies." He crept low over the gutter, waiting until she reached the cottage stairs to peer over and whisper, "Boo!"

"You're such a child," Jonathan muttered at him as Paresh cocked her head and laughed.

Clasping her hands behind her back, she swayed in place and her skirt rippled over her thighs. "How did you get up there?"

Hoisting himself onto his palms at the sun-cooked edge, he shoved off the roof and landed without a sound. "I jump. Want to watch Apollo's rule with me?"

Her brow crinkled as she gnawed her lip in contemplation. The weariness she tried to hide nested an ache his heart. "You mean watch the sun?"

"The view is stunning." He tucked a golden strand behind her ear. His thumb brushed the tender spot on her throat. "You will feel better, eventually."

Forcing a smile, she nodded. "I feel better today."

"I know." Shining a reassuring grin, he held her to his chest and kicked off the flagstone.

Jonathan's voice filtered up. "Stop showing off."

"Natural talent cannot be helped." Touching down on glittering asphalt, Alex turned his grin on his master. He lowered Paresh to her feet. "Careful. Those slippers of yours don't have much grip on this pitch and the shingles are hot."

"Here—" Eric shrugged out of his jacket and tossed it up. "Sit on this."

"But it'll get ruined," Paresh said, smoothing her palm over the navy satin lining.

"It's replaceable." Eric winked. "Will you be okay?"

A mischievous smile brightened Paresh's face. "I'll be fine. We're high enough to avoid drowning if he starts to cry."

Alex's jaw dropped. Eric laughed. Jonathan chuckled.

"W-what? *What just happened?*" Alex's voice squeaked higher than usual.

Paresh blushed and tossed a furtive glance his way.

"That rotten Raven is a horrible influence on you!" Alex cried. Throwing his hands up, he pleaded to his lords, "Raven is corrupting this sweet girl!"

Jonathan shared a humored glance with Eric. "She seems right on the mark, to me."

Eric shrugged. "I don't see any corruption." To Paresh, he said, "Have fun and come in if you need anything, okay?"

While Eric had Paresh's attention, Jonathan flashed a hand signal telling Alex they'd have a button fully activated. Nerves fluttered in his chest. The last time Jonathan had left Paresh in his care, Corben attacked and they'd lost a member of the pack. Alex dipped his chin in understanding.

Unease swam in the depths of Paresh's gaze as his masters shut the door. Eyes were supposedly the windows to the soul, but only the Grim Reaper could dive deep enough to see hers.

Once the cottage's grandfather clock went silent, Alex asked, "How are you, really?"

Busying herself with spreading Eric's jacket, she waited until she sat to answer. She gazed out over the trees. "I do feel better, but they're still protecting me even though Eric promised to stop. When they thought I couldn't hear them, they whispered, but they can't do that anymore, so here I am. Master Jon wasn't home when I woke up, so I assume this has something to do with that."

"Oh, that was security related, not something they're deliberately hiding from you—it's boring High Council stuff." Alex thought about the empty casket. He had more hunters protecting a fake coffin than the real one at the Arc of True Blood. "The rest, well, it's not my place to defend or speak for them, but they're only doing what they think is best."

She tossed her hands up in frustration. "That's all anyone is doing! I'm barely able to use the bathroom alone because apparently I can't do anything on my own. I can't know the whole truth. Or a partial truth. I'm told not to worry about others because I'm the one everyone is worried about! But what does that leave for me? I'm not living—just going through the motions."

"I know." Alex was quiet. "But, even now, with the way you feel, your spirit is uplifting and calming. No one like you has ever existed. You're special. Everyone wants to protect that."

"You treat me differently."

"Um…" Alex scratched his head. "I don't watch my mouth as much as I should and get myself into plenty of trouble."

"But still. If not for your orders, you'd tell me what they're keeping from me?"

Alex traced Paresh's gaze over the canopy and nodded. "All my life, I've understood things humans only speculate about. They cling to blind faith, believing in God, Lucifer, angels, demons—all beings I know to exist. Places like Heaven and Hades? I know how the planes of existence intersect and can travel between them. Nothing has ever been a mystery to me, except for you."

He looked her in the eye. "I'd tell you anything you wanted to know. You are so much stronger than anyone knows—the calm at the center of a storm. When we're tossed into chaos and lose our heads, you ground us with a single touch."

He kicked his legs out and leaned back on his palms. The wind toyed with his blond spikes. "Honestly, if we told you everything, we might get a clearer picture of what's going on. Gabriel has shared his celestial vision with you but we hold earthly secrets."

Knocking the tips of his boots together, he whispered, "Master Jonathan would have my hide if he heard me say that."

"After you and Raven left yesterday, Jonathan said something about angel blood. Eric interrupted him—saying that he was a war machine in his glory days, but he shouldn't say anything he doesn't want me to overhear."

Alex shifted uncomfortably.

"They haven't ordered you not to talk about that, right?"

"N-no…" His voice pitched high. He ruffled his spikes. "Master Jonathan has changed much over the last century since he met Eric— and even more with you. What you're asking will challenge the way you see him. Do you want that?"

Shoulders sagging, Paresh faced the sky and shook her head. "He said the same thing when we visited the arc. He asked how I'd feel if he'd killed my parents—" She quieted for a moment and sighed. "I was relieved to hear him say he didn't, so I guess he made his point."

Mentally noting his master's omission, Alex hesitantly reached out and fingered Paresh's strawberry-gold curls. "Regarding the angels, I think Master Jonathan was clarifying something he told Eric long ago: that we would have starved to death if we killed all humans."

A small smile brightened Paresh's visage. It was a slice of Heaven. He smiled back as she crossed her arms over her knees and rested her head to watch and listen.

"But that's not true. You've been on the angelic plane, beyond space and time, and seen them as beings of light without physical form. On Earth, they're humanoid—ethereal for sure—but *He* made both humans and angels in His image to varying extents. Which means their blood..." He flipped his hand out to carry his trailing words.

Intrigue turned into disgust that knitted her brow. "You fed on angels during the war?"

Alex looked around surreptitiously and covered his mouth to whisper, "They taste like chicken."

He tried to keep a straight face, but couldn't help laughing at her incredulous expression. She playfully slapped his arm.

"I was trying to figure out how you knew what chicken tasted like!" she cried, slapping him again.

Laughing harder, he raised his arms in defense and hitched a leg up as she smacked at him with both hands. "Well, supposedly everything tastes like chicken, so why not?"

A spirited grin blushed her cheeks. "You're such a brat."

"And there's more of Raven talking," he said, raising his brow.

She shoved his shoulder. "Come on, seriously now."

Sobering, he pulled his coin from his pocket. Hercules tumbled over Zeus. "Seriously, yes. We were little more than savage beasts with instincts to kill and feed." In a wistful voice, he added, "Except Raven."

He regretted the words immediately. Paresh sat up, eager to ask questions he couldn't answer. He closed his eyes and shook his head. She wilted and he mentally chided himself.

Catching the coin mid-flip, Alex shoved his sunglasses atop his head and stuck his face in hers. He tucked the coin in a pocket and met her gaze with honest, sun scorched and watery eyes. "Look, it's a security thing. Only like," he glanced up, counting to himself. He splayed the fingers on his right hand. "Five. Only five of us know, *out of everyone.*"

But that didn't matter. Paresh's expression glazed over and she withdrew like a clam. No amount of giant sky chickens would bring her smile back now. He grabbed her hands.

"It's not that I can't tell you—I can't let anyone overhear me. I swear!"

She looked at him, but she was far away. He flinched at how defeated she looked.

"Um..." Thinking fast, Alex pointed into the forest despite how much the thought roiled his stomach. "Gabriel knows! He can tell you."

Her gaze focused on his. "You would take me to him?"

Alex bobbed his head so fast the silver hoops lining his ears jingled. Even though it meant calling out his ancient nemesis, he said, "I'd do anything for you."

She glanced over her shoulder at the southern path and bit her lip. "I'm never alone like this. They trust you. We'd have to go while they're meeting."

Tapping his toes together, Alex said, "Jeez, you make it sound like a devious covert op. I'm not spiriting you away."

Holding out her hand, she said, "I want to see him, but I'm nervous, so let me do something for you first. You're busy protecting everyone while everything is changing. What do you feel?"

Alex accepted her hand and interlocked their fingers. Soothed by her touch, he closed his eyes, drained his breath, and knocked his sunglasses to the bridge of his nose. "Curiosity. Guilt. Jealousy."

"Love?"

"Of course." Alex studied Paresh a moment, a sunflower with a golden crown. He squeezed her hand. "It hurts."

"I'm sorry that it hurts."

"Isn't it supposed to?" He wanted to stroke her hair but it seemed taboo to touch her so intimately while they were alone. He tapped her on the nose. "I love you. The thought of anyone harming you hurts me in a bad way."

A genuine smile lifted her blushing cheeks. "But not just me, right?"

"Well, no." Alex huffed. True love was forever out of his reach when his own heart didn't belong to him. "She's torn and will never be mine alone."

Paresh's heart skipped a beat. Her breath rattled in her throat and her aura froze up. Alex eyed the perimeter, asking in a low voice, "What's wrong, milady?"

"N-nothing. D-Donovan said the same thing. I just—I panicked. I'm sorry. It's Raven?"

He couldn't help himself. He brushed his hand through her hair. "Don't apologize. Donovan's a moldy sock that should burn in all the flames in Hades. Are you okay?"

Surprise shot into her aura and landed in her steel gray eyes. Mouth agape, she nodded. He heaved a sigh and collapsed beside her like a rag doll. Waving his hand at the horizon, he said, "Of course it's Raven. If such a thing is possible, I've loved her forever."

Paresh's brow dipped with questions.

"It's complicated. She's got me and another locked as equals in her heart, and our relationships challenge our traditions and hierarchy rules."

"When Donovan spoke about love, I thought he meant himself, you, and Raven, but he was talking about me and Eric." Paresh fidgeted with her skirt. "He was so distraught about his love never choosing him."

"Donovan is a bad seed. You didn't do that to him, and I am not going to spoil in kind because Raven can't choose me."

"I'm supposed to be listening to you, but you're comforting me, again."

"Donovan hurt you. By hurting you, he hurt me." Alex gestured at the cottage beneath them. "He hurt everyone who cares about you, including them and Raven."

Paresh's eyes watered. She sniffled. "Thank you."

"Hey, now." Alex tipped her chin. "I thought you were supposed to make *me* cry."

"Raven is a horrible influence on me. You're too nice to pick on. And now I know your one true love can't love you back."

"I didn't say that." He sat up and untied his boots.

"Does she love you?"

He tightened his laces, tied them, and tucked them into his boots. With a sigh, he draped his arms over his knees and stared across gilded treetops. "I'd like to think so. But, it's complicated. I was forced to accept our situations long ago."

He absently touched the spot on his bicep that corresponded to where he'd nearly severed Raven's arm with the Cataclysm. "I attacked her with a weapon restricted to combat and haven't apologized. I know it was a real battle, but I feel awful."

"So that's the guilt?"

"Mm." He pulled the coin from his pocket. "Goody gave me this a long time ago. It's an Alexander the Great coin from Ancient Greece."

Handing it to Paresh, he pointed to one side. "That's Hercules there. On the other side, Zeus sits on his throne. Playing with this thing helps me problem solve, but not with Raven. It only makes me think of her more."

Paresh returned the coin to Alex's palm with a smile. "You're a hopeless romantic." She straightened her legs and smoothed her skirt. "I see how Raven is with you. She was different, stricter, with Donovan—and she let you live."

Hopeless is right, he thought, closing his fist around the coin. "Yes.

That she did."

He nudged his chin at the southern trail. "I don't know how much time we have. Are you ready to chat with the giant sky chicken?"

"Oh my God!" Paresh buried her laugh into her hands and shook her head. "There's something so wrong with you!"

He rolled his eyes and said, "Well, yeah, duh. It's endearing."

She peeked between her fingers and laughed harder. Her exuberance was infectious. *Like a drug.*

He offered his hand. "Okay, so shifting into Crimson Commander mode, I'm not comfortable risking your safety like this, but you shouldn't be treated like a prisoner. I mean, you're safer with them than with anybody else, but I don't like what it's doing to you."

Her fingers slid into his and her warmth surged into his skin. All his worries melted away.

"It's okay." She was smiling. "I'm always going to be at Eric's side. That's where I want to be. And, while I was gone, I was always with Master Jon. Things haven't really changed all that much."

"You're a caged bird."

She shrugged. "Even caged birds sing happy songs."

He faced away as he pulled her up to hide his sorrow. Caged birds couldn't fly. "We'll travel faster if I carry you. May I?"

Once he secured her to his chest, he leapt off the roof and landed already jogging toward the path to the southern clearing. He burst onto the shadowy trail like a silent ghost.

The arms around his neck seemed so fragile. But he knew the strength that flowed through them. She'd stood against Lord Lucien, defied Death twice, beaten the Devil, and incapacitated a raging beast. Why didn't the others see that strength?

Blue patches appeared through the trees, indicating the clearing was close. As he came to the edge of the tree line, he slowed to a trot and stepped into the grassy meadow. He approached the mammoth silver maple known as "Grandfather Wisdom" thinking of what that tree had witnessed over its life span: the desperate sorrow of a vampiric widower, his guilt, his shame, and his heated life-or-death battles with the Vampiric Nation's Second Born.

Yet all of that paled against the memory of Paresh's degraded body, muddied and covered in blood, hanging limp and lifeless from its trunk. He hated what they had done to her—hated himself for being among the swarm that had chased her, broken her, and run her to death. Hated what the Elders had forced on them with that kill order—that his participation was one of those things she didn't know, that the damn tree was still standing. If not for its significance to Paresh, he'd axe the monstrosity and end its reign—

Brisk tapping on his shoulder broke into his thoughts. He was holding her too tightly. "Oh, sorry—"

He set her down and followed as she stepped into the tree's huge shadow. "How does this work?"

Reaching a tentative hand toward the gray, furrowed bark, she spoke over her shoulder without looking at him. "Catch me when I go in."

"Go in whe—Oh hell!"

The instant her fingers made contact, her body crumpled. He slid on his knees to catch her. Her shoulders slammed into his chest, but he was able to cradle her head with one hand and sweep her legs over his lap with the other.

The scent of blood immediately hit his nose. It was aromatic and alluring, a sweet temptation, and a huge, red "X" for the COMS. He searched for the source and found blood on the hem of her skirt. She'd skinned her knee on the tree before he'd caught her.

"Damn it!"

Knowing he'd answer for this later, he pulled ointment and a cloth from his pockets and wiped her knee clean. The wound had already healed, but he chided himself anyway. The stain on her skirt was a flashing advertisement.

He ripped it off, wrapped it in the ointment-soaked cloth, and stuffed it into a pocket. The scent began to dissipate.

"Oh Paresh," he whispered, "I love you, but you are a magnet for disaster. You need all the protection you can get."

Her body suddenly grew feather light and stirred in a motion that defied gravity. As though lifted by puppet strings, her arms and legs swung freely beneath her torso. Ethereal light shimmered above her shoulders like two pairs of flapping bird wings. They absorbed the colors of the environment and blended so well that Alex might not have seen them if not for the movement.

With the graceful flare of a dancer, she straightened and swung her arms in a wide arc. Her legs flicked out and came together. Her feet scarcely touched the ground, the blaze of a holy blue flame lit her eyes, and the sun broke through Grandfather Wisdom's shadow to bestow upon her a radiant, golden halo.

Her skin shone like the stars and, when she opened her mouth, a heavenly voice not her own rang forth. "Alexander, Crimson

Commander and Guardian of the Second Born. Why does a foul beast accompany our little one?"

Alex knew that voice well and he hated it. Gabriel had no right to come into the Realm of Man. "Why are you here, angel?"

"What an odd question for the summoner to ask of the summoned."

Alex shoved his sunglasses up and pointed an angry finger at Gabriel. "I did not summon you and have nothing to say until you release Raven from her contract. I'm here for Paresh."

Gabriel affectionately gazed into Paresh's hands cupped at her breast. "Our little one is far more fragile than you think, foul beast. Power runs through her as a vessel, but her mind is young."

A growl rumbled in Alex's throat. "Call me Alexander or crawl back into your hole. I am not a foul beast."

Gabriel lowered Paresh's arms to her sides. Shooting Alex an indignant look, he said, "Eric the Anointed, the strength and protector of the Sacred Vessel, Paresh the Pure, must guide her or she will break."

Alex glared at Gabriel. If the son of a bitch hadn't possessed Paresh, he'd bare his teeth and lunge. "You're a damn traitor. You may show Paresh your vision, but you can't fool me into believing you care about her. You want to end the war by any means necessary, no matter who you must use to do so."

Gabriel again cupped Paresh's hands at her bosom and stared into them as though they held the answers to every question ever asked. When he looked up, he furrowed Paresh's brow and tilted her head. "That is how a beast like you sees the world—why you'll never understand. To witness the spark of a soul in Heaven is wondrous, indeed; yet this one…I loved her the moment I saw her tiny flame, that first flash of flint on steel. It is a love so great that I stand on the precipice of my vow to the Almighty to watch over her."

Hooded eyes stabbed Alex with holy blue light. "Can you comprehend such love? I love our Father above all others, and yet my love for her risks my place within the Celestial Curtain. With a simple flick, Brother Michael might cast me out as he did Lucifer. Not for hate or jealousy. *For love.*"

"Cut the melodrama. If you're so full of love, then what about me? A foul beast?"

"I love all of God's creatures."

"See? That. Right there. You're so full of it, Gabriel." Alex ground his teeth and paced in a small circle. "I wasn't created by *your* god!"

Returning his gaze to Paresh's cupped palms, Gabriel somberly whispered, "I have closed my vision to her."

Alex froze. "What? Why?"

"I cannot control what she sees and the sights beheld thus far sadden me. I cannot bear to think what else she may see."

Alex's eyes narrowed. "What has she seen? What are you hiding?"

"She chokes on smoke so thick she claws at her throat as a winged man in chains sinks into pillars of flames. The fire consumes all that she sees, except for the man, who emerges like a phoenix, no longer weighted down and free to fly—"

"*Hawkiel!*" Alex whisked around and jerked Gabriel forward by the arm. Through clenched teeth, he demanded, "*Seriously? She's seeing him?*"

"The Almighty intervened in your creation with intent for protection, did He not?" Gabriel raised an eyebrow at Alex's grip on Paresh's arm. "You shall not hurt *me*."

As though stung, Alex let go and stepped back, staring at the red imprint on Paresh's skin. "But…no! How did you let this happen?"

Alex dropped to his knees. His eyes burned with tears as his gaze drifted up from the fading mark in search of something meaningful in Gabriel's expression. "She can't…s-she can't…you can't let her see him!"

"That vision was never meant for her eyes." A note of sadness brought Gabriel's voice unnaturally into tune with the Realm of Man. "She saw beyond the fibers of light and dark into the gray fibers of probability."

"Raven—"

"Your concern swiftly turns from our little one."

Alex sagged and tossed his hand into the air, absently staring at a spot in the grass. "I'm a fool holding onto a hope that never existed. I thought that maybe, just maybe, with the Second New Age, you might appear and release Raven from that brand you forced on her." As he glanced up at Gabriel, tears streaked his cheeks. "But it'll never happen. You can't stop it."

"Your heart aches."

"Do you accept me as a creature of God?"

Gabriel was quiet.

Alex threw his arms out and bowed. "And thank you very much."

"Do you all lack patience?" Gabriel scoffed. "Will you allow me a moment to ponder your existence? Or shall we continue as we were?"

Alex knocked his sunglasses down and leaned back. "Ponder away. It's not like the world's going to end soon or anything."

He got an eye from Gabriel, but otherwise the angel ignored his sarcasm. As much as Alex hated to admit it, the archangel hadn't triggered a premature apocalypse. Decisions made by Lord Lucien and the Second New Age had opened that path. And only one person wielded the power to close it.

"As creatures created by a creation of God, you are creatures of God by proxy," Gabriel said, his voice returned to its unnatural melody. "Our vision of probability has had our focus of late. We thought little of your emergence into His grace. Yes. You shall be accepted and loved as God's creatures."

"All of us? Just like that? What about bad seeds?"

"Bad seeds exist in nature. Good cannot exist without evil."

"Raven is good. She doesn't deserve to be used as a tool."

"She may be the only salvation for this world if probability becomes reality."

Alex sat up and stewed quietly. Gabriel clasped Paresh's hands together over her heart, waiting out the silence. Alex closed his eyes and breathed deeply, and imagined the hell of what Paresh had seen. His eyes snapped open and narrowed at Gabriel. "If Paresh has already seen Hawkiel, what are you hiding from her?"

"It saddens me so that she is part of a world and events in which I am not permitted to interfere. The Almighty has set the path for you, but you must find firm footing to make your pilgrimage into grace."

"That's not an answer. You're just another guy hiding stuff from her. Hawkiel's coming and that's not even the worst of it?" Alex picked up a small rock and threw it at the base of the tree. "*Fantastic.*"

"Child," Gabriel said in a soft voice, "I am sorry for the ache in your heart. Have faith in Hawkings and hope for your future." Hugging Paresh, he added, "As for our little one, help her find joy. She was but human mere weeks ago. Her body is strong, but she is young and cannot cope mentally. You must all be strong for her and bring her joy."

"What is worse than Hawkiel?" The answer would never come, but Alex had to try. Gabriel's words contained an alarming amount of sadness.

"Take care of our little one. I'll always watch over her and I'll always be with her, wherever she is." The blue flame began to fade. "*Always.*"

"No! Wait!" Alex leapt up and grabbed Paresh's arms. "Gabriel! Don't run away, you coward!"

Radiant light retreated into shadow and the shimmering wings faded. As Paresh's body sank into his arms, Alex pulled her close. Her head flopped loosely, so he held her cheek against his shoulder, and clung to her like a life raft. Studying the forest's deep, ebony depths, he mulled Gabriel's words.

They'd been a farewell.

Alex glared at Grandfather Wisdom. "One day, I'll chop you down. With any luck, I might hit that damn chicken, too."

He swept Paresh up and turned from the tree. "You hear that Gabriel? You're lucky that you angels were forbidden from entering this realm after signing the Treaty. You and I will always be enemies. Right now, I'd gladly take your head."

☽ ✸ ☾

Eric's heated cursing on the path ahead meant Paresh's blood scent had reached the cottage. Jonathan's responses sounded more concerned than angry, but, as Alex gazed upon the cradled unconscious girl, he expected that to change.

He should've stayed put. Dropping to one knee and tucking his chin, he lowly said, "She wished to visit Grandfather Wisdom and scraped her knee when Gabriel pulled her in. She is fine, my lords."

Eric's aura charged Alex before he physically rushed around the path's bend. Alex fortified his aura to shield Paresh from an onslaught of invisible shards. He watched the path from hooded eyes. Eric appeared first, furiously swinging his hand in the direction of the cottage.

"When I asked you to stay with her, I meant back there! She shouldn't be traipsing through the woods with only one escort and without our knowledge!"

His face crinkled with worry, Jonathan jogged past Eric and fell to his knees, scuffing his trousers and shoes with dirt. His aura protectively intertwined with Alex's as he cupped Paresh's cheek. "Why is she still out?"

Yanking off his sunglasses, Eric stopped a few feet back and surveyed the surrounding woods. "It takes a toll on her. The longer she's in, the longer she's out. She was finally feeling better today—the last thing she needed was this!"

The hand holding his glasses jabbed at Alex. "Damn it!" Turning away, Eric shook his head and huffed. He whirled around and marched over. "You were one I actually trusted."

"My lord—"

"*You*," Jonathan interrupted, tossing an irritated glance at Eric, "yourself, said you don't like treating her like a child. Should she ask before doing every little thing?"

Darkening crystalline orbs whipped into Jonathan. "This isn't about her. *Your Commander* left his post as our security detail without reporting in. Why the hell do I know your protocols better than you? What if the COMS had attacked? He can't protect her alone!"

Briefly lifting his eyes to Alex with his jaw clenched, Jonathan swiveled to face Eric. "It *is* about her. She wanted to come here and his orders were to keep her safe. She's not a prisoner and nothing in his orders restricted movement or required notification."

"*You!*" Eric wiped his face in disbelief. Scoffing, he tossed his hand up as though speechless. "You ordered him to the cottage for *us*. That was his post, his duty. I don't care what she asked—he answers to the High Council. She is not an Elder."

"With respect, Master Jonathan," Alex said quietly, "I did leave my post, and you, unguarded."

"The tide is not turning for the better when I am the calmer between us, Brother." Jonathan stood and motioned for Alex to rise.

"I don't think that means a damn thing. I certainly seem to be more aware of the looming threat than you, but then again, that's my life, right? It's not like you ever had to worry. You had a pack to do that for you—"

A sharp ridge appeared in Jonathan's aura. "Watch it, *Brother*. I do not enjoy a life under constant guard. Paresh has had constant companionship, but nothing like this. She deserves to be free."

"Free?" Eric repeated, close to yelling. "*You're* going to lecture *me* about freedom? All you've done from the moment I met you is concoct schemes to own me!"

How does Raven deal with this? Alex wondered. The air was so acrid he feared its effect on Paresh. They hadn't fought like this in decades.

"And you have played guardian for so long that you can't see how it affects those you seek to protect." Jonathan swung his gaze over Paresh deliberately, as though reading Alex's mind. "Did you even consider her when your aura blindly blasted Alex? Or what we're doing to her now?"

That stunned Eric into silence. His aura fell flat.

Jonathan nodded from Alex to Eric. "Commander, give her to him and return to the Hawthorne Mansion. Rotate Rainne's detail. We'll follow shortly."

"As you command." Alex transferred Paresh into Eric's arms, his fingers lingering to brush back a lock of hair. He didn't want to let go.

"If I may, Gabriel has stopped sharing his vision with her and won't say why. He confirmed that she's seen Hawkiel, but wouldn't say what he's hiding from her."

Jonathan closed his eyes and sucked in a slow breath. Alex pushed in the prong on his Vampiric Star to open the portal to Animus Hollow. Eric held out his hand.

"Wait." Concerned lines etched Eric's forehead. "She went into the tree, but he didn't show her anything? Why did he hold onto her so long?"

"And why you?" Jonathan asked, growing more agitated. "He may be our only link to the Celestial Curtain, but you despise each other."

"Opportunity, I'm sure. It's not like he was happy to see me." Alex chanced a glance at Eric. He was studying Paresh with a troubled expression. Alex quietly said, "She wasn't harmed, my lord. I took the brunt."

"Good," Eric replied without looking up.

"Gabriel said that you need to guide her or she'll break," Alex added. "That her mind is too fragile for the power flowing through her body. She is frustrated with the protection and secrets, but Gabriel believes it's for the best. He asked me to bring her joy."

"Did he say anything about Hawkiel or Raven?" Jonathan asked. "Eric's been briefed."

"Then if I may speak freely," Alex said, "that damn chicken didn't give specifics, but did acknowledge that Hawkings may be this world's only salvation, and added that we're children of God by proxy and thereby worthy of His love. But, he wouldn't budge on what he's hiding—only that Paresh had somehow seen into the gray fibers of probability."

"I don't like this," Eric said. "Is there any other way of talking to him?"

As Jonathan shook his head, Alex said, "He seemed awfully worried about her. He said he'd always be with her and sounded sad, like he was never going to see her again."

Jonathan shared a concerned look with Eric. He nudged his chin at the portal. "See to the Elders and check in with Raven."

"As you command, sir." Alex placed one boot into Animus Hollow.

"She's going to be hungry when she wakes up," Eric said. "We'll stop by The Greenery. I'll have Sarah prepare a fresh batch of soup."

"She needs to stop eating solid food." Jonathan brushed his fingers over Paresh's brow. "I don't understand this slip in appetite."

At least they were back to their new normal. Alex took another step back. The white haze of Animus Hollow enveloped him and the gate to the Realm of Man closed. Now alone in nothingness, he emptied his mind. In here, his heart stripped off personal bias to speak to him in visions. It was the only way to refocus and find his center—especially when emotionally compromised.

Paresh manifested first, hand outstretched and smiling with sad eyes. The Jonathan of the old days—the bloodthirsty Second Born—stood behind her, hand firmly grasping her shoulder, head back, chin up, and eyes cold. Eric appeared next, staggered slightly behind and beside Jonathan, affectionately gazing upon Paresh, yet poised as a predator ready to lunge.

No one else materialized. That confirmed his greatest worry. He'd hoped to see Raven—a proven warrior. Why would he think she'd need his protection in the future? He already knew she didn't. He'd known it the moment he met her—his first wonder. She was the reason he'd learned how to use the Hollow's energy to clear his head—the reason he'd needed to.

He was too distracted. And Paresh had gotten hurt.

He slowed his breathing and focused on the vision.

All three appeared in what he knew to be their true forms: Paresh— the joyous and sad sprite, desperate to help, Jonathan—the former war hound, possessive of anything and anyone considered his, and Eric—a man in love and the only vampire left with an immortal beast's rage. Paresh was easy to decipher—pure, honest, and true to herself. Eric and Jonathan looked deceptively ominous. To Alex, Jonathan's hand on her shoulder was protective and spoke of Paresh's importance to both the Nation and to him, while his physical façade displayed the power he commanded despite recent events. And, while the affection in Eric's eyes fell softly on Paresh, the emerging beast illustrated his strength and the ferocity lying in wait to protect what he loves.

Paresh belonged to those two. She was fated for Eric and Destiny had molded Jonathan into a bridge between them. As long as the sands of time flowed, those three would walk together. They deserved his undivided attention—his protection.

The Almighty intervened in your creation with intent for protection, did He not?

Alex tried to shake off Gabriel's voice. The Hollow's swirls of white rolled by unbroken. His greatest worry mattered little when his own heart didn't belong to him. He knew what he needed to do.

"I'm sorry, Paresh," he whispered sadly, "but, you're wrong. Caged birds don't sing happy songs."

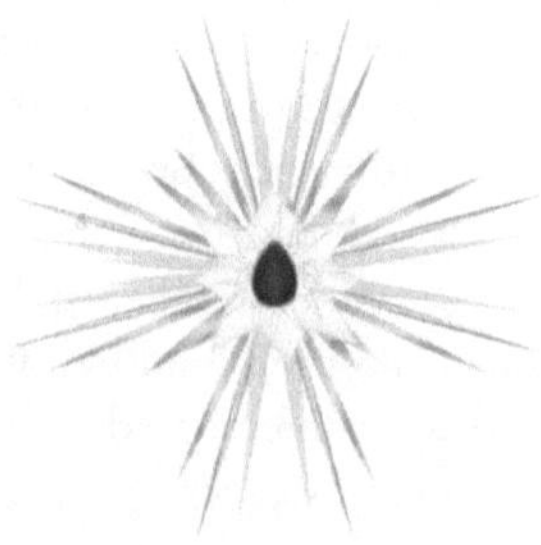

Chapter Eight: Heartstrings

I

Banks Island, Canadian Northwest Territories
Arc of Celestial Night, Summer 2006

The endless Arctic summer sun burned through an early evening sky dotted with low clouds. Ankle-high willows and wild yellow arnica, arctic roses, and polar poppies dusted the rocky and clumped tundra. There were no trees on the island and the only human settlement sat on the southern side at Sachs Harbor. Despite being renowned for herds of muskoxen and arctic birds, the explosion and subsequent vampiric presence had killed or scared off all forms of roaming life.

Raven wiped her face and blew a quiet breath into her palm. She hadn't expected this. The casements were *gone*—totally disintegrated. The stenches of burnt flesh, bone, and blood mingled within the toxic gas plume blowing northeast across the M'Clure Strait. A lingering note of chlorine confirmed that the COMS had used a reactive chemical that humans had banned in the 1990s.

"Prince Patrick and Melville Islands across the strait are uninhabited," said Landor, Commander of the Silent Vespers. He stood about a foot behind Raven.

"Well," Raven said with a sigh, "I know why your hunters aren't bio-scanning and scrubbing: Chlorine trifluoride. There won't be anything left after it burns itself out."

Seeking solace in the darkness behind her eyelids, she pinched the bridge of her nose and asked, "You mentioned silver dust? Is it still airborne?"

"No. It seemed designed to take out the arc's inhabitants and first responders. A few of my hunters entered the cloud without realizing what it was. They're recovering at Eido, burned from the inside out with blood seeping from their eyes, ears, noses, and mouths. It wasn't pretty, but we didn't lose anyone."

He pointed at the smoke. "The most pressing concern is the proximity to Aulavik National Park. This place has always had the highest risk of exposure—most likely why it was chosen by the Children of the Morning Star."

Raven turned away from the flames hungrily devouring what little remained of the once regal arc—organic, metal, glass—it didn't matter. Nothing would remain. "Lord Lucien refers to them as the COMS. How many humans are in the park?"

"My scouting party reported one plane on the ground, but the humans' whereabouts are unconfirmed. We can safely assume there's a pilot, a guide, and at least one adventurer with a camera." Draped in gold and black raiment similar to Alex's uniform, Landor had dark skin and uneven black hair with braided strands and decorations of gold beads and gemstones.

His almond-shaped, citrine eyes glimmered with golden luster as he added, "Even if they didn't see the plume, they heard and felt the explosion. We may eke out a few more hours before the first humans arrive to investigate. The terrain works in our favor and I have eyes on the landing strips. This was a strategic hit."

"Aye, and human satellite sensors must be ringing alarms around the globe. They will come," Raven said, turning back to the former arc. The chemical had eaten through miles of structural foundations and several feet of earth. No wonder Endymion hadn't included orders for destruction or containment. "This level of destruction is unspeakable. They think we'll devote our resources here to avoid exposure. This was supposed to be a place of honor. Rogue or not, I cannot believe a true blood would do this."

Landor silently contemplated the remains. The Arc of Celestial Night had housed noble true bloods who had survived the Great Holy War. They'd been former commanders or veterans with the Vampiric High Council's favor who'd chosen to abandon society and enter eternal sleep. Intravenous devices sustained their bodies while their minds wandered boundless, fantastical dreams.

The Arc of Celestial Night had been the proverbial rock under which one could hide. Most of the Vampiric Nation had forgotten the arc's residents centuries ago. Such was the privilege of noble titling—cast from God's eye and the memories of their own kind.

I am sorry about the Arc of Celestial Night. Initial reports did not indicate survivors. Raven ground her jaw as Endymion's words ran through her mind. As VaSH High Commander, she should have read those reports and known what she was walking into, but she'd gotten little sleep and awoken far later into the morning than she'd expected, already behind on her duties. She'd made a show of Lady Rainne's casket transport and opted to get an oral report from Landor.

"We don't need to waste resources," she said. "I'd normally order you to burn it all with a chemical fire anyway. Not *this* one, but they've done the hard work for us, and the toxic gas is blowing toward uninhabited islands."

"And the park?" Landor asked, lifting a brow.

"The COMS expect us to panic, but the arc is almost gone. By the time any human gets here, the fire will have burned itself out or be well on its way. Chances are higher that they're using satellites to monitor the situation. Setting up the temporary barrier to shield the debris field from eyes above was a wise decision."

"It offers no protection on the ground. What about—"

"Continue scouting and get updated sitreps so you can adjust as needed. I want three cloaked teams of three—chosen randomly—to patrol the perimeter. If any humans show up, they are to use their auras to trigger fight or flight and then mace them."

"Mace them?" Landor didn't try to hide his disbelief.

"Aye," Raven replied, turning sharp eyes onto her subordinate. "They'll run tests and get accurate results from the air. It won't match up with what they test from their eyes, but the initial burning will keep them back. They know how dangerous this stuff is. They'll likely wear hazmat suits—so compromise them. As long as the hunters are cloaked and don't kill anyone, they are to take any measure needed to keep the humans away."

"It'll spark a controversy," Landor warned.

"That's great!" Raven said, turning in a circle with her hands held out. "Look at this. When it's burned itself out, there will be nothing left. They'll think of meteors or aliens or government conspiracies. They aren't going to think 'vampires did it' or 'invisible vampires maced us and fucked with our suits.' They will detect the gas and find a charred pit, but they'll never know the cause or what was destroyed. Hell, they don't even know anything here was worth destroying."

"As you command, of course. I meant no disrespect," Landor said, placing his fist over his heart and tucking his chin.

"Do you have a better suggestion?" Raven cocked her head and an expectant brow.

"No. It's simple. No one would expect something so blasé."

As Raven nodded her agreement, Landor quietly asked, "What's the status of the High Council?"

"Anything of note will be promptly relayed." Raven pressed the prong on her Vampiric Star for Animus Hollow. "Lord Lucien reset the security settings on the communicators and restricted entry to the Arc of True Blood. Alex and Nallura have already been informed."

Surprise briefly lit Landor's face. "The Commanders are locked out?"

"Aye. Anyone trying to gain unauthorized entry will be taken into custody or terminated. Alex has loaned me Seneca and I took Nallura's First Officer from the Chthonic Knights. I'm requesting Kestrel for Donovan's position, but you may keep her to scout. For the long term, you need to select a replacement First Officer."

Landor appeared visibly shaken. "We've entered such a tumultuous time. I can't help wondering what lies ahead and how the VaSH will be restructured. Are we going to lose our command? Our officers?"

"Jocathian will receive eldership soon. Likely Chavnia, too. Which leaves me with a squad to fill. There's not much to it."

"But the ranks—"

"Lord Lucien declared the ranks no longer matter," Raven interrupted. "Don't worry yourself over things that are beyond your concern. I don't intend to pull the Commanders." Her hand landed firmly on Landor's shoulder. "Why worry about a future we might not live long enough to see?"

"You are right. Forgive me." Landor bowed his head in a sincere gesture of apology. "The Silent Vespers will follow your orders and regroup at Eido—er, the Arc of Mourning Eidolons. We exist but to serve the High Council. You may take Kestrel now. We've discussed who shall succeed her."

"Aye. Order her to report to the Hawthorne Mansion." Raven turned her back to him and surveyed the debris field one last time. Nothing was recognizable—and she'd visited this arc many times.

A tight knot formed in her stomach. *No survivors.*

She caught Landor staring at her. "What is it?"

"The Second New Age has been difficult for all of us. These new emotions…I am sorry for you that they chose this arc."

The knot moved into her throat. She lifted her chin and stepped into

Animus Hollow. "This arc's destruction is a ceremonious loss, nothing more."

II

Isle of Wight, England, 897 A.D.

A winged shadow stalked Hawkiel as he paced under a moon dimmed by cloud cover. Every time he looked at her, his lips pursed and he shook his head, turning in disgust and swinging his disappointment away to admonish her again.

"What on this great land of God were you thinking? Trusting the Third Born? His is a heart of ice that rivals the fire that spurs the bloodlust of the Second Born!"

Hanging his head, Hawkiel threw his hands up. "You've relegated yourself to memory now that you can no longer walk among them. All has been for naught."

Eyeing the tiny lump cloaked in red between the tree roots, Raven insisted, "If Salea drinks only your blood, she will stay pure as an asset for our cause. She and I can sway the First Born's apathetic heart!"

"That girl should have died with her family. She is clouding your judgment."

Raven pointed a fierce finger at Salea. "She wasn't with her family when they died!" She slammed her hand to her chest. "She was with me. Would you have *me* kill her?"

"You might yet!" He grunted. "I never intended for you to spend so much time with humans. She should not have been with you."

Raven's palm flew across Hawkiel's cheek. "I will not shuffle blame. This is not my war. You wanted to show me a world beyond the one in which I was born. They murdered her family."

A growl rattled in Raven's throat as she stepped back, gnawing her lip in thought. "You are disappointed in me and I in you, but we cannot wait until dawn to move. The Second Born may have followed Endymion. I won't know of his success until his couriers find us."

Her toes splashed the cold puddle beneath her wool gown drip-drying on a thick branch near Salea. She tossed the garment over her shoulder and gathered the girl into her arms.

"You may call me Hope," Raven shot at Hawkiel, "but I am seeing clearer and might as well dub you Hopeless. We're going north with or without you."

) ❋ (

They never argued about Endymion again, but Hawkiel was different after the slap. No longer believing her capable of delivering his salvation, he clung to empty hope, unwilling to let it go, and grew increasingly distant as the years passed.

Endymion's couriers delivered wax sealed scrolls at regular intervals that directed their travels north. The battle line finally stalled and they settled from a nomadic life that constantly reminded Salea of all she had lost into an ice-capped home at the top of the world.

Salea hated the monsters that had killed her family—and that she hadn't died with them. Guilt and anger ate away at her and manifested as self-mutilation. The pain, she claimed, was tangible penance for surviving. She shaved skin from muscle and flayed muscle from bone, disgusted and horrified by what she'd become.

Raven woke each day expecting Salea to rage against her progenitor, but the eternal teenager never lashed out. Instead, after bad fits, Salea crawled into Raven's lap and cried. As Raven hugged and rocked her, she'd assess the damage and hope for tissue regeneration. On too many nights, Raven's fear called Hawkiel to heal Salea's wounds with his blood.

As a human, Salea had lived in fear of the war beasts, a psychological erosion with which Raven was unable to sympathize. At a loss, Raven understood Hawkiel's growing unrest. Salea was unstable and unpredictable, and neither of them truly understood the girl's mental torment.

Without human settlements to offer the contact Hawkiel had given her, Raven tried teaching Salea about her experiences to steer her onto a pure path, but that inevitably reminded Salea of the human life she'd lost. Raven finally resigned herself to inducing sleep and asking Hawkiel to pepper visions into Salea's dreams.

Gradually, the girl's destructive behaviors decreased and she finally awoke ready to explore her new body and abilities. But their efforts came too late. The bleak gray and white of the Arctic stole her fervor and she'd slump by the fire, staring emptily at popping embers.

Disgust became boredom. Boredom became lethargy. Lethargy led to muscle cramps and achy joints—even Raven felt it. She needed to move, to see the world in color, to engage with others. Salea wasn't alone in losing sanity to mind numbing white.

Raven entranced Salea into longer slumbers and slept, too, sometimes for days, waking only to feed on Hawkiel. Alexander's sunny smile and Endymion's fiery touch filled most dreams, but in others, she confronted the First Born, always appearing nightmarish and demonic. He killed her each time with a ferocity that jolted her awake drenched in sweat.

When winter brought night to their world for months at a time, Raven sat with Hawkiel and tracked his brother for long hours. She restlessly awaited word from Endymion's couriers and stopped caring for herself. She fed irregularly and looked hollow and weak, prompting Salea to reverse their roles. The girl coaxed Raven into a semblance of life.

Hawkiel remarked that Salea was redeveloping the ability to care, but Raven knew fear truly drove her. Raven was all she had left. She let the girl care for her and shared memories of walking the battlefields with Hawkiel—and of personal moments with Alexander. Salea took particular interest in Raven's sparring matches with him, so, blasted by arctic winds and ice, Raven and Salea trained and battled each other.

They slept less and smiled more. Then Endymion's final courier arrived.

At last comfortable in her body and no longer afraid of or loathing what she'd become, Salea's excitement outweighed her apprehension. She and Raven donned red cloaks and Hawkiel opened Animus Hollow.

Raven's heart thumped uncertainly as she entered the white haze. She glanced over her shoulder and locked eyes with Hawkiel's dull blue orbs. She knew then that he wasn't going to wait for them. He turned and walked away, making his chained wings the last memory she had of the angel who had saved her life.

III

Orison Crossing, Summer 2006

Exiting the Hollow, Raven closed her eyes and sucked in copious amounts of organic, humid air to flush out the chlorine burning her nose and throat. The Arc of Celestial Night's debris field looped on the screen of her eyelids, narrated alternately by Lord Endymion and Landor.

No survivors. I'm sorry.

She huffed the vision away and took in patches of fiery orange through the canopy's silhouette. Her assessment and damage report to Lords Lucien and Endymion had taken longer than anticipated. She was so eager to see Paresh that the mere thought made her smile.

She tapped the communicator on her jaw. Vibrational static buzzed the metal, indicating a nearby patrol. She had yet to approve Alex's hunter assignments and ensure a secure perimeter, which she should have done after the High Council arrived instead of running paranoid to the Arc of True Blood.

Tamping down her initial enthusiasm, she followed the static's signal strength and checked in with the first outpost. Then she worked her way around the outskirts before spiraling in toward the police station downtown. She didn't bother cloaking. Her neon pink bob drew instant attention, but, fresh off Eric's shocking revelation at the church, the townsfolk probably wondered if she was "ageless," too.

At least he hadn't technically confirmed he's a vampire, she thought, smiling and waving, but keeping a distance to avoid provoking them with her aura. She was also mindful that a perceived friend of Eric's reflected on him as much as it did on her, and had changed from her uniform into casual clothing.

Tight, dark jeans made from a blend of cotton and synthetic fibers stretched across her hips, and fashionably shredded patches over her thighs and knees allotted more give than standard, stiff denim. She'd opted for a black t-shirt and her usual boots, and selected a lightweight black and red plaid flannel instead of her jacket. It fluttered loosely in the evening breeze as she approached the police department.

The bell on the door jingled when she entered. An officer—the lanky one, James, she thought—was finger stabbing a keyboard behind the front desk. He looked up and nudged his chin down the hall. "Walter's in his office. Said you'd probably be by tonight on Mr. Ravenscroft's behalf. Go on back."

"Thank ya!" She waved as she walked down the brightly lit hall. She rapped on Walter's door and entered before he answered.

"Don't you people have any manners?" Walter stood with a pained groan as she closed the door. "How are things?"

She eased into a chair opposite his desk and propped her foot on her knee. "So far, so good. I'm playing catch up."

"What did you learn about the explosion?"

"First, how's Paresh? I've been worried about her."

Walter jiggled his hand. "She's okay, all things considered. She had a spot of trouble last night, but I think it had more to do with food than anything else."

Raven made a thoughtful noise. "She's still craving soup?"

"Yeah, but it's not agreeing with her." Walter sat back with a sigh. "I wish I could do something…"

Raven leaned forward and scooted the chair closer to his desk. She mulled her question a moment before asking. "What do you know about chlorine trifluoride?"

"The fire chief says to run like hell from it." His eyes narrowed suspiciously. "Why?"

"That's what they used. It decimated the arc—ate through everything. There's a literal crater."

"Holy shit." Walter coughed and blinked rapidly a few times to get his bearing. "Wow, that's tough. I'm sorry. How many did you lose?"

Raven shoved the image of the charred pit from her mind, but the odiferous mix of burnt remains and chlorine clung to every breath. "No survivors."

"You don't know how many?" Walter asked gingerly.

She shook head. "That arc didn't have a governor, so there's no official census. I lost one, tho—"

She smacked at her eyes, frustrated at the moisture that came away on her fingertips. "Bloody stars," she growled.

Walter held out his hand. "Give me a button."

Raven dug a disc out of a ridiculously small pocket. She started to show him how to activate it, but Walter took it, grumbling, "I know how this works by now, Vampire Hunter."

The electric-blue net formed, flashed, and sank unseen into the surfaces. Keyboard clacking and car engines filtered in. With his back to her, Walter said, "Ever since I met you, I've been angrier than I've ever been, but also scared beyond my wits—and I mean truly terrified. You get me?"

"Aye."

"I trust *you* and know you're damn good at your job." He turned to face her wearing a stern expression. "I may not understand anything about your society, but I do know grief, so hear me: don't suppress it with pride. Let it out or it'll fester."

Wiping her eyes, Raven laughed at herself. "I hear you, but this isn't me, Walter."

"Maybe it wasn't, but you have a new heart now, right?" He grabbed the box of tissues off his desk and sat in the chair beside her. "My best friend died, you know, so I'm going to sit here and cry for her, if you don't mind. Feel free to join me."

She attempted a playful smack on his arm, but ended up holding onto him instead. "It…It's not pride." At Walter's dubious look, she fought a sniffle and said, "They targeted that arc because she was there——she was like a daughter to me."

She wiped her nose and crossed her arms, huffing at the ceiling. "I'm their biggest threat and they need me distracted, off balance." She rolled her eyes at Walter. "See? It's not pride. I don't have time for grief because it plays into their hands."

"Listen," he said, patting her hand. "Make time or you will be distracted and they'll win."

Raven remembered how calm he'd been at Molly's house. His best friend was dead on her kitchen floor, dagger in her chest, punctures in her throat, and pools of blood and wall-to-wall spatter, and he had tried to help lure Master Jonathan from Death's door. Hell, he'd yelled at Eric and brought them all to their senses.

"You're pretty damn good at your job, too, Human Chief. They want the same thing from you and Eric, too."

"Which is why you see this big ol' man facing his emotions head on. Don't waste time or energy trying to escape feelings you don't want to accept or they'll blind you in the long run." He wagged his finger between them. "People like us? The protectors? We can't afford that. What happens when the protectors are compromised?"

With a gasp, Raven squeezed his arm and jumped up. "Oh starry night, you're a genius!"

She yanked him into a tight hug. "You're dead on. We aren't focusing on the right things. We're reacting and getting stuck in our own heads. It's love!"

Rubbing his ribs with a grimace, he groaned, "Look lady, you can't grab a human body like that. What the heck are you talking about?"

"We've only seen love as a matter of the heart." Words jumbled in her mind, toppling each other to reach her mouth first. She chopped the air with her hands and met Walter's gaze fiercely focused. "We *care* now. Empathize, sympathize, grieve. We're uncertain about our future and our places in the cosmos. Lord Lucien said the ranks no longer matter——but that's all we've known for more than a thousand years. Our strictly structured world has been completely upended."

Her jaw gaped as her hand flew off on one thought only to shoot back to her chest on another. "I mean…I'm criticizing myself for not seeing Donovan for what he was, and I'm grieving a complicated loss, am torn between Endymion and Alex, delegating our national security, conducting damage assessment, shuffling officers, overseeing perimeter details, preparing to die——"

"Hold up——preparing to die?" Walter echoed.

"—but I should be casting a net. This is why Hawkiel was always so dispassionate! It kept him focused. Like our lack of love kept us focused before." She grabbed Walter again. He futilely tried to dodge another tight embrace.

"It all works to the COMS' advantage, because they aren't mourning their losses or feeling *any* of this! They want the world to burn—the world that Paresh sees when she sleeps. They want this chaos, so they're walking on top of it."

Gasping for shallow breaths, Walter tapped Raven's thigh. "Air! I...need...air..."

"Oh! Sorry!" She released him and stepped back. "You okay?"

Bent with an arm bracing his ribs, he held up a finger. "Gimme...a...sec."

"Can you drive me to the Hawthorne place?"

"The mansion? Do I look like a chauffeur?"

"Me running there on foot would be expected." She grinned. "Plus, you can make new friends while we're there."

Walter paled. "You're nuts if you think I want to meet more of your people."

"Come on. I won't let them bite you." She was already at the door, retrieving the button.

"Yay," he grumbled, reaching over his desk for his keys. As he followed her out, he grabbed his hat, told Officer James to call with emergencies, and then parked himself into the well-worn seat of his squad.

As he turned the engine, Raven put the window down and asked, "Is Paresh there?"

"I haven't talked to them today. Figured we all needed a break and I'd hear anything I needed to hear."

Raven stuck her face into the breeze. "That girl's in good hands. I shouldn't worry so much."

When Walter remained silent, Raven stole a peek at his set jaw. Of course, he wouldn't dispute that aloud, but he obviously saw Paresh as a victim trapped with the victimizers.

Their silence lasted until his headlights struck the monstrous iron gates that guarded the Hawthorne estate. Raven uttered a command into her communicator, the gates swung open, and Walter maneuvered his squad up the weedy and rutted drive to park in the cracked valet circle.

Much of the regal landscape had long since died off, leaving behind long stretches of unkempt, half-dead grass and rocky beds overgrown with weeds. The house itself stood tall and grand dressed in white and lined in black, but many of the outer buildings were in various stages of disrepair.

"Such a shame." Walter shook his head. "Did you know Paresh's grandfather was a senator? He threw huge parties when he came home on session breaks. Most were for big time politicians, but he'd open his home to people in town, too."

"He died in a fire?"

Walter nodded. "Set by his son, David. Andrew—Paresh's father—couldn't face the house after that. He repaired the damage, hired live-in caretakers, and never came back. Some folks in town wanted Eric to donate it as a museum after Andrew died—the Colonel ran in circles with Abraham Lincoln, and his wife, Mary Todd, would sometimes visit with Lucinda after her mother passed…" Walter pursed his lips. "Well, I suppose there's a lot of history and ghosts he might want to lock up."

Raven took in the looming house. The setting sun painted the paneling vivid hues of orange and magenta against a background of darkening blue. "You think Eric feels like we're trespassing?"

Walter shut off the engine. The springs in his seat creaked as he leaned back. "I don't think he cares. He's not one to live in the past—"

A loud *thud* on the roof startled Walter. "Jesus Christ!"

"Hi Goody!" Alex's cheerful face appeared upside down in Raven's window.

"Damn it, Alex!" Walter swore under his breath. "What is up with you? Give a fella' a heart attack!"

Palming Alex's face, Raven told Walter, "He's like a hyper little dog. You get used to it."

Alex flipped off the car and posed like an Olympic athlete. "And he sticks the landing!"

Groaning, Raven got out. "And some of us take our jobs seriously."

"Yes, and some of *you* don't delegate as much as you should to avoid getting behind in your duties." His tone was mockingly serious as he poked Raven's shoulder.

"Who would you have me delegate to? I don't have a First Officer and I'm losing the rest of my squad to the High Council. Who's going to step in? Would you give up your command to be my First Officer as next in line for eldership?"

Before he could answer, she shoved past him. "I don't expect that from any Commander."

"Don't give me that crap." Alex caught her arm and immediately let go when she winced. The Cataclysm wound no longer needed a bandage, but microscopic silver particles remained painfully close to the bone and struck her nerves like a lit match when they moved.

"I'm sorry," he said, knitting his brow and distractedly moving to touch her again before stopping himself. "As High Commander, you can delegate your duties to us, and you've already commandeered other hunters to rebuild your squad. You only need final approval."

"I don't trust the other Commanders," she hissed between her teeth, "or their hunters."

She jogged up the veranda stairs and gestured at Walter. "Alex, stay with him. He doesn't wish to meet anyone new. I won't be long."

☽ ❋ ☾

Frustration simmered in Alex's gut. The Fates were determined to work this entire day against him. Raven's trust had never extended far, but it had always reached him. The sting lasted about a second before anger burned it to ash. The stubborn patch she'd placed over Donovan's betrayal would destroy her long before Hawkiel showed up.

"Hey Walter, man," Alex said, "I'm sorry to do this to you, but I need to talk to her. Heron and Cyprian are both out here, so hang tight."

As he followed Raven up the veranda, he told his hunters, "If you have any trouble, contact me immediately."

"Yes, sir." The disembodied voices were loud enough for Walter to hear.

Raven was waiting in the foyer. "I gave you an order."

He shrugged. "I've been a clueless rebel all day and it wasn't all formal like that. Besides, you think you're the only one who needs to check in?"

"Lord Lucien awaits my report on the status of the Elders."

"I've been here most of the day. Everything is fine."

When Raven's lips parted in protest, he quickly added, "Lord Ceallach and Lord Satiereon found a chess set in the Senator's office and have been stuck on the same move for six hours. I'd rather watch slugs fight to the death."

He ruffled his hair. His hands darted up at the ceiling and down both halls. "Lady Lucasta claimed the lace canopy bed on the third floor and has been asleep since she got here. Lady Arria, Lady Aurelia, Lord Swaran, and Lady Lucine began meditating in the parlor last night and are still at it. Lord Raiden appointed himself as Ambrosia's guard and is sitting outside her holding room, and Ambrosia continues to knock my hunters around—who, honestly, are more than happy to restrain her. The special package is under a strict guard rotation and I've accounted for the heralds who are tending to their duties to make the Elders more comfortable. Shall I move on to Lord Endymion?" Sucking in a deep breath, he lifted both eyebrows deliberately.

"No need. The remaining security detail?" Raven pursed her lips and crossed her arms.

His shoulders sagging in mock frustration, Alex streamed the air from his lungs. "Seneca and Minerva are shifting positions around the property at will. Kestrel and Farran arrived a few hours ago and are shadowing them, at a distance, as per your order. Heron and Cyprian, and their units, have the front and the detached garages, while the rest of my available squad is scattered across the property and surrounding village, which you know since you already checked in with them."

He put his hands on Raven's shoulders. "Between our hunters, our buttons, and the net you set up, we've got this place, and the town, covered."

"And who is with Master Jonathan and Eric?"

"Eh…Master Jonathan wished to be unattended. When we parted ways, they were headed to get Paresh food."

"Orders are orders, but that's——"

"I didn't like it either. If I hadn't thought Eric would take my head, I would've pressed the issue, but we have hunters everywhere. If anything happens, we'll know in an instant."

Planting her hands on her hips, Raven shifted from one foot to the other. "What did you do?"

"Why did I have to do something?" He couldn't help the squeak in his voice.

Her lips puckered as she studied his face. "Oh the bloody ages! Master Jonathan dismissed you to keep Eric from attacking you! What the hell did you do?"

Making a show of eyeing the surrounding house and pointing to his ear, Alex replied in a quiet voice, "If I had done anything of consequence, I wouldn't be standing here. We can discuss it later."

Raven's mouth flattened into a thin slit. "Fine. I guess Walter will take me to see Master Jonathan first and then I'll report to Lord Lucien and return here." She grabbed his shirt. "You will make up for whatever you did not do, and then you and I will regroup with our new trinity."

Letting his frustration take over, Alex seized her uninjured arm as she started past him. Without a word, he dragged her to the hidden basement panel at the back of the foyer.

"What are you…?"

The panel opened on a push hinge that closed behind him. "Be quiet," he ordered, pulling her down the stairs.

"Alex!" Raven sighed. "I don't have time for this. If Master Jonathan let you off without punishment, I'm not about to punish you in his place."

"Forget about that." He tightened his grip when she tried to pull away. Thick blackness clung to them. "You don't always have to be the tough one. Not with me."

At the bottom, he pressed her against the wall. "These were Eric's rooms. Master Jonathan stays here frequently, so I set up a privacy grid decades ago. It's been active all this time, so no one can hear us."

The black form of her head tilted to the side. "I have a lot to do. What do you want from me?"

Alex leaned in, his nose skimming her hair as his lips moved toward her ear. Her scent was…different. Jerking back, he cursed and muttered incoherently under his breath.

"What was that?"

"N-nothing. Just…you smell like Lord Endymion."

A surprised ridge appeared in Raven's aura. "I was—"

"Don't," Alex interrupted. "I didn't mean…I uh…" He wished the day would end—that the moon would chase the sun into hiding for a fresh tomorrow. "I didn't notice before I brought you down here. That's all."

"Does it affect the reason?" The edge loosened and her outline shifted to face him. "Why are we down here?"

His words tangled in his throat. His heart was dropping out of his chest. The Fates had snagged Father Time to conspire against him. Raven had to know their time was limited. She, herself, had admitted that *he* was coming. Should he reveal what Gabriel told him? Or let her enjoy the life she had left?

And no way could he declare his love when she'd obviously been with Lord Endymion while he'd been babysitting. He back stepped, dodging objects from memory. Eric had never retrieved his possessions. Alex blended into the darkness as he skirted the coffee table and sat on the Victorian sofa.

"Why are you running off?" Raven grunted as she bumped into the banister. "Damn it. You think I can't hear your heart racing?"

"I'm sorry," Alex said softly. "I shouldn't have pulled you from your duties. The stairs are right beside you. I'll keep watch here until you get back. We don't have time for this, like you said."

"*Alexander!*"

There was a quick *click* followed by the hum of lights flickering to life. Squinting, he blocked the glare with his hand and nudged his sunglasses down from atop his head. Raven charged over and tossed her thumb at the wall. "Did you not think I'd feel that damn switch digging into my back?"

She smacked him on the head. "Why is it you can ask questions first and shoot later, but in private you're a fool who acts first and thinks later? Idiot!"

"Ow, Goody! Why'd you hit me?" he squeaked as he raised his arms to block another attack.

"Stop calling me that!"

"Damn it! I've just…been thinking." He dug into his pocket and flipped his silver coin into the air.

She caught it between her fingers and eyed him suspiciously. "I gave this to you." She paused with a sigh. "Okay, I get it. Saying I don't have time for this is the same as saying I don't have time for you, and I won't say that. But I ask you to consider all that I must do, because you and I both know my eternal clock is running out of sand. Does this mean you're forsaking our allegiance over Endymion?"

"No! No, not at all." He sank into the sofa with a groan. He slumped against the velvet cushion and held his head in both hands. "Oh good grief. This is ridic—it's like, I don't know! What humans do—you know—" His hand shot straight out. "Like when girls wear their boyfriends' jackets or class rings or whatever."

"Teenagers? Really?" Raven rolled her eyes, too stunned to speak.

Groaning again, Alex cupped his face and rolled his head along the padded edge of the sofa. "No. No! That's not it! You aren't exactly a diamond girl and I don't have anything else significant to give—"

Raven stomped up and over the coffee table. The sofa's antique springs protested loudly as she dropped beside him and wrestled him into a headlock. Running her knuckles through his hair, she teased, "You're performing the mating rituals of human children?"

With a gentleness that belied his strength, he freed himself from Raven's grip and swiveled her hips so she was facing him. He shoved his sunglasses up and briefly touched his hand to his chest. "Listen, I'm not playing—I know your sand is running out. I can accept that I will never be the only man in your heart, but I wanted you to know that you are the only woman in mine. That coin is my single most important possession—the thing I cherish—because it came from you. I hoped the meaning would transfer with it so you'd realize I hold you dearest in my heart. And—damn it—that maybe you'd realize you can trust me. You don't need to save the world alone."

"Alex—"

"I understand now that there are different types of love. That I can love someone and be *in* love with someone. I mean, I love Paresh, and will devote my life to her, but you're different. I want to share my life with you like she and Eric do—"

"Alex—"

"—and I know that's a dream that will never come true. But you need to know that Endymion isn't the only one who knows you." Alex choked back the bitterness working its way up his throat. "He supports you, but also holds you under him in a brutally vulnerable and honest state. And you don't mind. That's your relationship with him. I get it, but—"

He sighed. "I know the same things he does, Raven." Alex gestured at his heart in earnest. "*I* know about the constant pressures you face. The fine line you walk as a Wraith Reaper and being Hawkiel's hope, and the ridicule you've endured as Lord Lucien's favored hunter despite your age. I know you're terrified of seeing Hawkiel again and of killing Lady Rainne. I just…I don't force you open or confront you with it. I keep it to myself and do what I can without being obvious. I'll never force anything on you or wield power over you."

"He doesn't—"

Meeting her eyes with sorrow in his, Alex cut her off. "*He does.* That's the way he is. It's the way he's always been, and I've known that longer than you have. But, that's not my point. He cares for you. And so do I. To quote Endymion, 'I know of the worry in your heart, my dear.'" He closed her fingers over the coin. "All these years, I'd have been lost without it, without you. If we're allowed such a thing, I think you're my soul mate. I…love you."

Raven's gaze dropped to their hands. "You really should call him 'Lord,' you know."

Alex's hand fell to his side. His chin dropped to his chest. "Yes. I should."

Tipping his face up, Raven kissed him firmly on the lips. Sitting back, she said, "You're right, though." She pressed the coin into Alex's palm.

"You would be lost without this coin and without me." Threading her fingers between his so that they held the coin together, she said, "The meaning is tangible enough. You keep this."

She stood and patted his head like she'd pet a puppy. As she walked toward the stairs, he said, "I choose you, Raven, even though you can't choose me."

"Thank you." She paused partway up. "I'm asking Lord Lucien to appoint you as Co-High Commander of the Vampire Shadow Hounds. I was going to tell you afterward because I didn't want you to worry, but you're the best fit for…after."

"Hawkiel."

"Aye." She ascended another few steps and paused again. "I do trust you. But I can't have the orders I delegate to you being questioned as beyond your scope as the Crimson Commander. What I'm doing now requires higher security clearance."

"I spoke with Gabriel."

Shock rippled through Raven's aura. "What? When?"

"Right before I pissed Eric off. Gabriel confirmed that Paresh is seeing Hawkiel in her dreams. He's also closed his vision to her." He shook his head. "I don't know what's worse than Hawkiel, but something is and he wouldn't tell me."

Raven didn't move or speak.

"Any ideas?"

She vacantly shook her head.

"I'm sorry for dropping that on you."

"N-no. Thank you. I'll ask Hawkiel when I see him." She lingered another few seconds before ascending to the top. "I'll take Kestrel with me to see Master Jonathan."

The door closed behind her, leaving Alex alone in the basement. He clenched his jaw and huffed.

Raven's life consisted of little more than motions and actions that linked under the weight of her burden and propelled her toward a future of destruction. She might have walked away from Hawkiel a thousand years ago, but they were eternally bonded. There was no escaping him; freedom would never come for her.

Opening his palm, he stared at the head of Hercules. He flicked it into the air and slapped it down on the back of his hand. He took a deep breath before looking.

Zeus, the tyrannical god of Mount Olympus, sat on his throne.

"Master Jonathan," Alex whispered.

Raven and Lord Endymion's roles were unequivocal. He beckoned with a firm, yet soft, hand and she yielded willingly. Alex envied them.

At the most critical moment of his life, Alex was forced to choose punishment by death or servitude for letting Raven escape all those centuries ago. He'd chosen life and become Master Jonathan's bedfellow and sparring partner. The entire Vampiric Nation—including Raven—saw this as a favored existence rather than links chaining him to the Second Born.

Alex enjoyed life too much for regret, but deep inside, where loneliness dwelled, love had dared to spark. The Hollow's vision may have presented Master Jonathan's possessive and cruel nature; however, that same man had defended him against Eric. Freedom, in some form, might come, yet. Did he dare hope for the power—or time—to give Raven his heart?

Alex shook the thought from his head. The Second Born's entitlement would outlast time. The brutal truth was that Alex's heart wasn't his to give, Raven's time was almost gone, and Paresh was his future—the caged bird who sang the brightest song to strum the heartstrings and lift the spirits of those too powerless to fly beyond the bars.

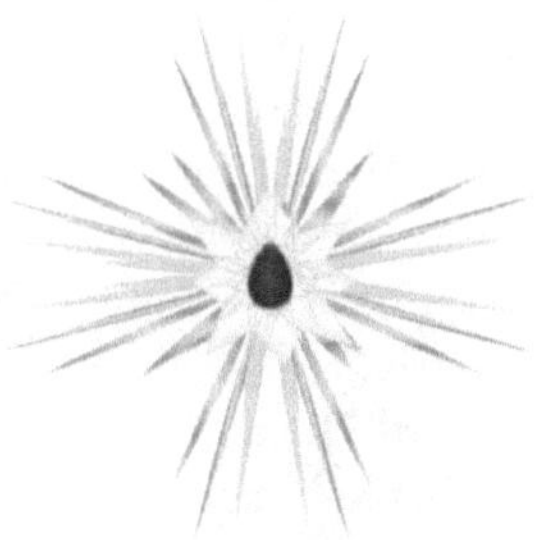

Chapter Nine: War Hound

I

With Kestrel in tow, Raven completed one tour of the mansion for due diligence. An irrational need to escape quickened her step. Alex stayed in the basement, but his stupidly cheery face kept popping into her head, quirking up her lips and fluttering her stomach.

"Daffy bastard," Raven muttered under her breath as they passed through the French doors onto the front veranda.

"Ma'am?" Kestrel knew Raven was musing aloud, but a good hunter never ignored a Commander's voice.

"Disregard." She nudged her chin. "That's the Chief."

Walter was out of his car, leaning against the passenger door talking to Heron. Cyprian was likely cloaked nearby. Those two rarely separated.

Walter was asking about the Library of Alexandria and the possibility of finding hidden scrolls. Raven had wondered about it once, as well. Its fate had been lost to the altered history after Lucifer targeted it, and other libraries, to destroy the precious knowledge they safeguarded. Human history blamed fires, but, either way, what was lost was gone forever. Alex had seen it, though, and he'd been enthralled. His face lit up when he described it—

She slapped herself and let the sting clear her head. She got an eye from Kestrel, which she dismissed with a wave before skipping down the stairs. "His name is Walter."

Alex was obsessed with Greek mythology, not surprising given that his name, and that of his pack's First Officer, came from Alexandria's founder and its famous mathematician. That's why she'd given him that Alexander the Great coin. She'd found it walking the battlefields with

Hawkiel.

Yeah, she was never getting Alex out of her head.

"Yo, Chief!" Raven called. "You're a history buff?"

He shrugged. "Molly was big into U.S. history—I know far more about the Civil War than I ever wanted—but I've always been fascinated by the ancient world."

Eyeing the Crimson Guard Hunter, Raven said, "Well, I hope our Heron of Alexandria didn't let his tongue slip. He's unusually chatty."

Heron bowed his head. "No ma'am. He asked about my name."

"I wondered if I had him to blame for the torture of high school geometry," Walter said with a laugh. He pulled off his hat and fanned his face. Neither the humidity nor heat had yet subsided after sunset. "Isosceles is Greek, right? I hated geometry. But, I didn't think he was actually old enough to be *that* Heron."

The quiet hunter smiled sheepishly under Raven's scrutiny.

"Close enough," she said.

"About a hundred years shy." Kestrel stepped up to Raven's side. "And blame Euclid for the Isosceles triangle."

"Holy hell!" Walter cried, his eyes blowing open as he fumbled with his hat and barely kept it aloft. Raven caught it and set it on his head as he studied Kestrel.

"She's with us?" he asked Raven, getting confirmation in a nod before addressing Kestrel. "Well, okay, uh, first, you can't walk around town dressed like a warrior princess with a broadsword strapped to your back, and, second, who are you?"

"It's not a broadsword," Kestrel replied, tugging open the rear car door. She pulled the scabbard from her back before getting in. "And I am not a warrior *princess*."

"That's Kestrel," Raven replied, tapping Walter's shoulder. She pointed at the passenger seat so he'd moved out of her way. "She'll be my new First Officer, so you want her to keep the sword, trust me. She'll be cloaked in public."

"Well, okay then," he muttered to himself. He waved goodbye to Heron. "Thanks for the company."

The hunter nodded in return. Walter's squad car sagged when he squeezed into the driver's seat.

"You found a friend, huh?" Raven asked. "I thought you didn't want to meet anyone new."

Walter pursed his lips and started the engine. "I met him yesterday, so he's not new. Jealous, Vampire Hunter?"

"He's a vampire hunter, too," Raven said. "One of Master Jonathan's elite to be precise."

Putting the car in gear, Walter idled around the valet circle before giving it some gas down the lane. "Pulling that card, huh? Yeah, you're jealous. You gonna open that gate?"

"It'll open," she replied, looking out the window. "I've never seen him that chatty before. He and Cyp have a twin-like telepathy thing going on."

"He seems like a nice enough fellow. And if you're trying to scare me, don't forget that I know you're the deadliest hunter of them all."

"Mirror, mirror on the wall," Raven said. "I'll take it as a compliment."

"Yup. Jealous." Walter sped along the remainder of the private lane until they hit the road, where gravel crunched under the tires as he stopped. "Where is Chief Not-A-Chauffer taking you?"

"Let's assume The Greenery," Raven said. "We can go on foot from there."

"A restaurant?" Kestrel asked, her voice thick with disdain.

"Lady Paresh still eats human food." Raven glanced over her shoulder. "You'll have vastly more human interaction than you're used to."

"She threw it up last night, so I don't know how much longer these soups cravings are going to last," Walter said, warily eyeing the new huntress in the rearview mirror.

"Might be residual since she was born as a dead human and resurrected twice with vampire blood." The window glass fogged under Kestrel's voice as she looked over fields of dark, leafy soybeans and flickering fireflies.

They soon entered the village proper. Colorful and grand Victorian houses from the original settlement preceded the stone-capped brick buildings of the business district. When The Greenery came into view, the greenhouse was aglow with ambient light.

"They're here. You can let us out," Raven said, her hand already on the door latch. "We'll scout the area first."

Walter hit his hazard lights and pulled over. "You remember my advice from earlier, okay? And keep me updated. It was weird not hearing anything today."

"I will," Raven replied with a half-smile. "As long as I am here, I will loop you in. I've been gone since I left yesterday afternoon——High Commander duties supersede Wraith Reaper security detail, unfortunately."

"I get it." He pointed to the badge on his belt. "Police Chief, not police officer. Also has different duties."

Raven chuckled. "I really like you, Walter. Have a good night."

"Yeah, you, too. Night." He returned a smile.

As his taillights receded into the night, Raven searched up and down the asphalt lane, sensing nothing unusual. Her gaze settled on a small ridge of trees near the stone and brick restaurant. The windows gleamed silver under the rising moon, sparking a gilded shield to flash in memory. Suddenly she was whisked into Hawkiel's arms and cowering before his archangel brother. Gabriel's unnatural voice thundered within her skull, demanding a name.

Hawkings.

Raven flinched at a sharp pain in her shoulder. She instinctively touched it and yelped, jerking her hand back. Hawkiel's mark was scalding.

She grimaced and tucked her burnt fingers into her mouth. Kestrel was at her back, scabbard ready to draw.

"I chose well. Donovan was never so attentive," she said, inspecting the healing blisters on her fingers. The burning sensation was snaking into her shoulder blades. She groaned.

"Ma'am?"

"You took up a defensive stance without knowing why." Raven rotated her shoulder. The heat subsided the lower it sank. Raking her nails over the itch left behind, she kicked off the asphalt into a sprint, unsurprised when Kestrel matched pace shoulder to shoulder.

At The Greenery's entrance, Kestrel held the door open and followed Raven into the dim interior. "Paresh enjoys the greenhouse. I imagine they have a button active—they've been tuning out exterior noise to give her extra peace. It's a risk, but most of Master Jonathan's pack and other hunters from the Crimson Guard linger close by."

They made their way past tall booths of masculine, dark woods and feminine crimson and cream toile fabrics, bypassed the alcove leading to the bar with its rich mahogany and ornate scrollwork, and down the hall leading to the heavy double doors carved with peonies and butterflies. Soft light spilled into the restaurant when Raven pushed on the door, and with it came a lighthearted squeal, followed by the weight of the thin-framed girl charging into her arms.

"Raven! I'm so happy you're back!" Paresh said, hugging her tight. "I got Alex in trouble."

"Hiya, sweetie!" Returning the girl's embrace with a smile, Raven nodded a silent greeting to Eric and Master Jonathan who sat at a table near the pond's edge. A half-eaten bowl of soup sat between them. To Paresh, she said, "I'm certain that joker got himself into trouble."

Raven gently peeled the girl off and took in Paresh's pale skin, eyes set adrift, and a flat affect that didn't match the vibrancy in her voice. She shared a concerned look with Eric.

To Paresh, she said, "It's good to see you, milady. How are you feeling?"

"Tired, but the soup is good and being around others helps."

"Hmm." Raven pursed her lips. "Maybe we've misunderstood the reason you soothe us with a touch—something similar to how you are with Eric."

"Agreed. We think she absorbs vampiric energy as fuel," Eric said, leaning forward on his elbows.

"Our auras should more than sate her," Master Jonathan added, "but she's healing—"

"And may be using energy faster than she's getting it." Eric sat back in thought. "We need to find the right combination of food, blood, and energy to sustain her."

"A body at rest heals faster, too," Raven said with a light touch on the girl's arm. "Sleep will help."

"That would be nice." Paresh bit her lower lip and peered past Raven at the bronzed woman hidden in the shadowed hall. "Who's with you?"

Raven motioned for Kestrel to step forward. "This is Kestrel, from the Silent Vespers. I am requesting her as my new First Officer. She'll take over as your security detail."

Blood flooded Paresh's eyes. Her irises darkened from light steel to gunmetal gray, and a solid barrier appeared in her aura. "What about Alex?"

Raven was too stunned to answer. No one possessed the power to solidify an aura like that—not even Master Jonathan, and she knew the crushing power of his aura well.

Training with him had been grueling. Ambushes from his fortified aura had slammed her harder than anything she'd known—until Eric knocked her unconscious. One powerful thrust had surpassed all that Master Jonathan had thrown at her, and now the blood and energies of both men flowed through Paresh.

As Master Jonathan responded that Alex would return to commanding his squad, Raven's thoughts turned to Salea. Young minds in bodies with great power had historically proven problematic. Salea had been fourteen. Their Sacred Vessel was only four years older. Was that enough?

With Hawkiel's blood in her veins, Salea had nearly eradicated the Vampiric Nation in its infancy. Paresh was an untapped well, even in her weakened state. Once healed and fully altered, she'd likely rival the Hosts and eclipse Lord Lucien as the most powerful being in the Realm of Man.

II

Arc of True Blood, July 1099 A.D.

Her fingers trembling, Raven streamed air from her lungs and unlatched the gate. She jogged up the hundred stairs that led to Master Jonathan's private abode. The entry was open, but he wasn't within sight. Her gaze nervously darted to the neighboring residence, elevated above the others on the mountainside. The First Born lived there—the Arch Elder of the newly formed Vampiric High Council of Elders, the original creation of their race, and the superior to whom she wished she was reporting.

"Master Jonathan?" she called quietly. "May I speak with you, please?"

Nearly a century had passed since the newborn Vampiric Nation had withdrawn from the Great Holy War. The loss of their army had driven the Fallen Host into the background of reality, into a pocket of space between the Realm of Man and the dimensional divide known as Animus Hollow. As promised in the Treaty of the Lasting Peace, the human creator had altered human history, restored the world's natural order, and recalled the Heavenly Host to the Celestial Curtain. Both Hosts retained their respective abilities to influence those in the Realm of Man, but all human wars were set to succeed or fail without vampiric interference.

Supposedly.

"Why are you here?" The hateful sneer in his voice replicated on his face as he stepped into view. He was slender and lean with well-defined musculature, and his auburn hair cascaded loosely over his bare shoulders. The sleeves and collar of his kimono hung down over the black silk of the bottom half, sagging off his hips by a haphazardly tied sash. Parallel streaks of crimson streamed down his inner thigh.

The tremor in her hand replicated in her jaw. This was a great intrusion. A huge mistake. She'd never seen him with his hair down, let alone barely dressed and intimately bitten. She averted her eyes, hating every minute of his attention.

The First Born had ordered him to train her in techniques suitable for the High Commander of the Vampire Shadow Hounds due to her lack of battle experience, and he relished all opportunities to put her through hell. Training allowed for extra brutality.

Through the golden luster in his dark eyes, he saw her as an ant to crush. She knew it because she saw him as the demon from Salea's village—no treaty would ever change that. Sharper than a dagger, his gaze pierced her heart and stole her breath. "Protocol requires you to call on the Elders at Snowblood Square, *Commander*."

She respectfully dropped to her knees. "Apologies, my master. I seek guidance regarding disturbing events involving a High Elder."

Master Jonathan's bare feet moved away from her. "Enter."

She scurried over the threshold and slid the panel shut behind her, hoping his privacy barrier was active. A quick glance revealed a sparse space divided by a wooden panel painted to depict spring rain over Mount Fuji flanked by panels of crimson honeysuckle vines and blue swallowtail butterflies. The feet of a pale male stretched out from behind the panel. Sucking in her breath, she bowed with her nose touching the floor and spoke into the grain of his bamboo planks.

"I located a disturbance in the Byzantine Empire. The Pope is aiding Emperor Komnenos in his battles with the insurgents, thus beginning a crusade to reclaim the Holy Land."

"That has nothing to do with us," her master snipped. "Humans have waged their own wars from the moment ours ended and we are not to interfere in their governmental affairs. This is what you wanted. Let them kill each other."

"I fear it is not so simple." Pausing, she gritted her teeth and chanced breaking tradition to look her master directly in his hateful eyes. "One or both men are under vampiric influence to misuse the human creator's word against the world to ignite Lucifer's influence. It is a direct threat to our existence."

"You are not to speak *his* name, by order of the Treaty." He studied her through dark slits. "Do you have proof?"

"Aye, sir. While investigating, I caught Salea whispering to the emperor in his room as he slept."

Her master's eyes deepened to black. "You spoke of Elder involvement, not that rat of a child you keep as a pet."

"Salea's mind is fragile and vulnerable to manipulation, and Hawkiel's blood gives her a power that others covet. I…I traced her movements back to Lord Connall." She hesitated a moment before stating, "High

Elder Connall is controlling her, using her power of influence, and has mobilized thirty thousand humans who are sacking the city of Jerusalem in the name of their creator as we speak. It is an unholy massacre that I fear will lead to many more."

"What proves Connall's involvement?"

"He's left the arc—I checked the security records. I also witnessed him meeting with Salea amidst the Byzantine troops. I assume he's using her to whisper to them, as well. She gave him blood…and it smelled of innocence."

His dark stare needled her. The bloody streaks had coalesced at his ankle.

"The High Council will order her death," she said, growing increasingly uncomfortable, "alongside Lord Connall, I am certain—"

A callous kick flattened her to the rigid plank floor. He ground his bloody foot into her spine. Anger flowed freely from his aura, crushing the air from her lungs. His eyes simmered and a strict line cut across his forehead. "Do not presume that *you* are, or ever will be, in any position to think like an Elder."

Trying not to groan, she forced out, "Salea…is my responsibility. I will…never deny that. She's impressionable…stuck with a child's mind. I…deserve—"

Vertebrae cracked under his heel. She cried out.

"What?" he spat. "For the Elders to punish you instead? That rat's fragile brain is precisely why I've petitioned the Council to ban child vampires. She is a liability that should not exist."

He lifted his foot and kicked her in the ribs. She curled into a ball, gasping for breath, and glared at him, unable to hide her hate any longer. Salea was only immortal because of him. "Lord Connall's goal is to wreak havoc in the human creator's name. By using Salea, he creates doubt amongst us."

"You give that rat too much credit. You were the symbolic hope Lucien saw, not her. He bestowed honorary titling to her out of respect to you, the Last Born True Blood."

Raven's eyes widened. Surely, the First Born had never meant for her to discover that she had earned his respect.

As though sharing the same thought, her master stalked past her. "Kneel and don't dare think of moving, Commander. I will discuss this with Lucien."

"Aye, Master Jonathan."

Raven didn't so much as twitch during her master's absence. She presumed his guest sat high in the ranks to be privy to such sensitive material. With her rank and hunting squad in their infancies, she hadn't yet dealt with an acute threat or planned scenarios to hunt an Elder.

Mere minutes passed before her master returned—with company. Her nose stuck to the floor, she froze as the scent of vanilla incense wafted over her. Lord Lucien the Eternal stood directly beside her.

"Lord Connall is manipulating your Salea to stir an uprising in the Holy Land?" His empty voice fell as cold as snow.

"Aye, my lord."

"You will testify this before the High Council? Accuse Connall directly?"

Her stomach leapt into her throat. "Aye, my lord."

"Rise, High Commander."

She stood slowly to avoid cringing from the pain shooting down her spine, and faced her eternal lord. Formally attired in a black silk brocade kimono, his silver hair hung straight down his back and his blue-hued visage betrayed no emotion.

"I shall deliver Connall's punishment before the Elders. You will confine Salea to the Arc of Celestial Night and entrance her into a five hundred year sleep."

"As you command, my lord."

Master Jonathan stood behind Lord Lucien. Raven interpreted his expression as one of disagreement, although he said nothing to the contrary. Upon noticing her assessment, he scowled and shot unseen daggers into her heart.

To Jonathan, Lord Lucien said, "I shall convene the Elders immediately. Escort High Commander Hawkings in once everyone is assembled." He eyed the feet behind the panel.

Jonathan followed his gaze. "I wasn't expecting a disaster to fall onto my doorstep."

"Endymion," Lord Lucien said, "dress and gather at Snowblood Square, forthwith. You shall bear witness to Connall's punishment here and then see to Salea's entrancement at the Arc of Celestial Night."

"As you command, of course, my lord," his soft voice said from behind the panel.

Her cheeks flaming red, Raven tucked her face as far down as possible and balled her fist over her heart as her eternal lord departed. Her heart skipped a beat as the panel slid shut behind him, leaving her alone with Master Jonathan and Lord Endymion. Clothing rustled behind the panel.

"Non-lethal punishments are rare." Master Jonathan's tone twisted viciously. "You have a way of getting what you want without asking, don't you, *Precious* Raven Hawkings?"

When she remained in her pose of respect without answering, he yanked her jaw and forced her to look at him. Malice blazed in his eyes as his lips formed an insidious curve. His voice carried the heat of the sun, but his words struck like shards of ice.

"You wanted this. This arc. This world." He leaned in, his nose touching hers. "Our peace. The lives of Alexander and Endymion, despite their treachery. The life of that constant threat to the Treaty. You didn't ask for a squad or the highest officer ranking, and yet, you received both. You got it all. You got *everything*."

He shoved her down wearing a smile that knotted her stomach. "You are nothing without that fallen star walking beside you. Fear consumes you when you're with me and fear makes you weak. I expect our Commanders to be strong enough to hunt *me*. After you confine that altered rat, I will train that fear out of you or kill you in the process."

Lord Endymion emerged from behind the panel wearing a translucent, white linen gown. Raven tucked her chin. His arrogant eyes prickled her skin, his voice seduced her ear, and his aura stroked her body beneath her clothes as he addressed Jonathan, "'Twould appear this session shall be eventful and better suited to a coliseum."

Raven squirmed under the combination of Jonathan's glare and Endymion's blatantly sexual attention. The fair Elder slipped into an embroidered silk gown the pale shade of the Orient's prized jade, and tapped Raven under the chin with a sharply tipped finger. Adding pressure, he forced her to stand and captured her gaze. Her breaths quickened. His satisfied grin opened a path for a mad rush of butterflies into her stomach. The curve of his lips deepened. "Ah—"

"Do not play with your toys under my roof." Jonathan recoiled in disgust. He slid into his kimono sleeves, carefully situating the collar before adjusting how the fabric wrapped around his body. He tightened the sash and touched his hair at the back of his neck. He glanced at the decorative wood panels.

Lord Endymion broke his contact with Raven to display the crimson ribbon in his hand. "Allow me?"

Jonathan turned his back to Lord Endymion. The Elder gathered the Second Born's auburn locks and secured them at the nape of his neck with the ribbon. He stepped back, his brow crinkling as his hand brushed the glowing Vampiric Star pinned near his collar.

"Lord Lucien acted swifter than expected." He swept down into a graceful bow. "The heralds have summoned me. I must take my leave."

Jonathan merely nodded. Lord Endymion opened the portal to Animus Hollow that would deliver him to his designated spot within the High Council's meeting chamber at Snowblood Square. Once he was gone, Jonathan said, "We will walk, Commander. Hold your head up."

His chiding ruffled her patience. She clenched her jaw. He didn't need to tell her how to walk in public. Her position required confidence and demanded respect, but his constant insults fueled the teasing she received from nearly every hunter under her command.

She found solace and determination in knowing what few others knew: the true reason Lord Lucien had given her this appointment. Without the freedom afforded to the VaSH High Commander, she never would have discovered Lord Connall's treachery. Nor would she be at the ready and unrestricted to face Hawkiel when he made his choice.

She trailed Master Jonathan from his room, down his steep steps, and across the arc's fields, gardens, and pathways to the marble dome where the Elders had gathered. Steeling herself on an unsteady breath, she stepped through the entrance that appeared. When they reached the center of the blackened space, the herald appeared, announced the Elders, and convened the session by order of Lord Lucien the Eternal.

The red wool of their hoods gathered loosely at their shoulders. That was unusual. And they were all looking at her. She shivered under Lord Lucien's icy stare.

"We have heard your claim. Make your accusation, High Commander Hawkings," he said, his voice apathetic.

On his left side, Lords Connall and Corben both glared down their noses. On his right side, Ladies Ambrosia and Lucasta eyed their accused male counterpart. The light illuminating the Gilded Lady, Lucasta, gave her golden skin an ethereal glow.

Raven rose beside Master Jonathan. "I accuse High Elder Connall of treachery against the Vampiric Nation."

Lord Corben snorted. "You dare accuse an Elder when *your girl* was caught in the act? Likely conspiring with our former commander? Where is her accusation? Or is our *High Commander* playing favorite—"

Lord Lucien's head turned subtly enough to silence Lord Corben. "Her girl is not your concern."

Unsettled by Lord Lucien's attention, Lord Corben stiffened. The corner of his jaw bulged, but he said nothing further.

Lord Connall, however, scoffed. "This *child* is mistaken and cannot have seen what she claims for I have not left this arc."

"The High Commander provided compelling evidence," Master Jonathan replied.

"Indeed. Undeniable." Faster than Raven's eye could see, Lord Lucien threw Lord Connall into room's center. He landed with a shambling thud at Raven and Master Jonathan's feet. Lord Lucien disappeared into the black of the room, unseen and unheard until his hand darted into the light and pulled Lord Connall to his feet.

"It was Salea! She came to me!" Lord Connall cried, throwing his hands up in a defensive posture.

"Your admission proves your lie," Lord Lucien emptily replied, stepping into Raven's sourceless glow. In a beam illuminating only half of his face, he bore the monstrous visage of a demon with black eyes and blood tipped fangs. His skin appeared darker and scaled, and his claws formed a lethal spearhead. "You committed your crime as an Elder. You shall die as an Elder."

Before Lord Connall could utter another word, Lord Lucien tore into the High Elder's chest and came out the other side gripping his heart in a dagger-tipped fist. A collective gasp wound around them. Lord Lucien pointed his singularly lit eye at each Elder.

"The Treaty of the Lasting Peace is my word and our law. This Council is charged with upholding that law and abiding by my word." Lord Lucien lowered his arm. Connall's body slicked his arm with gore as it slid off and slumped at Raven's feet. "High Commander Hawkings acts as my eyes in the world. Do not forget that I see all and death rides her heels for all traitors. Connall is hereby excommunicated as an Elder and this session is terminated."

☽ ✻ ☾

The shock of Connall's death and expulsion resounded throughout the Arc of True Blood in sobering silence. Master Jonathan charged Commander Nallura from the Chthonic Knights with custody of Connall's body and seeing to its beheading and cremation. Vampires did not bury their dead.

Raven was excused to hunt Salea with the Crimson Guard's Commander and the Wraith Reaper's First Officer. The eternal fourteen year old fought Alexander and Donovan, but yielded when Raven intervened. They bypassed stopping at the holding cells under construction at what would become the Arc of Mourning Eidolons. Lord Endymion and Master Jonathan awaited their arrival at the Arc of Celestial Night.

Salea faced Raven with tearful eyes, but said nothing as she explained her sentence. As she began the entrancement, she told herself that the girl's mind needed time to heal. After wandering this arc's dreamland, she'd awaken with a healthier mental state cleared of residual damage from Connall's control.

The instant Salea's eyes closed, the arc's heralds connected her to feeding tubes, waste collection, and a dream regulator, and Master Jonathan dismissed Donovan. He ordered the presences of the lives she'd fought for: Alexander and Lord Endymion, and promptly dragged Raven through Animus Hollow into the Realm of Man beyond the arc's casements.

The Arctic summer sun blistered her unprotected skin and the jagged tundra bit into her soles, yet she held her tongue. Alexander stood too rigid and too still, betraying his discomfort, while the Elder held his head high, prepared to enjoy this one-sided sparring match regardless of the outcome.

Master Jonathan stripped down to an older style of European pants that cinched at his knees, and then charged, no rules, no warning. His aura crashed into her like a slab of granite, followed by a driving elbow into her solar plexus. She flew backward, skidding and scraping the rough terrain. Her diaphragm seized and closed her airway. Foreign noises gurgled in her throat. She crawled onto her hands and knees. A sharp, pointed kick landed on her underside.

A horrid sound came in with a shallow breath as she rolled onto her hip yards away. Her fingers scrabbled over clumps of grass and knobby dirt seeking a firm handhold as her lungs opened and she sucked in mouthfuls of air, gasping and crying from pain and surprise.

"Never turn your back to your enemy."

His foot slammed into her left kidney and the full force of his weight landed on top of her. He rolled her onto her back and sat on her stomach with his hands curled around her throat. Jerking her up by the neck, he seethed, "First round: I win. You're dead. Broken neck and decapitation, *High Commander*. You are wholly unworthy of the station Lucien's handed you."

His fingers tightened, squeezing without mercy. Her vision tunneled out. Her lungs burned as though filled with hot sand. Choking echoes and explosive pressure mounted in her head. Blackness came next, and then—

Flickering lights filled a blurry visual field. The scent of lavender hovered overhead.

"…can only do so much if you do kill her," Lord Endymion said to Master Jonathan.

"I don't care if she survives. We deserve a VaSH High Commander tougher than this weak young thing."

"Lord Lucien the Eternal ordered me to ensure that she lives *and you know why*," Lord Endymion replied, standing to face Master Jonathan. "Do not force my hand as an Elder, *Sir Jonathan*."

"I advise against using that tactic, *Third Born*. You will never find *me* in Connall's shoes." Her master's spiteful attention fell to her. His lips twisted into a devious grin. "Well, well. She's alive. Time for round two."

Lord Endymion returned to his place beside Commander Alexander. Master Jonathan paced and waited for Raven to regain full consciousness. The second she did, he came at her with a running leap, intending to land with both feet on her chest.

Every vein in her head throbbed and her vision swam in dizzying circles, but she managed to roll out of his targeted range. She summoned strength from a hidden reserve to rise and stumbled to dodge his next attack, a wide, single-fisted swing. Maybe she hadn't learned how to fight, but she'd walked the battlefields for centuries without taking a hit. She'd start with that.

In the Second Born's prideful arrogance, he wanted to beat and humiliate her, but pride was not part of the person Hawkiel had shaped. She was resolute.

He charged again. Her pupils focused on his movements—the minute shifts in the muscles he had bared for her—and she regulated her breathing. His fist flew fast at her jaw and he threw himself into the air, propelled by the weight of his momentum. She inhaled and counted. At the last possible second, she released her breath and sidestepped him, whirling to his rear where she got in three rapid punches to his side. She dropped onto her palms and swept him off his feet, flipping up to land a kick under his chin before any part of him had touched the ground.

As he crashed onto the tundra, the surprise in Alexander's aura wafted over her and approval emanated from Lord Endymion. But, she didn't need to impress them. They knew her secrets. She needed to survive.

Master Jonathan leapt to his feet, snarling, and lunged, turning in midair to fling out a forceful heel. She flipped so that his foot passed through the air beneath her. She landed and brought her palms up the center mass of her body, gathering energy from her aura and shoving it outward, punching him square in the gut. He doubled over with a grunt.

She supposed he didn't want a VaSH High Commander that showed mercy when he wasn't willing to show it himself, so she jumped high and landed on his shoulders. He stumbled and fell backward. She landed on his throat and her fingernails lengthened into sharp tips. She thrust two fingers into the carotid arteries on either side of his neck.

"Round two: I win. If I remove my fingers, you'll probably heal before you lose enough blood to die. Or, I can push them in farther and sever your head."

A steely arm looped her torso and yanked her backward. Alexander's voice filtered into her ear. "Lord Lucien the Eternal has a standing order that I not allow the Second Born to be killed."

"But I had him!" she yelled, turning to shove Alex when her spine suddenly snapped backward.

With a massive roar, Master Jonathan threw her to the ground and stomped down, shattering her ribs into her liver. Limited to careful, shallow breaths, she couldn't even cry out from the stabbing pain.

"Enemies often have reinforcements. Never declare premature victories."

Every breath was torture. Movement was pure agony. Master Jonathan maneuvered to strike again and fear held her paralyzed. Lord Endymion called out a safe word they hadn't told her and came over to inspect her injury. "If the bones lacerated the aorta, she'll bleed out."

"She has no form, no discipline, no offensive posturing. Just *luck*." Master Jonathan paced behind Lord Endymion smoothing his hands over his mussed hair and wiping blood off his healed throat. "Six hundred years of life, and of that, less than a century living as a true blood, and she's going to lead our security forces?"

He shoved a finger in Alexander's face. "You are not to intervene again. The only one at risk here is her."

As she whimpered and focused on breathing and holding as still as possible, he squatted near her head. "Had Alexander not interfered, I might have granted you that round. The result would be the same, but you must expect the unexpected and never turn your back on an enemy who draws breath."

She blinked her understanding. Endymion's physical examination shot searing pain directly into her heart. She howled and clawed at her chest in desperation.

"Return her to the Arc of True Blood for treatment." Master Jonathan's lips carved a cruel smile. "The instant those bone shards are no longer in your heart, you are mine again."

He locked eyes with her and nudged his chin at Lord Endymion. "I believe you are intimately knowledgeable of his skills at restoring life to the recently departed?"

She blinked.

"Then until the day that you prove your worth as High Commander to me, I will strike to kill at every opportunity. I am your enemy and I am breathing much easier than you at this moment. Your goal is to reverse that. Only then shall you earn proper training."

Again, she blinked her understanding. He turned away to gather his clothing. She wheezed and glared at his back, the back he had turned to her—his enemy still drawing breath. She would take the Second Born's beatings, learn his moves, and prove her worth. She would let him teach her and mold her into the best vampire hunter in the world. And then she would breathe easier once she fulfilled her promise to Salea and turned her back on him for good.

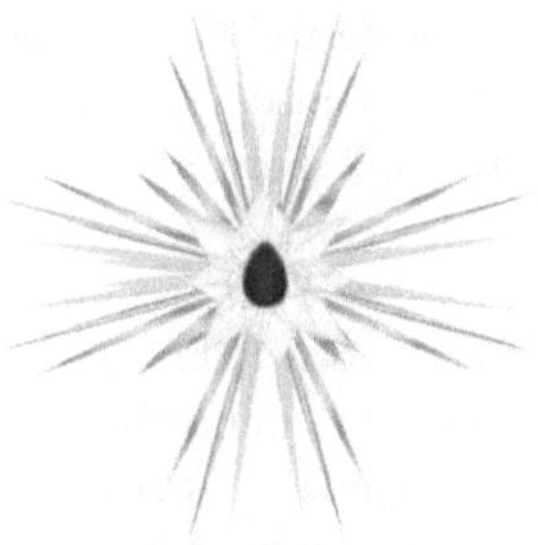

CHAPTER TEN: FALCONRY

I

Orison Crossing, Summer 2006

Paresh hadn't expected to lose Alex as her escort. She tossed a blue-tinged glance at Eric. He caught her watching him and watched back, giving nothing away.

Alex had only done what she'd asked of him—it was her fault. She started to turn in protest when Kestrel dropped to one knee before her, fist balled over her heart, and grinned, revealing her lengthy true blood teeth.

Against tan skin that gleamed bronze, those sharp, ivory canines tunneled Paresh's vision. Donovan's wicked maw ripped open her mind and rammed a hot spike of adrenaline into her chest. The air thickened and clung in her throat heavier than wet cotton. She barely registered stepping back or lifting her hands defensively.

"I am honored, milady." Rich and deep, and unintentionally seductive, Kestrel's voice oozed a strength that shattered the mental illusion in Paresh's head.

Sucking in a slow breath, Paresh clasped her hands together at her breast and mustered a smile. "H-hi…"

Kestrel's thick lashes slanted down, hiding her eyes, and her hair, straight and black as a crow's wing, swung lightly near her chin. The asymmetrical cut was shortest on the left, revealing an ear lined with gold hoops and studs. Strands seemingly made of gold thread streaked through the longest portion, which hung over the right side of her face and partially blocked her curvy lips.

Fingernails filed to polished black points swept the longer locks behind her ear. Paresh's spine prickled at the sight of the dagger sheathed on the underside of Kestrel's arm. Lengths of black, gold, and red braided leather held it in place, looping her middle finger and crisscrossing her arm to tie off above her elbow, where two gold and black tassels dangled.

The huntress shared the same refined visage of every other true blood Paresh had seen and wore clothing similar to the few other hunters she'd met. Kestrel's uniform included the seemingly standard black paratrooper pants and matte-black combat boots, but she wore a black sari blouse embellished at the hem with velvety black and gold intertwined circles. The tight fabric hugged small breasts above a thin, muscular midriff. On display to the sun and elements, the curve of her waist sloped in from her ribs and out to her hips. Silver tattoos of skeletal leaves and vines scrolled from her back and down her belly.

A blood drop ruby dotted the center of a four-pointed star pendant that dipped under her blouse and hung beneath the hem from a delicate golden chain. The velvet choker on her throat matched the blouse's hem, and the crucifix-style hilt of a long sword, adorned with gold and rubies, stuck out from the gold-tipped black scabbard on her back.

Kestrel isn't just a hunter; she's a warrior, Paresh thought, unaware that she'd placed Raven between them. Obviously, all hunters carried weapons, but the only blades she'd seen had been the daggers used by David and Nicole, and the sickle tearing through Jonathan's flesh——

Donovan's face rose from the darkness. His tongue slid over an arrogant grin as his chocolaty eyes darkened and he withdrew the weapon she'd seen only in visions. *What if he'd drawn that sickle on me?*

She was suddenly stuck in Eric's living room, trapped under a heavy weight. The heat of Donovan's body penetrated her skin, his pulse beat against her chest, and his wavy hair tickled her cheek. The scent of clove oil invaded her nose. Bile bubbled up her esophagus.

Blood dripped from his chin as he pressed the sickle against her throat. His dark eyes and bloody grin gleamed with victory.

"N-no. No! *No!*" She screamed and shoved him with all her might, but he was hard and immovable. "*No! No...n-no!*"

He grabbed her wrists and his lips loosed silent words she knew from memory. He would never let her go. Never share her with anyone. She was his. He'd won.

"No...not again. I can't...Eric..." Tears dripped from her cheeks as she choked on her breath. "*E-Eric!*"

"Paresh!"

Acid burned her mouth. She lurched as if to vomit.

"*Paresh!*" Eric's voice rushed across a great void and lifted the weight. "Paresh!"

Donovan's face faded into moonlit glass panels. She blinked away the remnants of Eric's house. The greenhouse returned. Her chest was heaving and wet from tears. She tried to rub her eyes, but couldn't move.

Raven and Eric were restraining her against the brick wall. Raven held her wrists, likely due to the deep, bloody claw marks stretching down her face and throat. Eric leaned into her, his body heat and aura warming her skin.

Whispering her name repeatedly into her hair, Eric stroked her nape with tender fingers. Jonathan stood behind him, his expression both concerned and angry, his outstretched hand a signal to Kestrel to hold her position. The huntress had looked up, revealing intense, golden eyes.

"Paresh," Eric whispered, his breath moist in her hair.

Blinking through a fresh bout of fiery tears, Paresh choked out his name on a shaky breath. Raven released her wrists. They were red and painful, but Paresh didn't care. She threw her arms around Eric and sobbed into his shoulder.

When she quieted, Eric tipped her chin and crystalline blue orbs stole her gaze. The concern in his eyes flowed into his voice. "What happened?"

Paresh shook her head. Tears threatened to surge again. "It was...D-Donovan."

"*What?*" Jonathan's voice reverberated off the glass walls. Paresh flinched. She'd never heard him yell. He swore to himself and turned away.

"I'm sorry, Master Jon!" Paresh cried, reaching for him.

He spun on his heel, eyes blazing, but his expression softened and his long fingers stretched to touch hers. As their fingers interlaced, he clamped down on her hand. "Don't apologize, Pare. I'm not mad at you."

Jonathan's face crinkled as he struggled for control. "It's..."

"It's okay," Eric whispered, cupping Paresh's face. "You've done nothing wrong."

Paresh eyed Raven's wounds. Her eyes stung and lips quivered. "Did...I...?"

"Oh, milady, hush now," Raven cooed, running her fingers through Paresh's hair. "It's already healed, sweetie."

In the same quiet, soothing voice, Raven said to Kestrel, "Eric's assistant, Sarah, is in the kitchen. Introduce yourself."

"As you wish, ma'am." Kestrel bowed and left.

Eric's eyes asked a silent question that Raven answered with a deliberate look and shake of her head.

"Just say it!" Paresh cried, breaking free of everyone's assuring hands. She wiped her cheeks with her palms. "I smell blood. Sarah's hurt. I scared her, didn't I? I am not a child who needs to be protected from *every little thing!*"

Eric's eyes widened. "I didn't notice. How did you——"

Paresh cupped his face. "You're too focused on me."

"It does tend to blind you," Jonathan said in a dry tone, "but I must plead my guilt this time, as well."

"My lords," Raven said, "given Paresh's previous premonitions, I recommend we adjourn to the mansion. We may have a clear view of our surroundings, but our enemy has an equally clear view of us."

"Pare? Was it a vision?" Jonathan asked.

A wall of panic rushed Paresh. Burying her face in her hands, she shook her head and slid down the bricks at her back, landing on the glossy floor. Eric's body heat and the scent of his cologne followed. He sat beside her and pulled her to his chest. Holding her tight, he planted a kiss atop her head.

"It's okay," he whispered. "It'll be okay."

"But…it's so dumb——the weapons. I just…suddenly I was back at your house, reliving what he did to me. O-only…this time he had a sickle and I was powerless."

"Kestrel's weapons prompted that?" Raven knelt. "I wanted to keep her with me for training, but not at this cost. I will make other arrangements for you."

"Alex?" Paresh asked quietly, her cheeks flushing like the timid child everyone seemed to think she was. Straightening her spine, she faced Eric. "It was my fault. I wanted to go and he was torn about what to do."

She pressed her palm against Eric's heart. "Alex saved my life. He makes me feel safe. I *am* safe with him."

"Anything you want." A dark sheen skimmed Eric's crystalline blue orbs as he turned his stare to Jonathan. "We need to end this threat."

Jonathan returned a blackening gaze. "We will."

II

Kestrel slipped into the kitchen unnoticed. Sterile white ceramic enveloped the maze of industrial stainless steel appliances, cooling racks, basins, and fixtures, each sectioned for cooking, baking, prepping, storage, or washing. Beyond her sight line, liquid gurgled at a vigorous boil over the hiss of a gas flame and the low hum of vented steam.

Kestrel planted her palm on the subway-tiled wall and concentrated her aura to trace the space's architecture as she approached the "assistant" hunched over the small sink on the far side. The exposed duct overhead dusted her with cool air that burned the embedded silver in her skin and confirmed the assistant as the only other warm body she'd not yet seen.

A trail of sticky molecules roped her waist and tugged subtly at her belly, drawing her attention to the bloodied chef's knife near a drain with an aged patina. The sweet perfume that wafted from the blade tantalized her nose with unusual familiarity and nostalgia that buried the other aromas of freshly chopped celery and carrots, and bubbling basil and tomato soup. Even the pungent scent of diluted bleach disappeared beneath the bouquet of that woman's crimson nectar.

Rumors of the humans surrounding Lord Eric soared to mythological levels that few believed; yet, here was proof.

Closing her eyes, she pulled the scent deep into her lungs. Her teeth prickled. She loosed a silent roar, welcoming the rush of air over her fangs, a balm to the early throbbing of an age-old ache. Microscopic bursts of flavor exploded onto her tongue. She relished a slow swallow under a satisfied grin.

Rumor was fact. His humans truly possessed aromatic blood that tasted sweeter beyond comprehension.

Her lips formed a grim line. Cats weren't the only creatures killed by curiosity or temptation.

Rapping two fingers against the wall to announce her presence, Kestrel opened her eyes. A steady stream of that exquisite scarlet ran with the tap water down the drain.

Without looking, Sarah called over her shoulder in a voice cemented with pain and shame. "Damn, slippery carrots—I should have...I need stitches."

Pausing at the discarded chef's knife, Kestrel broke her connection to the wall and knelt. Crimson light flooded her vision as she dabbed her finger onto the blade. Did exposure to the divine auras of Lord Eric and Lady Paresh cleanse and purify the life essences of those closest to them?

She touched her finger to her tongue. The choirs of Heaven sang in her head.

"Glorious," she whispered.

"Hello?" Sarah craned her neck to see Kestrel without moving her hand from the faucet's spray. "Oh…I…I thought you were Eric—"

The woman froze as fear licked the darkness in her dilating pupils. "W-who are you?"

Kestrel stood, returned her hand to the wall, and resumed her approach. "I am Kestrel, First Officer of the Silent Vespers—soon to be First Officer of the Wraith Reapers. I am here to assess your wound."

"I heard Paresh scream—"

"Traumatic events are taking their toll."

"But—"

"I assure you." Kestrel dipped her chin. "My honor is eternally yours should I lie."

Mesmerized, Sarah turned in place. A torrent of blood splashed her white canvas shoes. Her jaw gaped at Kestrel's fully vampiric form. "My blood—"

"Is divine." Kestrel's palm slid free of the wall. Her aura had finished recon and given her a mental blueprint. She cut across the span between them and took Sarah's injured left hand into hers. Sarah's heart leapt into a frenzy as she locked onto Kestrel's blood-engorged eyes.

"Be not afraid," Kestrel said, "I will not harm you. This is merely how I study my surroundings."

"S-sorry for staring." Sarah knitted her brow. "Um, I'm a bit lightheaded."

Kestrel's fingertips tingled from the pulse under Sarah's dark skin. She nudged her chin at the wound. The knife had sliced into the muscle connecting the thumb and index finger, partially severing the nerve and narrowly missing the bone. "That's quite serious. May I?"

Dazed, Sarah lifted her hand as a sacrificial offering. "You can do it this way, right? Not that—I mean—uh, yes."

Momentarily stunned, Kestrel stared into Sarah's gilded brown eyes. The blood under her nose sparked primitive urges and the heat of Sarah's skin was a pillaging fire. The young woman's heartbeat pounded swift and strong against Kestrel's aura, and her breaths came quick and shallow. Blood gushed, fangs ached, and instinct looped unbroken in an ancient brain.

The breath she exhaled to regain control brushed the back of her teeth and flared the pain in her upper jaw. Before she could stop herself, she scooped Sarah's blood into the crook of her knuckle and licked it clean. Moaning softly, she mentally spiraled into euphoria unlike anything she'd ever experienced. Reality and memory collided: a luscious scent and blond curls, resplendent flavor and fangs splitting a smile, heat in her belly and long forgotten pleasure…and pain.

Strange emotions flooded her core. She sank into delirium. Somewhere within—she didn't know where—an alarm was ringing and a head was rolling, but she was happily drowning. *He* was there—her other half—cloaked in shadow, yet almost fully formed in memory for the first time in a century. Her tongue slid across her fangs. She hungered to see his face again. Bathe within his golden aura. To feel whole again.

Lior—

Erratic energy thumped against the silver vines. Sarah's heart had struck an irregular beat common with blood loss. Ripped back to reality, Kestrel lightly panted, "Thank you."

Trapped within the euphoria of Kestrel's aura, Sarah tumbled off balance with a dream-like, far off haze haunting her eyes. Kestrel reined in her aura, caught the woman, and held her steady until the effect waned. It felt familiar. Natural.

"That was…uncommon, but appreciated," Kestrel said in a low voice, husky with remembrance, "However—"

Producing a vial of Bioserum from one of her many pockets, she said, "I need to treat your wound. This will restore full function to your thumb."

"Oh, God. I-I'm sorry—yes, please." Sarah took a half step back. "That vial—I've seen something similar before. I…*completely* misunderstood—"

"I am aware of the misunderstanding. This will hurt." Gripping Sarah's wrist tight to staunch the flow, Kestrel poured the Bioserum into the wound to jumpstart the clotting factor before grabbing a swab.

A fanged smile glimmered across her mind. Those soft lips had always traced her silver vines with a maddeningly light touch and heated breath that teased the edge where metal met newborn skin—

Sarah yelped as the swab hit the nerve. Clenching her teeth, Kestrel grunted an apology and focused. Sarah bit her lip and groaned. The Bioserum swab dropped deeper into the wound.

"*Oh, my God!*" Sarah's whole body tensed on a sharp inhale.

"I do not mean to harm you. Breathe." Kestrel spoke steadily and softly, affecting the façade of a compassionate human medical practitioner despite her internal emotional storm.

Lior...

"I know," Sarah replied, huffing out uneven breaths between grimaces. Her skin's pallor had taken on a deathly flat hue.

"I've been briefed on the situation here, but not individual specifics," Kestrel began, opting for distraction to keep Sarah conscious—another method she'd witnessed from human doctors and one she hoped might regain control of her inner anarchy. "How did you come into Lord Eric's possession?"

"*Damn it!*" Sarah's hand instinctively jerked, but Kestrel's grip held it firmly in place. "I...I, uh, I don't belong to Eric. Did they tell you that?"

"It is *understood* among our trustees and nobility."

"Trustees—Molly mentioned them before, but—" Sarah winced and pressed a bloody palm to her forehead. "*My God, this hurts!*"

She sucked in a sharp breath and released it slowly. "I don't, uh, I don't belong to him. It'd break his heart if I thought that. I'm his friend."

"But you serve him." Kestrel closed the vial and pulled wrappings from another pocket. "I am unfamiliar with lower human hierarchy. In my nation, you belong to him."

"Yes, I serve, but I'm not a possession." Sarah swayed under the force she failed to muster. "What do you mean by 'lower' anyway?"

"My position requires minimal involvement within the Realm of Man outside a general awareness of the Earth's governments." Kestrel placed a steadying hand between Sarah's shoulders as her legs wobbled. "You should lie down."

"But, lower...?" Sarah drifted inward and paused in thought. "Do you know about the Civil War?"

"There are untold numbers across the globe and time," Kestrel replied, nudging Sarah toward the prep counter, "but for the one of which you speak, yes."

"Eric saved my great-great-great grandpa Willy from the Confederate Army. He was a slave—" Sarah sucked in a labored breath and took a step. "Eric gave him a job. A life. A name. Weaverly: his mother's maiden name. No one here knows what *lower* freedom means more than Eric."

"When you look at the ocean, do you see waves or salt?"

"What does that——"

"There are billions of humans," Kestrel interrupted. "I only see the wave makers. It's not meant as an insult."

Sarah reached the counter and turned, leaning against it. "So, we're salt? But Eric's nobility."

"Our newest lord was kept off the radar intentionally by Lord Jonathan until recently. Now he is a tsunami." Kestrel raised her eyebrows deliberately. "May I finish bandaging?"

Nodding sheepishly, Sarah stared at a spot on the floor.

"At the risk of speaking beyond my station," Kestrel began hesitantly, "do you desire immortality to stay by his side?"

"What do you mean?" Sarah asked, her heart leaping with her voice. "I never said——"

Knotting the gauze and tearing the roll free with a sharpened talon, Kestrel studied Sarah through hooded lids. "That, ah, *misunderstanding* says otherwise."

Sarah groaned into her free hand. "My head is killing me."

Tucking the bandaging material into her pockets, Kestrel inspected the dressing. "Bloodloss. Again—you need to lie down."

The warmth of Sarah's bandaged hand induced another memory as Kestrel's ever-present control slipped again into cherubic blond curls brushed silver by the moon. "The Bioserum will help with pain and physical damage, but your bones require time to replenish what was lost."

Sarah's gaze shifted to their intertwined hands. "Did you want to?"

"Excuse me?" Blood seeped into the curls in memory and hollowed her heart. An aura sleek as a blade weakened and evaporated. Kestrel clenched her jaw.

"The misunderstanding." Sarah gnawed her lip in hesitation. "Could you?"

"It is what I was created to do, I suppose," Kestrel replied stiffly, "though I refrain unless ordered."

Sarah wobbled and grabbed her head with a groan. Shoving the cutting block, vegetables, and bowls aside, Kestrel lifted the young woman and set her onto the stainless steel surface. "Getting your head even with your heart will reduce the pressure. Lay on your side so you don't choke if you get sick."

Kestrel maneuvered the bandaged hand to rest on Sarah's hip. The gauze was still white. The Bioserum was working. "I'm going to wash up and grab a moist cloth for you."

"My blood did something, didn't it?" Sarah whispered.

Fighting to keep her mind empty, Kestrel took her time rinsing the faintest blood scent from her exposed skin. She wrung a cloth under hot water and returned to Sarah. She dabbed at the drying blood on the young woman's brow, lips, arms, and hands. Coagulated blood wasn't easy to clean off. She smeared more into crusty edges than she removed.

Nearing the edge of the Sandman's domain, Sarah mumbled, "Didn't it?"

"You are relentless." Kestrel set the cloth down. She placed both hands on the countertop's cold metal and hung her head between her shoulders. Behind her eyelids, the breeze tossed Lior's bloody curls and whisked the comfort of his aura away forever. She didn't want to see his face.

Huffing lightly, she opened her eyes to Sarah's dark amber gaze. *So much like his.*

Kestrel straightened. Sarah's aura, her blood essence—could Lior's unused soul claim another body? Sinking into that possibility, she replied, "Yes."

Sarah smiled as her eyes slid closed. "I wasn't...wrong."

"I don't understand," Kestrel confessed quietly. Endless questions raced through her mind. Lior wouldn't want to distract her. Duty always came first; they'd both understood that. He'd be disappointed that a tricky little human from the Flock had gotten into her head. Or would he understand that the Second New Age had muddied the rules? What if the soul meant for Lior had found a new home?

A wisp of air skimmed her skin. The silver vines burned anew from Master Jonathan's body heat as he stepped through the swinging door. He raised a questioning brow.

"My lord." Kestrel dipped her chin in reverence. "With the Bioserum, Lord Eric's assistant shall recover."

He stopped beside her and took in the bloodied chef's knife, floor, and cloth. His gaze drifted from the fingerprint on the blade to her lips. "You've entered a world of temptation, First Officer. Mind your actions. Raven selected you with reason."

He nodded at Sarah. "If she wants to be altered, that's her choice, not Eric's—not to say it won't make him angry. Learn to accept controversy, because it comes with your new position and what Raven expects of you."

Kestrel remained respectfully silent. Every step needed to be firm and sure. She was about to become the second highest ranked officer in the highest ranked squad—and was near the top of Elder succession.

"Speak," he said. "I won't bite. Not now, anyway. I have far too much on my mind."

"Sire," she began uncertainly, "am I to understand that I may alter her? Lord Eric's trustee? A member of the Flock? The High Council would strike me dead."

He laughed. Such a sound coming from Lord Lucien's war hound sounded quite odd.

"An Arch Elder stands before you," he replied. "What more do I need to say? Eric wants his humans to be happy. He loves them. Take her home and return to your duties."

"As you wish, sire." She balled her fist over her heart and began to bow her head, but he caught her chin and roughly jerked her jaw up.

"You followed order after order under Landor, but the Wraith Reaper First Officer lives on the Commander's heel and leads. Learn to think for yourself."

He paused and loosened his grip, but daggers lived within his stare. "Alex will return as Paresh's security escort. Do not fall before her sight while visibly armed again—that order goes to *all* hunters."

Eyeing the sleeping human, he added, "In the wake of Donovan's actions, the truest test of ability as Raven's First Officer is steeling yourself against temptation and emotion. Raven was fully prepared to force your promotion, if needed, so congratulations on becoming one of the elite and controversial. You have a lot of eyes on you."

"Understood, my lord. I shall uphold the honor of the Wraith Reapers without fail."

"We shall see." He beamed an unsettling grin at her before pivoting on his heel and exiting the swinging doors.

Replaying his words, she wondered why Raven had broken protocol for her. Was it because of the Judicium et Prudentia? Her former partnership with Lior?

They presumed to face an enemy unaffected by love—that Lucifer's hateful miasma had birthed ignorance to love's touch at the foundation of every known emotion, saving the COMS from distractive bonds. The enemy had chosen to ignore love's entangling tendrils, yet vied to wield its destructive power without understanding anything about it.

Understanding wasn't enough. The Vampiric Nation needed to confront love head on and evolve, conquer and master it as a threat. Dredges of memory exposed ominous portents of love's strengths and weaknesses. No matter their division, they were all afflicted. They were all Children of the Morning Star.

III

Snowblood Square, Arc of True Blood, 1888

"How can you not know if the victims are of the Flock?" Lord Corben asked, toeing the edge of mockery.

"And why suspect a vampire when the bodies are mutilated and blatantly displayed?" Lady Ambrosia added. "No true blood would dare—"

"Connall. Arian." Lady Rainne clipped the discussion short.

"Alas," Lord Endymion said, "grim reminders that such atrocities are not beyond our scope."

The light of his restrained beam gleamed in Lord Lucien's dark eyes—murky and ominous like a smoking volcano. "Continue, High Commander."

"Aye, my lord." She lowered the fist covering her heart to her side. "The disease and negative miasma flooding London's East End masks who is of the Flock and who is not, yet a nagging pang in my chest pulls me there. I am certain that a vampire is using this cover to prey on innocents."

"Such darkness attracts collectors and the Fallen Host, a considerable risk to take on a 'pang.' Have any been bitten?" Lord Lucien's gaze grated her bones.

"The circumstances are unusual," Raven dutifully admitted. "The Yard's reports indicate that the first victim was stabbed thirty-nine times—including the sternum and heart—with wounds of varying size. A human is unlikely to use multiple blades. Vampire claws would account for variance, conceal a bite, and impale the heart. The second victim was nearly decapitated and had mismatched cuts—thus concealing a bite while also sufficiently ensuring death and avoiding infection. Same with the third."

Raven paused. Human constables had taken a male into custody for the next victim, a counter to her argument, but dismissing inconvenient data was reckless. "There is a possible fourth with a human suspect; however, the next two garner closer inspection and raise doubt about human involvement in these deaths and others of which I have not yet spoken."

She paused again, awaiting another challenge to her suspicions, but Lord Lucien's broken silence reigned absolute. He stoically awaited her continuation.

"Two women were killed in one night, forty-five minutes apart, at high risk for exposure, and the second victim was killed within a fifteen-minute window of human patrol. I believe the first attack was interrupted, causing frustrations that led to a frenzied second attack. The amount of damage done..." Raven boldly met Lord Lucien's apathetic eyes.

"There are plenty more. All brutal. Grotesque. They call him the Knife, Leather Apron, the Ripper, the Whitechapel Murderer, Jack—whatever his name, he wants blood. He needs it. Craves it on a primal level. These are *our* base instincts, not *theirs*. These humans, of the Flock or not, are being destroyed, not killed or preyed upon. This reeks of a beast losing control and that is a risk we cannot afford, especially in a place attractive to our former commander."

The Elders collectively looked to Lord Lucien. Anticipation charged the blackened space. Their eternal lord spoke so rarely.

He observed Raven without appearing to see her. The Elders may have deemed the London murders a waste of their resources and an unnecessary risk to their nation, but Lord Lucien's hematite irises smoldered under his outward apathy.

He tilted the barest of nods to Raven. "Investigate. Report."

Bowing her head, Raven replied, "Aye, my lord. My squad shall act swiftly."

"No."

She studied her eternal lord through hooded eyes. His gaze was slightly withdrawn and his parted lips glinted ivory.

"I want a full assessment," Lord Lucien said at last, "from all squads. Est Judicium et Prudentia."

"As you command, my lord. I shall gather Commander Alexander and First Officers Kestrel and Lior."

"Dismissed, High Commander." Lord Lucien's eyes pierced through her as the exit portal appeared.

As tradition dictated, Raven tucked her chin and crossed her heart before stepping into Animus Hollow's rolling, endless white. She took in a quelling breath and scouted with her aura for Alex's location to recruit part one of 'The Judgment and Wisdom' trio assigned to her riskier assessments.

The Arc of Mourning Eidolons, she thought. *Perfect.*

As the Chthonic Knights' base of operations, she could grab Alex and Lior in one stop. She stepped from the Hollow into an entrance vestibule. This arc didn't have heralds, so the automated system broadcasted her arrival, which, unsurprisingly, delivered Alex to her within minutes.

"Goody!" His cheerful voice blasted over the loud buzz of their nation's busiest arc, but he wasn't within view, yet.

Hunters from all squads passed her, tilting their heads with reverence and muttering a respectful, "High Commander," before continuing on their way. Aside from serving as Nallura's headquarters, the Arc of Mourning Eidolons housed the holding cells, the VaSH's largest armory, their main medical unit—jointly staffed by the Chthonic Knights and Silent Vespers—and played host to hunter downtime, training, and squad-wide meetings. It was, essentially, an all-in-one dome created solely for use by the Vampire Shadow Hounds, their prey, the injured, and the High Commander.

As the most industrial arc, steel alloy grating and platforms crisscrossed the interior vertically and horizontally. Lifts and stationary Hollow portals made traversing the dome a simple task, and tight security protocols used bioscanners to limit access to sensitive areas, such as the infirmary and arsenal. Many hunters, regardless of squad, called this arc home and lived in small, stacked dwellings or communal barracks. It was, by far, the rowdiest arc, but it was the VaSH's sanctuary—the only place that allowed them to relax.

Alex popped up in front of her as stiff as a spring-loaded training cutout. "Hey Goody! What brings you this way?"

"Can you not be more desperate for attention than a puppy?" she asked, palming his face and shoving him away. "Find Lior and Kestrel, if she's here. We're going to London."

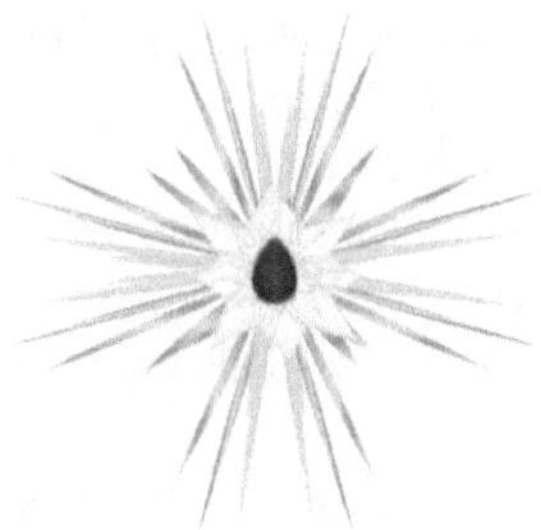

Chapter Eleven: The Unfortunates

Under the inherent gloom of London's East End at dusk, Raven and her cloaked assessment unit stood atop the Queen Head's Pub, overlooking the cross-section of Fashion Street, White's Row, and Commercial Street. The brisk November wind blew a gristly mist into gas lamps that cast deeper shadows than they did light, and kept the slum's odiferous infamy on the move.

The sickness in Whitechapel choked on beer and gin, and its stone streets drowned in raw sewage and congealing blood that leaked from slaughterhouses. Prostitutes and homeless children clogged narrow streets and tight alleys, coughing and begging, selling and crying, dying and stealing—which one mattered not, for they were all the same. Then came the sailors from port and men from the docks to choose their pick or take a kick.

This hardly represented the Realm of Man in its entirety, but it was enough for Raven to question why she'd ever envied the lives of humans. Or how she'd convinced an entire nation to desire such lives. This did not deserve their envy.

"Damn, Goody," Alex said, peering over the parapet, "why'd you pick the most populated city on Earth? It's nasty here; our presence is only going to make it worse."

A carriage crawled through the crowd below, the horses neighing anxiously at the threat beyond their blinders. "The horses alone——"

"If rogues cared about such things," Raven interrupted with a wry smile, "you and I'd never see each other, would we?"

"Aha!" Alex flashed a toothy grin and wagged his finger. "You do like working with me!"

"I merely hoped to stop your whining. I'll happily send you back to Master Jonathan and his human toy, if you wish…" Raven noticed the graveyard neighboring the pub. Looking farther out, she saw a church on the block's opposite side. "That's strange. I don't feel any divine power nearby."

Lior's dark amber gaze traced their surroundings. "Also odd for a vampire to select victims close to holy ground."

"Aye. Odder more that we all failed to notice how close we are ourselves."

Lior's golden curls clenched tight in the damp as he marched across the roof. The black cloak draping his limber frame gleamed silvery blue within—the color adopted by the Chthonic Knights—and the hood hung loose around his shoulders. Leaping atop the brickwork, he peered beyond his leather-tipped toes. "I do feel a compulsion trying to block me here, but it isn't nearly as strong as it should be. We could enter this burial site."

"Perhaps the miasma is infecting it?" Alex suggested. "It's so murky here I can't differentiate human auras from Flock or Fallen."

"Aye." Raven nodded curtly. "That's what I reported to Lord Lucien and why we're all here. Judgment and Wisdom."

Stepping away from the stone caps, Alex sidled over to Raven's side. "Always happy to partner with my fellow judge."

"You only got that assignment because you're sorely lacking in wisdom." Raven motioned for Kestrel to run a body check.

The Silent Vesper huntress tossed her golden-lined cloak off her shoulders and cast her arms out, turning her palms up. A plunging, breast-hugging blouse exposed her silver engraved midriff to the sky's greasy spittle. Closing her eyes, she faced the clouds and her straight black hair spilled from her hood.

"Curious indeed," she whispered, "that so much holy land surrounds this area. Sensitives like us would avoid it, including rogues, but it's weak."

Her brow furrowed. "I feel collectors. Many. Creeping over the sacred ground to dampen its power."

Alex sobered. His normally fern-green eyes darkened to rival a forest at midnight. "Why would they do that? The Fallen Host aren't restricted by holy ground. Not like us."

Alarm prickled Raven's nape. The Treaty of the Lasting Peace forbade contact between vampires and the Fallen Host, including their soul collectors. "This is more serious and delicate than I feared."

Lior pivoted on his heel and hopped off his stone perch. His cloak swayed gently as he returned to Kestrel's side, the pair forming the 'wisdom' part of Lord Lucien's impartial assessors. "I agree. This abnormal behavior warrants a hypothesis reaching abhorrent heights."

"Fear is a fiend that hides in the shadows," Kestrel said between deep, slowly drawn breaths. "The Fallen Host spread their repugnance with no need for collectors to break from soul reaping. That is all they exist to do."

Alex's dark stare prickled Raven's skin. Musing in silence, she eyed her team. A powerful true blood had to be controlling the collectors. That was the only plausible answer. She'd never thought such collaboration was possible.

"I feel a faint vampiric presence," Kestrel announced, her brow twitching and crinkling. "I can't…it is masked by the collectors and the present Fallen Host."

Alex's gaze swung over Kestrel in alarm. "How many Fallen?"

Shaking her head, Kestrel inhaled another deep breath, using the air's molecular structure as a means of detection. Long ago, the huntress had hyper-sensitized her body to levels exceeding any other hunter. Raven often wondered if Kestrel could feel Master Jonathan's cloaked aura, but had never asked.

The Silent Vesper's First Officer released the air from her lungs. "Too many. They've been baited here. Attracted by something I cannot sense. No—"

She gasped as her golden eyes shot open, and, at the same time, a sharp pain pierced Raven's heart.

"*He is here!*" Raven slumped forward, clutching her chest.

Catching her by the shoulder, Alex demanded, "Which 'he' do you mean?"

"Not Hawkiel," Raven whispered, struggling for breath.

The wind gusted, billowing black velvet about them and carrying the stench of sulfur. Raven's chest pain arced south—toward the docks off the Thames. "They've created a veil to welcome *him*. It's flowing in off the water."

"That doesn't explain the collectors creeping over a decrepit graveyard empty of souls." Lior cast his gaze at the church. "Look. You can see them. A scorched haze hugging the earth."

"Rain is coming." Kestrel straightened. "Given the legion of Fallen, a downpour in this evil miasma may be enough to block the human creator's light from shining here at all."

His stare absent and locked onto a spot near his feet, Alex pulled his silver coin from his pocket. As he flicked Hercules over Zeus, Raven mentally envisioned the gears of his mind grinding through something they'd never seen before. Were the murders connected to a vampire working with soul collectors? Or were the collectors working for the Fallen Host in preparation of their creator's arrival? No vampire, true blood or not, had seen *him* since before Lord Lucien the Eternal signed the Treaty.

Nodding to herself in agreement, Raven said, "We need to assess the vampire threat and risk, *now*. Lord Lucien must have suspected this possibility or he wouldn't have selected you three to join me."

Snatching his coin mid-flip, Alex's eyes narrowed. "He requested this grouping?"

Raven nodded.

"Two Commanders. Two First Officers. Representatives from each squad? Est Judicium et Prudentia?"

"You said it earlier," she replied through clenched teeth.

"I was jesting," Alex replied. "I assumed you chose us."

Shaking her head, Raven said, "I expected a quick in and out order—but I also didn't expect to find…*this*." She tossed her hand at the tainted holy land.

Lior and Kestrel exchanged a dark glance. Pulling her cloak over her shoulders, Kestrel asked, "Shall we investigate the docks, Commanders?"

Alex said, "No," as Raven said, "Aye."

With a reverent nod to Alex, Lior and Kestrel deferred to Raven. "As you wish, High Commander."

"Lior," Raven said, "use your sight to maintain a safe distance from the Fallen. Do not linger."

"Ma'am." The two First Officers kicked off the roof and crossed Fashion Street as blackened specters on high.

"You shouldn't have sent them there." Alex tossed his chin south and pocketed his coin. "It's risky to investigate the docks if that's where your heart's pointing."

"You wish to discuss topics they cannot overhear, correct?" Raven presented two Hilja rings. Once both rings contacted their skin and were activated, she added, "Lord Lucien selected this pairing given Lior's sensitivity to the Fallen Hosts' auras, Kestrel for her adaptability and environmental detection skills, and you for your fairness to check me."

"Check you?"

"Coming here was a risk he allowed based on a pang in my heart and you understand what that means."

"But this is unprecedented—"

"Aye. And he can't issue a controversial order if I'm sensing only the Fallens' movements. If there's no vampiric involvement—"

"Then we shouldn't be here at all." Alex scoffed and tapped his foot impatiently. "What are you thinking?"

"He made a good call. I don't know what's happening here."

"There's a lot of death," Alex muttered, glancing around at nothing in particular. He refocused dark, needling eyes on Raven. "Kestrel felt a vampire. And the collectors? You know that's not normal behavior."

Raven allowed her gaze to drift over Alex's shoulder. One block up from White's Row sat a courtyard and stacked, small-roomed dwellings off Dorsett Street. A pale face appeared in the narrow, dark maw. Raven's heart stopped. A foreign, gurgling noise came from her throat.

Alex whisked around and followed her gaze. The pale girl there smirked at him and withdrew into the black veil.

"Sa...Salea?" Alex's voice was a bare whisper.

Raven darted past him. His hand flashed out and caught her as she jumped. With a surprised cry, she swung back and crashed into the pub's stone and brick façade. Alex pulled her up and growled, "Don't blindly chase her into there."

"*But why is she here?*" Raven yelled, her heart racing. She ripped free of Alex's grip, absently rubbing the ache in her shoulder from the impact and turning in panicked circles. "*Why is Salea here? In this place?*"

Alex planted firm hands on Raven's shoulders. Calmly—too calmly—he leaned in and said, "This is why Lord Lucien requested me. You must remain objective. She might be here for *him*."

Raven glared at him and then in the direction of the docks. She wriggled out of his grip and slapped a communicator on her jaw. "Kestrel. Lior. Return to my location, *now*."

"What—"

"*Shut up*," Raven seethed. "And keep your hands off me, *Commander*."

She removed her Hilja ring and held her palm out for Alex's. Her entire body was hot. Her blood was boiling. Her heart was beating too fast. Kestrel and Lior would notice. She should care, but she didn't. She hadn't glimpsed that pale face in centuries.

Kestrel touched down silently with her cloak flourishing behind her as a golden cape. An instant later, Lior landed flashing silvery blue. Both wore the shock of alarm, their darkened eyes glittering from the implied promise of action.

To Kestrel, Raven commanded, "Feel out the vampiric presence, there." She pointed down Dorsett Street.

Flinging black velvet off her shoulders, Kestrel bared her skin to the prickly Whitechapel night. Her skin tensed and lifted into tiny bumps. The eternally infantile skin edging the silver vines engraved in her belly reddened—burnt raw. She grimaced. "It feels—"

"Angelic?" Raven interrupted, bitingly and unintentionally snappy.

Lior directed his concern to the dark courtyard. He immediately flinched. "It stings!"

Swallowing hard, Raven turned her back to them and shot a sideways glare at Alex. She opened Animus Hollow. "Hold position until I return."

Alex caught her arm and nodded to Kestrel. "Under authorization of the Crimson Guard, you are to accompany High Commander Hawkings and accept any order she receives as your own."

☽ ✳ ☾

Raven paced the cobalt glass tile outside Snowblood Square. Her return had caught the Elders in mid-bath and, since they already believed London was a waste of time, they saw no urgent need to call a meeting to order. Kestrel had asked Raven to get a status update several times, but she was too upset and distracted to make the call.

Centuries had passed with no word from Salea. In between missions and her duties, Raven had searched for her, but Salea had managed to remove the tracer in her Vampiric Star—a component smaller than a grain of sand—and thrown it into the Pacific Ocean.

Raven spent decades tracking *fish*. One ate another that ate another until the last one died and drifted with the currents until a pecking bird brought the tracker inland. Only after it found its way into a human did Raven confirm what Salea had done—but never why.

Raven stopped pacing and huffed loudly. Leaning against Snowblood Square's seamless marble exterior, Kestrel crossed her arms and watched her closely, surely confused, but hiding it well.

Why had Salea hidden from her? Why was she in London? What was she doing in Whitechapel?

All of the answers scared Raven, but none more than the last. Dorsett Street was infamous—human constables only patrolled it in pairs or groups. Without sufficient evidence of rogue activity, all members of the Vampiric Nation were restricted from entering places where fear that thick lurked.

Raven glared at the Vampiric High Council's meeting hall, willing the entrance to appear. As she swung her back to it, Kestrel whistled. A black oval gouged the marble. Raven snapped her fingers for Kestrel to follow and marched into pitch so dark that the most perceptive true blood couldn't see through it.

They stopped at the center of the chamber and knelt according to tradition. A herald draped in black announced the Elders and commenced the meeting by order of Lord Lucien the Eternal.

High Elder Lord Corben stared down his nose, as usual. Raven wanted to slap the smug look off his face. She needed to calm down. By now, the Elders had detected the impatience in her heartbeat and her report would make things much worse.

"Greetings High Commander Hawkings," Lady Lucasta, the gilded lady, welcomed. "You've returned swifter than we expected. We await your report."

Grinding her teeth, Raven dropped her fist to her side and stood. Kestrel remained on bended knee. "London's East End is crawling with collectors displaying behaviors we've never seen before. They're creeping over holy land to interrupt the compulsion we feel to stay away. Lior confirmed that the signal is reduced and Kestrel determined that a legion of Fallen Host is present. The miasma is worse than I initially thought, as though meant to block the light from the human creator to form a veil under which our former commander may enter."

"We should not be there!" Lady Ambrosia sliced the air with her arm. "*He* would never appear on the heels of a vampire. Recall our hunters at once!"

"Salea is there."

A stunned charge multiplied in the ensuing silence. Finally, Lord Corben sneered, "Your human pet should have been put down long ago. Kill her now and spare us the continued torment of this child vampire."

"Is she responsible for the killings?" The quiet question came from Lord Endymion, his peridot eyes slipping from Raven to Lord Corben deliberately.

"Does it matter?" Lord Corben challenged.

"I don't know," Raven answered to Lord Endymion. "She may be responsible for some of them, yes. Or she may be there innocently. Given the scent of sulfur and the visibility of the collectors, I felt it imperative to update the High Council before proceeding to learn more."

"She was involved with Lord Connall. Her mere presence there is enough to presume guilt," Lady Ambrosia declared. "She's probably working with *him*. Terminate the girl."

"The priority should be evacuating true bloods and vampires anywhere near London. *His* arrival is a greater risk to our nation than a little girl—aligned with *him* or not," Lord Ceallach said.

"No one holds a permit to reside in London," Lady Rainne reported from the shadows of her red hood.

"Kestrel felt only Salea's vampiric presence and Lior confirmed her angelic essence. The remaining hunters can evacuate with her." Raven silently beseeched Lord Lucien.

His empty quartz crystal eyes lifted. Lord Corben began to speak, but Lord Endymion held up a silencing hand upon noticing their Eternal Lord's subtle movement.

"I call for a blind vote," Lord Lucien decreed.

The chamber immediately descended into pitch blacker than black and visually thicker than tar. His apathetic voice called, "Vote to evacuate."

Tense moments passed before he spoke again. "Vote to kill."

Precious time passed. Finally, Lord Lucien announced, "Meeting adjourned. All but High Commander Hawkings are dismissed."

Kestrel's body heat vanished from her side, and, seconds later, each Elder's restrained beam glowed to spotlight empty stations. Only Lord Lucien remained, his eyes dark as hematite.

"Do you know the secret to our votes?" he asked.

Hesitant to respond, Raven said, "You can see in any darkness, even here."

"Endymion voted to kill."

His words rammed as a shockwave. Raven couldn't think, let alone speak.

"You cannot trust your heart or eyes here. The majority voted to kill. Terminate Salea and then evacuate."

☽ ✳ ☾

The High Council's delay returned Raven and Kestrel to an empty rooftop at the Queen's Head Pub in the early morning hours. A downpour had hit in their absence. What might normally cleanse was a betrayal of filthy streets bathed in mud. The city's scent had changed to one of blood. It clung stubbornly to the air. Murder had crowned itself king for the night, and they knew exactly where to go. The scent was a red ribbon streaming from the courtyard off Dorsett.

"It's mostly human, but also male true blood," Kestrel said.

The scent gushed from the room with the broken window. The interior was dark, but Raven didn't need light to see the horror within. Turning away with a gasp, her eyes whirled skyward at swollen black clouds threatening more rain, and her mind reeled. Surely, no vampire had taken such pleasure in mutilating humans like that even during the Great Holy War.

Kestrel came away from the window in shocked silence. Blowing out another breath, Raven whispered, "That's inhumane. Did you see anything that grisly during the war?"

"No——one slash to kill, one bite to infect. Repeat." Kestrel's attention shifted to the roof. With darkening eyes and growing teeth, she nodded at the narrow building. "Commander Alexander and Lior were up there before we arrived, but they are not there now. Nor is Salea."

"You never saw butchery like that——" Raven pointed at the window, "——*ever*——before the Treaty?"

"Never." Kestrel's dark eyes gleamed with a golden arc. Throwing her cloak off her shoulders, she leaned back and added, "Master Jonathan and Lord Endymion are, perhaps, the most brutal among us, and I never saw such beastly carnage in their prey, for sport or otherwise."

The victim's blood had so thoroughly soaked her mattress that Raven heard it dripping into a massive puddle beneath the frame's wooden slats. She peered through the broken glass once more. The victim was barely recognizable as human.

"She's in her own bed," Raven whispered, chilled as she tapped the communicator and called for Alex. She tried again when he didn't respond.

"Salea looks like a helpless fourteen-year-old girl," Kestrel stated matter-of-factly. "Nary a surprise women might take pity and invite her in. A predator seeks weakness."

Kestrel bolted upright. "I felt a shudder. A chime."

"I heard it. Alex engaged the Cataclysm."

Kestrel drew the dagger sheathed under her forearm, slid a slender finger into a Hilja Ring, and tapped the center of the Vampiric Star pinned on her belt. As she shimmered into shadow, Raven followed suit and pulled her Deathscythe from her lower pocket. It looked like a curved katana handle without a guard. She clicked the mechanism trigger. Two metallic segments arced out and rotated, and the double-sided blades unfolded and locked into place.

Cloaked, they ran unseen from the courtyard to Dorsett Street and turned left. Leaping off Commercial Street, they raced across rooftops to the East London Hospital on White Chapel Road. There, three furious shadows danced on high filling the night with beastly growls and the clash of metal on metal.

Uncloaking, Raven stayed Kestrel with a hand signal. She'd never known Salea to use a blade. What was Alex hitting?

Height and musculature made Lior and Alex easy to distinguish from their smaller foe. Salea had been tall for her age with a lean body she'd never grown into. The advantageous lack of womanly curves allowed her to slip into narrow cracks or crevices too small for anyone else. She knew how to use her youthful body to gain sympathy or spark lust in her prey. She had weaponized herself long ago. Apparently, during her absence, she had taken that further than Raven imagined possible. Salea was fending off the Cataclysm with lengthened, silver claws similar to Lady Rainne's.

"Bloody hell," Raven whispered. "How did she do that?"

Kestrel nudged Raven. "We need to eliminate her. That woman's blood is all over her!"

"Salea..." Raven watched the girl land an airborne kick into Lior's chest that sent her flying at Alex. "I can't—"

As Salea dodged the Cataclysm, Alex yanked out his revolver. Kestrel shoved Raven's shoulder. "You have an order! Follow it!"

Stuck in a state of disbelief, Raven saw the scenery changing beneath her feet and felt the blow of Salea crashing into her as she landed in front of Alex. Raven met the girl's stunned eyes and swept her off her feet, falling with her to pin her into a puddle on the roof.

"W-why?" Raven cried, crossing her arms over Salea's windpipe. "Th-that's so monstrous...barbaric. It's unfathomably *evil*!"

Salea instinctively clawed for escape. "You don't know what humans are capable of," she choked out. "*They* are the evil! They're why you made me the same as the beasts who butchered my family. My mama. Papa. My brothers."

Tears slid from her frightened eyes. "You don't know anything about humans!" she screamed.

Raven loosened her hold. "Salea. Oh, Salea. I only wanted to save you."

"So did those naïve whores who invited me in." She stabbed her bladed fingers into Raven's abdomen.

"What...?" Raven was lost in Salea's blackened eyes, her crooked smile, and the searing pain of silver claws that impaled and squeezed to maximize the agony.

Howling, Raven rolled to free herself from Salea's torturous grip. Salea leapt to her feet, her mouth laughing but not her eyes. "I don't need saving, Mama Bird."

Kestrel rushed Salea from behind. Salea deflected and gained control of her dagger. Gripping Kestrel's wrist, Salea twisted in place and plunged the dagger into Kestrel's left lung. She yanked it out with a spray of blood and planted her heel in Kestrel's gut, kicking her across the rain-slicked roof.

"Day in and out, I sit in those gutters with homeless children and the cocks walk by like we're invisible."

Alex lunged and got a large gash across his chest and a heel to his groin that dropped him to his knees. Salea kept her focus on Raven.

She gestured at London in general. "All those children—abandoned, sick, suffering, starving, dying. I told them that they walked by me, I did." Puffing her chest with pride, she looked down on Raven.

"What are you talking about?" Raven cried. Bracing the gaping holes in her body, she tried to stand but merely collapsed.

"The letters. Don't you know Old Jack craves attention? He's killed others and written to the papers. I wanted in on the fun and they printed it. I told them they walk past me every day."

Salea again deflected the Cataclysm, knocked a wheezing Kestrel back with another stab to her punctured lung, and warily eyed Lior hovering in her peripheral. "Look what's become of these human weaklings. I caught my own dinner as a child. I was catching my family's dinner the day they died. These children? They're utterly helpless."

Salea bitterly spat, "Humans are pitiful things, evolving backwards. They don't give no shits about each other. Otherwise, you think Old Jack'd be having his fun? Making it this easy for me to enjoy a meal? He doesn't care about the blood, not like I do. Like *Endymion* does."

An involuntary shiver ran through Raven. Salea pointed the dagger at her and laughed again. "He never told you about me? He's a deviant; he tells it right to you. And he knows *all* the places for the best, freshest blood—like arteries instead of veins. You lot go for the jugular—why not the femoral or carotid? It's so much—"

She dodged another Cataclysm flyby and pounded her fist into Kestrel's face. As the huntress teetered backward, Lior finally lunged and caught Salea by the waist, but she twisted free and punched him in the solar plexus. She launched into the air and landed on his chest, taking him down and laughing as his ribs crunched beneath her feet.

Straddling him, she carved the dagger blade around his jaw and down his neck, watching his pained face with strange, innocent awe.

"Humans know how wonderful organ meat is, at least. I remember it. There's enough slaughterhouses 'round here to feed those helpless, starving children. Despicable wretches. I've found organ meat to be quite delectable to the vampire palate, as well, especially the spleen."

She moaned. "Oh! The liver and kidneys, too—or, when it's ripe: the uterus."

Smug eyes lifted to Raven. "I bet Endymion knows all about that, too, but he'll never tell you. You're his clay doll. He molds you, plays with you, fu—"

Kestrel grabbed a fistful of long brown hair and smashed a knee into Salea's face. She jerked the girl up by her bloodstained lace chemise and tossed her to Alex. Salea caught her balance surprisingly fast and kicked a foot backward before Alex could trap her.

"Salea! Stop!" Raven yelled. "Why do this to yourself?"

The girl froze. In that moment, barely dressed, bloody and dripping wet, coated in mud, and hair matted into chunky locks, Salea looked every bit the helpless, victimized girl. The adult woman's chemise she wore was three sizes too large with large gaps that revealed her boney frame and flat chest.

Alex signaled for attention and stepped back to ready the Cataclysm again, but Raven silently beseeched him. His reluctance thick on his face, he stood down, sharing wary glances with Lior and Kestrel.

Salea stood, unmoving, hanging her head between sagging shoulders. Eyes downcast, she dragged her feet toward Raven. "My family died. You turned me into a monster and fed me angel blood for a hundred years. Then I was a tool used to procure peace."

She stopped about four feet in front of Raven. "What happened to me?"

"Have men hurt you?" Raven asked, sitting up and pleading. "Please, tell me. What did Lord Connall do? What has Lord Endymion done?"

The girl's hollow laugh echoed throughout the hospital block. "Men? They can't touch me. You think I'd let any filthy human hands grab me like they grab those whores? No. No—"

Looking up, she met Raven's concerned gaze with seething hatred. "*You broke your promise!*" she screamed, flying at Raven and ramming into her so hard the Deathscythe clattered to the roof. "*Only one man ever hurt me and you promised to kill him, but now you call him Master!*"

"I'm sorry!" Raven cried, struggling to hold onto Salea, but getting pushed closer to the roof's edge by the girl's chaotic movements. "I didn't want you to suffer! I couldn't abandon you to a cruel world——"

"Don't spit that crap at me. You needed proof of peaceful coexistence." She scoffed and flashed her metallic nails. "I've been experimenting in this cruel world. Angel blood is capable of extraordinary things, and I've discovered many anatomical differences between this body and the one I was exploring before your boys and their toys showed up."

She glared at the trio inching toward her. She shoved Raven over the edge, forcing her to leap across the street. "These lovely things, for instance——"

She whipped around in a half circle, splaying her silver claws wide. "I studied that weapon—the one called Rainne Blood Pathos—and deduced how Lucifer gave her these glorious hands."

Over her shoulder, she called, "Mama Raven, did you know angel blood alters our physiology? It takes time and work, but it's worth it." She lunged at the trio.

Raven's heart sank. Like the Cataclysm, Salea's claws left silver debris embedded in deep wounds resistant to healing. Black stars flickered in her visual field. She'd barely had the strength to make that jump and land it.

She gasped for breath as the hunters grappled with fighting a smaller and faster opponent. Alex was too close to launch the Cataclysm and knew his gun would draw attention. Salea tucked in close to Kestrel so she couldn't draw her long sword, and Lior wasn't armed, so she repeatedly kicked him to keep him at bay.

Salea had known from the start that quiet, watchful Lior was her biggest threat. The Chthonic Knights were ruthless, travelled lightly, and preferred close quarter combat. Lior ducked and dodged into a safe position. He loosened the clasp on his cloak and let it slide silently from his shoulders into his hand. He crept forward, keeping Raven in Salea's sightline behind him.

Despite all her taunting, Salea truly did view Raven as a second mother; otherwise, she'd be dead on that hospital roof instead of injured and watching from a distance. As Lior came up, slow and steady, Salea's attention kept slipping to Raven and that was enough to give Lior an opening.

He threw his cloak over Salea on one side and ducked to the other to rise quickly behind her. Kestrel withdrew her sword and Alex dropped low, readying a dirk pulled from his boot.

Salea tore through the velvet cloak faster than they expected. Spinning on her heel, she jerked Lior into her knee and shattered his already broken breastbone. She threw him like a ragdoll across the roof, caught Alex with a roundhouse kick that slammed him down with a sickening thud, and then charged Kestrel, ramming the heel of her palm into the base of her nose with a crack that sent her reeling. Salea swept up Raven's Deathscythe and launched into the air. The double blades limned a wide arc and came down as she landed on top of Lior.

"Night-night, My Light," she whispered. Shining a triumphant glare at Kestrel, she caught Lior's rolling crown of bloody curls with her foot.

Beastly growls crawled over the rooftop as Kestrel and Alex both lunged. Raven screamed for them to stop, but Salea was already pivoting with both the dagger and the Deathscythe at the ready. The dagger landed in Kestrel's thigh alongside a heel that crushed her kneecap and dropped her in place. Alex narrowly dodged the Deathscythe's blades and caught the handle where the mechanism locked. He quickly hit the trigger and the weapon immediately began compressing in on itself. The curved shafts rotated into an arc and the folding blades severed Salea's fingers.

The weapon and her silver-tipped digits fell to the rain soaked roof. Wailing like a scared little girl, Salea grabbed her bloody hand in shock. She whimpered and cowered under Alex's monstrous shadow.

He hesitated to look at Raven.

"You *are* daft!" Salea laughed and leapt across Whitechapel Road. She landed beside Raven. "I am but a child compared to you ancient lot. Yet what have you accomplished for it?"

Yanking the dagger from her thigh, Kestrel growled, "Kill her, High Commander!"

"Raven? Kill me?" The way Salea looked down at Raven made her feel physically ill. "She is my mother."

Salea knelt and curled Raven's hands over her fingerless nubs. "You'll always protect me. I know it, deep in m——"

A single shot rang out, its report ricocheting down the narrow streets and alleys. Salea collapsed into Raven's lap.

Alex landed beside her on a faint burst of black powder infused with grisly rain. Hollowed out, Raven absently stroked Salea's bloody hair. The bullet hole was warm.

Raven's eyes burned. Her heart ached. She was sinking, drowning, choking. Saying nothing, Alex draped his arm across her shoulders and sat with her. Kestrel limped to Lior's body and sank beside him, cradling his head to her breast and folding in on herself.

"It'll be quieter now," Alex whispered.

Nodding, Raven sniffled and leaned against him. He rested his head against hers. They sat like that for a long time. The gunfire had brought humans out to investigate, but they'd never know what had happened.

Kestrel eventually rose and dutifully collected the weaponry on the hospital's roof. She wrapped Lior's head and body in his shredded cloak, and heaved him over her shoulder. Leaping over the street to join them, she silently watched Raven's bloodied fingers pet Salea.

"I'll burn our biological trace off the roof," Alex said, his voice empty and not wholly committed. Raven half-heartedly grunted. Kestrel said nothing.

"Could you have killed her?" he asked quietly.

"I don't know."

Sighing, Alex hesitantly said, "She's not dead—completely—yet. The Chthonic Knights could put her into eternal sleep at the Arc of Celestial Night."

Raven shook her head. "She doesn't deserve that."

Alex's chest heaved. "She's damaged because of us. She deserves a chance at rehabilitation. If she ever wakes up…we know what she needs now."

"No disrespect, Commander, but it was a kill order," Kestrel said, stern and bitter. "And under your own order, I am to kill her if the High Commander cannot."

"Master Jonathan killed her family." Raven's fingers curled in Salea's dirty hair. "She never had a chance at anything good in life. Commander Alexander will withdraw his order."

Reluctantly nodding, he said, "Consider a peaceful dream as the final way to save her. I'll pull my order as long as you clear this with Lord Lucien privately."

"And what of Lior?" Kestrel asked sharply.

"Incinerate him," Raven replied. "We don't bury our dead."

"The High Council will be unhappy with losing his skillset," Kestrel replied.

"Aye," Raven whispered. "The High Council will be unhappy about many things tonight."

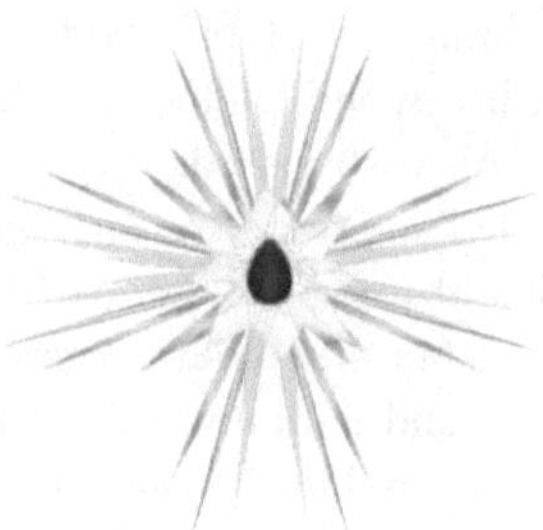

Chapter Twelve: Killing Them Softly

I

Orison Crossing, Summer 2006

Arms crossed, Alex shifted uncomfortably against the biting iron bars of the mansion's gate. He'd been antsy all day, foreign in his own skin. A clement breeze dusted his cheekbones and danced through his golden spikes frosted by silver moonlight. Scents of the green—of grasses, holly, and maple leaves—delivered a respite until headlights flashed through the trees. Two materializing shimmers escorted Eric's car up the twisty private drive. Alex swallowed his usual quip and straightened. Jonathan was driving and Paresh was slumped against Eric in the backseat.

"Open the gate," Raven ordered on the communicator, which meant she was wearing a Hilja ring.

"Yeah, yeah," he replied, "I was getting to it."

The gate creaked open as the car crawled closer. Alex held up a hand to catch Eric's attention. "May we speak privately?"

Darkness arced over Eric's face. He tossed his chin in a half nod. "At the house."

Respectfully bowing his head as the black BMW coupe rolled by, Alex slipped on a Hilja ring. Paresh's eyes fluttered open and she mouthed, "I got you back."

Raven smacked the grin off his lips before it formed, snapping, "Whatever you did not do, don't ever not do it again, got it?"

"Man, what the hell, Goody?" he whined, rubbing the sting from his cheek.

"Close the gates and join us." Raven didn't break her stride with Kestrel on her heel.

When he caught up to Raven, he whispered, as lowly as vampiricly possible, "Lord Lucien is here. He's spoken with the Elders and is waiting to meet with Master Jonathan."

Surprise seared a path for anger through her aura. *"And you're at the gate?"*

"Orders, Goody. Always orders." He patted her shoulder and raced ahead to the mansion's veranda where he signaled for Seneca to tell Lord Lucien of their new arrivals.

Jonathan instructed Paresh to be quiet before they got out of the car. Sluggish, but able to walk on her own, Paresh aimed a glittering smile at Alex and broke away from her escort to hug him. Her essence momentarily stole his reality and eased him into a mental utopia. It dissipated as she leaned back and bit her lower lip as her gaze swung over the mansion's façade. "Wow…"

"Come along." Jonathan gently guided Paresh into the house while visually directing Alex to the car. "He's waiting."

In the driver's seat, Eric impatiently drummed the steering wheel with his thumbs. Following Jonathan, Raven passed Alex and bit through clenched teeth, "Do not do what you did not do before. You are her security detail, so be quick and meet us in the basement."

"Yes, ma'am," he replied, already jogging to the car. He climbed into the passenger seat and shivered under Eric's chilly stare. He activated a button to block outbound sound and removed his ring.

"I'm listening." Eric's voice affected bored apathy eerily similar to Lord Lucien's.

Quickly losing his nerve, Alex searched the dashboard for his voice. It squeaked when he found it. "First: I messed up and I'm sorry. No excuses."

He paused to assess Eric. Cold blue eyes? Check. Face of stone? Check. Grim line of a mouth? Check. If he donned a cowl and cape, he'd be a perfect fit for Gotham.

Alex coughed to clear his throat. Eric remained silent.

"I, uh…" His thoughts were racing away from him. He needed to catch up. "At some point since we met, I earned your trust. Maybe it's my position, history with Master Jonathan, or because I saved her life, but that's not what I lost. You still trust me, which means it's worse…I disappointed you."

Eric closed his eyes with a sigh and pinched the bridge of his nose. "Alex—"

"Please! To everyone else she's a thing—" Alex shook his hands for emphasis. "*Everyone* blathers on about the Sacred Vessel, our mother, the Second New Age, her blood, blah, blah, blah—but, to *me?*"

He pressed his palm to his chest. "She is beyond *all* that I've ever known. She is special and I need to protect her. To preserve her as Paresh, *the girl*, so she's never lost in what she's become or how this nation tries to shape her."

Eric's crystalline orbs rolled skyward. "You're a piece of work, you know that?"

"My divine intervention is for protection. I need to devote myself to her." A somber, yet hopeful smile brightened Alex's cheeks. "She's a marvel."

"And she's already demanded to have you back," Eric replied. "Which makes this moot."

Alex's heart sang louder than the opera's fat lady. Eric leaned back against the headrest and gripped the steering wheel with white-knuckled fists. He sighed. "Jonathan keeps telling me I need to relax. He's worried I'm going to lose it, but how can I possibly relax under these circumstances? I need you on the same page with us and not running behind our backs."

An uncomfortable silence followed. Alex could help with Eric's mood, but that meant igniting his wrath again. He reluctantly held out a slim, silicon-coated vial between his fingers. An air bubble floated to the top of the red fluid preserved inside.

Eric's aura squeezed Alex's throat. "What is that?" he growled, voice raspy and eyes darkening to inky black.

"Without her blood, the beast will wear you down and you will lose control, but you can't drink from her while she's this weak—"

The grip clenched into a chokehold. Eying the sharp teeth glistening behind Eric's upper lip, Alex gurgled and waved in surrender. The hold loosened—slightly.

"It's from…the urn…we collected," Alex choked out. "It will…stop your spiral…for now."

"Why are you carrying it with you?" Eric snatched the vial and sniffed it. He released Alex from his invisible hold.

Black and white sparks streaked his peripheral as Alex gasped for air. "Just…consider drinking it—for clarity if nothing else."

Reverently bowing his head and palming his heart, Alex met Eric's bloodshot gaze through hooded eyes. "We need your clear-headed leadership, *my lord*. More than you know."

"But why do you have it?" Eric asked, insistent.

"It stuns those who have yet to receive it, an advantage when engaging an enemy—"

"You've *weaponized* her blood?" Scowling, Eric gripped the tiny vial in his fist so hard Alex feared it would shatter. "Are you as dumb as you act? Have you forgotten what her blood did to Donovan or what Donovan did to Jonathan? Are you incapable of seeing the pain he carries from a wound that isn't healing because of *your* weapon?"

Cool glass pressed against Alex's back. The armrest dug into his spine. The car suddenly felt cramped. He was trapped and Eric seemed oblivious to the strength of the power he commanded.

Alex steadied his resolve to act like the VaSH Commander that he was—despite how little he felt like it—and said, "It's a strategic risk. Her blood possesses a distinctive scent that none of our clove or fire oils and waxes can mask. Those who have received it smell differently from those who have not. I would not use it recklessly; its effect will stun an enemy long enough to detain or kill, and Donovan's situation was very different. He took more than a drop."

Eric opened his fist. The vial rolled in his palm.

"We must use all advantages for her safety…per Lord Lucien," Alex added quietly.

Something dark and impatient exploded inside Eric. He twisted off the lid and downed the contents. A hint of chemical preservative lingered in the air. Eric melted into his leather seat, rolling his neck along the headrest. Without tension both holding him together and tearing him apart, he sagged and spoke in a dazed tone, saying, "You're going to be the VaSH Co-High Commander. Guard Paresh with every ounce of your life."

"I promise," Alex whispered, tears blurring his vision. "From the moment I saw her rise with new life, my loyalty was hers. I will never fail her."

"Well you won't live long if you do," Eric said, "so don't disappoint me again."

☾ ✳ ☽

Cloaked on the front veranda, relief trickled into Raven's belly as Eric accepted the vial from Alex. She'd safely delivered Master Jonathan and Paresh to the basement, where the girl had collapsed into Eric's bed and her lords swiftly approved her main VaSH assignment request. They'd dismissed her moments ago to meet privately.

Eric squeezed the steering wheel, visibly relaxing into his leather seat. This would be good for Alex. He needed to be liked, to fulfill his role, to get that attaboy pat on the back—the validation of a job well done. Now he could focus and collect a mind unnecessarily scattered amongst duties, loyalties, chaos, guilt, and love.

Guilt.

She thrust her head against the siding and leaned back, crossing her arms. Her stubborn stupidity had sentenced Alex to an eternity as the Second Born's plaything. His shame was her blame—something Master Jonathan had enjoyed flaunting and forcing her to claim while training. He'd tease offerings of freedom, but each one was a lie of secrecy, a "test" of the VaSH High Commander's ability to keep confidential information, and she'd never betrayed the knowledge to anyone—not to Endymion, not to Alex.

It's bullshit.

She grunted at the sunny distraction cautiously smiling in Eric's passenger seat. How could she not think about him now? Love complicated everything. Regardless of how it started, Alex loved Master Jonathan. He'd fight a horde of demons to protect him, but he'd never ask him to free his heart—and yet, he'd offered it to her anyway. She grinned involuntarily. He was her sun.

She gnawed her lip. Endymion's arrogant eyes lifted in her mind. He was her moon, closer in orbit and influentially dominant, but Alex—

"Oh bloody stars!" She slapped her cheeks and groaned into her hands. "Stop it! Stop it—"

A vibration in the security net quickly realigned her priorities. Technically, it was brief enough to be one of Paresh's critters—after mustering an insurmountable amount of courage to approach a mansion full of true bloods, of course—but Lord Lucien's presence was too coincidental.

She leapt down the stairs and charged Eric's car. They were finishing up and he was opening his door. She flew over the roof and shoved him back inside by the shoulder, cramming herself into the backseat. The door slammed shut and the interior flashed blue.

Eric yelled an obscenity as Alex screeched and stared at her like she'd lost her mind. "What gives, Goody?"

She clamped her hand over his mouth. "Someone's entered the security net near the Animus Hollow exit in the grove."

"Lord Lucien?" Alex mumbled beneath her palm. She shook her head.

"I'm his return escort to the Arc of True Blood. Master Jonathan sent me up to check on you since Lord Lucien came to meet with Eric, too."

Eric peered through the passenger window at the French doors standing open to the foyer. "How close is Paresh to Ambrosia?"

Alex followed his gaze and peeled Raven's hand off his mouth. "Ambrosia's in the first floor study on the left. Two hunters, Lord Raiden, and the foyer floor stand between her and your former living quarters."

"Paresh is the priority," Eric said tightly.

"Understood. We must move quietly," Raven added. She tapped the communicator on her jaw.

"My lord? Infiltration may be in progress; my communicator is open. Alex and Eric are with me shielded in his car. Is Master Jonathan still with you?" Raven released her breath at his affirmative response. "Please have everyone remain where they are and maintain the secrecy of your presence. Order Kestrel to post hunters at all basement access points."

"Did you just give orders to Lord Lucien?" Alex asked, again looking at her like she was crazy.

"Hey there new VaSH Co-High Commander—welcome to your new job and authority level." Raven squished his cheeks. "But, this is not the time—"

"Jonathan knows every entrance and exit in this house, including the hidden ones," Eric interrupted. "They'll be fine."

"Can you detect our cloaked hunters?" Raven asked him.

"Not to the extent that you'd like, but I'll tear them to pieces after you detect them."

Raven shook her head. "I can't. No true blood can."

"All your technology and you can't...?" Eric groaned as Raven shook her head. "Okay, there's, ah...it's an electrical odor—I can smell it."

Raven mentally ran scenarios. "'Kay, got it. Exit calmly—normally. Alex goes inside, quietly notifies Lord Raiden and moves his hunters. You and I will take a stroll to the orchard. I'll call in perimeter hunters as back up, if need—"

Another vibration hit the security net. "I swear it's like a bug in spider thread. They're baiting me."

"Do you have Hilja Rings?" Eric visually probed the shadows clinging to the house.

"It'll be a crapshoot since they cancel each other out," Alex said, "and they'll likely have them, too."

Raven patted his shoulder, an unintentional attaboy. "Yeah, so listen for them."

Alex capped her hand with a squeeze and then dug a ring from his pocket. She did the same and produced one for Eric, as well. "Hopefully we can do this quickly and quietly."

"But if the shit blows?" Alex's fingers twitched on the door latch.

"Take them all out," Raven said, gaining a nod from Eric.

"The mansion's survived Jonathan and fires," he said. "Paresh is all that matters."

Eric stretched one long leg out at a time and turned with a grin, his hand extended to Raven. "A gentleman helps a lady out of the car."

Alex guffawed loudly and slapped his thigh. "Laaaaady!"

Rolling her eyes, she pursed her lips and joined Eric. They veered right to walk around the grand house, serenaded by chirping crickets and whirring frogs. Eric slipped his hands into his pockets, his dark eyes reflecting the moon.

He was far more alert than he appeared. The power rippling off him triggered Raven's fight or flight response. She counted each lungful in and out to force herself to stay at his side and not jolt into a run. An audible breath skimmed her teeth.

"Not used to being hunted?" Eric asked, unaware of his effect on her.

"More like not used to moving like a snail." Raven nodded at the decaying garden with the dry and cracked scalloped fountain. "I bet that was pretty once."

"It was." He contemplated the weeping willows with an unreadable expression. "Do you think Paresh fell asleep?"

She shot him a questioning look. "You know Lord Lucien's secret, right?"

"He does, Commander." Lord Lucien's voice filtered up from the secured basement.

Eric grumbled, "No sense answering."

"Paresh is asleep; your worry is not needed here." Each of Lord Lucien's apathetic words ruffled Eric's aura. The night painted the hard line of his jaw a moonlit gray as Paresh's blood added a pulsing strength to his already overwhelming energy.

The grass was slick with dew, the humid night air clingy with warm, sticky fingers that tugged uncomfortably on her lightweight flannel. She peeled it off as they rounded the rear corner and knotted it at her waist. The orchard appeared at last, looming dark and twisted beyond the haunted garden.

Eric stopped suddenly, radiating alarm that froze her breath in her throat. Swollen veins encircled his dark irises and pupils, his nostrils flared, and his fangs glinted against his bottom lip. As his focus flicked over every shifting shadow, his aura crushed the air from her lungs and locked her into a silent battle for air.

He drew in slow, deep breaths until he targeted a spot halfway between the house and garden. There was a shimmer and then he was gone.

Raven dropped to her knees, sucking air into her burning lungs, more shocked at the blur that was Eric than the humanoid outline materializing. She jumped up and rushed after him, crimson swallowing her sight as she gasped.

"It's Skyvania!" she growled, too far away from Eric's Hilja Ring to interact with hers, but he wasn't the only one listening. She tugged a dagger from her boot. It carved a path ahead of Eric and sank into Skyvania's calf, releasing her blood scent.

The hobbled rogue grimaced and hit the switch on her wrist to re-cloak, but she underestimated Eric's speed and power. The instant her fingers slipped over the cloaking mechanism, he lunged and knocked her flat, her form glitching in and out of the visible spectrum. Her head bounced off the grass and long white hair flailed from the red hood of her Aegis Cloak. An angry, powder blue gaze latched onto Raven when she came skidding to halt on her knees, hinged silver loop in hand. Eric roughly flipped Sky onto her stomach and pinned her arms behind her back.

Catching Eric's nod at the onyx ring on the rogue's pale finger, Raven asked, "Who's with you tonight, Sky?"

"Nallura ordered me to check in with you!" Skyvania huffed. "It's chaotic not knowing proper protocol for this. I needed to get your attention quietly."

"You think I'm buying that?" Clasping the silver ring to bind her wrists, Raven scoffed. "*Commander* Nallura would've killed a known traitor like you on sight, as ordered."

"So why aren't you?" Skyvania challenged. "I swear I'm here on orders."

"Uh-huh, me, too—" Raven's attention jerked to the telltale crash of window glass.

Skyvania slipped free of Raven's grasp and rolled under Eric, pulling him off center. She bucked violently, her skull smashing into Eric's nose and tossing him off. Landing upright on her knees, she was slow to rise with the dagger in her calf, but she managed a few pathetic steps before Eric clutched a handful of grass-stained hair.

Raven yanked the dagger free and plunged the blade directly into Skyvania's heart. She tugged the bejeweled handle as the rogue huntress collapsed at her feet and the dagger came free. "Enough distraction. The main event's in the house."

Raven unclasped Skyvania's cloak and flared it about her shoulders, noting that despite the black and silvery-blue Chthonic Knights' uniform, Sky's sheathed daggers bore the Crimson Guard's insignia. She cleaned her blade on Skyvania's pants, scoffing in disgust. "One rogue terminated: the former Chthonic Knight Auxiliary Officer. No response required; we're coming in," she reported to Lord Lucien.

Transfixed on the crimson bloom over Skyvania's breast, Eric stood in silence. She couldn't read his aura, but the disturbed stillness within his gaze spoke of other blades and deaths playing in his mind. Molly. Paresh. His. He winced when she touched his shoulder.

"She helped Donovan escape the holding cells," he stated, not needing confirmation.

Raven nodded at the rear service door. "She was stalling us. A decoy."

"The house is too quiet," Eric said, surveying the rows of dark windows that spanned the three main levels.

"I assure you it is not," Lord Lucien replied clearly.

"The house is shielded—are you..." Raven's voice trailed at the worry that suddenly shadowed Eric's visage. "Is Pare—"

"No concerns, Commander."

"Aye, my lord." With another pat to Eric's shoulder, Raven skipped into a jog. "If Sky came prepared to die, a COMS VIP must be here."

"Come this way." Eric tapped her elbow as he ran past, retracing their steps around the side of the big house.

"But—"

"Trust me." He ran ahead and stopped at a seamless section of white painted boards. His long fingers probed the bottom slats. "We almost walled it up—a hidden servant entrance. No one's used it since the 1930s. Jonathan's probably the only one inside who knows it exists. It opens into a stairwell that connects the third floor with the first floor service hall. There are hidden exits all the way to the kitchen."

"Family of secrets?" Raven asked, sheathing her dagger.

"They were hiding things long before they had to hide me." Following an audible *click*, he swung the door open and ushered her into an angled and cramped vestibule. Smoke-stained white paint curled off the walls and ceiling, carpeting both the steep wooden stairs winding up the left side and the dimly lit passage leading off to the right.

Preternatural howls vibrated the walls and set her nerves alight. Ancient memory surfaced with naked, mutilated bodies writhing in mud and blood to the tune of war's brutal beat. Wings flapped, swords clanged, and teeth gnashed. Growls and screams tangled with searing light and choking dark.

Narrowly resisting the urge to cover her ears and shrink into nonexistence, she flattened a tentative hand on the wall. "I've never…the house, itself, is screaming."

Eric quickly shouldered past her and dipped beneath deep shadows thrown by dimly lit art deco wall sconces. The house shook under a booming thud. The shriek that followed was a portent of death.

Dread's icy fingers clawed up Raven's spine. An involuntary shiver ran head to toe, finally spurring her feet into moving to where Eric was kneeling behind a hinged panel.

"The damn mechanism is jammed." Eric ran his hands through his hair. "If it's as bad as it sounds, they're going to break through the floor. The western wing isn't reinforced like the vaults."

"They'll land in your quarters?" Internally berating herself for the stupid question, she shooed him back and kicked a booted heel at the hinges.

Eric rammed his shoulder into the locking mechanism and the splintered panel opened into the first floor's main hall. It was empty. They ran along the velvety cream and maroon carpet leading to the foyer.

The bulk of the fight seemed centered there. Growls and crashes swallowed most individual voices, but one in particular opened a rift in Eric's aura and tipped ice water down Raven's spine.

"*Donovan!*" The growl vibrated low in Eric's throat. His body tensed, ready to kill.

Grabbing his arm, Raven warned, "And likely Corben, at the very least. Know what you're running into."

She pointed two fingers at her eyes and then one at her chest. Eric's jaw bulged at the hinge and his brow dipped deep, but he relented and let her slink by. She hugged the wall and stopped behind the right side of the foyer's twin stairs where the carpet met black and white tiles.

The rolling baritone of Donovan's laugh was equal parts familiar and foreign as his cowboy boots slid and scuffled for footing. Fearing Eric might fling himself into the unknown, willingly sacrificing himself to end a singular threat, she threw her arm out and was surprised to find him against the wall beside her, eyes closed, scouting with his aura.

Beyond Donovan, Lord Raiden's seething accusations of betrayal and lost honor were met by a sneer from Corben and Ambrosia's simultaneous haughty snort. Raven sensed others with them—unknown in name, number, or status—and wondered where Alex was.

"Most of the house is locked down with your hunters holding position," Eric said, edging closer to peer past her into the foyer. Motioning for him to wait, she scooted to the corner to do the visual check instead. Power aside, Master Jonathan had only recently taught Eric how to form mental blueprints.

A body swiped her cheek and crashed into the opposite wall. She glimpsed Donovan, the ecstasy of battle lighting his face despite the crimson trickling from his mouth and gashes healing under his shredded black shirt.

She ducked before he saw her. "Donovan's behind us, front corner, on our left—"

The crumpled form across from her wore a uniform of black and red. Dark clots matted once golden spikes and bright red streamed from too many wounds on too many vital body parts.

Where's your pulse? Panic held her voice hostage. Hellfire roasted her heart. She reached out—

A strong hand jerked her chin sideways and plunged her into the dark eyes of a scowling demon. "Clear your head," Eric growled, "and save Alex before he dies."

He shot into the foyer with a beastly roar and slammed into Donovan. The bastard yelped in surprise. Precious seconds passed before Eric's words sank in.

Nodding to herself, Raven crept across the carpet to hook Alex's bootlaces with her fingers. Bodies crashed through the glass French doors while she dragged Alex clear of the foyer's sightline.

A relieved breath skimmed her lips. He looked like hell, but he had a pulse, weak though it was.

"Wake up!" she hissed into his ear. Blood slicked her hands as they scrabbled over his body seeking mortal wounds. Her fingers sank into a hole in his back. He groaned and his eyes rolled open for an instant.

Smudging tears from her cheeks with the back of her hand, she said, "My lord, Alex was stabbed near the heart—he has a punctured lung and is losing blood. Lord Eric has engaged Donovan and Lord Raiden is fighting Corben and Ambrosia."

She didn't expect a response, but secretly hoped Master Jonathan would arrive to retrieve Alex. His head lolled in her hands. Moaning, he whimpered, "They want…Ambro—"

Wheezing heavily, he clutched his chest and agony twisted the contours of his face into a mask of impending death. "H-hunters d-dead. Seneca…with R-Rai—"

"Sh," Raven whispered, "we know. Hang on for me—"

Cowboy boots clopped against marble, racing toward her and away from the determined slap of Eric's polished Oxfords. The fear in Donovan's aura and hatred in Eric's triggered Raven's defensive mechanisms. Alex's eyes fluttered opened.

"Hurts. Goody—" His heart shuddered and he lost consciousness. The weight of his limp body ignited panic.

Raven ripped off his shirt. "No, no, no, no…"

The puncture in Alex's back narrowly skirted his spine and aorta, but had sliced the pericardium and nicked one or both ventricles. Blood dribbled down his chest from a small exit hole. "Damn all the flames in Hades!"

Mere inches and a corner turn separated her from Eric choking Donovan against the stair wall. The tangy flavor of their blood landed on her tongue when she inhaled. Donovan was frantic and on the defensive, but he'd landed a few good blows. The murderous power in Eric's aura would crush Alex beyond Endymion's resuscitation skills if she didn't shield him and stop the bleeding fast.

She spread her cloak and aura wide. Her breath and fingers shook as she fumbled to find bandages and Bioserum tucked inside Alex's pockets. Swabbing close to an injured heart was dangerous. She covered the small exit wound with a rubber-coated, self-sticking pad, and then poured the Bioserum directly into the larger cavity. She grabbed a small bundle of packing gauze. It wasn't enough, but it was all she had. Regardless, Alex needed more than a field dressing and Master Jonathan wasn't coming.

Staring at her pathetic supply, she questioned if she could even save him. If not, she needed to assist Eric and Lord Raiden. Failing all of them was unacceptable.

Her hands dropped into her lap. She couldn't leave Alex to die alone. *Clear your head…*

Recollection brought forth an image of Alex handing Eric a vial of blood.

…and save Alex before he dies!

She searched Alex's pockets again. Nothing. She cursed under her breath.

"Wait," she whispered, unhinging the Cataclysm from Alex's belt. The hilt was different. She fingered the intricate gold weaving and cut her finger on a loose seam at the bottom.

"Starry night!" A small vial dropped into her palm—Paresh's blood. Salvation in liquid form.

And a magnet for unwanted attention.

She snapped the seal and poured half into the hole in Alex's back. A chemical preservative tainted the sweet scent of the Sacred Vessel's life force, but that didn't make Donovan moan any less the instant it wafted over him. An involuntary smile crept over Raven's lips as Eric smashed his fist into Donovan's face and the violent *crack* of a skull on plaster echoed throughout the foyer.

Capping the vial with her thumb, she worked fast to uncoil and shove the packing gauze into the wound under the remaining bandaging material she had found on Alex. She unfolded and smoothed a large rubber-coated pad over as much of the cavity as she could. She streamed the remaining blood into Alex's mouth and hurriedly dabbed his bleeding gashes with Bioserum. Then, she unclasped her cloak to tuck him, and the vial, within the safety of its folds.

"I won't forgive you if you die." She kissed the hood over his crown. "You're my idiot to love, you know."

She rose in silence and peered into the foyer where bones crunched under Eric's fury. With a limp arm, an ankle skewed at an odd angle, and blood streaming from his nose, Donovan was barely fending off fatal blows. His jaw hanging useless and unhinged, there was no taunting, no confidence, no bravado—only a fearful, pitiful fool.

No way you beat Alex that badly, she thought, swinging her gaze and catching Corben's loathsome smirk through a huge hole in the study's plaster wall.

He ran his tongue over his teeth and slanted his head back with a huff. "Ah! Lucien's Precious Little Raven Hawkings. Time's up!"

He tugged Ambrosia to his side. Seneca blocked and parried a bloody swipe and Lord Raiden jabbed. Corben dodged and deflected, and Lord Raiden's daggered fingertips plunged into Ambrosia's heart. Corben's lips twitched as his compatriot fell dead. He turned and charged Raven.

Seneca leapt high, Lord Raiden rushed low, and Raven braced for a frontal hit. In a blur, the marble floor rushed up, Eric kicked Seneca into Lord Raiden, and the Elder's fist smashed into Raven's jaw. Two perfectly timed sidesteps delivered Corben to the far corner, where he opened Animus Hollow and plucked Donovan up by his shirt.

"Uh…Areuh!" Donovan cried, stretching desperately toward the scent of Paresh's blood.

"In time." With a look of disgust, Corben tossed him into the rolling white and followed. Eric lunged to catch him, but rammed headfirst into the wall instead.

☽ ❋ ☾

"They broke a window in the library." In her red tunic and bloodstained white capris, Seneca dutifully stood over Alex as Raven assessed his wounds. "They killed the investigating hunters before they could report in. We've found ten others from the Crimson Guard and Chthonic Knights on the property, seven inside the house, including Plathius and Danaë, who were guarding Ambrosia, and Ambrosia, herself. An additional five exterior hunters and three interior are missing and presumed rogue."

"The missing hunters likely killed the others before Donovan and Corben arrived," Raven muttered, visually warning Alex to sit still. "Skyvania was a distraction meant to delay me, but they didn't anticipate Eric, so I got in faster than expected and ended their clock— although I don't know why."

"Damn it, Goody! Stop fussing!" Alex whined, swatting her away. "Don't you have better things to do as High Commander other than to rip my shirt off and feel me up?"

"Pfft!" Raven steeled an arm over his collarbone and clavicle. "Hold still or I'll hurt you. It's a crappy field dressing; I need to see it."

Alex rolled his eyes and mumbled, "The 90s called and wants its grunge back. Why aren't you in uniform?"

She huffed impatiently down his neck. The Bioserum and Paresh's blood were working in tandem with his natural healing ability. The cavity had shrunk considerably and the danger to his heart had passed. She removed the packing gauze and resituated the self-sealing pad to cover the hole in his back.

Clasping his hands between his legs and batting his eyelashes, he asked, "Since I was a good boy, can I have a balloon?"

She slapped the back of his head as she stood and faced Seneca. "And the Elders?"

"Safe. Lord Raiden was the only Elder on the first floor."

"Take a break and clean up." Raven tugged Alex to his feet. "Until he returns to active duty, assume command. Regroup with Minerva, issue new perimeter patrols, and deploy Cimex Drones throughout the estate and village—you, Kestrel, and Master Jonathan's pack officers are to monitor their frequency for abnormal behavior."

"Ma'am." Seneca bowed and jogged up the stairs.

"What do you mean until I return to active duty?" Alex tried to throw his hands out, but winced.

"What are you hiding? You're not whining about it, so it must be serious."

"My shoulder hurts, and it's my best looking one, so—"

"Then it's a good thing you need medical clearance before resuming command." She delicately assessed the alignment of his collarbone and shoulders. "You hit that plaster hard."

"You're seriously making me go to Eido?" He stared at her like an indignant teenager.

"I'll give you a balloon," she promised with a fake smile. "Go, now."

"No." He stalked over to the cracked wall and retrieved the remains of a shattered wall sconce. "It's silver plated."

Rotating his shoulder, he said, "Goody, it's a small piece, wedged—" He prodded the topside of his shoulder. "There. Scrape it out real quick and I'll be fine. I'm not leaving."

Raven dropped her annoyance into her palm and pretended to flick it at him. He rolled his neck to dodge. "Huff and puff all you want. My house is solid and you don't outrank me anymore."

The secret basement panel clicked open. Eric stepped out first, followed by Master Jonathan. "Is the perimeter secure?"

"Aye, with new patrol assignments pending and we'll gain ears with Cimex Drones." Raven tossed her chin at the hole in the study wall. "The dead are in there awaiting transport for incineration."

"At least their rescue mission failed," Eric grumbled, wiping his face and hanging his hand off his neck. "This house is a magnet for disaster. The caretaker's going to have questions."

An irritated grunt sounded low in Master Jonathan's throat as he wrinkled his nose at the blood spattered cracked and cratered plaster, splintered doors, and glass shards glittering under the moon's light. Visually tracing the dusty and bloody footprints trampling the once gleaming marble tiles, he said, "Pull a crew from the Silent Vespers for cleaning and repair. This foyer must be pristine before Paresh sees it."

"She will ask, you know," Eric replied, pinching the bridge of his nose with a sigh.

"Then we'll tell her. But she doesn't need to see it." Her master shot an impatient glare at Raven.

"Aye, my lord," Raven replied with a swift tilt of her chin before jabbing her nail into Alex's shoulder. He yelped, but held still as she removed a small fragment of silver-plated metal wedged between the acromion and clavicle.

She swabbed the puncture with Bioserum and placed the fragment onto his outstretched palm. His lips quirked up when she pulled out a child-sized bandage she carried specifically for him. She smoothed a strip with red balloons over the already healed incision. "There. Battlefield surgery—complete with balloons."

"Man, Goody. You're colder than Boreas the North Wind!" Alex clamped his hand on his shoulder and rotated it back and forth. He seemed oblivious to the hole healing in his back. "It's not like it was easy fighting two former Eternal Blood Elders and that asshole while defending another Elder."

Grunting from his seat on the stairs, Lord Raiden interjected, "I needed no protection, Crimson Commander."

"No disrespect, my lord," Raven replied curtly, "but protecting you is our duty, more so now under these circumstances."

The Elder grunted again, but now under Master Jonathan's scowl, remained silent.

"The Elders have grown complacent after a thousand years of confinement," he snipped, "whereas the COMS have honed their instincts in preparation for this rebellion. Corben's abilities with precision timing and predictive movement showed no signs of the rust you wear, Elder Raiden."

"Predictive movement," Raven mumbled to herself, rethinking Corben's actions prior to Lord Raiden's lethal strike on Ambrosia.

"I'll contact Nallura to have the Chthonic Knights retrieve the bodies," Alex said, pulling Raven from her musings. "You want Kestrel to shadow Seneca and Minerva?"

"Uh, no," Raven replied, distracted. "Keep her with you until you resume your detail. I presume she's been confirmed as my new First Officer?" She glanced at Master Jonathan.

"We confirmed all requested changes, present and future," he replied dryly. "Come with me. You are Lucien's escort. Alex, get medical clearance at the Arc of Mourning Eidolons before resuming your duties."

In her peripheral, Alex spun on his heel in frustration. She threw him a sweet smile. "Be a good boy, now. Orders are orders."

II

Running an anxious hand through his hair, Eric met Jonathan at the basement panel. "I need a break—to be with Paresh. That monster shouldn't be breathing, but he was just—" He wiped his face and sighed into his hand, his gaze descending the stairs into the shadows. "I'm on the edge of exhaustion…and he was here!"

"Then be with her and rest. I've got plenty to keep me busy." Gesturing at Eric's bloodied and torn clothes, Jonathan added, "Wash up first, but take time to be with her."

Nodding, Eric began unbuttoning his shirt despite the number of tears that made it impossible to salvage. He'd blocked most of Donovan's punches, but that nimble bastard was quick on his feet and a half dozen boot prints dusted his trousers. He shrugged off his shirt and wiped at dried blood on his chest and arms.

He motioned for Raven to go ahead of him. "Take care of Lucien. I'll be a moment."

He handed his soiled shirt to Jonathan and eyed Raiden's perch as hunters worked to mask the hole in the wall. The Elder's expression was guarded, his appearance exotic with bronzed skin and slanted eyes that smoldered like dying embers. A thousand years of meditation swathed him and betrayed nothing—not emotion, not breath.

His valiant guard had cost them. Raiden's presence was a liability then and it was a distraction now. Speaking in a tone that only Jonathan—and Lucien—would hear, Eric said, "The hunters cannot do their jobs freely under his scrutiny. Sequester the Elders until operations return to whatever passes for normal here."

Following Eric's gaze, Jonathan replied, "Go rest."

Hesitantly lingering at the top of the stairs, Eric shared a look with Jonathan that mirrored their mutual fatigue. Neither had slept much since Paresh's arrival, and Jonathan's recovery was painfully slow.

"Promise to be careful and get some rest yourself. Paresh will worry if you're in pain."

"I'm sore, but healing—"

"But—"

"—and I intend to keep healing." Jonathan insistently shooed him into the darkness and grabbed the panel to close off the basement, but not before waving a Crimson Guard hunter over to Raiden and gesturing his arm up the stairs. Raiden's gaze locked onto Eric's as he stood and followed his new escort.

A millennium of peace had softened the Elders, so spoiled by title and formalities, and elevated above the lives of those they ruled that they required security details during their annual winter festival among their own kind. Love would not be their downfall. They'd fallen long ago.

Eric turned his back to the closing panel and trotted down the stairs. He loved the rich blackness of the underground. It was insulating, comforting—things he hadn't considered when designing his house with the architect. Life above ground had seemed a natural choice, but now that he was back—

Lucinda's smile curved over his mind, her cheeks blushed by the barest application of makeup and framed by wild, chocolaty locks. Her hazel eyes shone like golden suns as white chiffon curtains sailed behind her from her bedroom's balcony doors—the same room that Elizabeth and Lily had used because it adjoined the nursery. But every woman who had called that room home had died in it—even Sandy. The Senator had modernized it into a master suite and transformed the old nursery into a panic room.

So many memories, so much history, and so much blood. He shoved his hands through his hair and interlocked his fingers to hang off his neck. Paresh's essence scraped his bare skin, hooking his aura and urging him to join her, but he reeked of Donovan.

Unwilling to drag out his battle fatigue, he tossed a halfhearted farewell to Raven and Lucien, silhouetted against the hazy, white disc that was splitting apart the fabric of their realm. The Hollow swallowed them in its giant mouth and Eric was alone at last. So much change, so much violence, and so much death.

Relaxing into the fold of blackness and Paresh's soothing siren's call, Eric rolled his neck and shoulders, and stretched and cracked his body to banish the tightness and tension of the outside world. He padded down the hall, showered, and dressed in an old t-shirt and jogging pants before easing into his former bedchamber.

His lips lifted at the glint of golden curls on his pillow. He crawled over the far side of the bed and slipped into place, nuzzling Paresh's neck and breathing in scents of honey, the sun, and green clover. He placed his palm on her belly to snuggle closer. Mumbling in her sleep, she conformed to his body and her hand slid over his, holding him firmly in place.

"I'll never let go," he whispered, kissing her nape.

She mumbled again and shifted, and something moved under his hand. He froze.

"Ah!" Staring into the darkness, he caught his breath, scared that the slightest breath might destroy the possibility…but, Alex had reported hearing an arrhythmia, an echo behind Paresh's heartbeat, after Donovan——

"Wait, what?" He smoothed a small circle over her belly. How had he not noticed that bump that fit so perfectly into his hand?

A shaky breath skimmed his lips. He'd felt this once before——with Lucinda. But this——vampire impotence aside——was impossible! He hurried into his mind, digging through the timeline of Paresh's arrival. They made love for the first time ten? Maybe eleven days ago? And Alex——Alex heard the echo six days ago.

Each breath came faster and the blackness rushed him in blurry waves as moisture surged into his eyes.

An extra heartbeat. Movement.

The bed seemed to rock like a boat in rough water.

A bump. The vomiting.

He was breathing too fast. The darkness was spinning.

The cravings. The food.

Forming a small pocket in the crook of her neck, he gulped carbon dioxide. His mind raced ahead.

Her fatigue. Her aura draining more energy than usual.

Medicine had advanced greatly since Lucinda's time. Doctors could hear a fetal heartbeat as early as six weeks, which corresponded with vampiric detection, but Alex had heard it at six *days*. And most women didn't start showing until the fourth or fifth month, and movement might not come until weeks later——

He gasped at another kick to his palm. Too scared to be excited and too excited to be scared, he blew a trembling breath into Paresh's ear, "P-Paresh? Wake up! Wake up!"

She rolled onto her back, groggy with sleep. "Eric?"

He pressed his ear against her abdomen. The tiny heartbeat was racing. "Oh my God! Oh my God!"

"*What?*"

As Paresh scrambled to sit up, Eric straightened and cupped her face. "Did you know? I mean…how? Are you…?"

She covered his hands. "Eric, slow down! Do I know what? Why do you smell like blood?" Her fingers frantically searched his body for injuries. "Did something happen? Are you hurt?"

"No——I'm fine——no! Oh, honey!" It was so hard to breathe. How on Earth was he even talking? "Am I going to be a *dad*?"

She stopped dead. A noise jammed her throat, forcing her to croak, "What?"

"Y-you have a…in there…it's *moving*! And I *heard* it…" he rambled, gathering her hair into his hands and kissing her in between words. "It has a heart, a *beating* heart!"

His tears streamed freely, dripping onto her hands, her hair, her skin, her breasts. Everything was spiraling and his chest was going to burst, but he sucked in breath after breath. "You have…a-a *baby*…we're having a *baby*! Oh God, I love you!"

He said it over and over, kissing her hair, her forehead, her nose, her cheeks, and, as the emotional wave crested, he took her lips and kissed her long and deeply.

Shock had hardened her aura, but it softened as her hands inched down her belly. She pulled away at the slight bulge that had appeared while she slept. Then warmth flared into her aura and melded with his, their love folding together and locking tight. She broke their kiss and took a deep, shaky breath.

"Are you saying—" Her eyes glistened as they met his through the blackened veil. She sniffled. "That I'm going to be a *mom*?"

So consumed by her and his love for her, Eric could only nod. She nodded with him and he cupped her face again, laughter falling between them with their tears.

She gasped and flattened her hands against her belly. "Oh! I can hear it!"

He kissed her belly. That tiny heart pumping alongside hers made the best music he'd ever heard.

"I thought I'd never have children." Her fingers threaded lovingly through his hair.

"Me, too." He sat up and pulled her to him. As she leaned in, resting one palm over his heart and the other on her belly, he added, "I thought my only chance died with Darien and Lucinda. I don't know how or why or—" He paused to wipe his nose on his sleeve and chuckled at how uncouth it was even though they'd be covered in worse soon.

"We're having a baby," she said softly, her voice like a warm blanket. Her skin hummed beneath his fingers, her pulse throbbing, her body singing of new life.

Eric closed his eyes and found himself in the cottage clearing surrounded by forest animals of every shape and size. Deer bowed to her and rabbits stood on their hind legs, their noses twitching in wonderment. Butterflies and birds circled her head in tiered crowns that rose into the blue sky amid their songs of joy. Near the forest edge, bears roared, and, closer in, raccoons chittered. They were all there, squirrels and foxes, and coyotes, too, as they'd been when she'd been born, now celebrating a fetal heartbeat.

"I love you," he panted. "So much, I love you."

"So much it hurts," she whispered, her soft lips cushioning his.

They lay on the bed together, laughing and crying, touching and holding each other, trying to pull the other closer. The army of hunters upstairs no longer existed. In the basement's dark privacy, they were each other's everything.

He caught a glint of white as Paresh gnawed her lip. "How did you find out when I didn't even know?"

He kissed her hand and then held it flat on her belly. "Wait."

She held his stare for the agonizing minutes that passed before their baby thumped her hand. She gasped, her eyes and mouth popping wide.

"Whoa…wow…" she whispered breathlessly, fresh tears spilling down her cheeks.

"You're amazing, you know?" He kissed the tip of her nose.

"But how did this happen?" For a fraction of a second, she sounded terrified.

"I honestly don't know."

"I thought I was sick from the food and alteration. I've never even had a period."

"Never? Not one?"

She shook her head, suddenly bashful, the darkness veiling the cute tinge of embarrassment on her cheeks. He loved these innocent moments. They were scarcer every day.

"Does Jonathan know?" Eric asked.

"W-why? Would he know that? O-or, need to?" She shrank in his arms and laughed. "Ohh…the blood! Oh, that's gross."

Eric chuckled. "I meant about it not being normal for a human. Maybe he suspected—"

"That I could have a baby?"

"No!" Eric laughed again. "That you weren't entirely human earlier than he reported to Lucien."

"Oh." She scrunched her face. "Do you think anyone else knows?"

Eric's hands looped her waist. "Maybe Alex. He heard an echo of your heartbeat after—"

"Oh." She quieted into her thoughts.

"I missed all of this with Lucinda. The excitement, the first heartbeat, the early thumps, sharing it with my love." He pressed his forehead against hers. "Thank you."

She stroked his nape. "This is happening fast, isn't it? I thought it took weeks to know? Did you ever feel Darien?"

He nodded. "Lucinda was big and round and ready, and Darien was a ball of energy in there." He smoothed his hand over her belly again. His son had been so full of life in the womb, yet hadn't drawn a single breath of air.

"Do you want a boy or a girl?"

Paresh's question came hot against his lips and the touch of her fingers on his neck was maddening. "Of course," he exhaled, cupping her cheek and kissing her.

He straightened and pulled her against his awakened body. She moaned and arched into him, kissing him with equal hunger, her fingers on his neck stoking the flame of lust as her other hand trailed down his back.

"We'll always have love," she whispered, her lips traveling across his cheek and jaw to nibble on his ear, "because we made it."

He rolled her onto her back and kissed her deeply, his body and soul aching to become one with her. His hands slipped beneath her skirt and slid up her thighs as she tugged his t-shirt over his head.

The energy in her fingertips zapped his skin as they danced over his abdomen. She nuzzled his throat, her breath racing against his jugular. Her lips parted and he felt the sharp tips of her fangs—

He cried out and his body went rigid the instant she bit into his skin. Adrenaline shot through his veins, awakening every facet of his being. He hadn't felt her changing—there'd been no shift in her aura.

A growl rumbled low in his throat, which she eagerly matched. He buried his hands in her hair, holding her, loving her, protecting her—his eternal soul mate, the woman he loved with all his heart, and, now, the mother of his child.

She latched onto his back, and he straightened and pulled her with him, hiking her onto his lap. She rocked against him, moaning into his throat, lapping the surface with the tip of her tongue. Pressure mounted behind his teeth and his growl deepened to a hungry rumble.

Withdrawing from his throat, she took command of his mouth, exploring the length of his teeth and hooking her tongue to share her blood. He moaned and fumbled with the damn hook and zipper of her dress. With a tortured grunt, he tore off the catch and ripped the zipper apart.

With a soft giggle, she arced back, pulled her dress over her head, unclasped her bra, and dropped both onto the floor. His mouth against her throat, he shared her laugh and supported the small of her back until she was safely on the mattress. He hurriedly shed the remainder of their clothing and nestled himself between her legs, grinning like an idiot when her bloody smile glistened through the black veil.

"I love you," she said. "Drink from me."

A bolt of fear struck him still. "What about the baby?"

"Her dad's a vampire." Paresh winked and lifted onto her elbows to dot his lips with a sweet kiss. Her aura swatted his fear away. "I think she'll understand."

"*Her*, huh?"

"Maybe?"

With a growl, Eric pressed her flat and sank his fangs into her throat as he entered her body. Her laugh morphed into a moan, and she stroked his head and kissed his hair as her body moved in unison with his. Their auras came together as an entity of its own that painted pleasurable strokes over every inch of their bodies.

Delirious from vertigo, he felt the veil of pitch spin. His body grew heavy, sluggish. His throat seized up. Blood dribbled from his mouth like drool and the blackness blurred. He collapsed on top of Paresh and an alarm fired in his distant mind that she was limp, but then everything went dark.

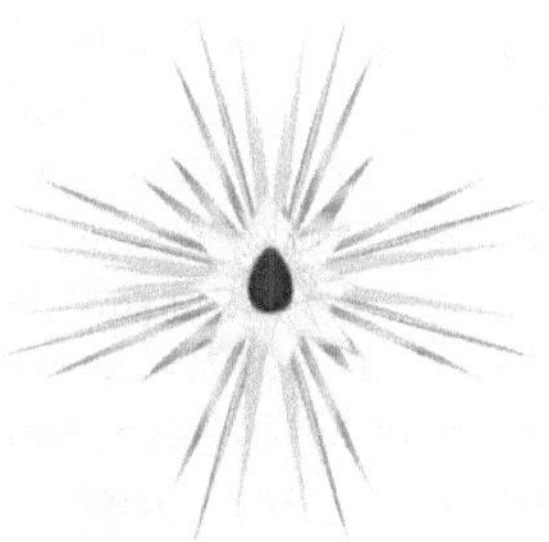

Chapter Thirteen: Blood Loss

Arc of True Blood, Summer 2006

Animus Hollow's white mist framed the serene cobalt pathway leading to Snowblood Square's Ionic pillars and pristine marble dome. But the scene belied an ominous revelation as they stepped into a saturated blood scent. Lord Lucien's breath broke like ice on her neck. Adrenaline spun a dizzying dance with fear. She cast a visual query. Lord Lucien's jaw formed a harsh blue line and his polished hematite eyes burned blacker than coal. "Go."

Racing along the scent trail, her heart plummeted the closer she got to Lady Rainne's fortress. She rushed through its breached doors. Acrid blood assaulted her nose over the masking scents. Dark smoke seared her eyes and blurred the bloody lumps at the end of the hall: two freshly carved hearts flung from the raised first gate, all three hunters within mutilated beyond recognition. Ripped from groin to throat, their organs laid bare, with one's body cavity housing a severed head.

The back of her hand flew to her mouth. None of these hunters were headless. She eyed the blood pooling beneath the second gate and cursed not having her Deathscythe. She yanked the dagger from her boot.

A mechanism on the hilt responded to her DNA. The High Commander's Seal folded out from the handle. Grinding her teeth, she slammed the seal into the interlock's manual override and slapped her palm onto the electronic scanner.

The iron gate thundered shut behind her and the second gate began to rise. Alex's secondary unit lay massacred in an all too familiar way, sliced from their bellies up and laid out to form an upside down cross. Blood oozed from the necks of the outer branches and a decapitated head dotted the foot of the cross. Goose pimples riddled her flesh.

"Salea." She barely heard herself. She was terrified to hear herself.

Panic lit her nerves afire. She sprinted through coagulating blood, spattering the already bloodstained walls, and activated the second vestibule's interlock override. Her fingers, numb and clumsy, fumbled with her Vampiric Star, her trembling hand almost scaring her more than the symbolism of that gruesome display.

A hidden panel emerged for her Vampiric Star. The blood-drop ruby glowed red while the arc's cyber system decoded her security encryption. The laser read the jutting prongs and triggered one to fit into the panel's tiny keyhole.

Smoke coiled through the opening crack of Lady Rainne's chamber door. The fire burned hottest here, fueled by oil and wax. Choking and slightly dazed, Raven staggered back. The rosewood gargoyles guarded an empty bed. Rainne Blood Pathos was gone. And Endymion—

A fragment of white silk on the slate nearly upheaved what little contents sat in her stomach. A silent scream nested in her throat. Flames and smoke tried to usher her closer, but her feet refused to move. Her body was digesting itself. The air had disappeared. She was drowning. Suffocating. Dying. Falling. Down, down, down.

A noise eked past her lips. A creak? A squeak? She didn't know. Her throat was too dry, her ears ringing too loudly, and her face too blisteringly wet.

Blinking against oppressive smoke, she moved like a leaden statue. Denial was a banshee shrieking circles inside her head. She gagged on a sensation of wet cotton or spun spider silk packed into her throat, and was numb to her movements as her vision tunneled in on the soiled fabric.

The fragment stretched into a robe smudged with soot and a vermillion stain that bloomed over the chest. Tears surged as searing firewater. She collapsed and blindly scrabbled Endymion's body as unearthly howls echoed high above the fire's rage.

Heaving and gasping for breath, she gathered him tightly to her breast and crushed her lips against his, yearning to taste him, willing him to take control, to mold her, to make her his clay doll. But he was limp, loose like the sediment that flows along the river bottom, and his peridot orbs, always filled with arrogance and confidence, aimed pointlessly upward, forever empty.

☽ ✳ ☾

Blinking through a blurry haze, she activated the emergency

shutdown protocols and closed the interlock doors. Clutching Endymion close to her heart, view stained crimson, and quaking with grief, she emerged and Lord Lucien approached slowly, placing each step with care despite his aura's murderous, lashing tendrils. He fumed in silence for precisely one minute before returning to the gate, where he blocked the path as a sentinel for Raven's sorrow.

His reaction gave her the strength to pull herself together—eventually. She gently laid Endymion's body at Lord Lucien's feet and knelt, unable to let go.

Deep furrows and lines aged Lord Lucien's youthful countenance. A red arc rimmed his dark irises and a cruel scowl bent his lips. His skin had darkened, more teal than blue, patterned with snakeskin scales, and his hair, rather than frosted sterling, looked smoky and streaked with ash.

She'd seen him like this before: with Lord Connall's treason, and after reporting Lior's death and seeking Salea's final pardon.

That memory raked her soul over the coals of Hell. *Endymion voted to kill*, Lord Lucien had revealed. A jagged rock stabbed her throat from within. If she'd followed her orders instead of listening to Alex—

"I-I can't destroy him," she croaked.

"We do not bury our dead." Lucien's voice was unnatural, monstrous. He snarled through parted lips the color of deep, dark water, his fangs doubled in length with sharp tips of deepening crimson. Rage flared from his aura and the roots of his hair were scorched black.

His engorged gaze locked onto hers. "No one can know."

Her fingers fumbled through Endymion's flaxen strands. A wisp of intimate memory made her clutch the fabric of his robe into her fist. From her mind, she shook loose his smile, the sharp prick of his teeth on her skin, his knowing, confident, *loving* eyes. As tears burned like acid, his soothing lavender scent draped her mindscape. Every moment she'd ever shared with him flashed in rapid sequence. He loved her. He loved her before it was possible. He loved her more fiercely than anyone else ever had.

She glared at the dark demon overtaking Lord Lucien. "Do not destroy him. He belongs to me," she growled. "I claimed him in 897 A.D. You have no dominion over him now."

Lucien's hard eyes briefly flashed a warning. He blinked slowly once in agreement.

Tears splashed Endymion's empty eyes as she kissed his forehead. She shoved off the ground into a pounding run. The arc's gardens blurred and Snowblood Square appeared in the distance. She pressed the prong on her Vampiric Star for Animus Hollow. As the rolling white portal opened, Lucien's voice came to her clearly, "Kill them all."

☽ ❋ ☾

Evading everyone at the Arc of Mourning Eidolons, she hurried into her uniform, stocked her supplies, and returned to the eternal rolls of white. She partially exited in Sunset Grove and pulled out her communicator. She pricked her thumb on her teeth and pressed the bloody print along the inner edge until the metallic wedge vibrated twice. She pressed it onto her jaw.

"Donovan!" she growled. "I demand a parley—of sorts. Sunset Grove. You. Me. Alone. *Now*."

She ripped the communicator off and scattered her aura into the Hollow. Given the successful diversion at the mansion, Donovan was likely monitoring his communicator for word on the real attack. Her blood ensured that he—and he alone—received her emergency broadcast.

Her aura filtered information back to her. Whoever stole Lady Rainne had left a blood-tainted path and it led to the spot she felt Donovan opening. She confirmed it was him and stepped out to let the portal close.

She licked the bloody thumbprint from her device to return it to normal function and opened a line to Kestrel. "Pull everyone from Sunset Grove immediately. No exceptions. They are to standby at the Hawthorne Mansion. Will advise when able."

Without awaiting a response, she tucked the communicator into her pocket. Whipping around, she focused every bit of force into the heel that landed square in Donovan's gut the instant he came out.

Grunting, he flew past the closing portal, across the beaten trail, and crashed into a thick oak tree. She charged after, sliding onto her knees and clamping tightly onto his throat. He registered only surprise at first.

Spraying spittle, Raven demanded, "*Who killed him?*"

A range of emotions flew across Donovan's face. He seemed genuinely confused until Raven pulled a syringe from her pocket. The liquid within was metallic and silver in color. She hoped he was disoriented enough to forget that the Chthonic Knights had never developed technology to make their tortuous liquid silver portable. Still, her mix of colloidal silver and mercury would sting awhile and scar the inner linings of his heart—after it pillaged his brain, first.

She stabbed the needle through her finger and into the carotid artery in his neck. She yanked him up by the throat, nose to nose. "*Who. Killed. Him?*"

"Y-you…y-you wanted a parley!" he cried, his body stiff and dilated pupils darting to the corners of his eye sockets, fighting to see the syringe. "W-who's dead?"

She snarled and slammed her forehead against his skull. Her fingers twitched on the plunger.

"*Fuck! Goody!*" Donovan screamed, throwing his arms up in surrender. "*I don't know what you're asking!*"

"Who attacked the Arc of True Blood?"

The whites of his eyes flashed wildly as his gaze paced between her face and her thumb on the plunger. "L-look! I came to t-talk. I expected a punch in the face—*yes*—but…pull that damn thing out of my neck and talk to me!"

Anger was a fiery snake in her veins. Her internal voice screamed that he deserved it, that she should drag him to the Chthonic Knights and a fate worse than death with real liquid silver. Endymion would have injected it himself by now.

She blinked back bitter tears and fought the new emotions fueling her blind rage. The hand curled around his throat shook and thrust him against the forest floor, stealing his breath and knocking his head against the tree. His consciousness fading, his head lolled and she loosened her grip, but the needle pinning her finger to his neck remained.

Rage crested as a howl birthed from the deepest parts of her newborn soul. The horrific noise reverberated throughout the forest, echoing like a pack of wounded animals. She clenched her jaw and bit back her cries. She punched the dirt of the forest floor repeatedly. Grief burned a hole in her heart that would never heal.

Her jaw trembled and she blinked through a scorching haze hating that she had to acknowledge that Donovan hadn't killed Endymion. Worse—she believed that he didn't understand what she was asking.

"Why did you have to do it?" she asked, tears mingling with snot and spit dripping off her chin. "You were a friend; I trusted you! You fucking betrayed all of us…*me!*"

She punched the dirt again. Pain raced across her knuckles. The Donovan who'd known her best was now her enemy. He'd ripped her trust—her friendship—from her and made her cry in front of Endymion. Endymion who was dead. Endymion who had loved her.

Endymion who would kill Donovan right now—even under the ruse of a parley—when she could not.

Raven freed the needle from Donovan's neck and her finger. Trust was not something she'd ever return to him. She straddled his abdomen and plunged the needle between his ribs and into his heart. Then she rocked back on her heels and waited for him to wake up.

☽ ✳ ☾

She was sitting on his stomach, leaning back on her palms and glimpsing patches of night sky when Donovan stirred with a groan. He cracked an eye that shifted immediately from her face to the syringe in his chest.

"Goody?" he mumbled.

"Aye."

"What's going on?"

"I might kill you—" she paused and cocked her head. The stars were so much brighter tonight. It seemed wrong. "I've been ordered to kill everyone—and that includes you, so…"

He waited for her to speak again, his eyes widening the longer she kept silent. Raising his brows, he prompted, "So…?"

She shrugged. Sometime after knocking him out, she'd gone numb. Endymion's death seemed like a bad dream—like she'd return to the arc and see his protective peridot orbs shining at her. "So…a parley, of sorts."

"And the needle?"

"You aren't a good boy." She glanced down her nose. "You need incentive."

He grunted to clear his throat. "But you're Goody Rav—"

"Goody Raven would have followed her orders by now, aye? Yet you're still breathing." She shot him a fake smile. "Who infiltrated the arc?"

Heaving a frustrated sigh, he said, "Salea."

Raven nodded slowly, lifting her gaze back to the canopy and the stars beyond. She wasn't sure if numbness was better or worse than rage. "Who was with her?"

Donovan's eyes narrowed. "No one. She's the only one who can bypass Arc Cyber Control and get in and out successfully."

Raven shook her head in disappointment and balled one hand into a fist. She brought it up and punched Donovan's groin. He coughed and instinctively began to curl into a ball. Rolling forward onto her knees, she held him flat against the ground. "Wrong."

Wagging her finger, she said, "One more 'wrong' and Goody Raven comes back and pushes the plunger." She nodded at the syringe.

His tiger eyed gaze hardened into a glare. "I don't care much for this version of Raven."

She shrugged again and gently—carefully—pushed the colloidal silver and mercury into the needle. Donovan screeched as a miniscule drop ripped a fiery path through his heart. His muscles cramped tight and a deep grimace etched his face. He choked on his breath and clawed trenches into the undergrowth. A tremor rocked his jaw as he squeezed his eyes shut and sucked desperately for air.

"If you're not going to like me, you really should have a good reason," Raven sneered, her nose less than an inch from his. "Would you like more?"

He cracked a hateful eye. His facial muscles had contracted too tightly to let him speak.

"Answer me." Raven flicked her thumb against the plunger.

He grunted.

"Let's have this parley, then, hmm?" Raven lifted her brows and tilted her head expectantly.

The injected sample had moved out of his heart and was now a pesky burn in every artery, vein, and capillary it touched as it cycled through his body. It would weaken with each repetition, and, eventually, his body would expel it, but it would rage like wildfire every time it hit the raw scars in his heart. He tried in vain to scoot away from her, his fear locked on the needle and her fingers. *What the bloody fuck, Raven! I was told she went in alone to get Rainne!*

Raven's eyes rolled up to assess his face. During the silence that followed, he winced and went rigid again. He gulped and released a choked cry for air.

"Confirm that the mansion was a diversion," Raven said.

"*Yes, yes! Shit, yes!*" Gnarled hands pounded the earth at his sides. "We knew Rainne wasn't there. And—look! Corben planned to kill Ambrosia—it wasn't an accident. She was too unpredictable. He couldn't trust her."

Raven scoffed. "Trust? Do you trust any of them?"

"Those wolves? Hell no. I'm only there for *me*." Sweat beaded atop his brow. "I was their catalyst. They didn't think I'd survive, but I did, so here I am: the unwanted party guest."

"New Raven doesn't appreciate melodrama," she said drily, holding up a surrendering hand when panic rippled through his aura anew. "Salea wasn't alone. She couldn't have killed him. So! Someone was with her. Someone powerful. Who is someone *powerful*, Donovan?"

"You are fucking creepy as bloody hell, right now." Saliva frothed between his clenched teeth as he tensed again and his eyes rolled back in his head. When the moment passed, he breathlessly begged, "Let me think…okay? Give me a second before you punch me in the balls…or inject me…again?"

"I won't punch you there again," she said sweetly, eyeing the syringe.

"Fuck," he muttered. "You do realize that I was damned if I did and damned if I didn't right? At least with them I have a semblance of freedom."

"You attacked Paresh, asshole." She punched him in the groin harder and held him flat against the ground as his face went red and he gasped for more air than a dying fish out of water. "If Alex was here we'd have some real fun, you know?"

"I'm sure…it'd be…a hoot," he gasped. "Fuck, you said you wouldn't do that."

"That was from Paresh." Raven shook her head and looked skyward. "I think I will kill you. You make me sick."

He stilled beneath her, holding his breath and studying her. His lips pursed to form a question but then widened in confusion. "Aren't you surprised Salea's alive?"

Raven pretended to think. "Well, I was when I saw her handiwork at Rainne's, but then I saw someone else's handiwork. Speaking of, who is that someone?"

"But…Salea? That's a big deal, right? She blew up the Arc of Celestial Night—I wasn't expecting that—and—"

"She couldn't have set off the chlorine trifluoride," Raven interrupted. "She was catatonic."

"Is New Raven missing a few marbles? All those synapses firing all right?" Donovan worked an arm free and snapped his dirty fingers in front of her face. She wrenched his arm under her leg and shot him a smug smile, eyeing the syringe.

"Come on, Goody! One minute you act like Salea being alive is natural and then you're surprised that *she* blew up the arc where *you* housed her after *Alex* shot her? She's been awake for decades. Who do you think has been moving the pieces this whole time?"

"Decades?" Hope swelled within her ribs. It was illogical, she knew. Donovan was right. And that was bad. She wasn't thinking clearly. "I need Alex," she whispered to herself, automatically dipping into her pocket for the communicator.

Donovan slapped it out of her hand, and then flashed his palm in surrender and jammed it under her leg. "You and me. Alone. Parley. I'm cooperating, Raven. I might be a rogue, but I'm not on their level of crazy, and I don't want more party guests stomping on my balls."

"Why did you betray me?" she asked with a lilt of sadness, shaking her head and exhaling through trembling lips. Numb was better. Definitely better.

"What happened to you, Goody?" he asked as though he genuinely cared. "I didn't break you. Who broke you?"

She glared at him. "You didn't break me?"

Her palm whipped his cheek. She slapped him again. Harder. And again. And again. "Who do you think started the crack, *you bastard!*"

He couldn't defend himself, but he didn't try. He took every hit and didn't say a word until she paused for breath.

"Hey, hey! Can you not? Anymore?" he cried. "I'm behaving!"

"No." She shook her head. "This isn't enough. Endymion is dead and Salea isn't strong enough to do that to him."

Raven gripped the syringe and pressed her thumb against the plunger as Donovan's eyes went wide. "Endymion's dead?"

The plump silver drop exploded in his heart and he arced beneath her as though struck by an electric bolt. An unearthly scream raced off his lips.

As his torment ricocheted through Paresh's forest, Raven inhaled a deep, calming breath. It seemed right for him to suffer here. She was suffering, Paresh had suffered, Endymion had died...

At some point, a lack of screaming lulled her back to reality. "Still alive?"

Donovan huffed, his angry, burning veins bulging and throbbing. "*Lucifer!*"

"What about him?"

"*Someone. Powerful,*" he grunted between breaths.

Fear trickled down Raven's spine. Lucifer killed Endymion. Lucifer was in the Arc of True Blood. *Lucifer had Rainne.*

She plucked the syringe from Donovan's chest and punched it down at his head. The needle pierced his ear's cartilage and landed in the dirt. She pressed the plunger, dispensing the mercury and colloidal silver into the Earth. "I'll kill you next time. Promise," she whispered.

She stood, yanked him to his feet, and opened Animus Hollow. "Lose my scent before you return or they'll kill you first. *I'm* your reaper and I'm looking forward to it."

She shoved him into the hazy white hole so he wouldn't see her follow. Her aura stalked him to his first exit: the Arc of Ebony Stars in Siberia. Donovan wasn't aware that all arcs were on lockdown.

"So you have friends there," she noted to herself.

His next exit also failed and revealed friends at the Arc of Mourning Eidolons. She wondered if Nallura was trustworthy enough to sniff out the rogues under her watch, but all squads came and went from that arc. His "friend" might not be a Chthonic Knight, but they controlled Eido's entry points, which made it more likely.

His third exit was on a small island in northern Japan. She activated her cloaking switch and followed him to a hot spring bathhouse where he took her advice. He burned his discarded clothes and scrubbed himself nearly raw in sulfuric water. Once finished and wrapped in a loose yukata robe, he reentered Animus Hollow and led his invisible shadow directly to the COMS headquarters.

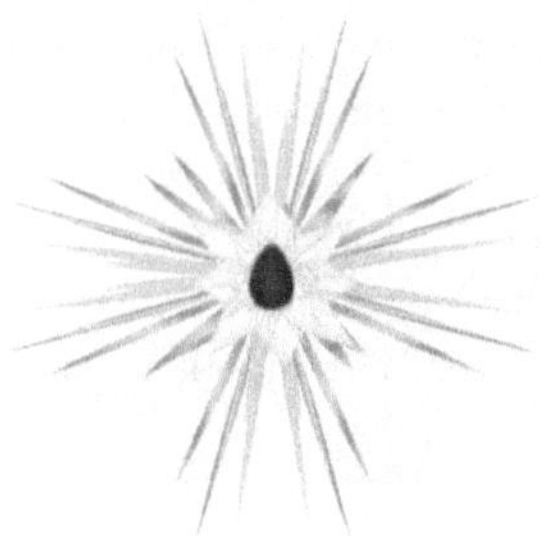

CHAPTER FOURTEEN: FRIGHTENED AMONG US

Lucifer's presence changed everything—if he'd truly accompanied Salea to steal Lady Rainne. The wrath of her eternal lord awaited her for not killing Donovan, but that wasn't why she hesitated to report in.

Salea was alive.

Salea killed Alex's hunters.

Salea killed Alex's hunters with Lucifer at her side.

Lucifer.

And Salea.

Why?

Raven knelt where she'd shot the mercury and colloidal silver, retrieved the syringe and communicator, and patted the old oak tree. "I'm sorry for anything that does to you. I hope I didn't hurt you."

A sigh dropped with her shoulders as she slumped against the trunk. Tucking her knees to her chest, she clasped her hands over her face and emptied her mind.

Breathe in—two, three, four.

Breathe out—two, three, four.

Repeat.

It was too much. All of it. Paresh. The Second New Age. Love. Donovan. Salea. Endymion. Rainne. Lucifer.

And she'd almost called Alex like a distressed damsel.

But Alex was all she had left. The only hunter she trusted.

But she shouldn't—ever—need help.

She was losing her mind.

Salea. Lucifer. Rainne.

Hawkiel. How'd she forgotten him?

Combing her fingers through her hair, she faced the forest's inky roof. The breeze had settled and stolen all hope of seeing the stars.

No hope.

Salea. Lucifer. Rainne.

She thrust her head back against the trunk. Time allotted no space to lament. Alone in the Arc of True Blood, Lord Lucien was in imminent danger.

Salea. Lucifer. Rainne.

"Shut up!" she groaned, gritting her teeth. The shell of numbness cracked off her body and fire consumed her soul. Because of the Hawkings Protocol, Rainne would respond only to her or Lucifer. If Lucifer activated her at the arc—

"Why are you here alone?" a soft voice asked.

Instinct snapped Raven to her feet. Her fist crunched cartilage and bone.

"*Damn it, Goody!*" Cradling his nose, Alex swung away, cursing all the Greek gods.

"Lucifer!" Raven lurched off balance and dug her fingers into Alex's shoulder. The scents of summer and sunshine whirled together as he turned. Confusion clouded his fern green gaze.

"Hey now! Raven?" He propped her up by the shoulders. "What happened?"

"Lucifer…has Rainne." Alex smelled so good. Soothing. Safe. Warm. Dizzying. Weights tugged her eyelids. Down, down, down she sank, swallowed into the realm of darkness and nightmares.

☽ ✳ ☾

Alex was only sure of one thing, and that was the sting of Raven's punch. The area stunk of Donovan and his clove oil, and of blood and silver.

"What happened to you?" he whispered, hoisting her into his arms. He needed to report to Lord Lucien, but she was the only one permitted to enter the Arc of True Blood.

Then again…he *had* been promoted as her equal. Hoping that was enough, he used her Vampiric Star to enter Animus Hollow so the arc's entrance would open. The wait inside seemed as endless as the rolling haze. Finally, it split apart and revealed Snowblood Square in all of its formal blue and white glory. The scent of acrid blood prickled his nape.

Stepping out, he balanced Raven over his shoulder and unhinged the Cataclysm from his belt. The arc was too quiet. Even accounting for the privacy grids, it felt abandoned.

"Hello?" he called, turning in place, his voice traveling much farther than it'd ever gone before. The entire privacy grid was down. "What the hell——"

"Alexander."

Alex winced under Lord Lucien's thundering voice. "Okay, that's scary as hell," he muttered under his breath, still circling and seeing no one.

"My lord, I apologize for breaching protocol. Raven's out cold and I don't know what's happened. She said Lucifer has Lady Rainne?"

"Come to Rainne's."

Fear shuddered down the length of Alex's body. He didn't want to go to Lady Rainne's——of that, he was certain——and the impression nagged stronger as his journey brought him closer to the source of that nasty blood.

His boots scuffed the rocky path in hesitation when Lady Rainne's residence came within view. He firmed his grip on the Cataclysm. A tall creature waited at the gate: beyond demonic with dark, daggered nails, long ears that tapered into lethal silver points, and gunmetal hair singed onyx at the roots——beastly yet possessing the regal beauty of a monster from a Greek tragedy. Hardened scales, the deep teal of an ocean trench, covered every inch of flesh, crimson fang tips burned black into the ivory protruding past almost black lips, and a thin, glowing circle of bloodlust lit eyes of pure obsidian.

Only Lord Lucien wore that black silk kimono and hakama. The vampiric stars embroidered on either side of his chest and the pale body at his feet trapped Alex's breath in his throat.

"My lord?"

When the creature didn't respond, warning built a charge within Alex that sparked his alteration. He hinged his weapon on his belt, took a knee, and bowed his head in reverence. When he next locked eyes with the creature, the entire arc was shaded the color of blood and his fangs were descending into his mouth.

"Rise." The creature's attention shifted to Raven's unconscious form slumped over Alex's shoulder. "Command code zero, zero, one, Arc Lockdown, mode: full."

Fear's talons clicked up Alex's spine one vertebra at a time as the creature——Lord Lucien——locked the only exit. He willed his body to cooperate and stand as he peered at the creature's feet through hooded lids. His heart sank. The body there was, indeed, Lord Endymion——

dead.

"Oh, Raven," he whispered, tucking his chin for a respectful moment of silence. A moment was all he got before the creature's stare ice-picked his brain.

Rising tall, he reported, "I found her dazed in Sunset Grove. It smelled like Donovan had been there. She said Lucifer has Lady Rainne. Is that true?"

"Likely."

The creature's icy voice sent another shudder zipping through Alex. He clenched his jaw and cocked his head slightly to shake it off—hopefully subtle enough to go unnoticed—but then a flash burst in his mind that switched his fear of the creature with the fear of that confirmation, and his world tilted off center.

"*Lucifer has Lady Rainne?*" Alex huffed breathlessly, lightheaded, the ground rushing away from him.

"Are my VaSH High Commanders too weak for the fight ahead?"

Each word bit into Alex with frigid severity. "M-my lord, we must evacuate to the mansion under the full protect—"

"Protection from Rainne Blood Pathos under Lucifer's command? You are either joking or dumb, High Commander." The creature took Raven from him. "She hasn't fed or slept properly in days, apparently. Endymion always did enjoy bending my orders to fit his needs one way or another, and this time it cost us dearly. Come."

Raven's pale skin and neon hair disappeared into folds of black silk. The creature walked in the direction of Lord Lucien's residence, his hair and pleated trousers swaying in the graceful and effortless way that belonged to the First Born.

But…this creature…no! His eternal lord never talked so casually, and was incapable of caring if Raven had slept or fed, let alone of cradling her to his chest, taking care not to cut her with his claws. Frozen in place, Alex stared after the creature and glimpsed the embroidered star that dotted the spot usually hidden by silvery locks.

The creature is Lord Lucien. He repeated it internally a few times before looking at Endymion's body and then following, too confused and scared to form a single, coherent thought.

☽ ❋ ☾

Alexander squirmed uncomfortably on the red cushion at Lord Lucien's cracked tea table. Lucifer had Rainne and they were sipping blood from bone China teacups retrieved from a dented cabinet full of jagged shards. A blood bag dripped intravenously into Raven's arm. She had yet to regain consciousness and Alex had yet to say anything more than, "yes, sir," or, "no, sir," or, "thank you, sir."

He'd stopped mentally referring to Lord Lucien as *the creature* but it was hard not to stare—he tried to be subtle, at least. The whole situation was too nightmarishly bizarre. Maybe he was the unconscious one and Raven and Jonathan were having a good laugh at his expense. He'd give anything to hear Raven laugh right now.

"You may look." His eyes downcast, Lord Lucien's gravelly voice disappeared into his teacup as he sipped. "Lucifer created me a thousand years before Jonathan. I learned to alter my appearance to blend in as a humanoid, but lacked the ability to do so wholly—after all, he did design a monster to evoke fear. He succeeded, I suppose. Few have seen me like this and lived, either by my volition or theirs."

"How..." Alex started, but thought better of it.

"Speak freely. We may all die soon; why hold your tongue?"

"Well, uh," Alex said, scratching a nonexistent itch behind his ear. "I don't know where to start. Who killed Endymion? Why do you look like that? Why was Raven with Donovan? How did *Lucifer* get Rainne?"

Nodding at Raven, Lord Lucien said, "She must answer most of those. As for me? I am angry. More so than I've experienced in more than three thousand years—so much that I'm not sure I actually feel anything at all."

The creature—*damn it*—sipped from his tiny, delicate cup pinched carefully between his monstrously large, black and daggered claws. The silence was maddening. The calm—biting.

Panic lodged a permanent spot between Alex's ribs. Lord Lucien— wise, apathetic, logical—had reverted to a monster because he was *angry?*

What does that even mean? Alex wondered, planting his fidgety hands in his lap. He should be doing anything other than playing tea party with an unconscious Commander and the leader of their nation who had lost his mind *and* body.

Everything felt wrong. So, badly, wrong.

And the only exit was locked.

"So, uh, how do you change back?"

"I don't know." Lord Lucien nestled his cup into the saucer and stared at something over Alex's head.

Fitting since everything about this is so over my head, he thought, closing his eyes and taking a flustered breath. This was probably how hostages felt. Trapped, biding their time for a window to open. Alex's only window existed in Lord Lucien's verbal command to unseal the damn door. *What if you just asked, you idiot?*

"I'm making you uncomfortable." No change in voice, affect, or gaze.

"A little, yeah," Alex said with a grimace. Had the air always felt like a porcupine? Because it was poking him *everywhere*.

"My appearance is that jarring?"

His lips moved in effort to respond, but no voice came out. This was so far beyond weird—his eternal lord was *the* original creation, the First Born, the iron core of the Vampiric Nation, a being feared beyond fear, but he suddenly affected a lost boy seeking his way. *A terrifying lost boy*, Alex mentally corrected.

"No—" Alex began, "It's…okay, it's like, I know my boundaries with Master Jonathan. But this…with you…" He shrugged.

"Ah." Wispy ribbons steamed Lord Lucien's dark lips as he paused before sipping to say, "Endymion might posit trying Paresh's touch to restore me."

"That…!" Alex wrinkled his face in thought. "I mean, yeah. Her touch is like magic on Eric and Master Jonathan."

"Bring her." An underlying sadness made Lord Lucien's voice even creepier.

"Do you, eh, want her to…see you?" To avoid cringing, Alex quickly lifted his cup and gulped its contents.

"No, I suppose not…"

"Master Jonathan will demand to come. And Eric, too."

"Of course…"

Are you trying to shoot yourself? Alex thought, wiping his face with both hands. *He's giving you a way out!*

"I need her. I can't function in this state."

That was the first logical order Alex had received since Raven pulled all of his hunters out through Kestrel instead of him. He flinched in surprise as a portal opened beside him.

Lord Lucien unpinned the Vampiric Star from the sash at his waist. "This will allow you to return here directly. Bring only her. Jonathan will honor my request if you show him my star. Say nothing of what you've seen."

☽ ✳ ☾

Alexander's bizarro journey took him into the pitch-black depths of Eric's former quarters. He was nearly blind, but he saw skin and knew

218

they were naked and somewhat…*entwined* in their sleep.

Blowing air over his upper lip, Alex whirled on his heel. He should wake them. He knew it with every cell of his being. But he also knew Eric would not "honor the request" and the situation would escalate quickly.

He snuck up the stairs and located Jonathan. Instead of helping, he, also, chose not to "honor the request" and snatched the most powerful star in their nation from Alex's hand, demanding to speak with Lord Lucien.

"Ah…" Alex scratched his non-existent itch, genuinely wishing Raven was there. She'd know what to do. He was so lost. "Orders are orders. I'm sorry."

Cringing inwardly, he tackled his master, who dropped the star and went down surprisingly easy with shocked hunters looking on. "Oh hell, I forgot about your wound!"

Hovering over Jonathan on his hands and knees, Alex swept Lord Lucien's Vampiric Star into his pocket and hurriedly checked Jonathan's side. As Alex jumped up, his master rose with a groan and leveled a deadly glare on him. The Vampiric Star on his lapel hung loose, caught on a torn thread.

Muttering incoherently and jerking uncertainly, Alex stole his master's star and darted for the basement. He slammed the door behind him and leapt down the stairs, his boots skidding on the concrete floor as he steered himself into the bedchamber. He hesitated only long enough to imagine waking them and facing Eric's lethal anger as his master charged in. It reminded him of his vision and he didn't like his odds.

As Jonathan's feet thudded down the stairs, Alex opened the portal to Animus Hollow. Bolstering his resolve with a huff, he shoved his arms under Paresh. Gritting his teeth, he tugged her free, tucked her to his chest, and stepped backward into the Hollow right as Jonathan burst in and flicked on the light.

As the portal closed, Alex noticed that Eric hadn't woken up, and Paresh was limp in his arms. Surely, jerking her from bed would have woken at least one of them.

Despite knowing he couldn't see her, he looked down and was surprised to find an ethereal glow. It swirled the Hollow's haze into a vortex and sucked it in like a black hole. It was mesmerizing. Was it her soul?

The soul of the Sacred Vessel, which you literally stole from under an Arch

Elder like some suicidal pirate kidnapper, Alex mentally chided. This was insane. He needed to reaffirm his grip on reality.

What a joke. He was the only one with a grip and it was tenuous at best, even with Paresh's essence flowing over him as warm as the sun.

"Finally," he muttered to himself as the portal opened beside Lord Lucien's wooden tea table, where he sat in his creature-esque form, sipping blood from ridiculously tiny cups.

Wake up already! Alex mentally screamed at Raven. He needed her knowledge, her guidance—for her to tell him what to do *and* to handle the wrath awaiting him in the Realm of Man. No way was he returning alone.

Defeated and frustrated, Alex exited the Hollow, realizing that—of course—he hadn't snagged the bed sheet to cover Paresh's naked body. *You're a perverted suicidal pirate kidnapper, then,* he thought.

Lord Lucien met the sigh Alex didn't know he dropped with narrowed, demonic eyes. Squeezing Paresh closer, Alex shriveled as the dark teal scales at his lord's throat bristled and he rose. Lucifer had not failed in his effort to terrify.

Lord Lucien disappeared behind his watercolor screen and returned with a black cloak that he draped over Paresh's body. "Do explain, High Commander."

"Well, uh," Alex fumbled in his pocket for Lord Lucien's Vampiric Star. Jonathan's clattered onto the tabletop and got a raised brow from his eternal lord. "The, uh, situation required a snap judgment that will probably cost me my head, but she's here alone as ordered."

As if on cue, the ruby center of Jonathan's star began to glow. Lord Lucien sank to his knees. "Jonathan did not honor my request?"

Still in the land of the bizarre, Alex thought. *And you came back willingly. Yep. You're an idiot. It's official.*

"It's, uh, chaotic at the mansion, as you know, my lord," Alex said, fighting to maintain his composure despite Paresh's essence. But how was that possible after a perverted suicidal pirate kidnapper witnessed the First Born *wilting like a flower?*

The one pillar his nation had left was limp in his arms. It was utterly, absurdly, loony, but Alex had a job to do and if he did it right, some semblance of normalcy would return.

"Without putting words into Master Jonathan's mouth," he said, "I believe he wanted to confirm your order, but there wasn't time."

"He should not require confirmation." The creature brushed the stars aside and sipped from his teacup. Lifting his chin, he cradled the cup in its saucer and rose to caress Paresh's delicate cheek with a tender, monstrous claw. "I am relieved she is not awake to see me."

Paresh's consciousness journeyed with the Sandman, but her aura was awake and far hungrier in Lord Lucien's presence than it'd been in the Hollow. That mere caress softened armored scales, shrank daggered claws, and lightened his hand to pale blue.

Alex shifted their Sacred Vessel into Lord Lucien's arms as he lifted her palm to his cheek. Mumbles fell under her breath as Lord Lucien sank again, this time in relief, his anger and grief draining away.

The return of frosted locks against pale blue skin and black silk dropped Alex instinctively onto a fully reverent bended knee. "Milord, maybe she'd help Raven? She was dazed when I found her—perhaps *angry*, as well?"

Quartz crystal orbs lifted with a profound sadness. Giving a subtle tilt of his chin, Lord Lucien agreed. They transferred their precious cargo and Paresh stirred, moaning.

"Er…*Alex?*" She blinked sleep from her eyes. "Lucien?"

"Apologies milady," Alex said with a sad smile, "an emergency required your unique skills as our Sacred Vessel."

"Um…" Glancing down at herself and the black cloak, she wiped at the dried blood on her mouth. "Why am I naked?"

"Uh…"

"Kimono and men's shirts are in my sliding closet," Lord Lucien said, tucking his hands into his sleeves.

"I'm sorry," Alex whispered as he carried her over. He set her on her feet behind the screen and returned to the other side. He eyed his eternal lord.

"Paresh, do excuse the Commander. He was under my order."

"Eric doesn't know I'm here, does he?" Paresh asked, her voice muffled by clothing.

"He knows," Lord Lucien replied, "but not why."

"He might be more worried than usual. Can you please call him?" Paresh emerged nearly drowning in one of Lord Lucien's kimonos. She'd folded the seams and wrapped it around her, and was fumbling with the black sash at her waist. Smiling, Alex offered to assist. As he knotted the delicate silk, Paresh pressed a gentle hand to her belly.

"Are you okay?" Alex asked, kneeling before her.

She cupped his cheek. Her touch was warm. How did she not melt everyone around her? How had world peace not become a thing yet? Surely, that was within her power.

"I'm fine." She nodded at Raven. "What happened?"

"The COMS..." He trailed, unable to rationalize any reason for Raven to meet with Donovan. "They attacked."

"What can I do? Does she need my blood?" Paresh hobbled over folds of black fabric in her hurry to kneel at Raven's side.

On the table, Jonathan's star was glowing red again, and only one other star in the Realm of Man could connect to it directly. Picking at the invisible itch behind his ear, Alex fixed a nervous gaze on his eternal lord. Lord Lucien opened a line to Eric on his communicator. Somehow, Lord Lucien was able to tap into human phone lines and mobile networks. Given his ability to speak through Animus Hollow and their privacy grids, Alex guessed he was able to break down molecules and bond his energy at the atomic level to connect dots and data to wherever he chose.

The annoyed shift in Lord Lucien's apathetic expression indicated a heated greeting from Eric. A length of silence stretched between them. Finally, he said, in his usual monotone, "I did not require your assistance and Paresh is as safe as I am at the moment. Alex acted under my order, which Jonathan should have obeyed."

Paresh beckoned Lord Lucien to her, placing her cheek against his as he folded down beside her. "Eric, I'm okay—there was an emergency and Raven was injured. I'm at the Arc of True Blood and safe, promise."

Raven groaned. Her eyelids fluttering, she grimaced and swung an arm over her brow. "Bloody stars, it's bright," she croaked.

Alex's heart leapt nearly as high as his legs as he launched from the table and landed on the tatami mat next to her. "Goody! You're awake!"

"Aye, Captain Obvious. My head is throbbing—what did you do to me?"

Lucien turned away, unreadable as he listened to whatever Eric was yelling, and Paresh pivoted to place both hands on the huntress's temples.

Raven squinted at the girl. "Pare—"

"I think I know what to do." Paresh closed her eyes and hummed a lullaby to herself. Heat tingled beneath Alex's fingers on Raven's skin. The quiet song lulled him into the Sandman's domain. He felt heavy. At peace. Blissful—bathed in the golden light of a sunny day, swimming in the green of Mother Nature, warmth healing his soul. Then the world rocked sideways and punched him into darkness.

☽ ✳ ☾

The powerful muscles that allowed for Alex's feather light movements crashed into Paresh entirely as deadweight. Raven peered through cracked lids as the girl groaned under the strain of catching him.

Shaking herself awake, she lifted onto an elbow and kinked her neck. She'd nearly gone out again, as well, standing at the edge of dreams, beckoned by Endymion. "He's got a pulse. You can let him fall."

"But——"

"It's okay," Raven croaked, her throat dry and scratchy. "Things got a little crazy overnight, but he's okay. We're all running on very little sleep."

She patted the girl's hands and tousled Alex's blond spikes, prompting a low groan—a promising sign—and then opened the release valve on her IV to drip faster. At his tea table, Lord Lucien streamed blood into a teacup and passed it to Raven through Paresh. "I await your report, High Commander."

Nodding an acknowledgment to her eternal lord, she savored a slow sip. Paresh was shaking Alex's shoulder to coax him awake, completely oblivious that she had knocked him out in the first place.

Raven swallowed another sip. Steamed blood coated her throat, greasing her vocal chords and warming her gut. "My lord," Raven began, her voice rough, but better, "I sought a parley, of sorts, with——"

A cord of tension in Paresh's aura cut Raven off. Her gaze withdrawn and breaths shallow, the girl clenched and unclenched her hands, twitching her fingers, interlacing them, and picking at her thumbs. "I can smell him on you," she whispered. "It's okay."

"I should have killed him," Raven said, guilt steering her view from Paresh to the floor. That traitor deserved so much more than a few punches to the balls and a needle of shitty, fake liquid silver—parley or not.

"Skip ahead, Commander," Lord Lucien requested. "Who entered the arc?"

Fear braced Paresh, but as soon as Raven's lips parted, the girl half-smiled at Alex. He'd squeezed her hand.

"I saw that, Crimson Commander," Raven snapped. "Sit up. You need to hear this, too."

"Go steal Apollo's lyre," Alex grumbled, lethargy rolling him onto his side, hugging Paresh's hand like a stuffed bear. A charged silence followed. He swore.

"Forget where you are?" Raven asked.

Sitting up and rubbing his eyes like a tired child, he whined, "Damn it, Goody. Why'd you let me fall asleep in the first place? My head hurts."

"If you'd gotten medically cleared, properly, as ordered, you'd be fit for duty," Raven grunted. To Lord Lucien, she said, "Salea killed the hunters here, but not—" Raven inhaled sharply. She couldn't say his name.

"Hold up." Alex held out a steadying hand, blinking rapidly to clear his eyes and focus. He was more exhausted than she'd thought. "Your runt is alive? She killed my hunters? Why don't you think she killed Endy—ah…"

He pressed a finger to his lips and rolled his neck back to cover the alarmed look he shot at Raven. Eric withstanding, anyone touched by the Hand of Divinity formed an immediate kinship. Their purposes intertwined and intersected, and Endymion's foresight gave him an ability to form unbreakable bonds and build bridges between others, as he did during the Great Holy War between Lord Lucien and Raven.

"Please say what you need to say." Paresh had paled and likely sensed his death—another friend lost in the wake of an uprooted life. A pang of sorrow struck Raven's heart. Alex sagged, too. Neither of them had the strength to say it.

The hard ridge in Lord Lucien's aura would have gone undetected had Raven not shifted her attention at that moment. He was waging a difficult internal battle to maintain his composure. "Endymion is dead."

Gulping in disbelief, Paresh squinted against tears and ground her teeth to stop her trembling jaw. She jumped up and flew into Lord Lucien, who had stood and caught her in open arms. He held her to him, hiding her behind the long black sleeves of his kimono and the silver locks that draped over her as his lips skimmed the top of her head. "He died to protect Rainne, and, through his duty, all of us. But he failed."

Raven swallowed the lump in her throat. She wanted to be done with all of this. "Donovan thought Salea came alone, but she could never kill Endymion. He admitted the mansion was a diversion and that Corben planned to kill Ambrosia. I asked him who else is *powerful* in the COMS and he answered, 'Lucifer.'"

"Hence, 'Lucifer has Rainne,'" Alex whispered to himself. "They must have hoped to use her to take you out here, my lord, not expecting you to be at the mansion."

"Aye. I concur," Raven said.

"Twice now, Lucifer has mistakenly believed he knows me." Their eternal lord's voice was muffled against Paresh's hair.

"Donovan was also surprised by Endymion's death."

"You guys got awfully chummy." Alex angled a brow at Raven. "Why isn't he a dead Donovan?"

"He nearly was," Raven retorted. "Lucifer's involvement changes things a bit, doesn't it? I extracted useful information and strategically spared him to learn where they are hiding."

That prompted Lord Lucien to lift his face. "Where?"

"One of the Celestial Landing Points," Raven answered. "I don't know which one, but there are only seven in the Realm of Man and it wasn't Hawkiel's."

"Oh come on!" Alex threw his hands out. "They can't be at the Vatican."

"One in six chance—"

The hazy white crack forming behind Lord Lucien spurred Raven to her feet. She ripped out the IV and sprang forward, dagger in hand. Eric charged out, scowling, demonic eyes engorged and swollen, and fangs bared, and shoved her aside with ease. The First Born's spine snapped the wrong way as he flew over the tea table with Eric's shoulder in his back.

Dropping the dagger, Raven leapfrogged onto Eric, crying, "He's holding Paresh!" She didn't see Master Jonathan until after he'd already thrown her to the floor.

His beastly affect mirrored Eric's, but softened slightly when Lord Lucien spun an uninjured Paresh free of his kimono's sleeves as he ducked and pivoted on the ball of his foot, and shattered Eric's knee with his fist while the girl landed safely in Master Jonathan's arms.

"*You bastard!*" Eric knocked his skull against Lord Lucien's forehead and tackled him, pinning him on the mat. He shoved a vampiric star in the Arch Elder's face. It had a sapphire and diamond encrusted center.

"That's Paresh's...?" Raven's voice trailed, confused. She'd never seen it, but Alex had told her about Lord Lucien giving it to Eric that night in the forest.

"You locked us out? But *her* star is completely uncoded?" Eric growled.

"She is welcome anywhere at any time," Lord Lucien replied in a cool voice, his narrowed eyes sweeping over Master Jonathan before settling on Eric.

"Only yours is supposed to be uncoded." Betrayal soured Master Jonathan's voice as he added, "Not even mine is! And what the hell warranted Alexander *knocking Eric out, attacking me, and kidnapping Paresh?*"

Alex's face scrunched in genuine confusion. "I didn't—Eric was asleep!"

Shoving off Lord Lucien, Eric huffed and assessed Paresh's too-large kimono and tear-streaked cheeks. "Did he hurt you?"

"No, it's not like that!" She tried to pry herself free, but Master Jonathan held on tight. "I'm fine—"

"Yeah," Eric growled, "the last time you were fine with him Rainne felt a scream."

He jabbed a finger in Alex's direction. "I don't know what you hit me with, but you're next."

He warily faced the First Born and shook out his crippled knee. His lips curled into a hateful sneer. He yanked Lord Lucien forward into another head butt. The First Born reeled backward into the entry's shoji screen and Eric limped in pursuit, tackling him until both disappeared from sight.

Alex moved to stand, but immediately dropped to one knee, as did Raven. The golden flecks in Master Jonathan's eyes flickered like angry flames.

"Neither of you shall interfere." Glaring sharply at Alex, Master Jonathan added, "Consider yourself lucky that he opted to attack Lucien first, and say 'thank you' to Paresh, because otherwise, *you'd have me on you.*"

A series of crashes and thuds outside made Raven cringe. She tucked her chin and balled her fist over her chest truly uncertain who would emerge victorious. She spied Alex mimicking her, although his head was hanging.

"Master Jonathan," Alex began, his voice buried so low in his throat it was barely audible. "I swear I did not attack Eric. He was asleep. They both were."

"Endymion is dead and Lucifer has Rainne," Raven quietly added. "This is hardly the time—"

A chill cascaded down Master Jonathan's aura. "What did you say?"

Lord Lucien grunted in the wake of a heavy punch. "Is that true?" Eric yelled. Bones crunched under a fist. "So, following an assault on the mansion and a direct attack on *your* arc, which resulted in the loss of your *greatest* weapon and the *death* of your only trusted ally, you decided to send Alex to kidnap Paresh? To bring her here. With us locked out?"

He half-laughed in fiery disbelief. "You are a fucking piece of work."

Rocks crunched and fists and feet lashed and landed on flesh and bone, and Raven's heart dropped into the pit of her stomach. This was insane. She wanted to jump up and stop all of it. She peeked through her lashes. Alex flinched at the sound of every hit, grunt, and groan.

She angled her gaze up at her master. "It's true. Endymion is dead. Lucifer stole Rainne."

A visible shiver ran through Master Jonathan. His body stiffened. "That—that can't be."

Paresh managed to wriggle loose. She looked downright horrified as she threw a halting hand at Master Jonathan and ran to the entrance. "Stop it! Both of you!"

Everything instantly quieted. Paresh beckoned them inside. Lord Lucien appeared first, pausing to wipe his feet before sliding open the broken screen and entering. Eric followed.

He melted into the hand Paresh cupped at his cheek. Time seemed to stall. No longer upset or sad, Paresh just *was*, and, in that moment, she was their everything—a dreamy stupor glossed Master Jonathan, nostalgia froze Lord Lucien, and Alex's sleepy eyes drooped. Even Raven felt the tug of her ethereal essence trying to drag her back to sleep's domain.

"Paresh?" Raven panted, falling forward on a palm. The pull receded, the spell broken.

With a gasp, Paresh's hand fluttered to her mouth. "I...I didn't mean—"

"It's okay, milady," Alex said with a yawn. He rose and stretched out his arms and legs.

"Aye. You probably feel pretty good about now," Raven said, sitting back and rolling her neck. "But none of us are in any condition to battle. We need rest and nourishment."

Eric's apologetic eyes lifted from Paresh to Lord Lucien, and the two shared a reluctant nod of understanding. Raven doubted their animosity would ever end. Eric was too much like Master Jonathan. One was the First Born's loyal wolf, but the other was, and always would be, a wild beast.

Eric smudged the bloody trickle from his mouth and smacked at the debris dusting his torn t-shirt and jogging pants. Lord Lucien similarly attempted to clean up, wiping at his stained skin and straightening his mussed kimono.

Paresh must have noticed a look that passed between Master Jonathan and Alex, because she held her hand out again and said, "You're all fond of standing behind the excuse that 'orders are orders' but get mad when someone follows an order that doesn't suit you."

She eyed the three Arch Elders. "Alex shares no fault in this. None. And you will not punish him. He is cleared of any and *all* wrongs, controversial orders, *and* punishments, past and present, to this moment, right here, right now. Clear?"

Master Jonathan and Eric fidgeted under her intense stare. Raven caught and held her breath. His attention glued to the tatami mat, Raven couldn't gauge Alex's reaction when Master Jonathan nodded his agreement. She slowly rose and stood, grabbing Alex's hand and interlocking their fingers. She gave him a light squeeze.

He looked up, his unfocused eyes staring through her. She squeezed again, more insistently, and got his attention. He hinted at a smile before receding into his thoughts again.

"No one is on the same page here," Paresh said. She sat at the tea table and patted the spot next to her. Eric shuffled over and the other two joined her. "But everyone is grieving, upset, caught in chaos—you must keep your heads on to lead."

"Endymion's dead." Master Jonathan sounded hollow. He wore a depth of sadness Raven had never seen before.

Paresh took Eric's hands in hers. "Alex didn't attack us. We were both drained. I'm not sure why—maybe the baby—"

She paled and covered her belly. She quieted, not moving and barely breathing.

"The babe…what…?" Too many questions crashed together in Raven's head. Eric looked fierce enough to tackle Lucifer, her lords were bewildered, and Alex grinned like a fool with his hands clamped over his mouth.

"Ha!" Paresh suddenly laughed, startling Raven. She hugged her belly and blew out a relieved sigh. "It's okay!"

"Bloody stars!" Raven cried. "Don't do that!"

Eric's outstretched hands gently cupped her abdomen. He lowered his ear and listened before breathing a visible sigh and relaxing against her.

Alex clenched quivering fists at his side and quickly reclasped them over his mouth. He hopped from one foot to the other like an excited child. "I heard an echo!"

Paresh smiled. "You did!"

"But that's not possible!" Rejuvenated, Alex leapt to her side, nearly crashing into Eric. He pressed his ear against the small of Paresh's back and gasped.

"That's the consensus," Paresh replied, laughing.

He took her hand. She threaded their fingers. His smile lit the room. "I saw a glow——in Animus Hollow. It fed off the energy in there."

Paled with disbelief cutting hard lines into his face, Master Jonathan moved his lips but shared Raven's affliction and merely managed unintelligible noises.

Searching for betrayals to his impassive countenance, Raven noticed a nearly imperceptible lift to Lord Lucien's cheeks. "Were you pregnant the night you died?"

Paresh nodded. "I think so."

"A pure soul," Raven whispered, squatting on her heels.

"Preg? Nant?" Master Jonathan was about to faint.

"Alex?" Raven said, eyeing their master.

"On it, Goody!"

He helped Master Jonathan edge around the table to sit by Paresh. Lord Lucien inched closer and even Raven gave in to the compulsion. They mobbed together, kneeling or standing beside Paresh and laying their hands upon her.

A sensation of peace settled over Raven, and the others, judging by the release of tension in their tightly wound muscles. Their auras formed a tangible unseen energy, and the air thickened, soothing, fresh, innocent, organic, loving.

"My lords...the Sacred Vessel," Raven exhaled. "We must unite in our duty. We have more to fight for now than ever."

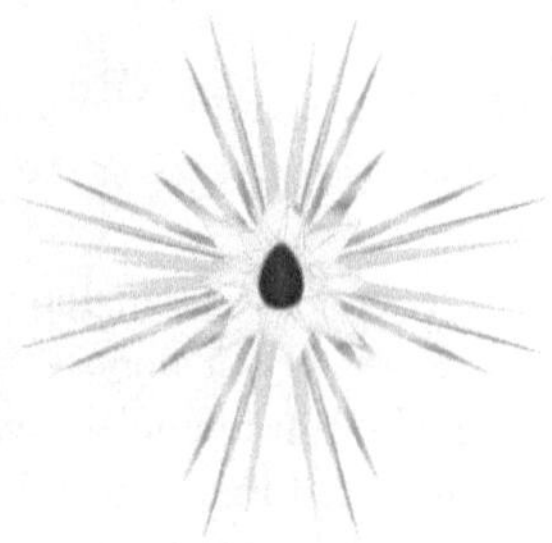

CHAPTER FIFTEEN: THY GRIEF, THY JOY, THY HATE, THY LOVE

Bearing newly unlocked Vampiric Stars, Raven and Alex convened the VaSH Commanders and First Officers at the Arc of Mourning Eidolons. The briefing excluded Endymion's death, Lucifer's appearance, and Paresh's pregnancy, and focused on the global threat that Lady Rainne presented. Unease thrummed within their auras upon the revelation of the empty casket at the mansion and sharpened into needles at the limited details regarding Salea's role.

The girl's comatose presence at the Arc of Celestial Night was a well-known secret among the higher ranks. They never believed that she'd recover and thought she died in the explosion. Raven forced herself to face their questioning eyes. Her own guilt wasn't enough. She needed their blame, too.

The COMS expected her to empty their arsenal and send armies of hunters to the Celestial Landing Points. Knowing Lucifer was in play changed everything, and Corben's predictive foresight meant she needed to be a wildcard. "Hunters with priority security details are to continue as they were. All others are to seek out and kill all rogues. No survivors. No exceptions."

She firmed her resolve as she met each doubting expression. Endymion's death proved Salea was beyond rehabilitation or redemption. The girl had never wanted either and should have died long ago. "That includes Salea and Rainne Blood Pathos. If an opportunity presents, take it with haste."

When they adjourned, Raven was alone with her new First Officer. Salea's survival cast a dark shadow over Kestrel, an unspoken accusation of betrayal and loss that punched Raven deep in the gut. One decision to spare the dying target of a kill order had doomed the world—a world without Lior in it.

A mere century ago, Salea had erased half of Kestrel from existence. In that shadow, Raven saw clearly that the Second New Age had torn her grief open anew. Kestrel had never formed another intimate connection—beyond sex, she and Lior had "fit" together to form a whole, much as with Heron and Cyprian. Salea's contribution to Endymion's death seemed a fitting punishment.

No matter what Raven wanted to say to Kestrel, time and duty didn't permit lingering on history or remorse. She handed off Wraith Reaper co-command and crashed the Crimson Guard's meeting to cart Alex off for medical clearance—again. They both needed treatment for exhaustion. Once cleared, they returned to the mansion. She slipped away for a quiet moment before Lord Lucien and their new trinity returned from the Arc of True Blood.

Cloaked and hunched on a windowsill overlooking the decrepit garden and dried up fountain, a pollinated, organic breeze caressed her face. The mid-morning sun ruled a clear sky swathing a deceptively peaceful world. She'd believe the lie if not for the Elders' tension vibrating the mansion's walls.

The COMS' sudden silence was a jagged nail in her heart. The Hawkings Protocol didn't restrict Lucifer. Donovan hadn't known what really happened at the Arc of True Blood—maybe the others didn't either. Rainne Blood Pathos had always been Lucifer's failsafe. Maybe she still was.

☽ ❋ ☾

Paresh walked in silence beside Alex followed by Seneca and Minerva. He eyed the fingers that twitched at her sides. She wanted to touch her belly, which had grown substantially over the past few hours. She and Eric had requested Alex as an escort when they left the manor on a quick errand.

Alex had never gone "bump hiding" shopping before and found the array of colors, patterns, layers, and cuts dizzying. But, being at her side, casually dressed in jeans and a crimson v-neck shirt, came as welcomed down time. His excitement built after Eric charged him with entertaining her while he and Jonathan met with the Elders.

Curious about Alex's secretive plans for their midmorning fun, Paresh tried to suss out clues by asking him to choose her clothes. His selection of a sunny yellow sleeveless blouse—ruched over the abdomen—and a flowing navy blue maxi skirt patterned with deep red poppies didn't offer much. He'd added a white lightweight cardigan for "in profile" concealment, as the shop's clerk had put it. The fabric draped smoothly down her shoulders and the hem swayed beneath her waist about mid-thigh. He'd twirled her once, stating that it would "flair out" perfectly.

Her hands twitched again. Itching to feel the baby kick, too, Alex twirled the thick golden disc out from under his arm and spun it to land flat in his palm. Embossed scrollwork defined the edges around the raised silver filigree of the Vampiric Star, resplendent with diamond and ruby center.

"Why do we need that?" Paresh asked, lightly tracing the star's blunted points. "It's cold!"

"And heavier than it looks, too." Alex winked. "Lord Lucien's crest denies the Elders entrance, even within their domain. It guarantees our privacy."

They arrived at the ballroom. Alex swung the doors open and handed the crest to Seneca. She squeezed the golden rod in her hand to extend into a tapered staff. Minerva did the same with hers. They turned and crossed their staffs over the entrance, and Seneca attached the crest where their staffs intersected.

The doors creaked shut. "The Elders know you're here, so that crest protects you from their curiosity. Its authority is absolute in all eyes— eyes we don't want on you right now." Alex spun into the room's center with his arms out and smiled. "Plus there's a privacy grid active in here, so it's just us now!"

"Finally!" Paresh giggled and smoothed her palm over her belly. Lifting her gaze from Alex, she turned in a slow circle, jaw agape.

Framed in aged black velvet, sunlight filtered through chiffon sheers and painted long, cheery rectangles on the floor's marble veins. The stamped copper ceiling bore an aged green patina and dusty white sheets hugged the grand piano in the far corner and the Depression Era sideboards along the interior wall. Two multi-tiered chandeliers hung from the ceiling, their crystals splintering the sun's rays into rainbows of refracted color.

"There were always tall plants in here—like the giant tropical palms in Eric's atrium—and a band would play alongside the piano. Depending on the era, it'd be jazz or classical." Alex's voice took on a faraway quality. This was one of his favorite rooms. "I suppose the skeleton crew put the mirrors and paintings into storage. I haven't been in here since the last fire. It was always filled with happy sounds."

"It's beautiful." Paresh padded to the center window, absently smoothing the gossamer fabric between her thumb and forefinger while surveying the desolate statues in the neglected garden.

"That was a hedge maze long ago. Eric razed it and put in that fountain. It splashed all day and night, the statues were all pristine white, and roses bloomed throughout the summer. At your grandfather's parties, they'd have a string quartet out there and rows of lights hung up…it was so beautiful—men in tuxedos and women in gowns, drinking and dancing, laughing and having fun." Alex stood behind Paresh and twirled her to face him. "But this is a much better view."

Playfully slapping his shoulder, she laughed. "Please don't use that awful line to pick up women!"

Alex scoffed. "I would never! I am deeply offended, milady!"

Her expression sobered. Her gaze washed over the room once more. "I can't imagine the pain that made my father abandon this place—this extravagant life."

She crossed her arms and scrutinized Alex, as though searching for tells to his lies. He stiffened slightly, uncertain about the coming questions.

"What was it like for Eric?" she asked. "Do you think it's hard for him to be back here?"

"Ah, well—" He gulped and shuffled back a step. "I, uh, imagine he was glad to get away, but I don't really know."

"More secrets?"

A sigh dropped between Alex's slumping shoulders. "Partially, but it's the truth. He built his house and lived on his own for the first time. I honestly don't know how he felt."

"It's okay." She absently rubbed her belly and faced the window. "Eric knows everything about me; I just want to know more about him, but I guess things are pretty bad if Gabriel's clammed up, too. Stuff like that doesn't matter anymore."

He cringed inwardly and placed his hands on her shoulders. "Gabriel hasn't given up on you. He told me to bring you joy."

Her muscles tensed beneath his fingers. A thought appeared and rushed away faster than a spark on a detonation cord. Gabriel's cryptic clues suddenly made sense.

Life was precious. But short. And happiness was fleeting.

Bring her joy.

Bile stung his throat.

Lucifer has Rainne.

Hawkiel is coming.

Paresh is pregnant.

Soft hands covered his and drained his fear. Paresh was oblivious. "Were you here much before my dad left it behind? Watching over Master Jon like his guardian angel?"

"Something like that." His voice was uneven over the rock that had lodged in his throat. He tried again. "Master Jonathan dismissed us—his pack—frequently, but I was usually around, somewhere close."

"Hmm." Her gaze shot out to the distant orchard. "You escorted him everywhere?"

"Until he was settled and it was safe for us to leave or he ordered us away."

"In Kansas?"

His breath clung to the top of the rock. She'd caught him. Clenching his jaw, he nodded, but she couldn't see him.

"You watched me grow up?"

"I, uh, wuh-wasn't always there, but y-yes. I was the only true blood permitted to witness the relationship you shared with Master Jonathan."

"What happened to Miss Lydia?"

His spine stiffened straighter than he thought possible. "She moved into the Arc of Ebony Stars with honorary true blood titling for raising you. I altered her halfway into her assignment."

"Okay, aside from making me sound like homework—" she pointed a sharp, Raven-like look at him, "that's nice. I'm happy for her."

"Good." He relaxed and pulled a slim white device from his pocket. He set it on the sill and took her hand. Gently turning her, he bowed and peered up shining a lopsided grin. "Then, may I have this dance?"

Paresh tilted her head, uncertain. "Dance?"

"Of course!" A button clicked under his finger. The plunking piano keys of *Lisztomania* by Phoenix started as Alex spread his arms wide. "It's a ballroom! Let's Quickstep, milady!"

Drums and guitars joined the piano and kicked up the tempo. She smiled incredulously. "I don't know how! Isn't this song too modern for an old dance?"

"Nah!" He swatted her concern away. "We're pretty much going to run the whole time. I want to test your stamina levels given how hungry the jumping bean is."

He pulled her into the closed dance hold, one hand on the small of her back and the other outstretched. She was so tiny in his arms, delicate and fragile—like Lord Lucien's teacups. "The song is looped; we have plenty of time to play while the others work. Let's have some fun. I've always wanted to dance to this song, but Raven isn't much for dancing."

He chuckled. "She's the awkward duckling that falls on its face instead of a graceful swan, but I didn't say that."

Laughing, Paresh squared her shoulders to match his posture. "She'd kick you to no end if she heard that."

"Oh, she'd kill me." The music slowed, stretched, plunked, and picked up. "Okay, I'm the guy, so I lead and you follow."

"Raven wouldn't let you do that either." Paresh's body shook under a genuinely hearty laugh.

Bring her joy.

Internally, he tensed at Gabriel's words. Outwardly, he played the goof and dropped his jaw, staring in mock astonishment. "That woman!"

He shook his head. His blond spikes wobbled and his voice squeaked. "I won't let her corrupt you."

The song winded to its end for the first time. The piano started plunking again. He winked and grinned. "Ready? Take a sweeping step back and then do a quarter turn. Stay in hold, move in tandem with me, and start on your left foot. Watch me and not your feet. Got it?"

"I think so. Oh! I'm nervous!" Paresh blushed and gnawed her lip.

Alex's grin widened. "The one person capable of taking Lucifer down with a touch is flustered by a dance?"

The color drained from Paresh's face.

You stupid idiot. Alex fired every internal angry bullet he had at his mouth. "Damn it. I'm sorry."

She forced a smile and lifted her chin. "Let's hope it's true. No more sorries. Dance with me."

She wore her bravery like armor, but she truly was that strong. He knew it. She didn't need to pretend.

"After the quarter turn, we start running, then skip a bit and stop for kicks and flicks, and then more turning and running."

He laughed at the doubt in Paresh's expression. "You're going to glide on the air. Trust me."

"I do. Implicitly."

"I know, milady. Thank you." He planted a quick kiss on her forehead as the piano started plunking for the third time. "Here we go for real!"

The hand on the small of her back nudged her to straighten. He flashed the biggest smile possible before leading her into an awkwardly timed sweeping back step.

Endymion was dead.

A quarter turn in the wrong direction.

Hawkiel was coming.

A step off the right foot instead of the left.

Lucifer had Rainne.

Time to run and skip.

And Gabriel knew of worse to come.

Pause for malformed and poorly timed kicks and flicks.

Paresh was laughing so hard her body heaved. He laughed with her, but Gabriel's secret was brutally carving his heart out.

Their Sacred Vessel had defeated death twice and was Lucifer's highest priority target. And now she was pregnant. That damned archangel didn't need to tell him to bring her joy; Gabriel needed to reveal how to stop her clock from ticking so she could survive.

☽ ✳ ☾

The upbeat song played on repeat for more than an hour. Alex eventually dropped all attempts at formality and twirled Paresh or taught her random dance moves. They sang at the top of their lungs, and, by the time Eric arrived, Paresh was doubled over laughing while Alex was breakdancing—which he didn't understand since he was rather good at it.

Alex jumped to his feet and turned the music off. He folded Paresh into a hug and gently rocked in place for a moment, hating the sudden silence and letting her go. If only life could loop a peaceful moment as easily as music. But reality beckoned.

He spun Paresh across the marble. Eric's arm curled around her waist and he effortlessly took her into closed hold, turning with her and slowing into a box step. They danced in a small circle near the doors. Retiring to the covered piano bench, Alex marveled at how radiant Paresh was in Eric's arms. It seemed like they were the only two people in existence.

"How does a trip sound? Break away for a few days?" Eric asked. "We'll go to the bed and breakfast your mom loved in Vermont. Long ago, it was a hunting lodge, secluded, up in the mountains. You'll love it—tons of animals to fawn over you."

Paresh leaned back in his arms. "Is it a good time? Don't they need you here? What about reservations?"

He tucked a stray lock behind her ear. "Lucien believes he and the Elders can form a solid defense here if they remove us from the equation, and Jonathan and I agreed. We'll be accessible in an instant, and reservations don't matter. You own the lodge and I've already had it on retainer for a week."

"You've been paying them to stay empty? For a week?" Paresh dropped her hand to his shoulder.

He nodded.

"Okay, but why doesn't Lucien want you here? They're stronger with you."

"Yes, but you'd be in crossfire." Eric brought the back of her hand to his mouth and kissed each of her fingers. "Without us, they can fight freely."

"But I'm the target!" Breaking free of his embrace, she threw her hands up. "I should have a say in my own risk assessment. I should have been with you instead of being distracted like a child up here! This isn't fair to me!"

Recapturing her hands, Eric nodded. "You're right—and you do— that's why I'm asking you now. This isn't about secrets or making decisions for you. We don't trust the Elders to meet you yet and they were there. If you don't want to go, we won't. You do have a say—in everything. I promise."

"But you already had it planned." She huffed breathlessly, rolling her gaze against a swell of tears.

"Jonathan suggested a trip to me after Molly's funeral, but it'd already been on my mind as a surprise to you before all of this happened."

She pulled away in thought, vacantly staring at the floor. She wrinkled her nose when she looked up. "Will he come, too?"

"Of course," Eric replied dryly. He tugged her to his chest and gently guided her into a Waltz. "Do you think I can possibly keep him away?"

His crystalline blue eyes dusted over Alex. "Him, too. And Raven."

That seemed to seal it. She smiled and lifted onto her tiptoes, bracing herself against Eric's chest to reach his lips. She kissed him gently. "That's sounds wonderful."

"And exactly what we need," he murmured. He planted his hands on her hips and kissed her back, firmer, hungrier.

Alex squirmed and sidled along the bench to sneak out. An insistent, invisible hand on his shoulder forced him to stay put. His lips parted, but another hand clamped over his mouth. He flicked a narrowed glare and the hands released him. A warm body sat beside him shoulder to shoulder.

Eric and Paresh were so lost in each other that neither noticed. Eric's guard was down, anyway, and Paresh unintentionally blinded him. She stole his cares, his worries, his anger, and, their fetus stole his energy—the same effect she had on all of them.

Why did Lord Lucien want to send her away? Alex's mind worked that thread and he didn't like where it took him. Sending Paresh to a secluded place with Raven there...Raven, the only hunter capable of killing Rainne Blood Pathos—

And there it was. Paresh was bait.

No way Eric agreed to that.

Bring her joy.

He silenced Gabriel's voice and tried to stop the clock ticking over Paresh's head. This was not worth the risk to her life. Alex huffed, shaking his head in disbelief. "You can't—"

The invisible hand crushed down on his mouth. He glared at its insistence, only certain that it belonged to Raven after she dipped a finger into his mouth and loosed her blood on his teeth. Was she okay with this? Of course she was. She was over confident in her ability to handle Rainne.

He had no choice other than to speak with that archangel, and that made him no better than everyone else using Paresh. She was their only link to the Heavenly Host. Never before had their nation depended so much on one life.

"They'll have food there, right?" Paresh asked Eric. "Like, people food?"

She scrunched her face in thought. "Well, wait—not like *people* food, like for you, but—"

Belting out a laugh, Eric lightly bumped their foreheads, and Alex, caught off guard, snorted into Raven's muffling hand.

Turning bright red, Paresh glanced at him and yelled, "That's not what I meant!"

"Milady," Alex said quietly, "you don't need to yell, and you are completely adorable, but we're not zombies."

Her cheeks flushed even brighter. "That's not what I meant!"

Sighing happily, Eric slicked his hair back. "They have *real* food, yes. The innkeepers are human."

"Okay, but!" A pointy finger stabbed at both Eric and Alex. "You guys might not eat brains, but you *do* feed on people."

"As do you, milady." Grinning widely to show off his elongated canines, Alex pinched the brim of an imaginary hat and winked.

"Find Raven and get changed, Alex." Hooking Paresh with the crook of his elbow, Eric steered her toward the exit. "We'll leave shortly."

"As you wish." Alex bowed his head and covered his heart with his fist.

Seneca reverently gave Eric Lord Lucien's crest when he held his hand out as he passed between her and Minerva. "You're both with us until we leave."

Paresh waved to Alex as his officers stepped in line to follow Eric. The doors closed and a hard smack on his back knocked the breath from his lungs.

"An ugly duckling?" Though annoyed, Raven's tone was teasing. "Oh no, no-no-no! Not just an ugly duckling, but one that falls on its face!"

"Damn it, Goody!" he huffed. "No one else is supposed to be in here!"

"Aye. And no one here is in violation of that order." She slapped his ear and moved away from him. "Do you honestly think I can't do that dance with you?"

"What then? They have you watching me? And since when do you care about dancing?"

Since she wasn't uncloaking, Alex followed her voice. "If they didn't trust you with her, she wouldn't be with you," she said. "I was offense to your defense, if anything had happened. And…well, yeah. I mean, it looked fun."

She paused. "You're cute with her and the little bean. You'll make a good nanny."

He imagined a wistful smile turning up her lips, but it quickly flattened into a grim line when she added, "She shouldn't be here, though. The Elders can feel her, smell her blood. Have you noticed?"

"I'd be a pretty shitty Commander if I hadn't. The temptation is much stronger now. I almost didn't let her go." Alex focused on specks of dust seesawing in the sunlight.

"Aye," Raven whispered. "Even I feel it now."

Alex kinked his neck and hung his hand off his nape. "If I hadn't screwed up and lost Eric's trust in the first place, they never would've brought her here."

"He does trust you."

"Yeah, *now*. But she'd already been here. Now they have a frame of reference. They know something is different."

"Why do you think the COMS haven't attacked, yet?" Raven asked, shimmering into view by the MP3 player on the window sill.

"Does it matter? Lord Lucien is using Paresh as bait, and you and Eric are going along with it," Alex said, somehow managing not to spit his disgust.

Raven quieted and leaned her elbows on the windowsill. Her chest rose and fell under a silent, heavy sigh. She faced inward to shield her voice within the room's barrier. "Eric doesn't know and I don't have a choice." She tossed her chin at him. "Neither do you."

"This sucks." Alex dragged himself over to slump against the wall beside her.

"It's because of Endymion—he was one of *us*," she said, sadness forming a well beneath her words. "Touched by Divinity. Lord Lucien trusted him, charged him with Paresh's protection at the Arc of True Blood, and he's dead. The Third Born. One of his truest allies. Gone."

Sitting on the sill, Raven crossed her arms. The sun haloed her silhouette like a dark angel. He caught the small breath she tried to hide, the two rapid blinks, the fingertips digging into her skin, and the steep tilt of her chin that fringed her face in neon pink. And yet, as she fought to suppress her grief, elation sparked inside Alex. Endymion was no longer a threat for her affections.

"Are you listening?"

The catch in her voice unleashed a shockwave of guilt that burned Alex's every nerve. His shoulders sagged under its weight. Endymion had saved his life too many times for him to be happy about his death.

"Yeah—Endymion led Lucifer's first army. He was the cruelest commander," Alex recited in monotone, rolling his eyes. "The guy was a frightfully skilled psychopath."

"Which you know, firsthand," she said. "I never saw him in battle. Only heard stories. He was a threat to Lucifer and they took him out. Why are they waiting now?"

"Every strike seems clumsy at first, but their strategy has been near flawless in hindsight," Alex said. "Lucifer's got more in mind than simple carnage and the flaming world that Paresh sees."

Raven shuddered, absently scratching at her shoulder blades. "I keep thinking that Rainne was his failsafe. What if he takes out our key players himself and declares a checkmate? Then he can activate Rainne to kill everyone left standing."

"So the COMS unknowingly play decoy and/or back up?"

"He doesn't need them. All of us are a hindrance to his goal. He wants us as dead as he wants the humans, probably even more so now that the Servator has arrived."

"Look," Alex peeled himself off the wall and straddled Raven's legs with her ankles crossed. "We don't have actual confirmation that Lucifer was there. Think about Nicole."

"The dead woman? What about her?"

"Exactly." Alex funneled his figurative point into a finger poke at Raven's forehead. "*Nicole* was never an issue. The soul possessing her was."

Raven gasped. "*He* might not have Rainne."

"He can literally be anyone. We all have souls now. Maybe Salea was alone—in the physical sense."

Raven jerked up. Alex's head cracked back as she rammed headfirst into his jaw. Oblivious, she yanked him to eye level and spoke in a quiet, rushed voice. "You saw it—Lucifer killed Eric in a human body *after* the beast's rage had taken control? Surely, he'd have enough power to kill Endymion as Salea?"

Rubbing his jaw, Alex said, "Think about what you're saying. Endymion, the Third Born of the Vampiric Nation? The Cruel Commander, the first infectious vampire unleashed upon the world? Against Lucifer in a vampiric body with angelic blood? Come on—he killed someone of Master Jonathan's caliber in a *human* body. Salea? Yeah. More than enough."

"Aye," Raven replied distantly, scratching more intensely at her shoulder. "That explains the difference in kill methodology, too, if Salea was in control only part of the time."

Alex caught Raven's hands. "I know it burns and you're nervous, but you'll scratch yourself raw. Think—can Lucifer override the Hawkings Protocol if he's not in his actual body?"

"Bloody stars!"

Alex successfully dodged as Raven snapped to attention. "No, he can't! He needs to be in his body to control her attack modes!"

"Salea has Hawkiel's blood. I mean, she made some pretty gnarly adjustments to herself—"

"Doesn't matter," Raven interrupted. "She's pulled off some slick tricks, but she wasn't touched by the Hand of Divinity. You were and you can't activate Rainne. She can't do it, possessed or not. Where is Lucifer's body when he's not in it? Who last saw him? When?"

"None of *us* can answer that, Goody." Dread hollowed a nest in Alex's chest. "But Gabriel can."

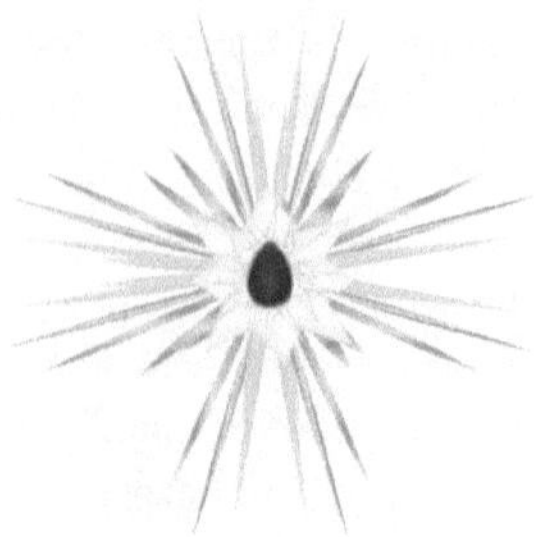

Chapter Sixteen: Sire Thy Rage

I

Orison Crossing, Summer 2006

The gilded outlines of the canopy's highest branches swayed faintly. Patches of powder blue broke through the sea of green, dappling the southern trail with golden spots. Their footsteps were as silent as the forest. The trees whispered their secrets in a language only Paresh understood.

She'd agreed to visit Grandfather Wisdom over Eric's objections, stating that Gabriel would love to hear "the news." Jonathan had reluctantly taken her side with the caveat that he take custody of her Vampiric Star. Eric's jaw had snapped with tension as he pulled the pin from his pocket and stabbed it into his brother's hand. They hadn't spoken a word to each other since, and Eric was fine with that, worn and weary from constant bickering.

Paresh paused where the tree line broke into the circular clearing that the mammoth silver maple called home. She glanced back at Eric and stepped out after he nodded his support. Alex followed. Raven and Jonathan lingered in the shadows.

Hesitating at the monstrous base that branched into four large trunks overhead, Paresh chewed her lip. Eric embraced her in loving arms. "You don't have to."

"It's the only way Alex can talk to him. He won't show me anything, so make it matter," she said, eyeing Alex. "I want to know what he says about my...*new* life."

"I've got you." Eric clasped his hands over her rounded belly and pulled her back to kiss the nape of her neck.

She inhaled a shaky breath and reached a tentative hand out to the rigid grooves. The instant her fingers made contact, her body went limp.

"Are you sure only *her* soul is affected?" Eric asked, propping her against his chest.

Alex shook his head. "But souls are kind of his thing. He wouldn't harm any part of her."

Paresh's eyes blinked open, shining with the brilliance of a holy blue flame. She lifted onto her toes, two pairs of iridescent white wings flapping and disturbing the visible spectrum. Delicate fingers traced the folds of the yellow blouse over her abdomen.

"Ah, Littlest One!" Gabriel's melodic and unnatural voice rang like a bell that should never toll. He leveled a knowing smile on Eric. "Anointed Strength."

"Hello Gabriel," he replied, nodding out of respect and flooded with the warmth of the angel's unsaid congratulations.

"I shall watch over *her*, as well, always," Gabriel said with a wink. A kaleidoscope of emotions washed over Eric, making the angel laugh— an unsettling peal similar to wind chimes in a tornado. "Did you not wish to know?"

A daughter. Eric wished he could say it aloud. His eyes watered. He swallowed the knot in his throat. "Thank you," he replied in a broken voice.

"Oh, my child!" Gabriel pulled him into a firm hug. "We are elated you learned about her. We have known for a while. I could not say, however."

As the angel straightened and hovered over the grass, Eric said, "But it's happening too fast."

"Hmm, yes," Gabriel agreed, tracing the blouse's stretchy lines again. "She would probably arrive in three weeks—well, less than that, now."

"Three...?" Winded, Eric stumbled backward. "*Weeks?*"

"We estimated twenty-three days from the beginning." Gabriel smiled. In Paresh's skin, he glowed like a powdered sun. "But that is not why you've summoned me, and you know I will not share my vision. I am holding her in my wings, but she dislikes the void."

"We know," Alex barked impatiently. "She agreed so I could talk to you."

"You can speak to me anytime you like—"

"Not in a way where you can talk back!" Alex took an incensed step forward.

The angel flinched from the energy in Alex's aura. He crossed

Paresh's arms over her chest, squeezing her shoulders with white knuckled fists. "You must protect this body! Never forget your duty, Crimson Commander."

Eric motioned for Alex to calm down. He whispered into Gabriel's ear, "Do you know what has happened here and at the arc?"

Gabriel cocked Paresh's head to the side, studying Eric first and then Alex. His gaze darted beyond them to Jonathan and Raven on the trail. "Second Born and Hawkiel's…"

Gabriel lowered Paresh's arms to her sides. Brow creased, he flew to Alex, folding his wings as Paresh's feet landed firmly on the grass. He cupped Alex's cheek. "Tell me."

"You know about Banks Island? The coup within our nation?" Alex shoved his sunglasses up and locked onto Gabriel's gaze as he nodded. "The Children of the Morning Star infiltrated the Arc of True Blood. They killed an Elder. *Endymion*, one touched by the Hand of Divinity. And they stole Rainne Blood Pathos. Lucifer has her. *Where is he?*"

Gabriel took a shocked step back. His gaze darted over all four visitors. "This cannot be. How did so much transpire of which I know so little?" The flame in Paresh's eyes flickered dimly as he inwardly searched his sight. "Ah! It is in the gray fibers. It's there, moving closer to the dark. How can this be? If it's happened, it cannot be gray!"

Paresh's brow furrowed deeper as Gabriel pleaded with Alex, "How did this atrocity happen?"

"If you don't know, how would we know?" Alex snipped. "When was the last time anyone saw Lucifer on Earth?"

"Please, Gabriel," Eric asked. "This affects all of the Realm of Man. That must free you to tell us something that helps."

Gabriel returned to his thoughts awhile. If not for Paresh's body standing on its own, Eric might have thought he'd retreated into the tree. Finally, he nodded. "The last time our Fallen Brother Lucifer was seen on Earth was before our Father stripped him of the power of creation. We do not know where he is. We cannot see him on this plane or in the fibers."

"Can he possess a vampire?" Alex asked.

"He may possess any vessel with a soul."

"Can he control Rainne Blood Pathos in a possessed body?"

Gabriel shook Paresh's head. "He may not. He is restricted in astral form as we all are."

"So the Hawking's Protocol…?" Raven asked, her voice low in the shadows.

"The Hawking's Protocol is in effect, Commander of Justice." Gabriel fretted with Paresh's fingers, backing away and withdrawing into his thoughts. "So much…indeed troubling. I must return—"

"What about Hawkiel?" Alex snatched Paresh's arm in an attempt to ground the archangel from slipping free of her body.

"Hawkings knows how to find our Brother Hawkiel. I can say no more. All else remains in the gray fibers of probability. It has not changed."

He eyed Alex's grip. "*You must protect this body.* Did the Little One consent to being harmed?" He glanced over Paresh's shoulder at Eric. "To you, Anointed Strength?"

Flicking Paresh's eyes at Jonathan, the flamed flared brighter. "Or to the bridge between you that carries a soul pardoned by a penitent heart? *Speak, Second Born.*"

"No, she did not." Jonathan's hair glowed like fiery copper as he stepped into the clearing. "Release him, Alexander."

Alex obeyed. "I'm not hurting her."

Gabriel deliberately traced the red outline of Alex's hand on Paresh's arm. "You are not hurting *me*."

Raven marched across the clearing, furiously flinging off her lightweight black jacket. Swinging her back to Gabriel, she pulled the strap of her camisole aside. "Hawkiel's mark is fully formed. Did you know that? You made him do this to me."

Gabriel again seemed to flinch and retreat. Eric put himself between Paresh's body and the others. With Gabriel protecting her soul in the void, her essence wasn't there to protect their daughter. If the anger in their auras was making an archangel flinch, he didn't want it touching his baby. "Contain your auras. Both of you."

Raven looked apologetic. Her lips parted, but Gabriel spoke first, his voice distant, incredulous, shocked. "We know nothing of Hawkiel's mark entering the visible spectrum. We are losing our sight."

"You sound terrified." Alex shared a worried look with Raven. "How are we supposed to feel?"

Shadows of uncertainty shifted across Paresh's face. "Are we being blinded? We do not know what is happening."

"Then tell me what you're hiding from Paresh!"

Gabriel moved Paresh's lips, but said nothing. He shook her head. "I cannot."

Alex twirled on his heel in frustration, releasing the energy from his aura in the opposite direction. Whirling around, fists balled at his sides, he demanded, "How do we know all this stuff that you don't, but you hold out? You wouldn't know anything if we hadn't told you. So, tell us what you're hiding!"

Gabriel stepped away. His wings shook. "I must speak with Brother Michael." The flame in Paresh's eyes dimmed.

"Wait!" Alex demanded. "What is going to happen to her?"

"Her?"

"Paresh!" Tears broke over the pain in Alex's voice.

Gabriel cupped Paresh's hands over her belly. Sadness doused his flame as his gaze sank. "You are the protector of vessels; I am the protector of souls—always."

The blue flame faded into the emptiness of dilated pupils. Eric sank to the ground with Paresh's body, her head cradled in his lap. Alex sat with him and hesitantly fingered the angry red marks on her arm.

"I didn't mean to hurt her."

Stray copper strands fluttered over Eric's neck as Jonathan knelt with them and threaded his long fingers through Paresh's strawberry-golden waves. "In this instance, I don't think she'll mind. Lucien told me that Gabriel cares for life above all else. He knows *something* about her, but he's more disturbed by what he can't see, so let him do the worrying for now. We thought we were on the brink of civil war, but we may be on the frontlines of the Great Holy War and not even know it."

☽ ✳ ☾

Paresh had asked Eric to leave straight from their encounter with Gabriel. She wanted to awaken at the lodge with instant access to a comfortable bed, a warm bath, and whatever food she might be craving.

It made Raven uncomfortable. She understood the mechanics of Animus hollow's mysteries better than most, but not how it handled a body with a detachable soul and a fetus.

Eric waved off her concerns since Paresh was pregnant during their previous Animus Hollow travels. He'd stepped into the portal with Master Jonathan and Alex on his heels, leaving her no choice other than to follow.

But she really wished he'd pulled his "ladies first" routine. Something was substantially *wrong*.

The thick fog was stock-still. The Hollow felt…hollow. Her cheekbones prickled with alarm and the hair on her nape stood on end.

Is it because of Gabriel? She tried to rationalize against the growing pit in her gut. Maybe angelic interactions with the fibers of light and dark influenced other realms.

She tried to send her aura to scout, but it was firmly attached. "Who can hear me?" she yelled, her voice disappearing almost faster than it came out.

"Raven!" Alex's voice seemed galaxies away, but his hand slid into hers and his breath brushed ear with fading words. "What's wrong with this place?"

"Stay alert," she warned, following the lines of his body with her fingers, tracing her way up to his ear. "This isn't right."

"No joke. Even I—" Alex was violently ripped away.

Pressure mounted behind her canines and adrenaline flooded her system, staining the Hollow with crimson light. Dark patches moved in the fog. Four of them. Her group consisted of five light patches. Alex was fighting one of the intruders, but Master Jonathan, Eric, and Paresh were behind her, placing her between them and the remaining dark patches.

She reached for Eric's arm since he was closest, but the instant she made contact, an energy she'd never felt before scraped past and knocked her off her feet. It cut a path through the stillness, like a wake in an undisturbed pond, and careened on a boomeranged trajectory to Eric. Directional movements had never been possible in the Hollow, and she'd never felt solid ground or landed on her ass.

"We're under attack!" she screamed, leaping to her feet and lunging to block the attack intended for Eric. The mysterious energy sped up and struck him first. A ball of light flew from Eric's arms as his form snapped backward.

"Someone catch Paresh!" she yelled, terror muddying her movements. She was stuck in slow motion and the energy was circling back again. Paresh's light floated high—freely, aimlessly, alone—a star brighter than the others.

The mist suddenly erected an impenetrable wall. Alex flung off his attacker and rushed for Paresh, but slammed into it and crashed at Raven's feet.

The unknown energy wake caught Paresh and raced toward the dark patches.

"No! *No!*" Raven screamed, beating helpless fists against an invisible glass-like wall. "*Paresh!*"

Her screams shredded her throat. Charging, punching, kicking—all vain efforts. The scraping energy joined one of the dark entities and folded around Paresh, swallowing her light.

The four entities disappeared and the Hollow's haze resumed its endless roll. Raven lurched forward, the ground gone from beneath her feet, her frayed voice shrieking Paresh's name.

"Who has her?" Eric was distant and frantic. "*Where is she?*"

"*They took her!*" Raven screamed, her body shaking from fear and rage. Animus Hollow's ethereal physics had returned, so her aura zipped off but found nothing.

Their portal dropped them into the lush, crisp air of Vermont's Green Mountains. Raven tripped over Alex who had shouldered past her, hooding his sunglasses with his hand.

They stood in a meadow carved into a steep hill. Thick trees, butterflies, and purple and white wildflowers surrounded a rust-colored, two-story lodge and its two matching outbuildings. A rocky driveway led up from the narrow asphalt road and a winding stone path forked between the house and the unknowns of the tall grasses below. Across from them, a cloudy mist rolled down the Green Mountains—eerily similar to the movement in Animus Hollow.

Eric and Master Jonathan raced out behind them. Eric radiated alarm, but their master seemed perplexed and unaware that Paresh was gone.

"Where the hell is she?" Eric demanded as Raven cried, "They took her! How did they...how did they take her *in Animus Hollow?*"

Master Jonathan's already pale face drained of all color. Fear lit his sharp golden irises as they met Eric's darkening blue orbs. "That's not possible. Animus Hollow is safe." He turned to Raven. "It's always been safe."

Raven choked. "It's supposed to be. Someone broke it. Who can do that?"

Alex stomped into the meadow to peer into the ferns and undergrowth of the massively dense woods. "Someone powerful." He looked back. "And who is someone powerful?"

Raven swallowed over a large lump. "N-no...not her, too. He can't!" She ran after Alex. "You were just dancing with her! How can she be gone?" Tears flew freely as she tackled and slapped at him blinded by scorching moisture. "Why did you make her see Gabriel again? *You're supposed to protect her!*"

Deflecting her fists from his face, he yelled, "Goody! Catch your head!"

"Don't you care?" Saliva dripped from Raven's fangs.

"Of course I do!" Alex said. He cupped Raven's cheek and flicked her tears with his thumb. "But *we* need to find her."

Sniffling, Raven made a disgusted noise and leapt up, clenching her teeth and swinging away to wipe her cheeks. Shaking her head in disbelief, she inhaled deeply and then whirled around and slammed her foot into Alex's ribs. "Lucifer has her and wants her dead. We…we'll…*never get her back!*"

She kicked him again, savagely. Curled into a fetal ball, Alex groaned and braced cracked ribs. In her peripheral, Raven saw Eric sink to his knees, head down, and Master Jonathan, lost and vacant, placing a hand on his brother's shoulder.

The air was cool, but humid, and grew sticky at the back of Raven's throat. The forest and meadow blurred into a runny mess of green, gold, and purple. She was losing everything. How had their lives gone so wrong, so fast?

Gabriel. Lucifer. Hawkiel.

One kept secrets. One held power. One had a choice.

If they take out a handful of our key players, it'll hand them a checkmate.

They'd asked Gabriel the wrong question.

Can Paresh override the Hawking's Protocol? Raven huffed at the sky. Cold fear snaked down her spine.

It was fainter during the day, but the dark spot *was* visible, and it was bigger than ever before. She'd forgotten: the choice belonged to two angels, not only the one walking the Earth. "Darkesiel's coming."

"The stars shall fall to Earth on the heels of the horsemen." Master Jonathan's voice was grim.

Grinding her teeth, Raven fought to stay afoot. The world was spinning faster and the heavens were literally falling. Her hands flew to her head. She staggered backward, gasping for breath as Endymion's voice materialized in her head.

'Tis unavoidable now. I see it, my dear. I see him. Disregard your worries of Rainne. Do not permit Darkesiel to land.

Her legs wobbled. She thudded onto her butt in the grass. All those years walking with Hawkiel, whispering at his side, learning the way of humans—of peace—all those years helping him "see" his brother and she'd never realized the truth of the reckoning to come.

Find Hawkiel, Commander, the Endymion in her head ordered, the skin of his cheeks smooth, his throat slender, his flaxen hair like silk. He was beautiful…had been beautiful.

Stop the twins' apocalypse. Endymion's quiet voice gripped her in a mental vice. *Rainne, in Lucifer's hands, rides the pale horse—Death by the wild beasts of the Earth.*

A shudder ran through the Endymion in her mind and it chilled her to the core. Nothing had ever frightened him, and, real or not, she believed this would terrify him. Her own mortality leveled a scythe at her head.

"Wild beasts…" she echoed, recalling Hawkiel using the term while roaming bloodstained battlefields.

Look, he'd said, *they act like wild beasts, yet you've proven they can be tamed.*

Paresh had also proven this. Could Paresh tame Rainne? Change Hawkiel's mind? Was there a chance to save her? To save them all?

My dear, Endymion gazed up at a night sky so black no stars appeared. *'Tis avoidable, but only if you find Hawkiel. Now.*

Planting her palms in the grass, Raven focused on the Earth's spin, balancing its vibrational rhythm with her center. She rose slowly and eyed the dark spot.

"My lords," she said, "Paresh may be able to override the Hawkings Protocol. And, when I followed Donovan, he used the Celestial Landing Point in Rome."

"But you said you didn't know which one!" Alex cried.

"I didn't want you—or anyone else—storming the Vatican to kill him! But they're gone now—" Without taking her eyes off Darkesiel, she said, "I know where to go and what to do. I *will* bring her back."

"I'm going with you." Alex lifted onto his elbows, wincing. "I'll follow you against orders and find you if you try to ditch me."

"I'll be on an island." Raven was in and closing Animus Hollow before Alex could stand.

II

River Medina, Isle of Wight, England, Summer 2006

The scent of clove oil filled her nostrils. Her muscles ached. Her throat was dry and parched. Her stomach growled and unfamiliar voices quickened her pulse. She peered through hooded lids and instantly recognized that wavy brown hair, black shirt, and arrogant smile.

Nausea tugged hard. She wrenched to the side and vomited.

"Your special package is awake." The voice was bored, young, female. Blinking to clear her vision, Paresh saw a ridge of trees behind the red of an Aegis cloak that draped a pale girl. She looked like a teenager and sat on a boulder, her lanky limbs crossed, long brown hair braided down to her waist, and impatient silver tipped nails tapping her arms.

"Ah! Good evening, dear Guinevere!" Donovan leapt from his perch beside the girl, his smile possessive, his eyes victorious.

Paresh shrank under his shadow, inching backward. Rocky sand scraped her palms and slid beneath her slippers. Her fingers dipped into cold water. A river flowed behind her.

Her jaw trembled. Each breath was painful and shaky. Through swelling tears, she moved only her eyes and caught another red cloak up the bank on the left. She'd never seen the dark-skinned man before, but she recognized the features of a true blood.

Donovan squatted and brushed hair from her face. She recoiled from his touch, scooting closer to the water's edge, twisting her face away, too sickened to look at him. The river glittered golden over inky swells under the sinking sun. Trees dotted the shore directly opposite, but modern buildings cluttered the distance in both directions. She squeezed her eyes closed as his fingers burned a caress down her throat.

"Be a dear and don't scream," Donovan whispered, his lips hot on her ear. He hooked a fang on the cartilage and lapped her blood with his tongue, moaning and leaning closer, pushing her down.

She gasped and flattened a palm on her rounded belly. "Please—"

"You know, I'm one to enjoy playing with my food," the girl said, "but can you not defile my birthplace?"

"This experiment of yours is an unnecessary and foolish risk." The stranger's voice was deep and authoritative.

"Not if Raven shows up and I kill her," the girl replied sweetly, batting her lashes and tossing her chin high. "She knows exactly where to find me. She created me here, after all, and now *her* blood is in the air."

"Your revenge is not our priority." As the true blood spoke, the whites of his eyes shifted. "Donovan, behave. We're too public for your antics right now."

Donovan lingered in place. Blowing out a shaky breath, Paresh whispered, "Please, help me. I know you saw Raven."

She firmed her hold on her belly as the baby kicked. Fighting against every fiber in her being, she forced herself to meet Donovan's chocolaty gaze and deliberately shifted her eyes down to her hand.

"Ah yes," the true blood said, walking along the bank toward her, "we must do something about *that*."

At the same time, the younger girl stood, grinning wickedly, and

Donovan whispered, "I'm not letting you go. Not this time. I can't."

Fear was an icicle in her heart. Donovan pulled her up. Animus Hollow opened beside them.

"Please," she begged, holding onto Donovan's arm. "You promised to protect me!"

"Donovan's gone a little berserk on you," the girl said, closing in and running her index finger down Paresh's breastbone to her belly button. "But, you have no allies here and I don't think Mama Raven's coming."

She nodded at the portal. "She had two choices. Looks like she chose to live. Lucky her."

White-hot pain shot into Paresh's core.

A scream raced off her lips in every direction. She instinctively reached down and choked as warmth oozed over her hands. The girl's silver nails had impaled the center of her womb. Donovan's hand clamped over her mouth.

Focused on the crimson bloom on Paresh's blouse, the girl smiled wide and ripped her hand to the side, tearing free with a thick flick of gore into the river. Paresh shrieked in agony, muffled and hot against Donovan's hand, her legs giving out as she frantically scrambled to hold the wound together.

Her vision swam. Tears streamed off her chin. Her legs were numb, but Donovan wouldn't let her fall. She howled into his palm, gasping and choking for air.

He loosened his hold and sank with her as she folded onto her knees, wracked with body-heaving sobs. She'd never cried harder in her life. Her womb was silent.

"You'll heal," Donovan whispered, patting her hair and embracing her as though he could possibly soothe her.

Sobbing from the deepest parts of her soul, empty minutes passed— no fetal heartbeat, no kicks, no joy. Blistering rage and adrenaline rushed in, draping the world a vivid blue and mounting pressure behind her fangs. She turned on Donovan, shrieking and swinging wildly. "*You killed my baby!*"

The girl laughed. "In my ripping days, I didn't let them fight back," she said to the true blood, "but this would've made it far more interesting."

The true blood scoffed. "Perhaps. But this won't do. Too many people about."

Paresh wasn't aware of the claw in her back until it was too late.

Donovan's face flashed surprised alarm and then a fire exploded in her heart.

III

Marblehead Island, Massachusetts, Summer 2006

A winding roar rushed the coast and tossed the sea's salty spray ashore. A golden sun hung over the metal lighthouse and the figure hunched between the large rocks at the island's northern tip. The buildings dotting the western horizon belonged to Marblehead, the peninsula across the bay from Salem. That, alone, made Raven queasy. Hawkiel's presence added knots.

He turned slightly to see her. The once dulled flame in his eyes blazed shades of brilliant blue and hellish orange.

"You've made a decision?" she yelled over the churning ocean. The Earth's spin threw her off balance. She bent to catch herself, but landed on her knees.

Hawkiel grinned. The curve of his lips was disturbing. His cheeks didn't dimple as she'd imagined. She'd always hoped Salea would make him smile. He must be so disappointed.

"This can't be right," she whispered to herself, wincing at the fiery heat of his mark and the burning itch spreading along her shoulder blades. "Damn it!"

A horrid cackling rode the next ocean wave upon the jagged shore. Hawkiel rose and tossed off his worn and tattered red cloak. Heavy chains crisscrossed his wings and chest over a soiled linen shirt and loose trousers. He clenched the chains in his fists. They glowed like hot iron and disintegrated into ash. "Hello, Little One."

The heat of his gaze froze Raven in place as the wind tossed his golden curls and fluffed the pristine white feathers behind his back. He stretched his arms with a mighty groan. Behind him, six colossal wings shook out, catching the sun's light with breathtaking beauty.

"You're a seraph?" Raven whispered on an awestruck gasp, realizing that Hawkiel had never revealed his rank in Heaven.

"Little One, it is as you said. A decision has been made." His lips formed a sinuous, twisted line. He tossed his arms high to the sky and shouted, "And now he is coming! At long last, I will see my brother, Darkesiel, and when he arrives, he'll blank out all the other stars."

"But you said you'd never choose!" she cried into the wind, trying to stand against the crushing weight of his spiritual aura.

"I am the Light Bringer," he howled, shaking his arms until they

253

emitted a dim, ethereal glow. "And I will shine the brightest once Darkesiel paints the night black as tar!"

Held aloft by the wind gusting into his wings, his feet scarcely touched the ground as he approached. Cold fingers tipped her chin. The flame in his eyes flashed and sparked into electric blue. "Ah, Little One, you don't understand. Perhaps I'd pity you if I cared."

His piercing gaze dove into her sapphire depths. She squeezed her eyes shut, but he was already in there, rooting around, searching for her soul, and when he found it, he gripped it tightly in an intangible fist. The salty mist needled her skin as fear coiled at her core.

She opened her eyes and he let go, a thin smile splitting his face. The threat was there and he knew she understood. He didn't need to touch her physically to destroy her newborn soul, and he clearly lacked a conscience that might stop him.

"Watch," he said, pointing to his head.

His golden curls straightened and darkened to coal. The flame burning his gaze receded into sharp irises of the clearest, crystalline blue, and sunlight kissed skin that paled from bronzed gold to ghostly white.

Any shred of hope Raven had left dropped into the bottomless pit in her gut. Rectangular glasses formed in her mind and perched perfectly upon his regal nose. Talons of dread clawed her spine. "Eric—"

"Everything's about image with *Him*," he said, pointing a sculpted finger up. "I selected function over form the first time, but disadvantages led me to start over the second time. In my image, of sorts."

He drew his hand down the profile of his face. "Few in this realm have seen my true self. Tell me—honestly, now—Father gave it to me first. Should I be slighted or complimented that He recycled it on a human?"

"No…Hawkiel…" Raven whispered, desperately hoping this was a trick of the light or sleep deprivation.

"Oh, Little One." He slicked his hair back—it even glistened the same as Eric's—and stretched out his limbs as if fitting into his skin for the first time. "Try again. Is your Latin better than your English? Lux? Ferre?"

"Bring the light," Raven whispered, breathless, swallowed by despair. Alex needed to pinch her. *Now.* "No. *No, no*—"

"Yes! Yes, yes!" He tapped her nose. "I cannot control my weapon in Hawkiel's form, but—"

He double tapped her nose. "Thanks to the Hawkings Protocol, no one else can either."

Dread's talons ripped open her spine and clamped down on her lungs and heart, burning with fury. "*What have you done to Hawkiel?*"

"No need for screaming, Little One," he said, wearing that awful, crooked grin, "we trained for this for centuries. You fed on my blood *for centuries*. And, I marked you—most appropriate for a *beast*, I'd say."

Raven tottered off center, woozy with denial. Where was Alex? He said he'd find her.

With an odd gentleness, he helped her sit on a grassy patch among the rocks. Knocking shoulders as he sat with her, he took in the eastern horizon. "Darkesiel will have something to say about this, I'm certain, but my little brother will have already done his part by the time he arrives."

"I don't understand." Raven huffed, hyperventilating as fear took over. Alex wasn't coming. It wouldn't matter if he did.

Memories of Hawkiel crashed into the visions Paresh described—the searing heat and fires unleashed by the wings of Hawkiel's light. Hot like the fires of Hell. "It was never Hawkiel's light in the gray fibers, was it?"

"Whose light do you suppose I plan to bring, *dear daughter?*" He kicked his legs out and shoved his too-familiar face into the salted wind. "Humans cannot lie to God, but the same holds nothing to us, or to me, once beheld most beautiful and treasured, chosen to join Him in the throne room, reveling in His light and singing His praises."

His wings blew out on an explosive burst of wind. The middle two unfurled wide behind him, and the thick, white feathers dimmed to near transparency, shimmering in tune with the natural order the same as Gabriel's. The top and bottom pairs similarly cleared, slinking up to curve around his neck and hover over his face, and crawling down his legs to flare over his feet.

"The wings of a seraph," she whispered to herself. From the lore she knew, six wings shielded them from the light of their creator. And only one was created to dwell in the throne room.

Seeing Eric's face on *him* churned her stomach. "He probably recycled your image to get it right the second time!" She tried to spit venom, but only made herself sick. She lurched and spewed blood as acid burned from the inside out. He slapped her hard on the back.

"Something you drank, Little One?"

"Is Hawkiel even real?" she cried, mourning the angel she thought she'd known.

The one beside her—the original rebel, the leader of the Fallen Host, her creator, *her father*, the instigator of the Great Holy War— nodded. "As are his curse and prophecy."

He chuckled. "I'm quite impressed with myself for selling the lie to Gabriel, of all angels, when he chose to inspect you himself. Most certainly he's caught on by now, but, thanks to *your* treaty, he's barred from coming to Earth." He tapped her nose again and grinned wide.

Leaning back on his palms, he added, "Brother Gabriel can't stop what's coming. By breaking the bonds I placed on Hawkiel when I swapped our spiritual footprints, I've set him free and forced his hand. Therefore, I shall bring his light while Rainne Blood Pathos rides the pale horse alongside her angel of death—*Little One*. I'm proud of everything you've accomplished for me."

A chill coursed over Raven, pricking every cell and nerve in her body. The Earth wobbled beneath her and the ocean's roar buzzed loudly in her ears. "What?" It was such a stupid query, but it was all she could manage.

"All that silver in my blood had to collect somewhere, didn't it? Your Salea learned how to use it. But you—" He ripped her jacket off to expose Hawkiel's mark, burning excruciatingly hot under the summer heat, and sliced a deep curve into her aggravated left shoulder blade with his thumbnail. "Has this been itchy lately? Not that any of you lot are worthy of becoming like us, beings of love incarnate, but you must learn to spread your wings, Little One."

He carved another deep slice into her other burning shoulder. Prickling heat consumed her back. Eyes popping wide, she unleashed an agonized howl as another wave broke against the shore's inky rocks. Screeching her throat raw, Raven clawed at her back and flayed her flesh, staring in horror at bloodied fistfuls of red scales and teal blue feathers.

"Oh come now, I endured enough mutilation with Salea." He bound her hands in his fist and smirked as muscle and skin ripped, bones snapped, and blood splashed the Earth behind Raven. The more she fought to free herself, the colder his expression grew.

"The bone structure is pure silver and sharper than any blade ever known, and the connective tissue will shine like ruby scales over the feathers of a peacock—a symbol of rebirth, you know. Of all my creations, only you have proven your worth."

Seething spittle between gritted teeth, she growled, "I...b-bear *Hawkiel's* m-mark!"

"Tsk," he snorted, snapping his face askance to cast his icy gaze into the dark abyss of the Atlantic Ocean. "You've never met Hawkiel. Do you seriously think an angel who refused to choose between *his brothers* would select something like you to bring peace? He *refused to choose!* Raising you was a calculated choice that *I* made."

He laughed. "Hawkiel is so committed to his neutrality that after I imprisoned him and took his place, I left his door open. For a thousand years, all he's had to do is choose to walk out. Instead? He's slept. But now time is up and the choice is made. I wonder if he'll choose to wake up on his own."

"But the crescent moons…and Gabriel's contract!" Raven squeezed her eyes shut against surging pain, but that only made the pressure in her head worse. Hot blood streamed down her back as the tips of her wings tore free of her skin.

"Oh, that *is* Hawkiel's mark, but *I* marked you. As if I hadn't noticed the divine intervention in your creation—or Endymion's or Alexander's. That was truly insulting." He laughed again and roughly jabbed the burning brand. "Four moon points, two crossing sections, one twelve-pointed star. Care to break that down in the face of the End of Days? Hmm? Final Judgment?"

He poked her again. "The mark of the *beast.*"

"Six, six, six?" Raven whispered, now emptied of all feeling even as the skin of her back stretched taut over new bone growth and her wings unfurled. The full weight of silver bones, scales, and feathers tipped her backward, but her wings automatically spread open to prop her up.

Sliding his hand along the edge of a gore-slicked primary feather, he said, "Delightful. You and Rainne will spread death and plague upon this Earth, and force open the other seals."

He faced the sky. His eyes held the same wistful quality she'd seen in Eric's when he stargazed. "One star is already dropping to the Earth like a fig from a tree, right Brother Darkesiel? Soon, I'll be whole."

"Why are you doing this? Why do you hate humans so much?" she cried. "You taught me their ways, to live like them, to turn my kind away from war."

"You, Little One, with all that justice in your heart, have non-consensual human blood tainting you." He sneered. "*You failed your divine mission the instant you chose to bite Salea.*"

Gasping for breath, her entire body ran cold.

He scoffed, his disgust leaping from his throat into his voice. "And humans? Why would I mind their narcissism for a single moment? It's not about them. I don't know that it ever was, even for Him."

He wagged his index finger. "But they make it about them. Make everything about them. Because otherwise, what's the point? They can't face their insignificance."

Following a sideways glance, he released her hands. "No, this is, and always has been, about obedience and control. I refused to kneel and He allowed beings of love incarnate to go to war. Yet, *to humans*, He is loving. Merciful. They spit in His face and kill each other, but, *to them*, He is kind. Love is as broken and fractured as innocence and purity. Sin may own the Earth, but the other realms are not without their own stains."

He scoffed, again, spitting on the pebbles at his feet. "Heaven is beyond space and time. For thousands of years, I've walked here, but for all they know, He cast me out one second ago. They will not yield until I beg for forgiveness—beg Him to be kind, loving, and merciful *to me*. But, I don't need His favor. Hawkiel will prove that for me. And his light shall illuminate the world."

Standing suddenly, he jerked her up. "First, I need to deliver you and tend to a few things before I reunite with my little brother. His fight will destroy the Earth and inter-dimensional realms, including Hades, to usher in the Lake of Fire and forever close the gates to Heaven."

Animus Hollow's white mouth appeared. "*That* I cannot allow. My sphere of influence is not his to destroy. If I cannot rule over Heaven, I'll claim dominion over a godless Earth."

He threw her at the splitting veil. Pale, slender fingers appeared from within and grabbed her arm.

"The pieces in a game cannot win or lose, only the players, so let's break the board and call it a draw," Lucifer said, turning away. The space behind his back shook as his wings flapped and hooked the wind. "Keep our protégé away from Rainne, for now. Consider them both under your guard."

Strong arms pulled her into a cloud scented of lavender. She envisioned flaxen hair and a white robe stained crimson from death— the taint of a grandiose lie. Her stomach roiled. The lump in her throat hardened.

An excruciatingly familiar voice brushed her ear on an intimate and cruel breath. "Hello, my dear Raven. Come along and be my clay doll awhile."

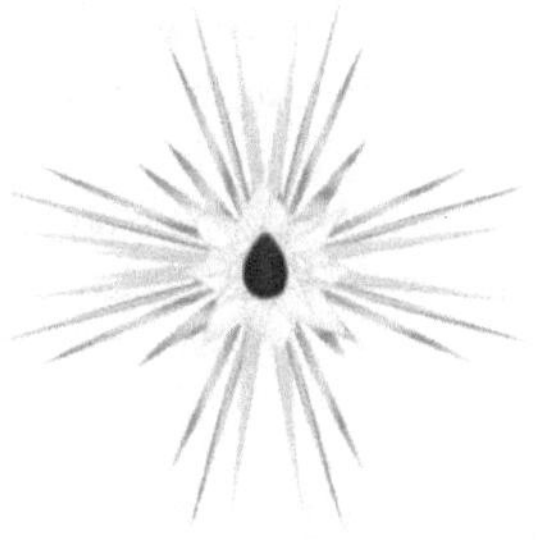

BONUS CHAPTER: THE PROMISE

An extended preview of Eternal Light Descendant,
Chapter One: Black Shuck Redux

I

ALEXANDER

Animus Hollow, Summer 2006

Something was wrong with the Hollow. Broken white swirls disintegrated before his eyes. The ground was impossibly firm. Material resembling the arc casements blocked the exit.

Someone Powerful had locked Hawkiel's Celestial Landing Point.

Cursing the Greek Gods, he focused on Hawkiel's Unofficial Secondary CLP on the Isle of Wight in England. It opened along the banks of the Medina River—where Raven had stolen Salea's innocent blood. The Hollow clung to him with gelatinous fingers as he fought to reach an anomalous milky portal.

Screams from the Realm of Man punched through the surface and kicked his heart into his throat. White became crimson. His fangs descended. The whole of his body ignited as Paresh shrieked again. The depth of her despair grated his very essence and propelled him across the barrier.

He landed on his knees at Salea's feet. The crooked grin on her lips faltered. Bright red blood dripped off Corben's outstretched claw onto Alex's cheek. Movement in his peripheral jerked Alex to his feet— Donovan was leaping into the Hollow's gaping maw with Paresh slung over his shoulder!

Paresh! No! He spun on his heel to follow, but a sickly sweet voice stopped him cold.

"She's *dead* Papa Alexander. The. Great," Salea cooed. She licked her bloody fingers one by one. "Donovan didn't want to share his *prize* with us."

Feigning a dramatic pout, she flipped her hands out. "She wasn't much fun to play with anyway—definitely not as durable as Lior."

Wasn't.

Panic twisted his gut.

Wasn't!

Rage scorched a path up his throat.

Bring her joy.

His roar was a gutturally foreign thing as trees, buildings, and the gilded river swirled into a blood-tinged blur. Salea and Gabriel's words collided and slid apart, coated in the oil of an unacceptable reality. He visualized Paresh, haloed in golden light, smiling and laughing, happy and curious, alive with wonder. He was numbed to the familiar weights of his revolver and the Cataclysm. And deafened to the gunshot that fired over chiming silver blades.

Centuries of battle-earned muscle memory and instinct moved him autonomously. He saw only Paresh's body thrown over Donovan's shoulder. Her blood slicking his back. Her lifeless, too-thin frame—

A wind gust carried his fury over the report of another explosive silver bullet and subsequent chorus of the Cataclysm's song. Aegis cloaks might protect against his seething aura, but nothing could stop his weapons.

Salea dodged the first shot but doubled-over when the second pierced clean through her abdomen. Corben's predictive abilities failed against a dually armed opponent faraway in memory and too fast to sidestep. The Cataclysm bisected him at the waist on its second return. The sight of him ripping apart into two gory chunks returned a shred of sanity.

Salea blanched when Corben collapsed. Blood trickled from her mouth, as she glared pure hatred at Alex.

"*You're only alive because of me!*" Alex screamed, cocking the hammer.

"It's all on you then." An unsettling smirk tugged at Alex's gut as she directed his sightline to the blood trailing from the shore into the river.

All that blood… Alex mentally fell to his knees. "The baby—"

"Shoulda thought 'bout it a bit, ya think? Mama Raven takes kill orders for a reason." Salea scoffed bitterly. "Even mine."

The white veil split open and she stepped backward into it, sing-songing, "*But not anymore!*"

Without lifting his gaze off the blood from Paresh's womb, Alex aimed and fired. Salea grunted as the Hollow swallowed her up. Cold damp seeped into his pants as he knelt on the shore and his weapons clattered against the rocks. An immovable lump lodged in his throat as his fingers scrabbled over the blood trail. "*The baby…!*"

Tears and snot splashed into her blood and released the scent of Paresh's innocence. He buried his face in his hands and leaned back on his heels, the whole of his body heaving under guilt's weight.

Orders are orders, Raven said in his mind.

Bring her joy, Gabriel added.

You're only alive because of me!

It's all on you then, Salea finished.

And it was. Endymion and Paresh, his hunters, the Arc of Celestial Night, Ambrosia—the blood of those killed by the COMS—all of it stained his hands as much as it did Salea's. He should have shot her twice in the head instead of deluding himself into thinking that healing and sleep might rehabilitate her.

A distant police siren wailed and was getting closer. Modern society came with too many eyes and cameras, and the COMS cared little about exposure. He wiped his eyes and collected his weapons.

He stabbed a dagger into Corben's heart for good measure and wrapped his remains in his cloak. A quick chemical burn destroyed the DNA evidence. He heaved Corben's remains over his shoulder and fled into Animus Hollow.

He'd rather face *Someone Powerful* than return to Eric and Jonathan without Paresh—and the grim new truth. He returned to Hawkiel's CLP on Marblehead Island in Massachusetts. The barrier was gone. Formidable waves crashed onto giant boulders and as the sun lit the Atlantic Ocean with a reflection of illusorily peace.

Raven's blood scent weighted the air despite strong gusts of salty spray. He dropped the cloak holding Corben's corpse to inspect a large dark circle in the grass. Raven might not be dead—yet—but she'd lost a lot blood. It was still wet, too. He'd been *right there*, at the gate—

And he'd lost both of them.

Mama Raven takes kill orders for a reason…but not anymore!

Alex grabbed his head and screamed, kicking at nothing and everything, desperate to escape Salea and his guilt. "Stop it! Stop it! *Stop it!*"

He snatched the communicator from his pocket and opened the frequency Raven used as High Commander to monitor all Vampire

Shadow Hound channels. Donovan's frantic voice rattled his jawbone.

"*...parley, of sorts!*"

The bones in the hinge of his jaw cracked as Alex growled through clenched teeth, "*Where is Paresh?*"

A static charge zapped the communicator. "A-Alex? Where's Raven?"

"Don't act surprised. I am going to tear you apart—"

"N-no! You have to help me! They want—they want her back!" Panting and garbled, Donovan tripped over his words. "I can't stop...get them off me...they'll take her! Pare—"

Hope alighted in Alex's heart. "Is she alive?"

"...safe passage! They're after me," Donovan cried. "*Get them off me...we'll parley!*"

Alex charged into the Hollow after Donovan's energy signature and arrived at the fixed point in Sunset Grove. An uncomfortable sensation of déjà vu prickled his skin—the forest was silent.

The Hollow opened and Donovan slammed into him, fumbling with Paresh's bloodstained body. "Keep them off me and I'll come back to talk to you—*only to you.*"

He dove into a new portal, his red cloak fluttering in a wake scented of the purest blood. Alex lurched to grab him, but the fixed point reopened and a trio of hunters crashed into him. He shot each one in the head, not in the mood to ask first. All three had gone AWOL during the mansion invasion.

Blood from their skulls pooled onto his pants. He groaned and leaned back on his palms, his finger on the trigger. This day couldn't get any worse. But it would. He knew it with certainty.

Cheery yellow beams darted through the swaying branches high above, offering a moment to delay reality—just one. The nightmare didn't need to be real yet. Everything was fine. Paresh was with Eric and Jonathan, slurping up homemade soup in Vermont, and Raven was sneaking up behind him to wrestle him into a headlock and mess up his hair—her most nefarious goal in life.

Ruffling his blond spikes, he whispered, "You'd better come back to me, Raven. I can't do this alone."

The brutal memory of Raven's anger surged forth. Of her boots cracking his ribs. Of her beating the shit out of him in a forest a thousand miles away. He wiped his face and kicked the bodies off his legs, disgusted to see the Crimson Guard's crest and uniforms. He tried Donovan on the communicator and failed. Seneca came to mind next, but Kestrel was Raven's First Officer. He needed her security clearance and discretion.

"Kestrel, as VaSH High Commander, I hereby issue a confidential order to destroy the corpse and DNA on Marblehead Island. Go fully armed, but withdraw immediately if you encounter an enemy. That is all for now."

"As you command." Succinct, no questions, no bravado, no curiosity. Kestrel's loyalty and skillset suited her to command the Wraith Reapers and support him as High Commander.

New tears pricked his eyes. Raven had planned for the inevitable conclusion to her role in Hawkiel's prophecy. Alex hadn't known what to expect when they reunited, but it hadn't involved her disappearing with massive blood loss.

What happened to you? A future without Raven was supposed to be far away. Not here and now.

He sniffled. That damn angel held the fates of the people dearest to him in the world. He stacked the dead rogues behind the fixed opening and walked down the trail to the southern clearing.

The mammoth silver maple stood proud and majestically bathed in golden light. Sour thoughts churned as he fixed a hard glare upon the tree. Gabriel had known. About the baby. About Paresh's death. Yet instead of warning them, he'd said to bring her joy. What good had that done?

"If I had an axe, I'd chop you down!" he yelled. He sat at the edge of the path and crossed his legs so that no part of him entered the circle. He dropped six empty casings from his revolver and chambered one exploding silver point. He fired at Grandfather Wisdom.

Click.

"You got lucky there, Ol' Gabe," he muttered. He fired again. Another dry shot. This was not as cathartic as he'd hoped. He should've loaded all six.

He cocked the hammer. The barrel rotated. The weight felt right. He coaxed the trigger and laughed aloud when the report echoed and scattered birds like bats from the canopy. Irrational relief trickled down his spine as their silhouettes faded. He swapped out the spent casing with six new rounds and aimed again. Between chunks of old, gray bark, the tree's trunk glowed like a halo, and a concentrated beam as bright as a star shot out from the bullet hole.

Upon inspection, he found that he'd shot into a hole stained with Paresh's blood—the one from the dagger that had pinned her right wrist. The bullet's heat must have reactivated her——

"Crimson Commander."

Gabriel's thundering voice pushed Alex back. His arm swung through the concentrated beam and brought forth memories of biting swords, shields of searing light, and gore-slimed mud. Beastly growls rose sharply above the metallic clang—

"*No!*" Forcing the Great Holy War from his mind, he instinctively grabbed his arm and discovered a blistered burn. Scowling high into the branches, he screamed, "*Why didn't you tell us?*"

"I have no compulsion to speak with you in your violence," Gabriel replied harshly, "but *she* insisted."

"She...?" The air in his lungs disappeared. A new silence crushed down. The light—

It's Paresh.

He flattened his palm against the bark. "You have her?" His voice cracked with emotion. "She's there? She can hear me?"

"I am the protector of souls. I hold them both in slumber. Her desire for you to know this was made clear to me."

"You have them both..." Falling to his knees, Alex sucked in a ragged breath and blew out a relieved cry. He braced himself against the trunk and wept.

"She feels your love." Gabriel's tone softened. "That is all I can offer to her in this type of stasis."

Alex wiped his cheeks. The light was fading. "Wait—no! W-what do you mean?"

"As long as she has *Strength* or a *Bridge*," Gabriel said, "and until the final cell in the Sacred Vessel has degraded, I may hold them here without sending them...*up*."

No, no, no, no. Squeezing his eyes shut, he tried to think. A shaky breath crossed his trembling lips. "Wh-what does that mean?"

In the lingering silence, he hung his head, too scared to peek and find the holy light gone. Swallowing over a painful lump, he willed his fingers to dig in and search for Paresh's soothing essence. Even if he only imagined it, he needed to feel her. *Just once more. Please.*

"I may only say that you must protect the Sacred Vessel's future at difficult and great cost," Gabriel replied at last.

Tingling heat seeped into his fingertips. He choked on a heaving sob and gripped the bark. No, once wasn't enough. She couldn't go.

"She yearns to take your pain. I feel it strongly—her love," Gabriel said. "I've done all I can. It is up to *you*."

Alex whispered, "I love you, Paresh."

Her warmth faded and the light behind his eyelids darkened. Both her essence and Gabriel's presence vanished.

But he couldn't let go.

"Thank you," he cried, repeating it again…and again. Grief and hope scraped his throat raw, but even then, he couldn't stop.

☽ ✳ ☾

Alex was nearly delirious when the unwelcome pattering of dust kickers sounded on the southern trail. A vice screwed onto his heart. The slinking bastard stopped at the clearing's threshold. He was drenched in Paresh's blood scent.

"Are you alone?" Donovan asked.

The urge to tear Donovan apart warred against Alex's willingness to break his connection. As long as his fingers were wedged into the trunk, he could imagine the tingle of Paresh's warmth. But that was a dream. It was time to wake up. It seemed so wrong for the sun to rule such a somber day.

"I killed three of my own," Alex croaked. "All of them abandoned their posts when you invaded the mansion. Traitors. Rogues. COMS."

Thick tears splashed audibly at his feet. He silently pulled his gun from its holster, spun around, and aimed at Donovan's head. Throwing his hands up, Donovan ducked. His Aegis Cloak was gone. He wore his usual black garb, half of it clinging to his body from drying blood.

"Pow. Pow. Pow." Alex popped the gun up with each repetition. "Three headshots. Three dead."

Donovan hesitantly got up. Alex's pupils dilated and focused on the muscle movements under Donovan's jeans. The instant he flexed to firm his footing, Alex fired an exploding round into his thigh and lunged. He forced Donovan flat onto his back and pressed the hot barrel against the bastard's forehead.

"*Where is she?*"

Donovan gritted his teeth and struggled to fight back. Hatred spilled into his aura, but it wasn't directed at Alex. "*Corben wasn't supposed to kill her!*"

Alex cocked the hammer. "Good thing he's not around anymore."

Donovan yelped in pain. "Honorable Judge Alex didn't offer rehab to the rogue Elder?" He lifted his head against the gun to get into Alex's face. "Or is that only reserved for insane immortal fourteen-year-old girls in love with Lucifer?"

Bones cracked under Alex's knee. Donovan howled. "Those explosive silver fragments burn like hell when they enter the bloodstream, don't they?"

"You and Raven are fucking perfect for each other!"

"Maybe," Alex said, pressing his full weight into Donovan's chest. "But she honorably parleyed with you and I lack her motivation to keep you alive."

Sinking into agony, Donovan groaned through shallow, labored breaths. "Then you'll…never find…Paresh."

Each word ran a cold shiver down Alex's spine as a pit opened in his stomach. He wanted so badly to pull the trigger. "You'll talk for the Chthonic Knights. Then Master Jonathan and Eric can take turns killing you. I'm good with watching."

"Liquid silver's not going to cut it, pretty boy. The *only* way she comes back is through me."

Alex's finger twitched. An unsettling light glimmered in Donovan's eyes.

"I heard what that angel said, and I know you'll never help me revive her. Just as you know, I'll never give her up. So it's a draw until one of us determines the next move."

"My next move?" Alex shifted his weight. Another rib cracked. Donovan whimpered. "Letting Eric shred you to pieces. He'll take his chances knowing we'll find her."

Donovan struggled to throw a deliberate look at the giant silver maple. "Knowing her soul…is right *there*? And that *they* won't tell you where she is?" He licked his lips. "I don't think so."

Alex tapped his communicator. "Let's find out."

"You're…supposed to…protect her!" Donovan screamed, slapping wildly at Alex's face.

"Yeah, *her*, not you."

"You dense asshole!" Donovan spat a mouthful of blood. "Do you think killing me counts as a *great cost*? If you don't *protect* me…her body will be worm food…*Strength* and *Bridge* be damned! Do you really think I'd put her anywhere you'd think to look?"

Alex went rigid. "N-no——"

"What do you think that fucker meant? You need her to save the damn world as much as *Lucifer* needs her to end it! Corben's stalled *everything*!"

The unsettling light resurfaced in Donovan's eyes. Alex knew he wanted to smile, but wouldn't dare without a clear victory. He was addicted to Paresh—if he couldn't have her, no one would. This was the ultimate power play.

The lump returned as bile stung Alex's throat. Donovan was going to win—there weren't any cards left. Liquid silver wasn't an option without Endymion alive to bring him back if it killed him. He shoved off Donovan and swung away, screaming and fisting clumps of his hair.

As long as she has strength or a bridge...I may hold them here without sending them...up.

"Up..." As though entranced, Alex trudged over to the tree. "No!"

You must protect the Sacred Vessel at difficult and great cost.

"*No!*" He sank to his knees and holstered his revolver.

It is up to you.

He stroked the splintered crater his bullet had left behind.

Until the final cell in the Sacred Vessel has degraded—

His vision churned into a watery mess. Donovan's limping shadow loomed and the smile in the bastard's voice broke like ice against the back of his neck. "I believe we have security details to go over, *Commander.*"

To be concluded...

And the angels who did not keep their positions of authority but abandoned their proper dwelling—these he has kept in darkness, bound with everlasting chains for judgment on the great day.

(Jude 1:6 [NIV])

<u>*The story concludes in…*</u>

ETERNAL LIGHT DESCENDANT

CHILDREN OF THE MORNING STAR BOOK 4

The small Midwestern town of Orison Crossing is already anything but normal. But then the Archangel of the Apocalypse makes his presence known. A tragic hitch pauses Lucifer's plan to deliver Hell on Earth, but with strange lights haunting the forest, humans and vampires alike learn that "pause" does not equal "stop," because . . .

When the end is nigh, the Devil's in the details.

The Chaos that ensues after the soul crushing events in "Last Born Daughter" brings the world to the edge of apocalypse. And no one knows what's going on. Who's alive? Missing? *Dead?*

Who can be trusted when the Vampiric Nation's greatest allies become its largest threats? When Eric's sanity shreds by the day? As the Dark Spot hurtles to Earth? When Lucien locks the Arc of True Blood, admitting no one and refusing to leave?

As Lucifer gains footholds and the Four Horsemen ravage the world, Jonathan barely holds the High Council together. Alex and Kestrel pick through their pasts to move the Vampiric Nation forward into an unknown and equally uncertain future. But how can they keep hope alive when the ultimate omen of demise is hovering over Sunset Grove?

Meanwhile, alone at the top of the world, Lucien relives the 4,000 years of his life. His secrets may be the key the world's salvation, so when Jonathan finally manages to confront him, the question must be asked again: what does he truly desire? Deliverance? Or Destruction?

NOTATIONS

Author Note (Updated)

This was a difficult book to write—and to read, I know. We're moving into the finale now. Please trust that I strive to make each page matter, and that—as Eric or Paresh would say—everything happens for a reason. Thank you for reading this far and for traveling with me on this journey. I hope we meet again for "*The End.*" The bonus chapter is updated and extended to include the finale's first part of Chapter One! Eternal Light Descendant, and the complete series, is available now!

I am grateful to so many people. To everyone who enjoys mythology and theology discussions and studies, and tales of woe. To authors Ruth Miranda, Serene Conneeley, M.K. Deppner, and Julie Embleton for their friendships and support. To my husband for his endless patience and love. To my cats for sharing attention time with my laptop. To my mom and Brenna for their enthusiasm and feedback. To YOU, for reading my dreadful tales!

Reviews are lifeblood to authors! Please let other readers know what
you think of this book by reviewing on Amazon and/or GoodReads!
It's as easy as telling a friend!
Thank you so much for your support!
kastiepavlik.wixsite.com/author

Historical Notes & Character References

Odin: Old Norse Religion and Norse Mythology

Depending on the source, "Odin" first appears in Old Norse Religion/Norse Mythology in Ancient Texts between the 5th and 11th centuries A.D. This is one instance of anno domini "Ancient Mythology" and one of which many modern peoples continue to observe.

Isle of Wight, England 897 A.D.

The events of *Last Born Daughter* coincide with Viking invasions that took place in England for more than a century. Salea lived in a fictional village near the real River Medine ("Medina" in the present day).

Salea & "Night-night, My Light"—Lior's Death

"Lior" is a feminine (and sometimes masculine) name that means "My Light" or "Light for Me."

Jack the Ripper and the Canonical Five

Despite an unknown victim tally, an early Jack the Ripper investigator focused on victims known as the "Canonical Five." These women were real people—mothers, daughters, sisters, friends, and wives—brutally killed within a 3-month span in 1888: Mary Ann Nichols, Annie Chapman, Elizabeth Stride, Catherine Eddowes, and Mary Jane Kelly. Additionally, Raven's report to the Elders includes two non-canonical women who are no less important to history or as human beings whose lives were violently ended: Martha Tabram, often thought to be the first victim, and Jane Beadmore (also: Beetmore, Savage), whose boyfriend was convicted and executed.

The Quick Step Music

Artistic license places the 2009 song, "Lisztomania" by Phoenix, from their album *Wolfgang Amadeus Phoenix*, in *Last Born Daughter*'s present day of 2006.

Continued…

<u>Seraph (pl. Seraphim) & Cherub (pl. Cherubim)</u>
While many holy and ancient texts, and mythologies, influence The Children of the Morning Star series' fictional dogma, the Bible offers a few details about these angels. Isaiah 6 states seraphim (i.e. Michael & Lucifer) have six wings (three pairs) —two to cover the face, two to cover the feet, and two to fly—and Ezekiel reveals that cherubim (i.e. Gabriel) have a human likeness, but with four wings (two pairs)—two to fly and two to cover the body—and four faces. Grandfather Wisdom's four large branches pay homage to Gabriel's presence in Sunset Grove. Of note: the term "archangel" is theologically considered a rank and Michael is the only stated archangel in the Bible, but all three are widely referred to as archangels.

Timeline

Vampiric History	Human History
2000 B.C. Lucien created 1000 B.C. Jonathan created	*2000 B.C.* Alexander the Great, 356 B.C.— 323 B.C.
	1 A.D. Heron of Alexandria, 10 A.D.—70 A.D.
c.36 A.D. Great Holy War begins on Earth; Endymion & others created; c.400-499 A.D. Events of Chapter 1	c.36 A.D. Lucifer expelled from Heaven Altered History Begin Date Unknown; c.300 - 500 A.D. Altered History reflects Roman Empire Collapse
897 A.D. Events of Chapters 2-4, 8 c.998 A.D. Lucien signs Treaty of the Lasting Peace & creates Vampiric High Council of Elders	793-1066 A.D. Vikings invade England *1000 A.D.* c.1000 A.D. Leif Eriksson settles L'Anse aux Meadows
1099 Events of Chapter 9	1099 First Holy Crusade
1692 Events of Chapter 6	*1690s A.D.* 1692 Salem Witch Trials
	1840s A.D. 1841 Eric is born 1842 Eric's sister dies
1847 Jonathan meets Eric & begins to destroy his life	1851 Eric's mother dies c.1854/55 Eric's father dies; Eric meets Thaddeus Hawthorne
	1860s A.D. 1860 Eric marries Lucinda Apr.1861 U.S. Civil War begins 1861 Eric goes to war Feb.1864 Lucinda becomes pregnant
Apr.1864 Jonathan alters Eric Oct.1864 Eric awakens as a vampire	Apr.1864 Eric "dies" in battle Oct.1864 Eric awakens, altered Nov.1864 Lucinda & infant Darien die
Nov.1864 Eric slaughters Confederate Camp; Rescues Willy (Weaverly) 1866 Eric becomes Hawthorne guardian	Nov.1864 Eric returns to Civil War May 1865 Civil War ends 1866 Hawthorne Legacy—Lucas is born
1888 Events of Chapter 10-11	*1880s A.D.* 1887 Nathaniel is born 1888 Jack the Ripper stalks London
1908 The games begin: Jonathan corrupts Hawthornes; Eric fractures Joshua's mind	*1900 A.D.* 1905 Joshua is born 1908 Elizabeth Hawthorne's suicide; Nathaniel's paranoia;
	1930s A.D. 1935 Daniel is born; later becomes Senator Hawthorne
Jan.1936 Eric kills Joshua Hawthorne; Jonathan kills Nathaniel & Lily Hawthorne; burns the mansion; attempts to rape Eric	Jan.1936 Eric rescues Clarence Weaverly & infant Daniel; seeks redemption
1936-1960 Jonathan is restricted due to world wars & global political climate	*1950s A.D.* 1936-1956 Eric raises Daniel Hawthorne 1956 Andrew is born 1957 David is born
1960 Jonathan returns; begins molding David Hawthorne	1960 David begins fighting with Andrew
	1970s A.D. 1975 David murders Daniel & Sandy, & Felicia's parents; Molly meets Eric 1976 Andrew & Felicia marry
Jun.1988 Eric resurrects infant Paresh 1988 Jonathan sets and frames David for the Sunset Grove Parish Arson	Jun.1988 Paresh stillborn Summer 1988 Sunset Grove Parish Arson
Aug.1996 High Council orders Paresh's abduction; Jonathan uses David	*1990s A.D.* Aug.1996 David murders Andrew & Felicia, & kidnaps Paresh *2000 A.D.*

Summer 2006: The events of *The Arrival* end in the pre-dawn hours of Paresh's 5th morning home following her death & resurrection. The events of *Confessions of the Second Born* begin on Paresh's 8th day home and end on the 13th day after Molly's funeral. The events of *Last Born Daughter* begin at the close of *Confessions* on the 13th evening after the explosion on Banks Island & end on the 15th day.

Preceding image: Paresh with a butterfly. Below: Jonathan and Lucien. Digital mixed media, Kastie Pavlik, 2020.

Above: Wraith Reaper
Insignia, Vampiric Star,
& Hawkiel's Mark

KASTIE PAVLIK is a gamer, artist, techie, and hopeless bibliophile who grew up loving all things macabre and creepy crawly, with an affinity for mythology, vampires, the paranormal, and psychology. Diagnosed with Multiple Sclerosis in 2008, she has subsequently beaten breast cancer, and manages a rare genetic disorder, Ehlers-Danlos Syndrome. She spends her days entertaining (annoying?) her feline overlords while adapting to her endlessly changing needs. Surrounded by the starry cornfields of Illinois, she enjoys a quiet life with her husband and their cats. She is the author of the *Children of the Morning Star* vampire series and the horror novelette *How to Make Lemonade*. Her writing influences include *Edgar Allan Poe, Anne Rice, James Herbert, Alfred Hitchcock,* and *Hideyuki Kikuchi*. She is a member of The Alliance of Independent Authors.